I0593203

THE RELUCTANT BRIDE

DUTIFUL WIVES

BEVERLEY OAKLEY

SANI
PUBLISHING

ABOUT THE AUTHOR

Beverley Oakley has written more than thirty sweet to sizzling historical romances, laced with mystery and intrigue.

She also writes Africa-set aviation romantic suspense, with a dashing pilot hero (based on her husband) as B G Nettelton.

Visit Beverley's website - www.beverleyoakley.com - to sign up for her newsletter and receive a free Ebook.

f

CHAPTER 1

S*pring 1813*

'IT'S NOT A SIN, *unless you get caught.*'

The gentle breeze seemed to whisper Jack's teasing challenge, its soft, silken fingers tugging at Emily's ingrained obedience. She put down her basket and stared longingly at the waters below, sweat prickling her scalp beneath her poke bonnet as desire warred with fear of the consequences.

'*Where's your sense of adventure, Em?*'

Still resisting, Emily closed her eyes, but the wind's wicked suggestiveness was like the caress of Jack's breath against her heated cheek; daring Emily to shrug aside a lifetime of dutiful subservience – again – and peel off her clothes, this time to plunge into the inviting stream beneath the willows. She imagined Jack's warm brown eyes glinting with wickedness. Taunting her like the burr that had worked its way into the heel of her woollen stockings during her walk. Exhaling on a sigh, Emily opened her eyes and admitted defeat as she succumbed to the pull of the reed-fringe waters.

Desire had won, justified by practicality.

If she had to remove one stocking to dislodge the burr she might as well remove both.

Scrambling down the embankment, she lowered herself onto a rock by the water's edge.

Her father would never know.

If he glanced from his study in the tower room, where he was doubtless gloating over his balance sheet, he'd assume she was a village lass making her way along the track. Emily had never seen him interest himself in the poor except …

Like most unpleasant memories, she tried to cast this one out with a toss of her head, still glad her father had never discovered what she'd witnessed from her bedroom window one evening five years ago: the curious sight of Bartholomew Micklen ushering the beggar girl who'd arrived on his doorstep into his carriage.

Then climbing in after her before it rumbled down the driveway and out of sight.

Now was just another of those moments when Emily was glad her father remained in ignorance. Her insurance, should she need it, was that she knew a few of her father's secrets the excise men might just want to know.

By the time the first stocking had followed Emily's boots onto the grassy bank she was bursting with anticipation for her swim.

What did one more sin matter when she'd be Mrs Jack Noble in less than a week?

The second woollen stocking came next. Fine enough quality but ugly and serviceable, like most of her clothes. Jack had promised her scarlet silk stockings spun with salutary Bible story scenes on his return from his covert mission to the Continent. This, he'd suggested as he'd debunked her father's theory that all women's flesh was vile and corrupt, would enable her to feel as dutiful a daughter as a wife: sensuous silk for sinning with her husband-to-be, saintly stories for her sanctimonious father.

Jack liked to shock her.

With water up to her shoulders, Emily raised her arms above her head in a swift arc, splashing for the pure pleasure of it and glorying in her sinful nakedness. Who would ever know?

Finally she acknowledged she was living on borrowed time. She dried herself with her chemise, which made it thoroughly damp by the time she pulled it over her head, then sat down on the rock again and stretched out her bare right leg, pointing her toe as she pretended to ease on a scarlet stocking emblazoned with winged chariots. Exhaling on another sigh of pleasure once she'd pulled on her dress, she raised her face to the sun. When she was Jack's wife, she'd contravene every sin she could think of. He would buy her gowns that stretched the limits of decency. She'd dance naked with him on the lawn.

Grunting with irritation when she was unable to ease her boot over her damp foot, Emily hurled the ugly lump of leather over her shoulder. Though she'd have to climb to the top of the embankment and put it on later, it was catharsis not to be called to account for giving vent to just one of life's daily frustrations.

'Good God, what was that?'

The outraged expletive, followed by a peevish whinny, confirmed she was no longer alone. Feeling foolish, Emily scrambled up the river bank.

'I presume this is what you're looking for?' A tall, straight-backed soldier regarded her from the saddle, her boot dangling from one gloved hand. He was dressed in the green jacket of one of the two Rifle battalions and Emily's heart fluttered with excitement as she looked past him.

But Jack was not there and her disappointment was quickly replaced by embarrassment at the soldier's unsmiling scrutiny. The unsettling effect of his dark gaze was intensified by a thin ridge of scar tissue which slashed his left cheek in a graceful arc from eye to ear.

Lowering her head so the brim of her bonnet kept her face in shadow, Emily accepted the boot. 'I had no idea anyone was on the path,' she mumbled, hoping he'd put her lack of grace down to the poor manners of a country rustic. Not that it mattered. His restless gaze, caught in the glare of the sun, had barely registered her face.

The young soldier waved a dismissive hand, then shaded his eyes, straining to see into the distance as if uncertain of his present course. 'I'm looking for Micklen Hall.'

Emily's foreboding increased. What business had this man with her father? Worse, what if he should recognise her if her father called her to attend to him to pour tea? Unlikely, but not impossible.

She briefly considered confessing her truancy, begging him to refrain from mentioning their meeting, but the soldier's erect bearing and forbidding expression suggested he'd condone her behaviour no more readily than her father would. Her next thought, that perhaps he was a friend of Jack's, was quickly dismissed. He might be roughly the same age but all similarities ended there. While his regular features and strong chin combined to create an effect of rugged handsomeness, enhanced, surprisingly, by his scar, his frosty demeanour was as different as possible from her easy-humoured, roguish betrothed.

She pointed behind him, over the hill. 'You took the wrong turn when you came out of the beech wood, sir.' Bobbing a quick curtsy, her manner was deferential. She was not dressed according to her rank. He'd forget her the moment he left. He'd barely looked at her and the sun was in his eyes. 'It's only a few minutes on horseback.'

He thanked her, and she watched him wheel his horse around, urging it into a gallop until he was a speck in the distance.

Emily waited until he'd crested the hill before she set her reluctant footsteps in the same direction. She'd be half an hour behind him, but if the stranger were not gone by the time she arrived she'd slip in through the servants' entrance and keep to her room until dinner.

If she were as lucky as last week, no one would even know she'd left the house.

If she were as lucky as last week, her latest sin would have no repercussions.

Major Angus McCartney was out of his depth.

He glanced at the clock on the mantelpiece. Only five minutes in this gloomy, oppressive parlour after the women had arrived and he was questioning his ability to complete his mission, a feeling he'd not experienced before Corunna four years before.

He'd been unprepared for the assault on his senses unleashed by the beautiful Miss Micklen. He shifted position once more, fingering the letters that belonged to her. For two years he'd carried the memory of the young woman before him as a confident, radiant creature in a white muslin ball gown with a powder-blue sash. Now her tragic, disbelieving gaze unleashed a flood of memory, for in her distress she bore no resemblance to the paragon of beauty at the Regimental Ball, a bright memory in an otherwise tormented year after he'd been invalided out of Spain. Clearly Miss Micklen did not remember him.

She'd remember him forever now: as the harbinger of doom, for as surely as if he'd pulled the trigger he'd just consigned her hopes and dreams to cinders.

She turned suddenly, catching him by surprise, and the painful, searing memory of the last time he'd confronted such grief tore through him.

Corunna again. As if presented on a platter, the image of the soldier's woman he'd assisted flashed before his eyes, forcing him to draw a sustaining breath as he battled with the familiar self-reproach which threatened to unman him.

He reminded himself he was here to do good.

'A skirmish near the barracks?' the young woman whispered, resting her hands upon her crippled mother's shoulders. 'Last Wednesday?'

'That is correct, ma'am.'

Mrs Micklen muttered some incoherent words, presumably of sympathy. Angus pitied them both: Miss Micklen digesting her sudden bereavement, and the mother for her affliction. The older woman sat hunched in her chair by the fire, unable to turn her head, her claw-like hands trembling in her lap.

He cleared his throat, wishing he'd taken more account of his acknowledged clumsiness with the fairer sex. He was not up to the task. He'd dismissed the cautions of his fellow officers, arrogantly thinking he'd be shirking his duty were he not the one to deliver the news. It was condolences he should be offering, and he had not the first idea how to appeal to a frail feminine heart.

Nor was he accustomed to the lies tripping off his tongue as he added, 'A tragic mishap, ma'am, but Captain Noble acquitted himself with honour to the end.'

Miss Micklen's gaze lanced him with its intensity. Tears

glistened, held in check by her dark lashes. 'I can't believe it,' she whispered, moving to draw aside the heavy green velvet curtain and stare at the dipping sun. 'Jack told me he was on the Continent.'

Choosing not to refute Jack's lie, he said carefully, 'An altercation occurred between a group of infantry in which I was unwittingly involved. When Captain Noble came to my assistance he was struck a mortal blow to the head. I'm sorry, Miss Micklen.'

He wished he knew how to offer comfort. The beautiful Miss Micklen of the Christmas Regimental Ball had seemed all-powerful in her cocoon of happy confidence. Unobtainable as the stars in heaven, he'd thought as he'd watched her skirt the dance floor in the arms of the unworthy Jack Noble. For so long he'd carried Miss Micklen's image close to his heart and this was the first time he'd been reminded of Jessamine.

God, how weary he was of war.

Two women, torn apart by grief at the loss of their soldier protector.

This interview was part of his atonement.

Angus dug into his pocket and held out a bundle, tied with red ribbon. 'Captain Noble's letters, ma'am.'

She took them with one graceful hand. The other fingered the brooch fastened to the collar of her high-necked gown. Angus was surprised by its modesty. Jack Noble's taste in women ran to the ostentatious, though perhaps it was not surprising he would choose a wife as different as possible from his doxies.

'Bear your sorrow with dignity, Emily.' The old woman spoke in French. 'You come from noble Normandy stock.'

Angus studied Miss Micklen's shapely back as she gazed silently at the letters before raising her head to stare into the gathering darkness. The calm before the storm? His mother's propensity for the vapours had taught him that females were wont to give vent to their wounded passions with no thought to present company.

Miss Micklen was stronger than that.

She turned. 'What was Jack was doing with *you*, Major McCartney, in Chester,' she challenged, 'when he told me he was traveling directly to the Continent?'

Angus wished he'd thought of some other excuse that did not involve himself in order to preserve the gilded image she held of her false fiancé. 'A confusion of dates, I'm sure, Miss Micklen. Captain Noble was with his regiment, *in Chester*.' At least that part was true.

Her lip trembled and she lowered her voice, suddenly contrite. 'I'm sorry, Major McCartney. Jack was your colleague. No doubt your friend, too.'

He felt his own heart respond and flower. She was no longer the careless beauty whose gaze had failed to register him during the spate of balls they'd both attended that memorable season. In her most painful hour she was capable of compassion.

She extended her hand. 'It's a painful cross you bear, Major McCartney. Jack was denied the glory of giving his life in battle for his country, but you saw your comrade struck down'—her voice broke—'to save your life.'

She pulled on the bell rope then turned to the thin, weary-looking parlour maid who appeared. 'Show Major McCartney out, please, Lucy.'

'If there is any assistance you require ...'

'No, but thank you, sir'—she sounded as if she might break down at any moment—'for giving me the comfort of knowing Jack died a hero.'

With a heavy heart, he bowed himself out. The comfort of lies. They sat ill with him.

But then, lying was the least of his sins. He'd lost his soul the day he laid eyes on Jessamine.

GATHERING her cloak and bonnet the moment the dust had settled upon the major's departure, Emily slipped out of the kitchen door and fled across the meadow. There'd been no hint that Major McCartney recognised her as the lass on the road, preoccupied as he clearly was by his impending mission. Not that it would have mattered if he'd unwittingly implicated Emily in this afternoon's truancy. Her father had looked as if he were about to punish Emily, regardless, the way the tendons of his neck had swollen about his bitter face, red with suffused anger, when he'd heard the news.

As if Emily were to blame for Jack's death.

At the top of the hill she glanced down at the church in which she and Jack would have married the following week. She didn't stop. Only when she reached the old, disused woodcutter's cottage, deep amongst the elms, did she feel safe. Throwing open the door, she hurled herself onto the pile of hessian sacks in the corner, the setting for the delights she'd shared so recently with Jack.

Her heart had been ripped in two. Without Jack she had no buffer against the harshness of her world.

When her passion subsided, Emily dragged herself into a sitting position and rested her head on her updrawn knees.

Jack, the man who had wooed her with such tenacity despite her initial reluctance, the man who had breached her defences with his teasing humour and whose twinkling eyes and boyish grin never failed to make her pulse beat faster, was gone.

Wiping away her tears, she bent to pick up a half-smoked

cheroot lying nearly obscured beneath an old log. Jack had smoked it just over a week ago. Clenching it in her fist, she closed her eyes and pictured the scene: Jack's smooth, muscled chest upon which she'd rested her head. With loving reassurances he had coaxed her out of her fear. Tenderly he had massaged her temples with his long, sensitive fingers; fingers which had taught her that not only lips could show what joy and delight there was in loving. Her body burned at the memory, but not with shame, for she was proud to have loved a hero.

An image of grim-faced Major McCartney intruded, pushing aside her recollections of smiling, tousle-haired Jack. The scar puckering the soldier's cheek and his stiff, military bearing only reinforced her aversion to men with no sense of humour. Men who did not know how to wring the joy from life. Unlike Jack. But Jack was dead and her world had fallen apart. There would be no more joy for her now.

Wind rattled the shutters. Distracted, Emily noticed the rain had begun to breach the meagre defences of the crudely constructed hut. She exhaled on another sob. She didn't care if the water rushed under the door and drowned her.

After a few minutes, rational thought returned. How could Jack have been in Chester when he had intended crossing the channel on another secret assignment the day after his visit to Emily?

If only she'd quizzed the Major more thoroughly. He'd said he was putting up at The Four Swans and to call on him if he could be of assistance.

Emily shuddered. She never again wanted to lay eyes on the tense, awkward soldier whose life had been saved through Jack's sacrifice.

CHAPTER 2

Autumn had set in and the surrounding patchwork of fields looked barren.

Angus shivered, despite his army greatcoat, as he and his brother navigated the narrow cliffside path on horseback. He glanced at the base of the froth-fringed sheer drop far below him to his left and wondered when the bridle path would be swallowed up by erosion. This was smuggler's territory. No doubt the excise men would have a field day if they only knew which caves and caverns harboured the contraband he had no doubt sustained the local community.

'How was mama?' Jonathan, older by a couple of years, twisted his head. His ready smile was amiable, differentiating him from the sibling he had once most closely resembled.

That, and the now generous coating of flesh, a legacy of his comfortable seven-year marriage.

'Same,' Angus replied shortly, drawing level once they'd reached more hospitable terrain. Then, as if remembering he addressed his brother who really was interested, and not some cavalry man who expected only a monosyllabic answer, added, 'In delicate health, of course. Apparently only a visit from her dear boys stood between her and her eternity box.'

Jonathan chuckled. 'Forever susceptible to the damsel in distress, aren't you, little brother? Incidentally, I hear you were in these parts not so long ago.' He indicated the emerald turf on the chalk downs with a sweep of his arm then directed Angus a candid look through a pair of myopic blue eyes. 'Rather an out-of-the-way place to find yourself?'

Angus shrugged, not feeling it necessary to give any reasons. 'Not really.'

'Business? Military? By the way, how are you faring on half pay? I understand you want to assess your future after fighting so long for king and country, but you'll have to make up your mind what you're going to do before much longer.'

Angus gave another non-committal shrug. 'I'm a half step ahead of the creditors. Tedium's the worst of it, though without Johnson it's the very devil taking off my own boots.' Angus had not yet replaced his loyal batman who'd been pensioned off to a small cottage in Norfolk since Angus had given up soldiering as his main livelihood. 'Thought I might go to Africa and be a mercenary.' He gave a wry smile. 'You advise me, Jonathan.'

'Find yourself a wife.' Jonathan put a hand to his expanded girth. 'A rich one. You look half starved.'

'Don't pity me.' Angus glanced towards the beech wood.

He hated it when his brother broached this topic.

Jonathan gave a snort. 'I wouldn't dare.' Reflectively, he added, 'Can't pretend to know all the answers either, though I *do* know you never chose the army willingly and wonder why you don't pack it in altogether.'

'It doesn't suit me as ill as I'd once supposed.' The truth was, Angus didn't know what to do with his life. War held no appeal. Hostilities with France had been a fact of life for as long as he could remember and men of his calibre were always needed to repulse the Corsican invader. 'I was hardly cut out for London revels, and as a military man I have some purpose.'

'Unlike the rest of your ramshackle family?' A grumble of laughter escaped his brother as they forded a shallow stream. 'You haven't answered my question. What brought you here?'

Angus was uncomfortably conscious of their proximity to the honey-coloured pile of stone which housed the beautiful, bereaved Miss Micklen. She'd occupied so many of his waking thoughts these past months. He wondered how she did.

And wished he didn't care.

Unconsciously he fingered the scar that puckered his cheek, an old habit of his when thinking. The disfigurement did not trouble him. No point concerning himself with his physical appearance when he could do so little about it. Jonathan had once remarked it was as well Angus did not aspire to be a Corinthian like the rest of their brothers.

'Military business,' Angus said shortly, shifting in the saddle.

'Distasteful, I would gather, by your reaction?'

'Oh no,' responded Angus with an uncharacteristic curve of the lips as he compared Miss Micklen with the wives of other officers. He turned his head away, irritated with his lack of discretion.

Obviously Angus was getting too comfortable. Jonathan had been his only champion during a lonely childhood, but now he was an adult Angus had learned the folly of letting down his guard, even with Jonathan. Especially with Jonathan. They had been on the road for more than two hours, returning from a visit to a prospective boarding school in Dover for Jonathan's eldest boy. The small town of Deal where Jonathan had business was just coming into view, after which they'd turn their mounts west and Angus could enjoy his sister-in-law Caroline's hospitality for one night of comfort. The thought of returning to his sparse soldier's lodgings in Maidstone brought Angus no joy.

Silence lengthened and when Jonathan continued to direct his enquiring gaze at him, Angus replied stiffly, 'It is always unpleasant reporting a casualty to loved ones.'

Staring ahead, he was conscious of the flush that stole up his neck as his brother remarked, 'Didn't know that fell within the line of duty. Thought correspondence was the usual. After we've taken a nuncheon at The Four Swans why don't we call on the young lady and see how she fares since she's in these parts?'

'I'd rather not. The nature of her betrothed's death was not …' Angus left the sentence unfinished. Trust Jonathan to have guessed it was a female. At his brother's raised eyebrows he sighed and continued. 'The man she was to have married, a fellow officer, died in a brawl over a camp follower. A woman.' The hard look he directed at Jonathan was meant to convey his desire to end this line of questioning.

Jonathan continued to look enquiring.

Angus gave in, realising as he spoke a kind of catharsis in unburdening himself. 'The woman's protector came upon the pair *en flagrante.* He seized Captain Noble's sabre which was lying outside the tent, and I arrived at the scene in time to see the cut which ended Noble's life.'

The image was branded on his conscience. Noble was a deceitful, untrustworthy braggart but he hadn't deserved to die. Angus forced out the words. '*I* directed the man there. He was a foot soldier who regarded the female with whom I suspected Captain Noble was dallying as his wife. Right-eously, I admit, I felt that Noble, affianced as he was, ought to be brought to task.' He cast a beseeching look at Jonathan. 'I therefore hold myself partly responsible, but of necessity have had to put another light on the incident … for the sake of Miss Micklen.'

'As your brother *and* as a man of the cloth, I grant you absolution.'

To his surprise Jonathan appeared not the slightest bit condemnatory. He went on, 'You might be *insufferably* right-eous, as you put it, at times, but you are not vengeful. There-fore,' he added, patting his horse's neck, 'I strongly believe it will help your conscience to know how his lady fares while lightening her grief to be reassured her sacrifice is appreciated.'

It took a great deal of persuasion before Angus reluc-tantly agreed to the detour.

There was, however, no friendly welcome for them at Micklen Hall.

'You wish me to convey your respects to my daughter?' Mr Micklen, standing by the mantelpiece, was an intimi-dating character. Like his bristling eyebrows, his thick thatch of hair was pure white, his eyes an unsettling pale blue. Though slightly stooped, he'd clearly once been a hand-some, commanding figure. Now any claim to handsome-ness was obliterated by the ugly twist to his mouth. Angus could imagine men quailing like girls when subjected to such sneering, belittling scorn. It was hard to know how to respond to a reception that all but painted him as Jack Noble's murderer, but the sooner he took his leave, the better.

He added sympathy to the other feelings he harboured for Miss Micklen. Noble must have offered a welcome escape from her father's house. In the uncomfortable silence, Angus went over what his investigations had revealed about the old man, though why he should have been interested was a moot point.

Bartholomew Micklen was not, by birth, a gentleman, but

in just a few years he'd trebled the fortune brought him by the French bride he'd rescued from the guillotine and brought to England in the midst of the revolution in France twenty years before. Micklen's detractors hinted at nefarious dealings that went beyond the smuggling that contributed to the livelihoods of so many who lived along this part of the Kentish coast.

Shortly after Angus had returned from his condolence visit, a subaltern in his cups had eagerly supplied Angus with some background to the circumstances surrounding the impending marriage of the beautiful Miss Emily Micklen.

When Miss Micklen had refused her father's initial choice of bridegroom—an elderly viscount—the old man had withdrawn the generous dowry that was a condition of his daughter marrying a title. White's Betting Book had Miss Micklen earmarked for an earl at the very least, given her father's ambition.

So Micklen's subsequent endorsement of the impecunious, raffish Jack Noble was a surprise.

Angus wondered how the pair had met since he gathered Miss Micklen had spent a year in isolation following her initial rebelliousness.

His host kicked a burning log into the grate, then turned to glare at his visitors from beneath his shaggy white eyebrows. 'And your regrets? It's *my daughter* who has regrets!'

Mrs Micklen, who was staring into the fire, made a convulsive movement. Her hands trembled in her lap and her eyes were glazed. Clearly she was following the conversation but her husband had not addressed her.

'Lucy! Show the gentlemen out.'

'My apologies for troubling you, sir.' Angus bowed as the parlour maid opened the drawing room door to usher them into the passage. Stiffly, he added in parting, 'I had wished merely to enquire after your daughter, sir, since it was I who broke the news of her bereavement.'

Micklen grunted.

The maid, whom he remembered from before, handed them their coats, then waited with frightened brown eyes as they donned hats and mufflers.

'Please, sirs,' she whispered with a furtive glance behind her. 'Miss Micklen is staying with the master's sister, Miss Gemma, in Sussex.' Her mouth trembled. 'Don't know as I'm doin' the right thing telling you, but me brother was a brave soldier what fought at Corunna – only Charlie never came home. Well, he were a hero too, what rescued a lass in sore need of a friend just before he left with his regiment ... A lass just like my poor Miss Emily, so I feels it only right to beg you to do the same.'

'Seems as if poor Miss Micklen's fit of the dismals has sent both parents queer in the attic,' remarked Jonathan as he vaulted into the saddle. 'Sussex? To pay a social call? I don't think so.' Picking up the reins, he glanced at his brother with a droll look. His mouth dropped open. 'Good Lord, Angus,' he said, 'you have got it bad.'

EMILY SAT on the edge of her bed chewing her finger nails, cursing the fact her curiosity had got the better of her.

To be seen at the casement by Major McCartney of all people! Why he should wish to call on her, she had no idea. But it was beyond anything to be caught out in such a shameless snub which reflected more on her, yet would no doubt be taken personally by him. Not that she was in a mood to care greatly for anyone else's sensibilities. She had enough to worry about.

Resting her forehead into the palm of her hand, she

hunched over the bed and tried to think sensibly. Well, regardless of how far he had travelled to see her, or why, she was not going to receive him.

It was at that point she received the summons from her aunt. Interfering, controlling Aunt Gemma who was not one to be thwarted, as evidenced by her threat to fetch Emily down herself.

Emily crossed to the dressing table. What a sight she looked. Was there any point in taking pains with her appearance, to at least make herself a little more presentable? The major would leave, shocked, either way. But moments after Mary had withdrawn there was Grummidge, Aunt Gemma's personal dresser, upon the threshold.

What on earth was Aunt Gemma up to?

Emily made her appearance in the blue saloon ten minutes later, dispatched by the thin-lipped, stiff-backed retainer with the dubious reassurance that she looked as good as she ought, under the circumstances.

And those circumstances were not the most auspicious, anyone would agree.

'Major McCartney.' How she managed to retain an aura of calm dignity in the face of the almost instantaneous fiery blush that rushed up from his shirt points, Emily never knew.

And then, suddenly, Aunt Gemma had abandoned her and she was left alone with the tongue-tied soldier.

Almost defiantly she stood in the window embrasure with the light behind her, throwing her silhouette into relief. There really could be no hiding the swollen belly that proclaimed her spectacular fall from grace.

'Miss ... Micklen,' he stammered, bowing, his eyes seemingly reluctant to travel upwards from the tops of his boots. So ludicrously apparent was his discomfiture that Emily actually laughed.

'You see how it is with me,' she said harshly, smoothing the loose, unflattering garment over her stomach. 'I don't wonder you are struck dumb, Major. Nor do I know why my aunt, who has been at such pains to keep me hidden, should have me flaunt myself before you.'

'When I told her I'd come from Kent she seemed to realise my interest was sincere. My—'

'Commiserations? Condolences?'

The young soldier bit his lip. 'Did Captain Noble know?'

'That he was to be a father? No, Major McCartney. He was killed before even I knew.'

'I'm sorry.'

'Sorry that he never knew? Or sorry for my predicament?' Crossing the room she lowered herself awkwardly into a chair, gesturing him to be seated while she poured the tea that Mary had just brought in.

'Both.' Frowning, he leaned forward to accept the dainty china cup she offered him. 'What will you do …?' Clearly too embarrassed to complete the sentence, he coloured once more.

Emily regarded him with wry amusement. 'You have no sisters, do you, Major?'

'No, ma'am,' he confirmed.

'But you ask me what I will do?' She sipped her tea and said with the faintest shrug, 'I am ruined, of course.'

'You were to be married the week after I visited you, I recall.' Quickly, the young major added, 'I'm not judging you, Miss Micklen. It was ill'—he reddened further—'luck.'

ANGUS'S EMBARRASSMENT abated with the realisation Miss Micklen was using proud defiance to mask her fear. He was suddenly brought to mind of that other young woman whose dark hair, pale skin and light blue eyes reminded him so much of the fair bereaved Miss Micklen. Jessamine had done the same.

'Miss Micklen, whatever happens, let me assure you of my discretion.' He wanted to believe she had hope, but his brief interview with her father was not reassuring. Angus knew it was easier for a parent to cast off an erring daughter than a husband a wayward wife. His own parents' troubled union had made that clear enough.

'Thank you, Major. You are, of course, a gentleman and'— her voice trembled—'have shown uncommon kindness in visiting me so as to reassure yourself as to my welfare ...' The bravado slipped. She looked close to tears as she whispered, 'I'm sorry if I have embarrassed you.'

Suddenly she was no longer the proud, unobtainable beauty whose confident gaze about the ballroom did not even register his presence.

Ruined. Her grim assessment was true enough. She would be forever barred from respectable society for a transgression no unmarried woman was ever forgiven. Without a timely marriage to legitimise Jack Noble's child she would lose everything that constituted a life even bearable.

Miss Micklen regarded him silently. Proudly. Despite her swollen belly she held herself like a queen. Her porcelain skin glowed and her inky black hair shone.

It was her regal hauteur which decided him.

A graceless soldier such as himself could never hope to win a wife of Miss Micklen's calibre.

Unless she were desperate.

Reason banished the uncharacteristic and impulsive madness.

Become father to another man's child? What's more, a man he despised? No, Angus did not act rashly.

He returned his gaze to her lovely face. It glowed with

energy and serenity, tinged with defiance. Yet he sensed she wished for his approbation.

She had it, and surprisingly, without disgust. Miss Micklen could only be considered a blameless victim of her betrothed's selfish coercion. Jack Noble would be better remembered for his shameless want of conduct with regard to the fairer sex than his heroism.

He opened his mouth to speak. Like the uncharacteristic impetuosity that had driven him to ride two days to get here, he was again driven by impulses beyond his control, to speak words he had never imagined he was capable. Words that would, he now hoped, change his life forever.

He turned as the door opened.

'My apologies, Major McCartney. Emily, a quick word if I may.'

With the ghost of a smile upon her thin lips, Miss Micklen's aunt beckoned from the doorway. 'Cook is in a pet over some disturbance in the kitchen. You are so much better at restoring domestic calm. I'd appreciate it if you went to her.'

As the door closed behind her niece, the venerable Miss Gemma Micklen waved Angus back into his seat while she folded her lanky frame into the chair opposite.

'So Major McCartney ... You see how it is with Emily,' she said bluntly. 'Captain Noble is dead, but she might just as well be, too. Her father has cast her off without a penny. He will not forgive her. Emily came here in a dog cart with one trunk, and no more. The workhouse was her only alternative, and that's the truth.'

Angus's thought that perhaps France might offer a safe haven was nipped in the bud by her next words.

'Madame Guillotine disposed of the French side of the family twenty years ago – except for an aunt rumoured to have bestowed her favours upon Napoleon, or some enemy of that nature.'

Miss Micklen fixed him with a steely look. 'Now, Major McCartney, what I have to say might sound somewhat peremptory. You have met Emily but twice. No doubt she expects that after today's morning call she will never see you again. I, however, have other hopes.'

ANGUS HAD NEVER LOST his nerve in battle, but facing the lovely Miss Emily Micklen in the same grim parlour the next day tested his mettle like nothing ever had.

It was not that he had expected to be thanked. He had not, however, expected to be scorched by such a fulminating look, and subjected to what amounted to a violent diatribe.

Immediately after his interview with her aunt the previous day he had coldly taken his leave, sickened by the woman's steely determination and handsome inducements. She had implied that the honour of her family was beyond price and that he, an impecunious soldier, who clearly had a personal interest in her niece, would be well rewarded for salvaging it. Miss Gemma, as frightening in her own way as the brother she obviously despised, had said farewell with flint in her hardened eyes.

The satisfaction that flickered in their cold grey depths when he had been announced just now was equally sickening. But Miss Gemma could not be helped. It was Miss Micklen he had come to see, Miss Micklen for whom he had a proposition. One that came from his curiously affected heart.

Now that it had been delivered in the most artful terms of which a man of his self-acknowledged romantic clumsiness was capable, he was receiving a dressing down of almost hysteric proportions.

'She can only have lined your pockets with gold to induce you to saddle yourself with … well, with soiled goods!' Flinging herself round from the window embrasure to which she had marched, chest heaving, her beautiful eyes luminous, Miss Micklen presented a terrifying manifestation of feminine outrage.

Before he had a chance to call on his experience with his quick-to-take-offence mama, she'd turned on her heel once more, grating out, 'Let's not tiptoe around the truth. I am what I am! Yet, sir, let me tell you I'd rather be on the streets than suffer the humiliation of—' Interrupting Angus's stammered protests, Miss Micklen was checked by a rasping sob. 'Oh, the indignity! How could Aunt Gemma?'

'Miss Micklen, your aunt had nothing to do with this—'

'I didn't cut my wisdoms yesterday, Major. Only bribery could have induced you to make an offer for me.'

Her vulnerability, which she dressed up as anger, was so stark he had to stop himself from bridging the space between them to comfort her. His nerve endings tingled with a sensation he could not identify and again he found himself stepping forward to take her hands in his and declare he was motivated by feelings of love and admiration, but he stopped himself in time.

Shaken by his momentary lack of control, Angus drew in his breath and fixed his gaze upon Miss Micklen's fierce loveliness. With businesslike calm, so at odds with what he felt, he said, 'Since yesterday's interview I've been unable to rid my mind of the conviction that making you an offer of marriage would not only solve your immediate problems, it would salve my conscience.'

The words sounded wooden but the conviction that welled up in his breast was almost overwhelming. He had the power to save Miss Micklen from ruin. From an inauspicious start he could foster love. He didn't want gratitude. Jessamine's gratitude had been a poisoned chalice. He wanted salvation through atonement and Miss Micklen offered him a chance to be better than he was.

The force of his longing powered through him though he stripped the emotion from his voice. 'Quite frankly, I am in need of a wife.' It was easier to stare through the window than at her.

The myriad of extraordinary sensations Miss Micklen unleashed in him when he'd first met her at the Regimental Ball two years ago had him once more in thrall. If anyone had told him then she might one day become his wife he'd have scoffed at a notion that surpassed his wildest dreams.

Quietly, he added, 'I am not a glittering match, but I have prospects.'

The fact she did not interrupt gave him courage. 'My lodgings in Maidstone are small, but I plan to sell my commission. We might then find a bigger house.' He paused, meaningfully. 'A home for both you and your child.'

Her eyes resembled her aunt's with their flinty coldness. 'My child and I can do very well without you *or* my aunt's interference.'

He had not reckoned on her intransigence. It only served to heighten his desire. *Desire*. His upbringing had taught him desire wrought disappointment and destruction. He had thought himself well trained in not desiring what he could not have, did not deserve. He swallowed, the need for her acceptance like fire in his veins. He would be raising a cuckoo in his nest, a bastard, but what of it? Hadn't he, too, been a cuckoo? His mother's revenge on a husband who nevertheless treated Angus no differently from his blood-born sons? Though Emily Micklen's child was Jack's and would have inherited Jack's faults had Jack lived to rear it, it was Angus who would rear and mould it. Give it love and a promising future.

He longed to give the proud, hurt, beautiful woman before him love and a promising future.

As a soldier, Angus had enough experience of intransigent prisoners to know when to press the advantage. Gaining confidence from her silence he said, smoothly, 'You realise, Miss Micklen, that unmarried you will be in no position to keep your child?'

Of course she'd know it.

She took a shuddering breath. 'Aunt Gemma—' she began. Then obviously perceiving that if she threw away the only opportunity she was likely to receive to legitimise her child Aunt Gemma may prove less dependable than hitherto, she covered her face with her hands and slumped against the window.

'I know nothing about you, Major McCartney.'

'I am a soldier and a gentleman. I need a wife. You need a husband. I am offering you my name and a home, Miss Micklen. It's intolerable you might be stripped of your child,' Angus called on reserves of creative logic he'd not thought existed to further his cause, 'when I am the indirect cause of your hopeless situation.'

She raised her strained, weary face to his. 'Your actions defy logic unless you are to be handsomely recompensed.'

'Your acceptance is recompense enough.'

Sighing, she looked at him steadily. 'I am not a fool, Major McCartney, and I would be one were I to reject your offer out of hand.' Her eyes were glazed with misery as she turned to stare through the window.

In a dull, flat voice she added, 'Allow me a day in which to consider it. I will see you tomorrow – providing you, yourself, are not struck by just how outrageous your proposal is.'

Exultant, he took a step forward. He wanted to take her

hands, press them to his lips and reassure her he would be a kind and loving husband.

He could not. Her despair was too overwhelming. His smile died before she turned. 'Then I shall call again tomorrow, Miss Micklen,' he said stiffly.

Bowing, he took his leave.

CHAPTER 3

When Emily was a child it seemed she could do no wrong. Her father had bounced her on his knee and called her his little beauty. She'd believed she was loved.

Lucy Gilroy, her nursemaid, had painted a glowing picture of Bartholomew Micklen as a man of courage and integrity who'd created a family dynasty of which Emily must be proud.

Each night, as Lucy brushed out Emily's long, dark hair prior to being presented to her parents before bedtime, she'd weave magical stories about her heroic father.

Young Bartholomew Micklen had been an Englishman with revolution in his veins, the familiar tale went. After he'd risked his life to whisk Emily's mother and aunt from the chaos of the French Revolution which had claimed the heads of the aunt and cousins with whom the Laurent sisters had lived, Bartholomew had married the crippled younger Margeurite. Emily's mother.

Margeurite's elder sister, the exquisitely beautiful Fanchette, had elected to remain in France and her likeness hung above her mother's writing desk, a tantalising link to an exotic past.

When Emily was twelve and no longer a child, her father's attitude towards her changed.

The indulgent papa who'd praised her childish exuberance became the stern disciplinarian. Lucy was put to work as a general maid in Micklen Hall and a series of governesses became Emily's only link with the world outside. At night Emily would hug her rag doll, Fanchette, to her chest and dream about the exciting life her mysterious aunt might be living.

Her own existence seemed stifled and dull.

One night her father had burst into her room, shouting that Emily was too old for such childish props as he'd torn faithful Fanchette from her tight embrace before tossing the rag doll onto the fire.

Her parents had been arguing over her Aunt Fanchette. She'd heard whispers that her mother's sister had been found guilty of a sin too wicked to repeat.

Her father's seditious activities, which had required him to leave England hurriedly, to travel to France when he was a young man, were, she thought sourly, nothing compared to Tante Fanchette's immoral liaison with one of Napoleon's trusted generals.

Emily and Fanchette's greatest sins were not the transgressions themselves, but the fact that *they had been caught.*

Now Emily gazed from her bedroom window in her Aunt Gemma's house and despite the lies and secrets that whispered through the corridors of Micklen Hall she still longed to return to her old home with its surrounding green fields edged by the familiar high, rocky cliffs that fringed the sea in the distance.

But Emily no longer had a home. Even if her father did renege and open his doors to her, she knew that unless she married Major McCartney, life under her father's roof as a sinner would be as intolerable as her only other option: the workhouse.

Having had all night to ponder the inescapable truth, following a fraught interview with her aunt, Emily awoke with a pounding megrim and a heavy heart, shot through with the inescapable knowledge that she had no choice regarding her future.

Jack had given her a glimpse into a world of unexpected pleasures and mutual love but those doors were now shut.

Two minutes after the stiff, unsmiling and clearly nervous Major McCartney had been ushered into the drawing room, Emily accepted his suit.

NOW EMILY LISTENED to the vicar intone the wedding service as if she were trapped on the outside of a large bubble, watching herself within. Her fate was beyond her control.

Just as it always had been.

Aunt Gemma and Major McCartney deemed it in everyone's interests that a hasty marriage be contracted between the introverted soldier and herself. In order to proceed with all due haste, a Common Licence had been obtained and now, resting her hands on her swollen belly – because there was nowhere else to rest them, these days – Emily stood beside the man who was in the process of becoming her husband.

Staring fixedly at the rector, she tried not to cry.

She heard the major solemnly repeat his vows. She dared not look at him in case she saw … what? Satisfaction? Aunt Gemma was a wealthy woman who set a great deal of store by appearances. She'd have paid Major McCartney a large sum to maintain family honour.

Though glad, Emily was perversely piqued he did not try to touch her. No comforting caress, or even the slightest attempt at showing her that he was aware of what she must be feeling. She choked on a sob which she managed to turn into a cough. How large had Aunt Gemma's inducement been to see her niece respectably married?

The major carried himself ramrod straight, his eyes the only hint that he felt any emotion at all. When Emily ventured a glance beneath lowered lashes she saw they burned with some indefinable fervour she was too afraid to wonder at. His tall, well-built frame and broad shoulders made him a commanding presence. It was not a complimentary thought.

Not when Emily had envisaged a domestic future with loving, easy-natured Jack by her side and a brood of lively children.

In a toneless voice she repeated the vows that stripped her of any rights as an individual and made her the property of her husband. That she would be a conscientious wife was not in dispute. Only a fool with no mind for her future comfort and safety would offer intransigence as her part of the bargain. If her husband beat her or otherwise abused her she would have no recourse. He would be legally entitled to the fruits of their marriage – including the child she was to bear.

Major McCartney had said he was ready to take a wife. It would seem a well-connected, financially endowed wife was, under normal circumstances, beyond his means. No wonder he considered her a bargain.

The intoning stopped and Emily realised with mild shock she was married. She raised her face to look at him and saw his diffidence as their eyes met. Of course he should kiss her, and she would expect no less, although it would mean nothing. But the poor man looked both reluctant and quite unsure of himself. She caught a glimpse of Aunt Gemma; she who was always one for observing the niceties. And so, with a small, resigned smile, Emily raised herself on tiptoe, stiffening at the fleeting brush of the major's lips.

Fear of what the next few hours would bring made the hairs prickle on the surface of her skin. Here, Major McCartney was on public view. But what of the privacy of the bedroom?

The bedroom of the Four Leaved Clover where he'd bespoken a room for the night.

THEY BARELY TALKED during the slow, uncomfortable journey to the inn. Angus suspected Emily used the pretence of sleep to avoid any exchange.

Miserably, he reflected on his failure to offer his wife the comfort she needed, even if she would let him. The carriage was a hired post chaise with poor springs and the inn was recommended by little other than its position as a halfway point to his lodgings in Maidstone which, God forbid, were as unsuited to housing a woman like Emily as he could imagine. During their one brief meeting before the wedding Angus had tentatively sought his future wife's thoughts on what she required in a dwelling. It was perhaps just as well her reaction had been lukewarm. Until he sold his commission he hadn't the funds to lease something more commodious, and even then he'd still be pinched in the pocket.

The carriage jolted over ruts and bumps while concerns as to what would be required in the privacy of the bedroom nagged at him. He was still discomposed by the unfamiliar stirrings of his body in response to the touch of her lips.

The uncertainty and resignation in Emily's wide-eyed look at the altar had affected him curiously. He'd needed every bit of willpower not to cup her cheek or reassuringly stroke the inside hollow of her bare arm. It was the fear she would misinterpret his actions that stopped him. Indeed, perhaps she had good reason to misinterpret them, he amended, feeling again the unfamiliar heat in his loins as he drank in her pure, unspoiled beauty.

Only briefly, and then it was accidental, did his eyes drop to her swollen belly. She had been ill-used by Captain Noble. Well, Miss Micklen need not fear *his* brutishness. Or his feelings towards the child she had misbegotten. He was glad for it. Likely as not he would never have married had it been left to him to follow through with the niceties: a proper courtship, then a proposal.

What did a scarred, taciturn soldier with no ready funds have to offer anyone, much less a beautiful, virtuous female like Emily?

He assumed – hoped – they would have children of their own, but he would not be guilty of the arrogant selfishness which had led to Emily's downfall.

'You must be tired,' he said above the shouts of the coachman demanding the attention of an ostler as the carriage came to a halt in the stable yard of the Four Leaved Clover. He saw wariness replace weariness, noted the determined lifting of her drooping shoulders. 'It's been a long day,' he added.

'Yes,' she agreed in a lustreless voice, allowing him to help her out. Closing her eyes briefly, she stretched, her hands tracing the outline of her belly. As if realising what she was doing, she straightened, her whole body seeming to snap to attention. Then with a regal tilt to her head she put her hand on Angus's arm and swept up the stairs to the inn without another glance at him.

As the publican led them to their room a shout of recognition arrested them upon the first stair.

'Major McCartney! Thought it was you!' A tall, blonde young man in regimentals appeared on the threshold to the tap room, grinning, his expression turning to one of surprise when he took in Emily.

Or rather, her condition.

Angus acknowledged the intruder with a stiff nod. Smiling at Emily, he managed the introductions with, he thought, commendable smoothness under the circumstances. 'My dear, may I present Captain Nigel Hartley. Hartley, my wife, Emily.'

'Good Lord, I'd no idea you were married. I admit it's been some months since I last … When was the happy day?'

'Five months ago.' Angus spoke the lie with barely a falter. At least he knew what was required to preserve honour. He patted Emily's hand before turning to his comrade. 'If you'll excuse us, it's been a long journey. My wife is very tired.'

'Aye, you look like you need an early night, Mrs McCartney. In which case, perhaps you'll not object if your husband joins us for a game or two of Faro.'

Angus was not sure who was more relieved at the reprieve. 'Yes, why don't you go and lie down, Emily? I'll organise the luggage and … I'll be up later.' At her obvious gratitude he added, 'I promise not to disturb you.'

He could declare this with conviction for he had no intention of laying a finger on her in anything but tentative affection while she was breeding. What civilised husband would?

It was well after midnight when Angus made his way to their chamber. He'd drunk to keep up with the rest of them, but he had an iron constitution and his head was clear.

Now, as he stood quietly upon the threshold and gazed at his brand new, beautiful wife, he felt himself sway. He was overcome; had to hold onto the bed end to keep himself steady, in fact.

The candle on the wash stand guttered, sending long shadows dancing upon the walls. Emily lay on her side in the gloom with the covers pulled up beneath her chin.

Angus moved closer, fascinated by the lush curve of lashes brushing her cheek. She was breathing softly but evenly, in a deep sleep from which he knew she would not wake easily.

Quietly he reached into the trunk at the foot of the bed and withdrew the tools he required so urgently: charcoal and parchment.

Then he stood above her and drank in every detail.

One long-fingered hand cupped her cheek. Her plait of glossy dark hair was spread upon the pillow beneath her lace-edged nightcap. The strain of her wedding day had been erased from her expression. She looked as if she were enjoying a pleasant dream, for a small smile played upon her lips.

Angus heaved a sigh of relief. He'd been afraid he would find her cowering like a frightened animal, jerked awake from a fitful sleep by his arrival.

He bent down to study the arch of her eyebrow. No artist could have rendered it better. They were fine, expressive brows. She'd used them to good effect when giving him her dressing-down for presuming to make her an offer.

Now she looked as peaceful and innocent as a child. He could not believe she was his.

However, better to dwell on her regal carriage and fine eyebrows than the fullness of her lips. He longed to press his own against hers again and feel them yield in chaste acceptance of her new husband.

He would not think of anything beyond that, right now. Nothing except committing this precious image to paper. Settling himself in a chair beside her he got to work. It was surprising how easily the image transposed itself. Battle scenes were his forte though he'd once done a poor rendering of his mother at her insistence. Now he was enraptured by the idea of doing justice to this exquisite woman. His wife.

A faint murmur made him freeze. No, she'd not woken. She was still smiling in her sleep. Smiling as she had when she'd first greeted him, when she'd misinterpreted his visit for a social call.

She had not smiled since and his heart contracted at her distress, her vulnerability, her unhappiness.

And once again, for the fact she was his.

How tranquil she looked with her pale skin and glossy, dark plaited hair. He felt safe in this clandestine perusal of her, shielded by the fact her lids were closed; her expressive eyes, which flashed like sunlight glancing off his Flintlock pistol when she was proud and angry, had been lustreless today.

She did not want him or this marriage, but by God he wanted *her* and one day he would make her proud of the husband another man's sin and selfishness had forced her to marry.

The candle guttered and the sketch was done. Stretching, rubbing weary, strained eyes, Angus concealed the drawing in his trunk before rising, his gaze shifting to the empty space in the bed beside her.

He groaned softly, feeling more a prisoner than he had when he'd been incarcerated for all those months within the damp stone walls of his Spanish fortress.

How in God's name could he insinuate himself between the crisp white sheets of the same bed and be responsible for his actions?

They hardly knew one another.

The candle was about to go out. Rather than light

another, Angus sat down on the seat in the window embrasure and quietly removed his boots.

In stockinged feet he moved closer to the bed for one final look, and noticed that she clasped something. Sick disappointment churned in his stomach as he recognised the red ribbon that tied the love letters exchanged between herself and Captain Noble protruding from beneath the pillow.

This was her wedding night. Tonight she should have become Mrs Jack Noble. She should have married the father of her child. She should have married Jack Noble, not Angus McCartney. She'd made that very clear.

Retrieving his sketch from the trunk he sat down again and grimly returned to work. He needed to amend his sketch, remind himself of every detail of this wedding night, including the fact she slept with another man's love letters. This was the stark truth and one day he'd look back and remember. Either he'd have to concede he'd made the biggest miscalculation of his life, or …

He tapped the end of the pencil against his teeth at the thought.

… or that force of will could triumph over the greatest adversity. Jack Noble was a man of honeyed words. He'd won Emily through charm and cajolery.

Angus would win her through honour and action.

Finished, he leaned back and closed his eyes. Jack Noble would have made Emily a slave to his passionate impulses. Angus would treat her with care and consideration. He would shield her from the brutish reality of the marriage bed. She need never fear her new husband would be ruled by the ungovernable impulses which had made Jack Noble so dangerous to know.

Folding his length to fit the confines of the window seat, Angus tried to settle down to sleep. He was used to discomfort; had bivouacked in the coldest, stoniest of resting places. He had always prided himself on being able to sleep anywhere, under virtually any circumstances.

But tonight he slept with the fitful awareness of one who suspects a potential enemy is lurking just beyond the shadows.

CHAPTER 4

E mily jerked into consciousness of her surroundings at the flat metallic sound of the copper pitcher being quietly placed upon the marble washstand.

'Good morning...'

Her husband, shaved and dressed, did not meet her eye as he finished his ablutions. Emily suspected he was even more embarrassed than she. Blearily, she took in the chiselled planes of his face, the dark wary eyes, the tight line of his mouth. A stranger's face yet it would have been nice to have woken to a smile. She extinguished the thought quickly. Major McCartney was and always would be a stranger. She was not insensible to the fact she owed him something... but it was too much. Too great a bargain to honour as one day she must, for right now her grief and lack of control over her life was overwhelming.

'We should make an early start unless you don't mind spending another night on the road.'

She pulled the counterpane up to her chin, aware he would be conscious of her aversion, her horror at waking to find a strange man in her bedroom. Still, it was better than finding one in her bed.

Releasing her breath on a sigh, Emily closed her eyes. Thank heaven her wedding night was over. Clearly her new husband was repulsed by her condition since he'd not forced himself on her when such close proximity afforded such an opportunity. She could only hope he'd be unlikely to try once they were … where? Ensconced in their new home?

With the money Major McCartney had received from Aunt Gemma he must have made arrangements for a house that boasted quarters for each of them.

Separate bedrooms.

A baronet's son – with money, now, thanks to Aunt Gemma's inducements – would not expect Emily to accept anything so common as a shared bedchamber.

Emily dragged herself up into a sitting position. 'No, I shall get up,' she said, taking the damp flannel he offered, discovering she still clasped Jack's letters in one hand. Surreptitiously, she pushed them under the pillow and out of sight.

'The carriage is ready whenever you are.'

'You're not riding ahead?' What did it matter if he heard the hope in her voice? This was a business transaction for both of them.

He hesitated. 'No.' He seemed to deliberate before adding, 'I was forced to shoot my horse, Gallant, two days ago.'

She waited, expecting him to leave the room or at least turn his back so she could rise. Irritated, she glanced up and saw the workings of his mouth.

'Gallant was with me in Spain. He was a grand horse.'

'I'm sorry.' The words sounded trite for she could see he was battling some emotion beyond her comprehension. Emily had never owned a horse. Or a dog. She'd given up begging her father for a pet – or anything else – by the time she was twelve.

Briefly, she contemplated telling her husband about her doll Fanchette's fiery end, then thought he'd not consider her loss in the same league as his. She forced a smile. 'You'll have to get another horse as soon as you can.' She wouldn't want him bouncing around in the same carriage more than neces-sary when he could be riding ahead. Besides, surely most husbands would hate the idea of being closeted for hours on end with their wives.

Distracted by the sound of voices in the passage, she glanced at the door, hoping to waylay a serving girl who could help her dress. When she returned her gaze to her husband's face, she was surprised to find him looking at her oddly.

'Gallant will not be easily replaced.' He cleared his throat. 'I'll await you in the breakfast parlour.'

'One moment …' Emily sent a desperate look in the direction of the door as two maids passed by.

He looked at her, enquiringly.

'You'll call someone to help me?' She noticed his confu-sion and felt heat sting her cheeks as she added, 'To help me dress.'

Oh dear Lord, did he really have so little idea of the needs of women? She saw his own colour rise as he muttered, already halfway into the passage, 'I'll get one of the servants to attend you.'

AND WHO WOULD DO it when they were ensconced in his highly unsuitable lodgings? Angus wondered as they lurched along in silence during the final leg of their journey. Miranda, his servant, lived in the village and came in each day. She would not always be on hand to help Emily with all those laces and buttons she could not reach.

The more Angus dwelt on how ill-equipped he was to satisfy his new young wife the less inclined he was to attempt conversation.

It was only as they forded a small stream and lurched out of the dip that he turned at her sharp intake of breath. Alarmed, he leant forward and took her arm as she doubled over, gripping her belly.

'No, please,' she said, shaking him off. 'Sometimes the bigger bumps—' She gasped again as the carriage bounced into a rut, taking a bend on two wheels before it regained its balance.

'We still have another two hours of this. Would you like to stop and rest?'

As Emily was emphatic they continue, Angus did not press it. Instead he suggested, 'If you lean against me I can cushion the jolting better than the squabs. They're old and the leather is hard.'

She did not answer but nor did she draw away when Angus changed seats to sit beside her. Gently he drew her across his lap and forced her head against his shoulder.

He knew she needed respite from the pain. 'Try and relax. For the sake of the baby.'

She stared up at him, mute, her eyes reflecting her misery; and recalling Gallant lying on the cold ground with his fractured leg beyond repair, staring trustingly at him as he loaded his pistol, Angus felt the bile rise up in his throat.

Jessamine, too, had looked at him like this. Needing something he could not give.

He closed his eyes. He could not think of Jessamine now. Not when Emily consumed him. Swallowing, he realised he held her too tightly as she twisted and whimpered against him.

He reached over and drew the blanket up around her, making a soft cushion for her back and midsection. The blanket also ensured she remain unaware of the effects on him of such close physical proximity. The last thing he wanted was to terrify her further.

'Better?' he asked, smiling, and she replied, stiffly, that it was.

It wasn't long before he felt her body go slack. It took all his strength to hold her against him so she wasn't jolted to the floor.

When they reached Maidstone Angus was exhausted.

AND AT MAIDSONE EMILY received the shock of her life.

She could barely move when the carriage ground to a halt. Angus had to lift her out and carry her up the shallow flight of steps to his lodgings.

Lodgings! Like those of an unmarried soldier of limited means. Her revulsion grew as he showed her around. Not that there was much to see.

She didn't care that she was unable to hide her feelings – she was beyond showing any sensitivity to anyone – so that his embarrassment grew by the minute.

'As soon as I sell my commission we can move to something larger.' He could not meet her eye. She knew it was her duty to reassure him that she understood his difficulties in finding suitable accommodation at such short notice, that she was grateful to him for taking her and her unborn child on at all. Calming platitudes and gratitude were required of a wife in her situation. But she could not find the words.

Instead, her exhaustion and disappointment threatened to find an outlet in tears. She tried to breathe evenly to stem the sobs. Perhaps Aunt Gemma had agreed to release the money only when they were properly married.

Perhaps the major had already spent the funds on gaming debts! She wanted to scream and cry. Instead, she could only stare at him, silent, while horror and despair at the long, awful future looming ahead of her twisted in her gut.

'I know it's not what you're used to.' His cheeks were burning as he set her down on a threadbare sofa so hard it made the carriage seem commodious. 'But it'll be only for a couple of weeks. I wanted to wait until you could help choose where we would live.'

She struggled up to follow him into the bedroom after he'd retrieved her trunk which he set down at the foot of the bed.

'Of course you're at complete liberty to redecorate as you wish. You may not find the battle scenes conducive to sleep.' He reached up to remove the crossed military swords above the mantelpiece, turning a battle scene to the wall.

Emily shuddered before looking away. 'It's your home. If this is how you like to live ...' She shrugged, pretending it was of little concern to her.

And yet, it was ... a nightmare.

One step up from barracks, she supposed as she stared at the lumpy double bed.

As he busied himself removing the battle scenes from the wall, Emily stole a glance at the scar that disfigured his left cheek and felt something close to hatred. But for him Jack would have been at her side.

Wouldn't he? She wanted to ask so much but couldn't. She'd scream and rail at the injustice of life, proving what her father had told her since she was a child: that madness ran in her veins and woe betide the man who allied himself to a Laurent woman. Misery and misfortune would be their lot.

Suddenly her anger at Angus dissipated. If he didn't

already, he'd soon regret marrying a cursed Laurent woman. She clung to the plain iron bed end and forced back the tears.

'I'll leave you ... Emily.' He stumbled over her name. 'You should rest.'

'Yes.' She swallowed. Forcing her way through her grief, her inertia, she glanced around, frowning. 'Is there no one here to help me unpack?' She had been going to say undress but disliked putting notions into his head.

'Miranda, my servant, will be here later. She comes in from the village each day, but we've arrived earlier than I'd anticipated.'

Emily ran a weary hand across her brow. She was so tired now she no longer cared what became of her. Presenting him with her back, she murmured, 'In that case you'll have to unfasten my dress.'

She smiled grimly as he fumbled with the buttons. What-ever pleasure he discovered as he caressed her flesh would be as hollow as she was. She knew with dull certainty that with Jack dead she had nothing but a husk to offer him. When the last button was unfastened, Emily gripped the bodice to stop it slipping down and with a sigh, asked him to loosen the laces of her stays.

With this done, she raised her hands above her head and asked him to pull off her dress. So many layers, she thought wearily. Though still in her chemise when she turned to face him, his face was flaming.

She didn't care. She didn't care about anything, not even her pride.

'I need to rest,' she murmured, close to crumpling to the floor and too ungainly to climb into the high bed, unaided.

Wordlessly, he pulled back the bed covers and took her wrist, helping her onto the mattress which wasn't as lumpy as she'd feared, before drawing up the covers. Strangely, his actions were efficient and soothing.

Desperate for release, she plunged into a deep sleep before he'd even left the room.

Emily was relieved to find her new husband had already left when she awoke after more than ten hours' thankful oblivion. For the next week she was asleep before he took his rest and he was up before she awoke. During the day they spoke little to one another while dinner was largely silent conducted over the plain fare Miranda provided.

ON THE FIRST day of the following week, Emily struggled out of bed feeling larger and more ungainly than ever and listened for sounds of Angus's servant. The previous day she'd overheard the woman grumbling to Angus that her extended hours did not suit her since she had six children of her own to tend.

The weather had grown warm so after washing she pulled on a light, loose morning dress from the trunk she had not yet unpacked. Fortunately the garment, which had been refashioned from one of her mother's old gowns, buttoned up the front.

Consciousness usually brought with it a wave of misery and desolation, but before Emily had time to assimilate her thoughts there was a loud rapping at the front door. As Angus appeared to be out and Miranda had not yet arrived, it was Emily who finally responded to the repeated pounding.

'Good God!'

It was hardly the kind of greeting she'd expected. A tall, handsome young man, with a very young, attractive female wearing far too flamboyant a costume to be respectable, stood upon the doorstep.

Emily drew herself up and fixed them with a flinty stare. 'Can I help you?'

The young man, blushing to the roots of his flaxen hair at her frosty response – delivered in the cultured tones which marked her out as a lady, not the doxy she suspected he must have assumed – stammered that he was here to see his brother.

'Whom do I have the pleasure of addressing?' asked Emily, dismayed at not having been informed. Morning dress was not the attire for entertaining visitors and although she had few presentable gowns, she'd have at least made an effort had she known Angus's family intended paying a call.

The young man bowed with a flourish. 'Bellamy McCartney, Angus's youngest brother, at your service, ma'am. May I present my friend, Miss Nellie Galway.'

Emily managed a barely perceptible nod as she stood aside so they could enter. 'As you may have gathered,' she said crisply, 'I am Angus's wife, Emily. Please, come in.'

Emily was under no illusion that Bellamy suffered from a congestion of the lungs. She could quite imagine that a fit of coughing, or was it choking, could easily be brought on at the delivery of such news. Angus, she'd already gathered, was not the marrying kind.

She led them into the tiny parlour and bade them sit, excusing herself to 'arrange for tea' since Angus's lodgings had nothing as sophisticated as a bell pull.

Nor the house, it seemed, a servant, though she prayed either Miranda or her husband would appear to help her.

She found both, and soon Miranda was seeing to the tea while Angus sat beside her on the tiny sofa, his thigh pressed insinuatingly close to hers as they faced their visitors.

'Thought I'd take Nellie for a bit of a bowl through this neck of the woods and stop in on you,' declared the youth.

'Lord, I never knew you'd got leg-shackled, Angus. I mean, married! Does the pater know? Well, does anyone? Beg pardon, ma'am,' he added, for Emily's benefit.

'I've not informed them, no.' Like Emily, Angus clearly did not embrace the intrusion.

'But married! Good Lord, out of all of us I never expected ... well, never mind. Congratulations and all that. Hope you're very happy.'

It was clear he was thrown by Emily's highly pregnant state. Every time he glanced at her his gaze dropped to her belly before a deep blush spread up his neck and he hastily looked away again.

It was not a successful visit. Angus glowered each time the simpering Miss Galway offered her unsolicited opinion on every subject under discussion, and in the most ill-bred of accents. Emily wished Bellamy would stop repeatedly marvelling at the fact of Angus's altered matrimonial state.

'Good Lord, you didn't even tell Jonathan? I only saw him the other week. When was the happy day?' he asked, adding hastily, 'Of course, it must have been some months ago, naturally ...'

'Naturally,' Angus replied, dryly.

When mercifully the guests had departed, Angus turned back from the front door and looked at Emily who was bending down to clear away the tea things. 'I cannot apologise enough for any embarrassment caused you. For both my brother's imprudent speech and for his bringing such a highly unsuitable female into your company.'

His apology did not provoke the response he might have expected.

With deliberate care Emily set down the plates once more and turned to look at her husband through narrowed eyes.

'For contaminating me with a lady of dubious repute? But Angus, how much worse a contaminant would *I* have been

47

had you not married me?' She patted her swollen belly. 'You'd be apologising to your brother. A fallen woman—'

'Don't speak like that.' His wide-set eyes burned with undeserved defence of her. 'Men's impulses can be ungovernable, but ladies do not suffer such … urges … You were … taken advantage of.'

Emily stared at him. She sucked in a long, quavering breath as her simmering anger came finally to the boil. Is that what he believed? That she was insensible to passion? And that was a *good* thing?

'What would you say if I told you that my impulses were every bit as ungovernable as Jack's?' She could barely control her anger sufficiently to speak. For days she had forced her feelings into the background, using the same emotional device against her unwanted husband as she had when her father insulted her, shutting out the hurt by erecting a barrier as impenetrable as steel.

Now, feeling surged through her, blackening her vision and causing her to sway. She put her hand on the back of the sofa to steady herself.

Angus stood awkwardly by the door, as if unsure whether to move closer to support her, or beat a tactful retreat.

Emily glared at him. 'What if I told you that I was so consumed by passion in Jack's arms I would not have heeded the Blessed Virgin Mary cautioning me against the temptations of the flesh?' She tried to regulate her breathing, but the rage was clawing its way further up her body, threatening to make her its puppet. She, who never lost her temper. 'I loved Jack. I was his slave in passion, every bit as culpable as he. If you are so concerned for virtue, spare your condemnation of innocent Miss Galway. You need only cast your eyes upon your wife to be singed by my sin. There! I have confessed my true nature. Whatever you thought of me before, you cannot but think worse of me now.' She registered the horror in his eyes and was glad for it. Much better that she banish any pretence between them.

She'd never expressed anger as poisonous as this. At first it frightened her, then it sent exhilaration pulsing through her. Her love for Jack had been cut off at the root. Now hatred filled her veins, making her feel alive again.

'And so you know, I care nothing for your opinion,' she added. She managed to remain upright, though her vision came in waves. She could feel her strength leaving her, but she had to spit out the truth so he'd have no illusions as to the kind of woman he'd married. A woman no good man deserved. 'You married me because you needed a wife. I married you so I could keep my child. We made a contract. My body is yours to do with as you please, but that is *all* you will ever have. My thoughts, my feelings, my love will be forever out of bounds to you.'

She flinched from his touch, saw concern replace his horror as he gently pushed her down onto the sofa. She did not want his compassion.

'My dear, you are overset—'

'Overset? I speak the truth. Wives do not talk of ungovernable passions. Not to husbands who know absolutely nothing of passion!' She flicked away his hands which had settled on her shoulders. Awkwardly, she managed to rise without his help this time. 'But I know my duty. You shall be well tended to. I know what I owe you.' She shook her head as if to clear it, casting her gaze around the room. 'Those plates,' she said, adopting a tone of briskness. 'Yes, they're the last things to be taken to the scullery and then all will be in good order once more. After that I must see to some bread.'

She took a couple of steps before doubling up with pain. But still she would not let him help her. Brushing past him, she left the room.

❋

ANGUS CLOSED HIS EYES, gripping the sofa back as yet another wave of misery swept over him. With an effort he swallowed down the lump in his throat as he assimilated the magnitude of all she had just said. The sounds of his wife struggling to acquaint herself with the scullery were further recrimination.

So she thought he'd sought a wife in place of servant and doxy, to tend to his practical needs and physical desires.

Unconsciously he had been crumpling the missive Bellamy had delivered on behalf of his mother. Now he drew it from his pocket, broke the seal, and, because Emily did not want him, scanned the two blunt lines.

Your father is dead. Please come.

The churning in his stomach which had started during his encounter with Emily assumed volcanic proportions. He had to sit down, reread the words and decide what to do.

His father was dead. Not the father whose name he shared with Bellamy and Jonathan and his other brothers, but the remote stranger he shared with one half-sister he had never met.

And then he heard a splintering crash, as if the entire contents of the crockery cupboard had hit the floor, followed by the unmistakable dull thud of a body.

CHAPTER 5

Angus crossed the threshold of the scullery, skidding in the growing pool of dark, sticky liquid to crouch beside Emily who was curled up on the floor by the kitchen fire, gasping. She jerked her head up at his touch, her eyes wild.

Dear God, she reminded him of a terrified enemy soldier with a sabre at his throat.

'I'll call for the doctor. He'll be here soon,' he reassured her, turning his head from her pain and fear to seize a piece of flannel Miranda had left over the back of a chair. Right now, stemming the flow of blood was his most urgent task. When Miranda clattered in through the rear door only seconds later Angus sent her to raid his linen chest for its meagre resources, then next door to dispatch Mrs Cooper's boy to fetch help.

Now Emily lay on the bed with her legs raised upon a cushion, a bloodied blanket between them, whimpering that she needed to cover her soiled dress for modesty's sake.

'Mrs Cooper is fetching blankets,' he hedged, knowing he had no more linen unless he tore down the curtain.

'Cover me, *please.*' Emily clenched her fists and Angus recruited his heavy, none-too-clean greatcoat which he snatched from the hook on the back of the door.

'Hush. Be calm. The doctor will save the baby.' Angus stroked her brow, calling on platitudes to comfort her, knowing how much more she'd hate him if his reassurances were empty. He stared out of the window, preoccupied with the best course of action, unaware he was unconsciously now stroking her swollen belly.

Surprised at the warmth that penetrated her gown, he glanced down.

He'd never touched her so intimately before and was suddenly overcome by the desire to feel the living, breathing unit that was his wife and the child. Without considering her reaction, he placed both hands on the taut mound. A weak, indistinct movement fluttered beneath his hands, and in sudden excitement he cried, 'I can feel it moving,' before dropping his hands as Emily convulsed, shivering.

The flowering of hope was quickly extinguished and his stomach contracted. Emily was going to die of cold unless he got her out of her sodden, blood-soaked clothes, and soon. He strained to hear sounds beyond the squawking of chickens and masculine shouts of the farm boys which drifted in from outside. Miranda and Mrs Cooper had been gone a long time.

'What are you doing?'

Angus glanced down at her terrified face and registered the knife in his hand, poised at the fastenings of her gown. He'd lost patience with the promise of help and had raised Emily into a sitting position, but now he dropped his arm so the knife was out of her line of vision while he attempted a reassuring smile. 'You'll catch your death in those sodden garments.'

She retreated into the pillows more furious, he thought,

than fearful. 'You will not use a knife to rip my clothes from my back! I have precious little to wear, as it is.' Her voice contained an edge of hysteria. 'What do you know about delivering a baby? Where's Miranda? Where's the doctor?'

'They'll be here soon,' he soothed, although her questions echoed his own concerns. Despite her protests, he sliced off the buttons that ran down the front of her gown. Then, taking a fistful of linen in each hand, he tore the garment from neck to hem.

'How dare you?' she shrieked, collapsing into tears as if it were catharsis to channel her fear into anger.

He'd seen reactions like it before in the army and was more concerned that she was shivering like a jelly, her skin now icy to the touch. Once he'd rid her of her blood-soaked garments he'd have to find more blankets.

'Do you make a habit of tearing women's clothes from them in wartime? Do you enjoy listening to their protests as you take a knife to them?'

In another situation her words would have been wounding barbs, but Angus was familiar enough with blood, fear and urgency to remain unmoved by Emily's terror-induced taunts.

Once he'd peeled off her outer wear he inserted his knife beneath the drawstring of her chemise and again, shredded that in half. For a brief moment she lay still and naked before giving an outraged shriek as she brought her hands up to cover her breasts.

His gaze did not linger. There was no room for sentiment and this was no seduction scene.

'I'm sorry, Emily.' Gently, he again covered her with his great coat. 'It's hard to be so helpless.' He squeezed her wrist before stepping back, but her gaze was blank.

When Mrs Cooper arrived bearing an armful of blankets for which he paid her handsomely on the spot, she told him the doctor was attending a breech birth and would come as soon as he could.

Angus relayed this to Emily who chewed on her knuckles and muffled her sobs as she moved her hips to try and shift the pain.

'I'm losing the baby, aren't I?' she whispered.

'Not if I can help it.' Angus sat on the bed beside her, listening to Mrs Cooper boiling more water downstairs.

He reached for her hand, but she pulled it from his grasp, turning her face to the wall. 'It'll be a relief if I die, too,' she whispered. 'A relief for all of us.'

He didn't know how to answer. Did she want soothing, or fierce rebuttals?

So he said what was in his heart, understanding her rage at her impotence and the power he had over her. It was a strange relief to be able to unburden himself to her like this. Careful not to touch her, he was also careful to see she was attending to him.

'We're strangers, Emily, but we won't always be.' Her body was an indistinct mound beneath a pile of coverings but she was still, her eyes open. Alert. He placed his hand on top of her covers, somewhere in the region of her shoulder. 'And this won't always be where we live nor will this coarse woollen great coat be your only comfort. One day I will buy you silk and cashmere and you will know I love you and perhaps even be glad for it.'

She did not answer and he sighed, preparing to let her be. Then reconsidered. He would not be deflected by her cold-ness. This was not the Emily he'd fallen in love with: the dazzling, joyful creature whose movements on the dance floor had held him captive as if she were a proud Spanish beauty performing her finest for her coterie of admirers.

Insinuating his hand beneath the covers, he searched for her hand. This time she did not pull away.

'Silk and cashmere,' she repeated in a murmur. He felt the splash of tears before they fell upon her wrist, though there was no trace of them in her voice. 'Why would I deserve silk and cashmere when I'm lucky just to have a roof over my head?'

It had gone quiet outside. It was just him and his wife. 'I suppose your father said that.'

With her other hand, Emily reached out to touch a mark on the wall. 'And that I am beyond redemption,' she whispered. Another large tear oozed from the corner of her eye. Angus could see it in the dull light.

He squeezed her hand. 'No doubt your father deeply regrets what was said in a moment of anger.' His own father was remote and distant to all his sons. The one he called father. Angus thought of the note his mother had written and knew he'd have to dispatch a reply shortly. He still wasn't sure how he felt. Disconnected. Unaffected. He'd only met his real father twice. Had not known who he was until his mother had told him and then he'd been so consumed by anger he'd not spoken to her for a week.

'Papa never says anything he doesn't mean.' Emily sounded like a young child. Angus felt the bond between them grow. The only interest his real father had shown in him was when he'd bought him a commission in the prestigious Rifles. Angus had written to thank him but there'd been no contact since.

'Shall I send for your mother?'

Emily gave a mirthless laugh. 'Papa would never let her come.' She moved restlessly. Sighed. Added listlessly, 'Papa had such plans for me. I tried so hard to please him but I couldn't marry the man he chose for me. I just couldn't.' She swallowed and her sorrow dissipated, her gaze suddenly luminescent. 'Then he introduced Jack to me. Perhaps it was atonement ... I don't know.' She shrugged. 'I couldn't believe he'd sanction such a match for Jack had no title or fortune.' Her mouth curved at the memory though her eyelids grew heavy. 'But it was love at first sight and for the first time for as long as I could remember, Papa seemed happy. As for me, all my dreams had come true.'

He could see she was drifting. Her eyes fluttered shut and her voice was indistinct as she added, 'Papa said I'd made an excellent choice.'

Angus stretched out his legs as he stroked her brow. Let Emily reminisce about Jack, though when the child was born it would be raised to call Angus Papa and Jack would have faded from Emily's mind.

God, he hoped it would come to pass.

Emily stroked her belly. Despite the fact it was an effort, she was clearly disposed to talk. About Jack. 'Jack knew how to charm people. He told me that in France he lodged with a family called the Delons when he was doing his government work—'

'Government work?'

Emily opened her eyes and clasped a hand to her mouth. 'Did I say that? I swore I'd never—'

'Then I'll ask you no more.' Angus smiled as if the indiscretion meant nothing, but he was surprised. He knew Jack Noble for a womanising braggart. Not the kind usually recruited by the Foreign Office.

'Well, Jack was so charming that the Delons considered him like family after his first stay with them.' Emily shifted and stared at the ceiling. 'If the child is a girl I want to call it Madeleine. The Delon family had a daughter Jack was fond of. She chose the ribbons Jack used to send me. He said if we had a daughter we would call her Madeleine.'

'If it's a girl you can call her anything you like,' Angus murmured. 'But if it's a boy, we must choose a name together, for it will be a McCartney and we McCartneys have a proud naming tradition for our sons.'

'But—'

He put a finger to her lips to stay her protest. Forgetting his diffidence, he leaned over her and cupped her face. 'Emily, like it or not, your child will be a McCartney.'

No, he was not a true McCartney, but he'd been reared as one. He drove his point home. 'Regardless of how many children we have, Emily, they shall all be reared without distinction but with love and affection. You surely didn't imagine it would be any other way when you married me?'

He'd hoped for a flicker of appreciation. Resting her hands on her swollen belly she said woodenly, 'Papa says I am beyond redemption and you will forever despise me.'

'It's not true.' Before he could reassure her further she twisted her head away from his touch.

'I thought I'd found happiness and a few days wouldn't matter. Now,' she lowered her voice to a whisper, 'I'm in Purgatory.'

He gripped her wrists almost roughly so that she opened her eyes in surprise.

'Purgatory is when there is no hope, which would indeed be the case if I despised you. Now count your blessings, Emily, for here is the doctor.' He put his hand around her waist to support her into a sitting position and drew back the curtain to confirm the truth of his words.

'Forget about what your father says and start believing what I say, for like it or not, I am your husband.'

He was not ashamed for the rough edge to his voice. Though her slavish devotion to her dead betrothed was understandable there was a limit to how long he'd indulge her.

Angus had his pride.

❄

EMILY AWOKE to the sound of splitting wood outside. She raised herself, blinking in the light that gleamed through the curtains from a sun that was high in the sky. She was not usually such a late sleeper, but then she'd been in bed for five days and her life and that of her child had been hanging by a thread.

Her hands went to her stomach. It was huge and taut.

And she felt movement.

Joy battled with grief. With a shuddering breath, she swung her legs over the edge of the bed, silently blessing the conscientious young doctor who had attended each day. Jack's baby lived. Her last link with the man she loved still breathed within her.

She managed to dress herself unaided, tidied her hair which Miranda had freshly braided two days before, then went in search of Angus.

He was working near the wood shed. Emily hesitated upon the back step, reluctant to approach him and ask whether she were required to provide breakfast now that she was up. She wanted to thank him for all he'd done but hadn't the words. Angus had stayed with her, reassured her and tended to her physical needs. Angus, more than the doctor, had ensured she'd kept her child, but Angus was still a stranger.

… though not such a remote one.

Stripped naked to the waist, her husband wielded the axe with strong, rhythmic movements.

First glance caused her to blush and lower her eyes, but then she strained for a closer look. She was surprised at the bulk of muscle, and the thick sinews of his arms which stood out at each stroke. This almost ascetic man was unexpectedly the athlete beneath his uniform.

Unconsciously she stroked her stomach as she leant her weight upon the door frame, watching him. There was something cathartic and relaxing in the sight.

'Mrs McCartney?'

She gasped at the interruption, guilty embarrassment burning her cheeks.

For a moment her visitor appeared as discomposed as she. *'Miss Micklen?'* Rising from his bow, banishing the astonishment from his tone, the soldier before her added formally, 'Good morning to you.'

'Good morning, Major Woodhouse.' Emily forced a smile for the young man she had met on a handful of social occasions. A friend of Jack's and now, it seemed, wanting Angus.

'I'm here on business, though … your husband'—he made it sound a question—'is not expecting me.'

The last time Emily had seen Major Woodhouse she'd been on Jack's arm at the Christmas Regimental Ball. She remembered his courteous admiration, had thought him handsome and likeable with his brown curling hair and open expression. Now his green eyes darted to her stomach and his smile seemed assessing – although perhaps that was only her imagination – as he remarked, 'Major McCartney is a lucky man. I did not know he'd married.'

'A whirlwind engagement, Major Woodhouse.' She wished her voice sounded stronger, for her tremulous whisper only emphasised her position as an object of shame. She indicated the half-naked man at the bottom of the garden. Angus's torso glistened with sweat in the morning sunlight. Engrossed in his task, he was unaware he had a visitor.

From a distance he looked strong and manly. Her heart seemed to shift a little, as if the heaviness of her unhappiness were almost too great a weight for it to bear.

'If you want to make yourself known to my husband I

shall organise tea.' Turning, she went inside, wondering if she would be able to find what she needed, even for so simple a matter. Major Woodhouse could draw his own conclusions, but it was best for them all – her unborn child, included – that her domestic clumsiness not reveal just how new a bride she really was.

Angus let the axe fall and turned as he sensed a presence, which he knew was not Emily. She'd looked like she could sleep for a hundred years when he'd checked on her early this morning after he'd risen from his makeshift bed on the floor by the scullery fire. An odd spark he was reluctant to identify burned in his chest at the memory of her face, lovely and serene in repose. Emily and her child lived. Emily was still his wife and he could still look forward to the little family that gave him hope there might be happiness on the horizon.

'Woodhouse!' Wiping the sweat from his brow with his forearm he smiled and looked past him to the house. He was about to – dubiously – offer refreshment, but the other man cut in.

'A brief visit, Angus. Strictly business so it would be best if we were not interrupted. Thing is …' Major Woodhouse drew level and rested his boot on top of the newly split pile of logs. 'A rather urgent problem has cropped up and we need your help.'

Angus waited. Several years before, he had been involved in a reconnaissance mission in Spain, scouting out the mountains ahead of their unit before the troops advanced. He'd been commended for the detail and accuracy of his intelligence but had resisted becoming involved in similar operations.

Though Woodhouse had never declared direct involvement in the government's clandestine efforts to destroy the

French Republic, Angus knew he sympathised with their desire to restore the Bourbons to the throne once Napoleon was defeated; that he passionately believed it to be in England's interests; however, he did not know how closely involved Woodhouse was in covert operations.

It didn't take him long to find out. 'The Foreign Office advised me one of our agents was attacked in Bern last week.' Major Woodhouse came straight to the point as he withdrew a leather drawstring pouch. 'I'm looking for a dependable envoy to supply him with replacement papers.'

Angus betrayed nothing. Not his distaste for subterfuge when he was comfortable on the battlefield where he knew exactly who and where the enemy was. Nor the unexpected frisson of excitement that he was about to be offered a mission that would give him something meaningful to do after so long on half pay, doing nothing.

'Francois Allaire, wealthy banker, is his alias.' Major Woodhouse tapped the pouch. 'You'll find passports and letters of introduction for both of you. In just over a week he's due to meet the Paris prefect of police, but without the right papers he's in a perilous situation.' His brow clouded. 'Some months ago and in similar circumstances we lost a valuable and long-serving agent. We can't afford the same to happen, which is why I'm approaching you to help us.' He sent Angus a searching look. 'There is no one I'd trust more than you.'

Practicality and a healthy dose of aversion to lying, even for so good a cause, made Angus hesitate when only moments before he'd all but embraced an opportunity to feel useful and serve his country.

'And my disguise? The green jacket of the 60th?' He shook his head. 'Sorry, Woodhouse. While I'm no friend of Bonaparte's, you need a diplomat, not a soldier.'

The man he'd known and respected for so many years

since they'd joined as recruits contemplated him a moment. When he spoke again there was a brittle note to his tone.

'My apologies. It never occurred to me you'd decline.' With a brief but pointed scrutiny of the back of Angus's humble dwelling he added, 'I thought if your patriotism were not inspired you'd at least view affairs differently in light of your changed domestic situation.'

Angus put a conciliatory hand upon his friend's sleeve. 'I am still in the pay of the British government and my loyalty will always be towards my country. I'm just questioning whether someone else would do *this* job better than I.'

Major Woodhouse kicked at a chicken pecking his boot before fixing Angus with a level look. 'In Spain you spent three days and nights in rain and sleet lying out ahead of Bonaparte's army. Your intelligence was first rate. When you were eventually caught and interrogated your quick wits saved your life. You were promoted to Major. Since then you've continued to serve the army with distinction.' He paused, assimilating his argument. 'It's because I knew you planned to resign your commission, and in consequence would be champing at the bit'—he sent another contemptuous glance, this time towards the scrapheap by the back door where Miranda was scraping out the remains of a bowl of gruel—'that I thought you'd be open to my proposal.'

For the second time in a few days Angus felt mortification at his inadequacy. The dwelling was supposed to have been a short-term abode after he'd come back from war. Stretched for funds and with only himself to worry about he'd not bothered to look for something else.

Major Woodhouse's tone became cajoling. 'This mission is part of a complex campaign to ensure homeland security. Our agent, in his guise as a Swiss banker and funded by the British Government, is proving that English gold is an effective tool in turning the loyalties of key French generals who are themselves starting to predict the fall of Napoleon. If Allaire's cover is blown, every agent we have recruited throughout Switzerland, Spain and France is compromised.' Woodhouse looked grey as he added, 'For he *will* be induced to talk.'

Angus digested this in silence. He was no coward, but espionage did not sit well with him. He would have preferred a mission that involved straightforward tactics.

Woodhouse clicked his tongue. 'For months you've been searching for something worthwhile to do, anyone could see it, Angus.' He sounded impatient. 'All I'm asking of you is to help ensure we don't lose another valuable, long-serving agent.' His lip curled as his glance encompassed Angus's dwelling briefly once more. 'I can't imagine a man of your pride relishing your current situation.'

He could see Angus was wavering. He cast another disparaging look, this time at Angus's worn boots, before warming to his theme. 'Our British agents are in league with French generals disenchanted with the Corsican invader. Together with representatives of the House of Bourbon we are confident of soon toppling Napoleon. But to ensure success we need to send someone who speaks impeccable French; someone dependable – and fast – to furnish Allaire with the necessary papers.' He cleared his throat. 'On a more practical note, the job I'm offering you comes with a government pension after the war is won.'

A pension. Instant remuneration. Angus stared at the lowly lodgings to which he'd consigned his beautiful wife and registered that he was not insensible to his friend's rising passion; and not only from a pecuniary point of view. He missed excitement.

'All we're asking of you on this mission is to play the messenger. Play yourself if you're uncomfortable with charades: the painter who won't let a war raging across

Europe interfere with his passion.' Major Woodhouse's tone became more persuasive. 'Tuck your easel under your arm and dust off those letters of introduction to the curators of the world's finest art collections to which the war denied you access.'

Angus shifted, the frisson of excitement within tempered by the reality of his changed circumstances. Even a veritable host of galleries could not outweigh his concern for Emily and his desire to see her safely delivered of her child. Some naïve part of him kept alive the hope that through his steady dependability Emily would develop for him some small affection.

He realised it was a pipe dream. Emily would appreciate him far more if he were playing the hero abroad than slavishly attending to her meagre comforts at home.

'My wife is in a delicate condition. How long am I likely to be away?'

'Once you've delivered the requisite papers to Allaire your mission from this side is completed.' Woodhouse muttered over the calculations. 'Two hours hard riding to the coast; the packet leaves every Tuesday and Friday; the channel crossing might be done within three hours, if you're not becalmed, and then another two to three hours to reach the home of Monsieur Delon. Perhaps you'd be looking to return to England several days after that.'

'Delon?'

Woodhouse raised an eyebrow. 'You are familiar with the name?'

'I have heard it mentioned in connection with Jack Noble.' Woodhouse's momentary confusion was replaced by suspicion. 'Miss Micklen ... I mean, Mrs McCartney, spoke of this?'

Angus tried to dilute his friend's objection by returning

to the matter at hand. 'I presume there will be future requirements?'

Woodhouse hesitated, then replied, 'For many years the Delons have assisted foreign emissaries who would see a Bourbon monarchy reinstated.' He stared at Angus as if determining his friend's commitment. 'If you do accept, yes, this will be the first of further operations. It is likely they will introduce you to other members of their association.' Clearing his throat, he added, 'I will therefore need reassurance that your loyalty to the cause extends beyond this first operation.'

Angus hid the frisson of irritation swept over him at his friend's pomposity. Although Woodhouse was the first he would turn to in a crisis, the man had the ability to get under his skin like no one he knew. Yet Angus also knew he had more to lose by rejecting the opportunity being presented. Not only from financial considerations.

'And this unfortunate soul you mentioned previously. Should I not know the circumstances of his death if you fear Allaire faces the same peril?'

Woodhouse reddened. 'Initially we attributed the late Monsieur Perignon's death to his well known voracious ... carnal appetites, however it appears he was betrayed,' he hesitated, 'though we have no proof of this. Then all went smoothly until Allaire was attacked. Again it appears Allaire's perilous situation is due to betrayal within our ranks. He sent Angus a searching look. 'So you will help us?'

Angus needed no further persuasion. Betrayal from within was an insidious threat and in a different league altogether from simple espionage. He nodded. 'I assume you wish me to leave at the earliest. Tomorrow? Anything else I need to know?'

'If Mrs McCartney questions you, say nothing of the real

nature of your business.' Woodhouse frowned, as if imagining the lengths to which a woman might go to have her curiosity satisfied. 'She may try to persuade you that Jack Noble kept her apprised of his activities. Do not be swayed. Noble was under the strictest instructions to say nothing.' His scowl deepened. 'If you heard the name Delon mentioned by Mrs McCartney it is clear she has no understanding of the need for discretion.'

'I'd have thought the charge of indiscretion was better laid at Jack Noble's door,' Angus muttered.

Woodhouse appeared to be making an attempt at mastering his exasperation. 'Noble was recommended for his position by no lesser personage than the Foreign Secretary himself.'

'Then I fill esteemed boots,' Angus replied with heavy sarcasm for he knew Woodhouse would consider Noble's selection as unlikely as Angus did. 'And the risks? There are always risks it is well to be apprised of.' He was thinking of the perils that dogged him in Spain: the silent, deadly wraiths of the night that could slit a man's throat before he knew what had happened.

He was not expecting a woman's name.

'Madame Fontenay … Fanchette Fontenay …' Wood-house's look turned to contempt. 'She's been a thorn in the side of the English for years. A blood-thirsty revolutionary responsible for the deaths of countless British agents … including our lately departed aforementioned agent in Paris.' His lip curled. 'I've heard she had a rare ability to inveigle her way into the trust of the most cynical using her vast arsenal of apparently limitless feminine wiles.'

At Angus's undisguised interest Woodhouse continued, 'She was last seen heavy with child many years ago before disappearing into the shadows. Then within the last twelve-month a woman fitting her description was seen in the vicinity following the deaths of Perignon and several fellow compatriots.'

'Anything else?'

'She married, surprisingly, some unwitting nobleman. Whether he knows it or not, he now funds her zealous hatred of the Bourbons and all who try to return them to their rightful throne.'

Angus nodded thoughtfully. 'A physical description would be helpful.'

Woodhouse raised his eyes heavenward. 'Hair like a raven's wing, eyes like liquid amber and skin like honey … despite not being in her first flush of youth. If you can enlarge upon that lyrical tribute you're not likely to pass it on, I'm told. Word is she was once mistress to one of Bonaparte's trusted generals and that she and Bonaparte remain on good terms. Well, I think you've heard enough.' He turned on his heel and preceded Angus up the garden path that led around the house. 'Take care when it comes to this Fontenay woman, Angus,' he said over his shoulder. 'Though it's not your immediate mission, we rely upon her capture. That said, if she entered your orbit you'd have no chance. Her kind is only successful through an instinct for sniffing out a man's susceptibilities, and I know damsels in distress are yours.'

Now that the serious business had been discharged he was in a lighter mood. Near the back steps he stopped and turned. 'Don't glare at me like that, old chap, when I've gone all out to praise your many fine qualities.'

'Madame Fontenay—'

'Madame Fontenay is, as I told you, another mission altogether. Right now, all you need do is deliver Allaire's papers.' Major Woodhouse pulled out his timepiece. 'Perhaps you'd better acquaint your – er – wife with matters as they stand and be ready to sail on the Friday packet. Everything you need to know is contained in there,' he added, pointing to the pouch which Angus now held. 'Allaire is at a safe house. Monsieur Delon's address is amongst the papers I've given you.'

Emily was relieved when she glanced through the window to see Major Woodhouse mount his horse, doff his hat in her direction, and ride off. Glancing up once more as she removed the kettle from the hob she was even more relieved to see Angus had resumed wielding the axe.

She found the end of some rather stale bread and a hunk of cheese and ate it with her tea, sitting on a stool in the scullery while she contemplated her sparse surroundings.

Miranda entered with a clatter of pattens – for the backdoor opened onto a veritable quagmire – her apron filled with wood which she added to the fire. Not a woman of many words, she jerked a nod of greeting in Emily's direction before picking up her scrubbing brush.

Emily chewed thoughtfully on the end of the bread. With renewed health came a revival of her spirits. Aunt Gemma's funds must be coming soon for Angus had spoken of their new residence. He was a decent man, she would allow him that. He had been kind and his decisive action had saved the baby. He'd made plain his concern for her. For both her and the baby. But she couldn't rid herself of the conviction that their present discomfort was due to Aunt Gemma's money being withheld due to some stipulation she was unaware of. Who knew what the two had plotted as fair recompense for

Angus to salvage Micklen honour?

She tried to rein in her scattered thoughts. Marriage was a contract for most couples of her station and she must get over the bitterness of losing out on love, for she had been provided with what most fallen women – yes, she must not forget that was what she was – could not even dream of: a marriage to enable her to keep and legitimise her child, and a home.

Hopefully a commodious home with separate apartments for each of them so she could reflect in privacy, read Jack's letters without fear of interruption, sing songs to the baby about its father—

She pictured Jack's roguish grin, her breath shuddering as her daydream was swept away by an image of Angus bending over her, his dark-brown eyes blazing with intensity as he vowed to save her child and protect Emily.

The sentiment and his actions were those of a good man and she must try to keep that at the forefront of her thoughts rather than hug her grief to herself over Jack's death. Yet how could a man as upstanding as Angus care for and respect a woman so steeped in sin as she? Could his concern stem only from the fact that if she died too soon he'd lose out on Aunt Gemma's money?

'Get back to bed with ye, girl,' grumbled Miranda, looking up from her scrubbing. 'Yer as white as a ghostie.'

Emily swallowed the last of the dry bread and fixed Miranda with a level stare. Soon she'd be in her own fine residence with servants who treated her with respect.

But it was true. She was feeling suddenly light-headed from her modest exertions. She accepted that Miranda, also, had been good to her, when the servant had every reason to despise her new mistress for being no better than someone's fancy ladybird with her swollen belly and too fresh wedding ring. Lacing her hands over her bulge, Emily waddled back to the bedroom, closing the door and reaching up for her shaw on the hook.

Then the pain struck again.

She regained consciousness in her husband's arms. Eyes closed, she remained limp as he covered the distance to the bed. He was still shirtless. The direct contact of her cheek against the coarse hair of his chest, beneath which she could feel the beating of his heart, evoked an indefinable, confusing response. She'd never been close enough to him to smell his fresh sweat, to touch his skin. Whereas Jack's chest had been smooth and hard, Angus's was dusted with dark hair.

'How do you feel?' he asked, realising she had come to.

'There's been no more bleeding, but I've sent Miranda to fetch the doctor, in case.'

Embarrassed by this clinical assessment and wondering at the nature of his examination while she'd been unconscious, she heard the tightness of her voice. 'Clearly you're accustomed to blood.'

He smiled his tense, thoughtful smile as he tucked her in, smoothing the pillow and again she wondered who had caused the scar that sliced his cheek.

'It comes with the job. Would you like a mug of sweet tea?' 'Perhaps later.' She sighed, though his concern was reassuring. There was no doubting the constancy of his feelings and she took comfort in his presence, she realised, but she was exhausted. She felt wrung out, emotionally and physically. Closing her eyes, she felt for the reassuring movements of the baby.

'Two more months, Emily.'

At the intensity of his tone she blinked to see him crouching beside her, his eyes level with hers. The room was dim with the curtains closed against the sun, but even in the gloom his eyes glowed. If she didn't know how ridiculous a thought it was, she might have said, with excitement.

'Two and a half,' she corrected him.

'He only needs another two to have a fighting chance.' 'You think it's a boy?' Despite herself she couldn't help smiling just to contemplate the living, breathing creature within her. Then she remembered it was Jack's child. Stiffly, she added, 'Besides, what would you know about such things?' and was immediately ashamed of her churlishness.

'I've delivered a baby.'

He must have seen her shock, for he laughed softly as he resettled himself on the stool at her bedside and took her hand. 'The battlefield isn't only about death. There's a huge contingent of women and children who follow their menfolk around the globe and they endure terrible hardship.'

Emily stared at him. 'You delivered a baby?' she repeated, trying to imagine how a commissioned officer of the prestigious 60th Rifles came to be involved in some sordid camp follower scenario. 'Your … mistress?' For some reason she'd never imagined Angus having a mistress.

'Her friend,' he corrected her.

So he had a mistress. Or once had. She digested this startling information in silence, unable to give voice to the multiple questions chasing themselves around her head.

He smiled. 'We were in Spain and although a fierce battle had just been fought, the irony was that, with calm restored, the poor woman had fallen in the river when doing the washing and was wedged between two rocks. The birth pangs were well advanced by the time I arrived. Now I have a godson, a lusty boy who'd be about four.' He rose, obviously amused by her shock. 'Don't fret over what you can't change, Emily. You're my wife and whatever happens, I promise to look after you.'

'And where is your mistress now, Angus?'

She heard the tartness of her tone and added quickly, almost meekly, 'I beg your pardon, Angus. That is not a question a wife should ask her husband.'

His look was difficult to read as he answered from the doorway, 'You may ask me anything you like though I do not promise I will always answer you. What I do promise to offer you, however, is the truth.' He was silent a long time before he said softly, 'Jessamine is long dead after a liaison of very short duration. Now, regrettably'—he cleared his voice—'I must go away for a few days. The doctor will be here soon and I shall make arrangements for your care.'

The surprise that he'd had a mistress whom he'd even discussed with her was replaced by astonishment that he should suddenly announce he was leaving, followed by fear that he'd consign her to living in these squalid lodgings during his absence.

'You're leaving me, alone? At a time like this?' she gasped.

'I'm on my way see my brother and his wife who will take care of you,' he reassured her. 'They live in great comfort. It will be far better for you to remain with them in the interim. Major Woodhouse has offered me an assignment abroad I was not in a position to refuse.' With a sweep of his arm, he added, 'One that will soon see us out of here and ensconced in something far more fitting. Besides,' he gave a self-deprecating laugh, 'I'm sure you won't deny that a little time away from me will hardly break your heart.'

This was true enough, but she was still dismayed by the circumstances in which he left her, not knowing how far away his brother lived, for he surely did not refer to Bellamy. 'I'm …' She closed her eyes and shook her head as she forced out the words, 'to go to your brother's house? But of course, for where else can I go? Certainly not home.'

From the doorway he fixed her with another of his almost disarming level gazes. She wanted to dismiss his words, his actions, as the platitudes of a man who had secured his comfort through her wretchedness, but increasingly her conviction that Aunt Gemma's bribes were somehow involved seemed without substance. Angus really did consider her comfort and safety as his first priority rather than an inconvenience now that adventure beckoned from across the channel.

'Home is with me, Emily. One day, I hope, you will feel that. I shall ride to Honeyfield House to see my brother, Jonathan, and ask him to fetch you'—he offered her a rueful smile—'as I obviously have no conveyance and his carriage is a great deal more commodious than any equipage I can hire locally.' At the look on her face he reassured her, 'The journey is less than an hour and my sister-in-law, Caroline, is a charming, accommodating woman. I'm confident you shall enjoy every comfort while I am away. To be perfectly honest, Major Woodhouse's proposition couldn't have come at a more fortuitous moment.'

She was surprised at how touched she was by his smile when he added, 'I hope it won't be long after I return from abroad that we shall move into a house worthy of you, Emily. I hope, then, that the rift between you and your father might be mended. You deserve to take your rightful place in society and to have your father's respect. It is every good daughter's right.'

With his attention focussed on the peeling walls he did not register her horror.

'If you think he'll forgive me you know nothing of my father!' She jerked forward in the bed. 'Reconciliation is not possible!'

Instead of declaring roundly, as Jack might have done, that he'd make sure it all came to pass, Angus took a while to gather his thoughts. 'You are respectably married,' he said slowly. 'The child will be born legitimate. You've brought no shame upon your family. Restoring ties between you and your father is important.'

'No, you don't understand.' She was close to tears as she gripped his hands which were suddenly clasping hers. 'Papa is vengeful. I sinned. If he could find another way to compound my suffering, my shame, he'd do it.'

Angus hunkered down to take her in his arms and as she

was squeezed gently but firmly she felt a strange sensation in the pit of her stomach. Not the movement of the baby and something that was quite definitely more than just gratitude for his concern.

'You belong to me now, not your father,' he soothed. With her ear pressed against his bare chest once again, Emily could hear the strong staccato beat of his heart. The strength of his arms around her was strangely comforting, for indeed the domineering spectre of Bartholomew Micklen did seem diluted.

Gently he lay her back down on the pillow and for a long moment she stared at him as if he were not the husband forced upon her whom she despised.

Still, it was important Angus understand. She clasped her hands and pleaded, 'Don't petition my father for forgiveness. It will only give him another focus for his dissatisfaction with me.' She turned her head away.

'Then I want to be the means by which you are reconciled. I can do that, Emily.'

She sucked in a quavering breath. 'I don't know why you're so concerned that I mend ties with my father. It's not as if I came with a dowry dependant upon his goodwill.' Almost viciously she added, 'And it's not as if you married for love.'

In the lengthening silence she regretted her words, but it was too late. Miserably she stared at the wall.

Angus stroked her hands which plucked at the bedcovers. Then, leaning over her, he kissed her brow, his murmured words filling her with immediate warmth only to be swept away by fear of her own failings. 'My dear Emily, I married where I hoped I might find it.'

CHAPTER 6

Angus found his brother and sister-in-law strolling hand in hand amongst the roses when he reached Honeyfield House.

'Already you're abandoning the new Mrs McCartney in her highly delicate condition?' Jonathan chided him. 'A gently born woman, alone in your lodgings, Angus?'

He was not surprised they'd heard from Bellamy of his marriage and Emily's circumstances, but Angus was quick to defend himself.

'You make it sound as if I were tying her to a stake beneath an oak tree with rations and a club to fend off wild animals,' he retorted, glad of the diversion when his young nephew bounded out from the stables.

'Uncle Angus! Papa's bought me a prime piece of horse-flesh. Come and see him!'

'I'll see him later, Jemmy. I have a long journey ahead of me and was going to ask your father if I could borrow a fresh mount. Perhaps you could saddle him for me if your father's agreeable while I explain my visit, indoors. This horse is borrowed and his owner will fetch him this evening.'

'Could I, Papa?' implored the boy. 'Joseph need only *tell* me what to do.'

This agreed, Angus and Jonathan made their way to the drawing room while Caroline set about ordering a hasty meal.

'Now tell me what this is about,' Jonathan demanded, not yet prepared to accept Caroline's gentle chiding that Angus may not deserve his censure. Easing his comfortable frame into an armchair beside the fire, he harrumphed.

'You've been mighty havey cavey, Angus. You know I'd deny you nothing within my power, but I think we're owed an explanation.'

A quick précis of events had Caroline's kind, homely faced creased with concern. 'I shall fetch her myself. Lord only knows what terrors the poor woman is suffering, knowing she'll soon not have you by her side.'

Jonathan was more interested in what Angus was not telling them and asked, as they repaired to the dining room a little while later, 'So you're to France, you say?'

'Did I say that?' Angus smiled as he sat down in a velvet upholstered chair. 'I'm taking tomorrow's packet across the channel at any rate.'

Three plates of steaming beef broth were placed before them. Jonathan's spoon hovered as he said, 'Honeyfield House is open to your wife for as long as required, there's no argument there. Even you, Angus, must realise a woman can't be expected to survive in those lodgings you've always deemed comfortable enough. But you're leaving her within a fortnight of your marriage?'

At Caroline's fresh objection he checked himself: 'I mean five months. At least, Bellamy told me, *sotto voce*, that this is what must be put about if reputations are not to be besmirched.'

Angus smiled at them both. 'I gladly entrust her to your care. Another thing,' he added as he picked up his spoon, 'on my return from France I intend paying a call upon Emily's father.' He looked at Jonathan. 'I daresay you recall Bartholomew Micklen. His welcome was not one that is easily forgotten. He's disowned Emily, but I believe a reconciliation would restore her spirits like nothing else I can think of.'

Jonathan looked surprised. 'The girl's better off without him.' He spooned up his broth. 'Since you made plain your interest in her when we called at Honeyfield House that *memorable* afternoon, I made enquiries. Fact is, I've heard much since that doesn't reflect too well on Micklen. Lord, and now you've married the girl!' he added in an undertone.

Caroline was more sanguine. 'Your honourable actions saved Emily's family from disgrace, Angus. She's as respectably married as any expectant bride and I've no doubt your father-in-law will extend to you a warmly reconsidered reception and, indeed, welcome the opportunity to restore ties between himself and his daughter.'

Directly after he'd left Honeyfield House and with the light still bright, Angus paid his mother the necessary duty call.

She lived a further twenty minutes' hard riding from Jonathan and Caroline and his visit to his bereft mama could wait no longer.

After being ushered into her darkened private withdrawing room he sat on the chaise longue beside her, holding her hand while she, in a laudanum-induced stupor, repeated the litany of gushing eulogies to her one true love, Angus's biological father with whom she'd conducted a torrid year-long affair when her husband, Sir John, had been in thrall to his latest mistress. Within an hour Lady McCartney was sleeping peacefully and, after a short and cordial conversation with Sir John, the only father he'd known, Angus rose from the leather sofa before the study fire.

'I hope to broker a more conciliatory relationship between Micklen and his daughter,' he said in answer to Sir John's inquiry regarding his in-laws. 'Their home is not far from where I take the boat to France.'

His marriage had been discussed in oblique terms. Angus assumed Bellamy must have regaled all with a highly coloured version of events, for Sir John merely grunted as he walked Angus to the front steps.

'How do you propose to keep this unhappy creature in your current straitened circumstances since I gather she's brought no dowry? Whole affair's decidedly out of character, my dear boy.'

'I'm about to resign my commission, and I hope it won't be long before I realise the funds.' Angus pondered how much to tell him. 'My trip abroad is on His Majesty's Service and well remunerated.'

They shook hands, Angus halfway down the stairs when Sir John stopped him. 'I haven't given you a wedding present.'

'I didn't expect one, sir—'

'Nor should you. Unbecoming secrecy.' Something like a smile played about Sir John's lips. 'Your wife ... Bellamy says she's a beauty. No doubt her eyes'd sparkle at the prospect of owning a choker of pretty stones?'

'I hardly think—' Awkwardly, Angus tried to deflect him.

'Bellamy also tells me you're in need of horseflesh. So what'll it be: the pick of my stable – except for Milton and Bess, of course – or the McCartney choker?'

Angus stared at him. 'But won't mother—?'

'Good lad, you've not disappointed me. So you wish to

add to your consequence in your new wife's eyes. The future of your union augurs better than your poor mother's and mine. Don't worry, I'll see what I can do to get you saddled in the meantime, regardless. As for the diamonds, it's been a long time since they could fit around your mother's neck and she'll not begrudge you them. You've always been her favourite.'

Angus returned from his visits to find the household in uproar.

'Thank the Lord you're here, Major!' Miranda dropped a bloodied sheet upon the hearth and wiped her forehead with her hessian apron. 'She's losing the babe, sir. Oh, Lordy, but it would come too early. Doctor's on his way so you must go up to her.'

Angus took the stairs two at a time and flung himself onto his knees at Emily's side.

'Help me up,' she whispered, her face white as chalk. 'I need to move. I can't bear the pain just lying here like this.'

'But shouldn't you—'

'Just help me to my feet!' She clenched shut her eyes and flinched as another spasm of pain gripped her.

'Emily …' He didn't know what to say, but he did as she bid, supporting her weight on his arm, helping to keep her upright. 'The doctor won't be long.' He had no idea when the doctor would come but he had to give her hope.

'He won't be able to do anything.' Her eyes flared with another sudden pain before she resumed her rhythmic circuit of the small bedroom. 'I can feel the pangs. The baby's coming too early and there's nothing anyone can do,' she sobbed.

God! He could almost feel her pain. 'Please know how much I want this baby, Emily.' He held her to him for a brief moment before she pulled away, compelled, it seemed, to keep moving. It did not deter him from saying what had to be said. 'This baby will unite us. I *wanted* to marry you, Emily, but you'd not have had me unless you had no other choice. I'm sorry that's the way it was. I'd have wanted you to accept my suit on my own merits, but—' He bore the weight of her as she paced, hoping she was registering his words though she said nothing. 'That's why I rejoiced in this child. It was *because* of it that we could become united. A family.' Anguish clawed at him. She had to understand the truth of it.

'Well, it's too late,' she sobbed between clenched teeth. 'I'm losing the baby and there will never be another—'

'There will be more.'

'Not Jack's baby!' She clapped her hand to her mouth. 'I'm so sorry,' she gasped, on another spasm of pain.

He rubbed her shoulders as she pressed herself against the wall, seemingly to escape the pain. Dully, he said, 'I heard nothing.' It was the only response he could think of, but her words cut deep. Jack had been dead nearly six months and still her heart cleaved to him with as much passion as she obviously rejected her marriage to Angus. Swallowing, he begged her in a low voice, 'Come, sit down on the bed, Emily. You should rest.'

'You know nothing of what it is to suffer birth pangs!' she cried, pulling out of his grasp. 'I cannot sit down. I'm a prisoner to the pain. I must move.'

She continued to pace, clutching her stomach while she muttered, 'I should have known I'd not paid my dues. My father told me I would pay for my sins. He said I got off too lightly by marrying you.'

Angus stared at her, helplessly. 'This is not your punishment, Emily. For reasons we'll never know, the baby is coming too early, but it's not your fault.'

She forced a smile and he felt a pang to his very core as she reached out and briefly touched his hand. 'You are a good man, Angus,' she whispered. 'I wish I could love you, but you must leave for France tomorrow and I am glad for it. I don't think I could have borne this sorrow with you by my side.'

CHAPTER 7

Not even the beauty of the passing elms, bright in their sunset-coloured foliage amidst fields of golden corn in a new and different country, could dispel Angus's gloom.

I don't think I could have borne this sorrow with you by my side.

Her words scored his heart like the pain of a thousand lashes, but at least she wasn't going to be alone. The baby had been born during the night and had breathed for half an hour before it had died. Before the priest had come.

Caroline, as good as her promise, had been there, arriving only an hour after he had. Instead of putting up at the Black Crow in modest comfort, she'd insisted on attending Emily so that Angus could leave first thing in the morning on his mission to France.

She'd also promised to lay out the dead child.

Angus delayed his departure until the last moment although Emily seemed not to register his parting kiss.

He would visit Emily's father on his return, certain that

despite what Emily declared, nothing would be more calculated to restore her spirits than her father's acceptance.

With Emily in the good care of his capable sister-in-law, Angus realised he must turn his attention to the future. His and Emily's. Fantastic possibilities had opened up his horizons. He was about to direct his talents towards the good of his homeland while his personal rewards extended well beyond that. He could provide for Emily: a fine home, a carriage and a wardrobe full of gowns.

He slumped back against the squabs of his post chaise.

What good were fine trappings if Emily did not love him … and perhaps never would now the reason for their union was gone?

Restlessly, he shifted in his seat. He wished he'd chosen hard riding to this endless jolting over rutted roads, but he'd decided there were advantages to not arriving travel stained and exhausted wearing muddied riding clothes. Even if riding clothes *were* pretty much the extent of Angus's wardrobe these days. Lord knew, he was on few invitation lists.

He swallowed, his throat dry. He must make an effort and emerge from his reclusive ways to promote his lovely wife into the arena she deserved. Once he'd settled upon a handsome house, ideally not far from Honeyfield House, he envisaged the determined-though-nurturing Caroline directing operations with her usual efficiency, grooming Emily for her new role as one of the foremost ladies of the district.

If this pleased Emily, Angus didn't mind swapping his riding breeches and boots for formal attire, on occasion. That was a small price to pay for seeing her smile.

As he consulted his timepiece he wondered rather gloomily if he'd ever see Emily smile again.

The countryside was changing and he remembered

Woodhouse's description that indicated the distance covered. He should be at Monsieur Delon's within the next hour, but exhaustion was fast claiming him. Angus knew his strengths and the few traits that he believed recommended him: he was tenacious, discreet and he could sleep anywhere. But he was a terrible sailor, and by God the crossing had been slow and rough.

THE DELONS LIVED in a handsome stone house in the centre of the pretty Cathedral town of Saint-Omer, twenty-eight miles, or three hours' travel from Calais. French aristocrats, they'd survived the Reign of Terror, fleeing Paris twenty years before, making connections in England, and then being reaccepted by France's new regime. Monsieur Delon was a canny local politician and, Angus had been informed, a secret campaigner for a Bourbon restoration, a goal shared by the English bureaucrats who'd recruited him.

Peace. Angus had spent too much of his life at war and he relished his role in this mission. He remembered the euphoria that had gripped him and his countrymen eleven years before when the Treaty of Amiens had brought short-lived peace. As an eager art student he'd been on the verge of seizing the opportunity to indulge his passions when suddenly the treaty was dissolved and hostilities were again the order of the day. As one son amongst so many, the army had offered him a livelihood.

Since then he'd seen too much horror. The thought he might in some way contribute to a more permanent peace between warring nations would make him feel his life had been good for something.

The house was silent as Angus was led by the parlour maid to an elegantly decorated drawing room. He recalled

Emily's mention of the Delon daughter, Madeleine, and listened for the sounds of playing. The thick stone walls filtered the noise from outside and he could have heard a pin drop, indoors. Madeleine must have no boisterous brothers. He knew nothing about girls but supposed that one small one, alone, would make little impression on a household like this.

The silence of the Delon residence, disturbed only by the tick of the grandfather clock in the hallway, reminded him of the Micklen household, but he was relieved that his greeting from Monsieur Delon was a good deal warmer.

As the parlour maid announced him, the exquisitely attired Monsieur Delon rose from his wing-back chair before the fireplace, declaring in perfect, accented English that any foe of Napoleon was a friend of his.

'A message came last night that we were to expect you, Monsieur McCartney.' From beneath Monsieur Delon's elegant, grey eyebrows a pair of bright eyes regarded him with interest and good humour. 'My daughter and I have been eagerly anticipating your visit.'

Angus judged him to be in his sixties. He spoke with pride of his daughter, before outlining his plans to present Angus later that evening to the most important figure in their operation. 'Count Levinne heads *Le Congregation de la Roi* and we greatly anticipate that your delivery of the necessary documents on such short notice is a prelude to greater involvement in an operation that aids a cause which we hope is as close to your heart as it is to ours: freedom and peace. Ah, Madeleine, our guest has arrived.'

Angus turned as his nostrils were assailed by a waft of peony scent, the assault on his senses intensified as he beheld an exquisite apparition in white, her lovely pale arms holding an arrangement of hot house blooms which she placed on the sideboard, her long dark hair simply bound in an ivory comb. Smiling, she swept back an escaped tendril.

For a moment Angus was speechless, the sudden constriction of his airways forcing him to straighten while he composed his features into registering nothing but neutral, courteous interest. Meanwhile his mind whirled and the surface of his skin tingled with an extraordinary combination of admiration and disgust.

Madeleine Delon was remarkably like Emily on first glance, with her glossy dark hair, clear-eyed gaze and perfect skin and features. She was also at least a dozen years older than the child he had been expecting.

Her simple white muslin gown moulded her shapely body, which she moved with an obvious understanding of the allure she must hold for most men.

'A pleasure to meet you, Monsieur McCartney,' she murmured as she curtsied before advancing towards him with the languid grace of a young woman confident of her powers of attraction.

'I see it was not a good crossing,' she added, raising one eyebrow in amusement as her eyes met his.

She was exquisite but he forced aside the admiration, imagining her instead sizing him up like a well fed cat sized up its prey; wishing he didn't care that she'd found him wanting after the rigours of his journey.

'I shall have the kitchen prepare something soothing.'

In only a glance she'd accurately summed up the reasons for Angus's obviously pallid looks. Now she took his arm and led him to a chair while her father set about procuring them both a glass of Madeira. 'Poor Major McCartney,' she crooned, 'We shall do what we can to make you feel better.' Angus was uncomfortably aware of his vulnerability.

Mademoiselle Delon exuded an incredibly powerful magnetism. After arranging the cushions to facilitate his comfort, the young woman moved to the mantelpiece from where she regarded him with sharp interest as she draped one arm languidly along the marble. 'Captain Noble, now he was a good traveller, *n'est ce pas*, Papa? We were saddened to hear of his death but are very happy such a brave man has replaced him. Our cause needs you, Major.'

The perfect symmetry of her face reminded Angus of a Gallic Madonna with impish eyes. Now she no longer reminded him of Emily, though both were of similar height and build, each with a smile notable for their small, white pearly teeth.

To his embarrassment he realised he was looking directly at Madeleine's mouth, full and sensuous, the lips moist and slightly parted, and he shifted and swallowed, feeling the heat in his face as he realised Madeleine was studying him with equal interest.

He forced his thoughts under control. Madeleine, the poised beauty with her raven tresses and confidence of her place in society and appeal to the masculine sex, was no match for Emily's purity and modesty.

He returned Madeleine's smile with the courtesy required while his skin prickled with the knowledge that this was the Madeleine after whom Jack would have Emily name their child. What duplicitous swine would do such a thing?

'Though the crossing was bad, I hope you recovered while riding over our excellent roads, Monsieur.' Mademoiselle Delon smoothed her glossy coiffure, smiling at Angus as her father handed him a drink.

And although Angus replied appropriately, he could only wonder how much Madeleine knew about Jack Noble's betrothed and whether she'd entered into the malicious fun of deceiving Emily.

After refreshment had been taken, Monsieur Delon laced

his hands across his neat, round, beautifully upholstered belly and gave a sigh of appreciation.

'You would, Major, probably care to rest for an hour or two before dinner. I'd hate Madeleine to weary you with her childish prattle.'

Father and daughter nodded in familial accord, and Madeleine swayed against her father's side as she focussed her amusement upon their visitor.

'I would, sir,' Angus said stiffly, his thoughts turning to how much Monsieur Delon knew about his daughter's dealings with Jack Noble and whether the personal deceptions practised in this household compromised the operation.

He forced a smile. 'As you accurately surmised, Mademoiselle Delon, the crossing was diabolical but the carriage ride was not as bad.'

'Perhaps you'd like me to rub your neck with lavender balm,' the young woman suggested. Her bright amber eyes raked him with undisguised appreciation. 'Captain Noble found it helped ease the ill effects of his journey.'

'I'd prefer to sleep, but I thank you.'

'Then go to your bed, major,' his host exhorted him. 'Madeleine will show you the way.'

Monsieur Delon's words sounded a hundred miles away. Angus forced his chin up as Madeleine placed her hand in the crook of his arm.

'Count Levinne is looking forward to meeting you at tonight's *soirée*, Monsieur,' she said as she led him from the room. 'The loss of Monsieur Allaire's papers has put us all in a difficult, if not perilous, situation should his identity become a matter of curiosity.' Leading him through darkened corridors, she stopped and pointed. 'Your room is in the attic. If the house is for any reason searched, the ladder can be pulled up. Many brave men have been housed here but none so brave as poor Captain Noble and now'— fleetingly,

seemingly unconsciously, she ran her fingers down his arm—
'yourself.'

Even in his current state of exhaustion, her smile sent uncomfortable tremors though him. She was so like Emily in certain lights.

Ignoring Angus's protests that he needed no further help, Mademoiselle Delon insisted on accompanying him to his chamber.

He finally gave up protesting when Madeleine pushed him back upon the bed and knelt to remove his boots. The truth was, he didn't think he could have torn off his Hessians without help in his current state of exhaustion.

'No doubt you have someone to do this for you at home.' The look she sent him when she glanced up as she knelt at the base of his bed was sly, the fleeting touch of her quick, deft hands both horrifying and uncomfortably erotic. Jessamine had been the last woman to have removed his boots. He closed his mind to the thought.

'I manage,' he mumbled.

'You do not have a wife?' She arched an eyebrow. 'Poor Monsieur. Every man needs a wife and you are so handsome—'

'I have a wife,' he cut her off, wincing at the relief of lying on a comfortable bed in stockinged feet, aware of the unintended sharpness of his tone.

She straightened, stepping back to regard him curiously from the centre of the wooden floor. With speculation in her eyes she looked nothing like Emily, though he wished Emily would look at him like this.

'Ah yes, but you are newly married, *non*?' Obviously she had been well briefed.

'Newly married, Mademoiselle, and very tired.'

'Yes, you must sleep.' Her lips curved in a secretive smile as she leaned over him, her breast brushing his cheek as she tucked the blanket under his chin. 'You have important work to do if you are to satisfy our organisation and to make your new bride proud. When you have rested you must tell me all about her. I take great interest in the brave men who lodge with us, and the women at home who make their own sacrifices.'

CHAPTER 8

Consciousness lapped at the periphery of Emily's brain and although she knew someone was in the bedroom she wasn't ready to emerge from the nether world just yet. She held her dream fiercely to her as she gave her mind free rein to wander. She and her infant son were tumbling in the sweet green grass beneath a clear blue sky surrounded by a dozen gambolling lambs. Jack's eyes stared out at her from her child's cherubic face as he extended his chubby fists to be picked up. Invisible bonds that could never be broken bound them together.

She bent down to scoop him into her arms, her heart filled to bursting at the anticipation. The thought of his soft curly hair tickling her cheek, his little arms wrapped about her neck made her breath come more quickly as she savoured the excitement.

She opened her eyes suddenly. He must have darted out of reach. Stumbled perhaps.

But no. He was not there and this was no rose-coloured reality or even a wonderful comforting dream. It was her reality. Her painful reality: a cramped bedroom in a soldier's barracks, devoid of physical comfort or friends or love. The only thing to recommend it was that it was free of the man who now had complete control over her.

She gave a sob. The child was to have been her future. It was to have been a little Jack protecting her from loneliness, providing her with a reason for existence, a reason for her marriage. It was … everything.

Groggily, she forced herself to confront the truth beneath the covers of a strange bed belonging to a man she'd known less than a few weeks … in her husband's house and more heartsick than she could remember.

She registered once more the rustle nearby, smelled the familiar smell of chamomile and the strange one of – what was it? Orange water? – and finally acknowledged she was not alone.

A tantalising aroma of bacon wafted through from the rear of the dwelling, and when she half opened one eye she saw someone sitting on the chair at her bedside. For a moment she thought it was her mother and excitement surged through her, quickly extinguished as an unfamiliar voice directed the maid, 'Miranda, a nice cup of tea, please. Mrs McCartney's awake.'

Mrs McCartney.

Emily jolted upright and stared at the stranger, a plain, pleasant-faced woman in her early thirties. Her cream muslin gown was simple but fashionable, her fair hair drawn back from her face, a style which accentuated her best features: fine, hazel eyes through which she regarded Emily with a mixture of interest and compassion.

'I'm Caroline McCartney, your sister-in-law, and you've slept a long time but I think it was just what you needed.' When the woman smiled she no longer looked plain and efficient. Her smile was the most heart warming smile Emily could remember in a long time, but she clamped down the flowering she felt in her heart and imagined Caroline must be a fine actress to hide the disgust she'd no doubt be feeling. She'd regard Emily as no better than a woman of easy virtue, a fallen woman, a Cyprian … and goodness knows how ghastly it must have been for her to have tended to her for all this time.

Giving no indication that this was the case, her sister-in-law went on. 'I came here the day before yesterday and you've been in and out of consciousness. We were worried and loath to move you.' Glancing around, raising her eyebrows at the pictures turned to the wall, she added, 'I think you will be more comfortable with us. My husband, Jonathan, is preparing the carriage for your removal now. In case Angus hasn't told you, Jonathan is his older brother and rector of St Barnabus, a little over an hour away. Less, of course, on horseback but although the carriage is slow, it *is* comfortable.'

Although Caroline withdrew the hand she'd extended towards Emily, her smile remained, despite Emily's lack of response. 'I believe you have no wish for your mother to be sent for, but if there is anyone …'

Her mother. Emily quivered with longing at the thought. Even if her mother could manage the journey her father would never sanction it.

'There is no one,' she whispered.

Nevertheless, she regarded Caroline with interest. Like herself, she was Mrs McCartney – the eldest brother's wife. And she was being kind to Emily.

Her sister-in-law took the steaming cup of tea Miranda handed her and said, as if reading her thoughts, 'Angus asked me to see to your comfort, Emily, but I think you also want someone with you who understands your grief.'

To Emily's surprise, Caroline touched her cheek, her eyes full of sympathy. This was not what she expected. Her dead child meant nothing to anyone else; except as an interloper by family members doing the arithmetic.

Emily did not withdraw from Caroline's touch this time. It had been so long since she'd enjoyed the comfort offered by another human being without fear of what she must provide in return.

'I understand your grief, Emily, for I lost my first child within a week of giving birth and my third was stillborn.'

Emily felt the tears begin again but her heart was like a bitter almond, though she tried to appreciate Caroline's words in the spirit in which they were intended.

'I'm sorry to hear it, ma'am,' she murmured, closing her eyes. 'It must have been hard for you.'

'I thought I would die of the loss.'

Emily was aware of being scrutinised in the silence but she refused to open her eyes. She didn't care, now, if she never left these awful soldier's barracks. If she died right here it would be a good thing.

Sighing, Caroline patted her wrist and Emily heard her rise, saying, 'Let us speak no more of loss for now. No doubt you imagine you could die of it at this moment, but I know better. I know that time will lessen the pain, only it's too early to try and persuade you of that. Now—'

Emily, opening her eyes, was surprised to see the obvious distaste with which Caroline regarded the sparsely furnished room.

'Angus is disappointed his arrangements for a new house have been delayed but he promises you shall be comfortably installed directly after his return. A good thing, too, though let me assure you, he's doing his best.'

Emily's eyes alighted on the threadbare rag rug by the doorway.

Caroline, following her gaze, gave a short laugh. 'When you both have repaired to something more commodious than these bachelor's quarters I've no doubt he'll give you full sway with the decorating. Angus is generous to a fault when his feelings are aroused.' She put her hand on the door knob. 'I see there is not much to pack, so perhaps when you've finished your tea I can help you dress in something suitable for travelling so we can be home in time for dinner.'

A minute ago Emily had embraced death. Now she decided she didn't care where she was going as long as it was away from these dreadful quarters, so perhaps she did have the energy to get out of bed.

Ten minutes later, without objection, she allowed Caroline to help her up and into an old gown with far too generous a waistline, for she possessed no appropriate travelling clothes that would fit her.

Reverend McCartney, a plump, friendly man with an open smile, was waiting by the side of a handsome equipage drawn by four fine bays. A crowd of ragged village children had gathered, staring in awe at the dark-blue vehicle. Such a sight would be a rarity in this neighbourhood she thought, before her heart clutched at the sight of the tiny coffin strapped to the back.

Caroline gripped her shoulders as she swayed, her sister-in-law's words of comfort finding their mark as she whispered, 'Jonathan will bury your child in consecrated ground and you will be there tomorrow for the ceremony. He will not be forgotten.'

Dazedly Emily allowed herself to be helped by Jonathan into the carriage.

'You must tell me if you are uncomfortable so we can stop or rearrange the cushions,' Caroline told her as they set off, taking the bumps and ruts with the smoothness of a royal coach.

Emily had forgotten what it felt like to feel cosseted. 'Your carriage is a good deal more comfortable than my own bed,' she remarked, running a hand over the rich plush cushions. 'I've my wife to thank for that.' The reverend, sitting opposite her, smiled fondly as he patted his wife's arm. 'You see, I married money.'

'Just as long as you don't tell people you married *for* money, Jonathan,' Caroline said, lapsing into what Emily soon came to realise was the familiar, bantering tone they used with one another. Even preoccupied as she was with her own feelings, the observation came as a shock. She'd not seen married people behave like this. When she found it too exhausting to offer more than monosyllabic replies to Caroline's efforts at engaging her in light conversation, she listened to the couple discuss their own concerns: Anthony's new school, Jeremy's preoccupation with horses, Jane's wicked toddler ways, the anticipated crop from the apple tree.

They spoke of domestic matters like they were the best of friends, not always agreeing, but with an overriding affection foreign to Emily. Plain Caroline was transformed into an engaging, quick witted and affectionate wife; Jonathan into an amusing, incisive husband with a teasing manner and a gentle self-deprecating wit.

She closed her eyes, enjoying the swaying motion as the carriage rolled along, so different from the hellish journey she'd endured just after her marriage; then heard Caroline whisper, 'Jonathan, tuck up Emily's feet and put another cushion behind her,' and Jonathan's tentative, 'Do you not think I might disturb her, my love?'

To this Caroline agreed, after which there was a long silence followed by her plaintive sigh. 'What has your brother done?'

Emily was not about to indicate she was awake. 'He's fallen in love.'

'Clearly,' came the quick rejoinder, 'but surely even you

can see he's set himself up for a good deal of heartache. He's not one to act impulsively so it's a pity he's done so over his marriage.'

'You're forgetting Jessamine.'

After another long silence Caroline said, quietly, with a finality that brooked no returning to the subject, 'Love had nothing to do with it. Hush, now, Jonathan. We don't want to wake the lass.'

Jessamine, again. Interest pricked though she told herself Angus's amours were of no account. Still, she was astonished that Caroline should know anything about Angus's illicit liaisons and even more so by her cryptic discounting the possibility that emotion had anything to do with the union. Everything Emily knew of Angus suggested he was man who'd only become involved with a woman if his emotions were deeply engaged.

The thought only intensified her guilt as she shifted restlessly, still feigning sleep.

'HOME AT LAST!'

Emily stirred at Caroline's jolly tone, allowing Jonathan to help her out of the carriage and set her down at the bottom of a flight of shallow stone stairs.

Gazing with surprised delight at the beautiful, honey-coloured vicarage with its mullioned windows and cloak of ivy, she turned at the sound of running feet on gravel.

'Jemmy, my sweet!' cried her sister-in-law, embracing the grubby-faced little boy. Setting him away, she added with a smile, 'Jeremy, meet your new aunt Emily. You didn't know Uncle Angus had married, did you?'

A choking lump rose up in Emily's throat but she extended her hand towards the lad who gave her a shy, gap-toothed smile. 'Where's Uncle Angus?' he asked, clearly disappointed with the answer that he was away on business before running off.

The next hour passed in a blur as Caroline showed Emily her room, instructed a parlour maid to unpack the trunk, sent her own dresser to help Emily wash and change, insisted Emily return to her bed after the long journey, then finally came to visit her, the maid in her wake bearing a supper tray. 'I'm sure you're done in after the journey so I've arranged for your refreshment to be taken here,' she said, easing herself into a stiff-backed chair by the bed.

Emily's room, like the others in the rectory she had seen, was decorated in the latest style and while she had grown up in comfort, she was enchanted by the bold decorating of her new surroundings.

'Angus asked me to write every day to inform him of your health.' Caroline smiled as if expecting some tender response from Emily. When this was not forthcoming she said without missing a beat, 'He was terribly concerned at having to leave you at such a time.'

Emily turned her head away and stared at the ceiling. The silence lengthened. She knew a polite response was expected. Something along the lines of how glad she was to hear it, or how she missed him. Instead she whispered, 'It is very hard to be a good wife.' Turning back to Caroline, she went on with difficulty, 'You must know that I was to be married to another man before Angus. A brave soldier.' She drew in a difficult breath. 'I mourn him still and now I mourn the baby, yet I know how much I ought to be grateful to Angus.' She swallowed. 'But it is so very hard.'

'I know.' Caroline's tone lacked censure as she handed Emily a handkerchief to stem the tears that spilled onto her pillow. When she touched her arm Emily felt a frisson of warmth and gratitude. A fallen woman was irredeemable and wasn't that what they all knew her to be? Yet Caroline went on as if Emily were not damned. 'When Angus returns it will be a new beginning even if part of you is in mourning.'

'When Angus returns I will have to do my duty as his wife and'—Emily slanted a glance at her sister-in-law—'I don't know how I can bear that.'

Caroline looked thoughtful as she smoothed Emily's pillow. 'When you have exorcised your grief, Emily,' she said slowly, 'embrace the good things life is offering you. Including your husband.'

Turning at the door, she added, 'I've known Angus more than seven years. He's the last to advertise his fine qualities but believe me, Emily, there are few men finer than he.'

CHAPTER 9

'My daughter killed any good opinion I harboured towards her.' Time had not softened Bartholomew Micklen, Angus noted as he accepted a glass of sherry, wishing the interview over and heartily regretting the deviation he'd made on his return from France. He'd so hoped to broker a reconciliation, but Emily had been right. There was no forgiveness in Bartholomew Micklen's heart.

Beneath a jutting forehead over which dangled the tassel of his smoking cap, Micklen's eyes appeared slits of malice which he focussed on Angus whom he'd directed to a low chair while he chose to stand. 'I'm sorry, Major, but if you've just left Emily's bedside with her petition ringing in your ears, you've come in vain.'

Angus looked down at his glass and wondered how to terminate his visit. The room was warm and stuffy. He ran his finger around the inside of his stock, forcing himself to mount one final appeal.

'You don't know how much your forgiveness would mean to her.'

'Really?' The older man's laugh was ironic. 'Emily is like all the women in her family.' He jerked his head towards his wife, bent in her chair by the fire but clearly following the conversation. 'She'll say whatever she thinks is to her benefit, regardless of truth. My daughter doesn't value my good opinion. Never has.'

Angus placed his sherry on the little side table and rose. It was not often he was roused to anger. Prudently, he decided it was time to beat a dignified retreat. 'I'm sorry to have troubled you, sir—'

'No need to be so hasty. I haven't ruled out my forgiveness entirely.' Mr Micklen waved Angus back into his seat. 'I simply want Emily to understand that her behaviour has consequences.'

'I think she is well aware of that, sir.'

Mr Micklen's smile did not have the effect of making his expression any pleasanter. 'I confess I am surprised by your visit but I'll consider your request. Emily has learnt a painful lesson. Perhaps she is not yet beyond redemption.'

When his son-in-law had gone, Micklen stared thoughtfully through the window into the orderly garden beyond. He knew it was pointless waiting for his wife to break the silence and for once regretted terrorising her to such an extent that the sport of cutting her down was now a thing of the past.

'You are surprised by my softened heart, Margeurite?' he asked, not turning.

'Nothing surprises me any more, Bartholomew.' Her voice was deliberately neutral; it amused him to think of the efforts she'd be expending right now to subdue her fear. He could hear it, as carefully controlled as a bow across a too-taught violin string.

'I can only think you have some motive for pretending to grant Emily latitude. You've never loved her.'

'How astute, *ma chérie.*' He turned. 'Perhaps if she'd been my daughter ...' He left the sentence hanging.

Margeurite swivelled her eyes to meet his. 'You see benefit in courting Emily's noble husband, yet I cannot see why, for he is nothing like Jack Noble.'

Micklen sighed. 'Jack Noble was the ideal son-in-law, it is true: greedy, unpatriotic and amenable to reason.' He left the window and began to pace in front of the fire.

Margeurite twisted in her chair to follow him with her gaze. 'Angus McCartney is none of those things. Certainly not amenable to the kind of reason you would have him see. Don't risk Emily's happiness a second time, Bartholomew, I beg of you. Major McCartney will be good to her. She may even come to love him. But if you—'

'Silence!'

Obediently, Margeurite Micklen pressed her lips together and lowered her eyes. Their exchanges rarely came to this. She had learned her place long ago.

Bartholomew rubbed his chin. 'Emily is half French. Why should her patriotism be confined to English interests? You heard the major. Like Jack Noble, Angus McCartney has been sent across the channel. Why?' He chuckled. 'It stands to reason Woodhouse has recruited McCartney in place of our ignoble lately lamented Major Noble.' He turned to warm his back, his smile contemplative. 'Fanchette is in need of assistance.'

'You have heard from Fanchette? After all these years ...'

Micklen smiled at the strangled surprise in his wife's voice before answering roughly, 'Fanchette deserves to be punished for foisting her useless sister upon me. Granted, there were benefits at the time, but now you are a millstone around my neck.' His lip curled. 'A hideous cripple.'

Margeurite's breathing quickened in defence. He could almost smell her terror as she croaked, 'The only reason you stand where you are is because of Fanchette.'

Micklen clicked his tongue. 'Reminding me of my place, eh? My, my, you are becoming bold, Margeurite.'

Margeurite lowered her eyes to her trembling hands. 'You are rich thanks to Fanchette's generosity—'

'Thanks to her treachery, I think you mean. She sacrificed her family to the guillotine for a fortune which she spent on those she loved. God knows why she was so fond of you, but the fact you still have a head on your misshapen body proves she does have some redeeming qualities, I suppose.'

Gratified by the fear his wife was unable to hide, though disgusted by the drool she hurriedly wiped from her trembling mouth, he added, 'Fanchette parades herself as the heroine of French liberation, but her black, immoral soul is a foul canker on all society. Should such a creature be rewarded?'

Margeurite managed to raise her voice above a whisper. 'All I want is the best for Emily. It's all I've ever wanted ...'

Micklen laughed as she began to sob. Rubbing his hands together, he said, 'The time has come for Emily to join the family firm, my dear Margeurite. Noble was supposed to be the means to bring that about, but the fool got himself killed. Now it's time Emily started paying her mother's dues, eh Margeurite? For twenty years you've been nothing but a drain on me ... an affliction I've been forced to bear.'

His wife's distress always afforded him great sport and tonight he was particularly restless, so when she managed, between gasps, 'Why so many secrets, Bartholomew! Tell me who came knocking at the door ... when was it, five years ago? You took her away in your carriage. Emily told me but I was too afraid to quiz you. Was it Fanchette? Was it my sister?' Micklen just laughed louder. 'Cripples must discover these secrets for themselves.'

'Lucy was too afraid to tell me, too, until I made her. You threatened her, didn't you, Bartholomew? It was Fanchette, wasn't it? Lucy said she never learned her name but that she was French and in rags, half starved.' She shivered.

Amused, Bartholomew watched her battle with the desire to challenge him and her well placed fear of the consequences. To his surprise, she pressed on. 'If it wasn't Fanchette it must have been Jessamine. Lucy said she had dark hair and large eyes. Fanchette told me in the last letter she wrote me five years ago that Jessamine had run away.' A choking fit bent her double.

Disgusted, Bartholomew turned from the sight of her spraying spittle, yet despite her apoplexy, Margeurite struggled on. 'If I had known how incapable you are of forgiveness, Bartholomew ... and your capacity for evil, I'd have chosen to be ripped apart by the mob in the Abbaye rather than become your wife.'

Bartholomew laughed louder. 'You should speak your mind more often, Margeurite. It's infinitely more diverting than watching you hide your quaking terror. As for forgiveness, I do not forgive those who have wronged me – and your sister wronged me greatly.' He fixed her with a level look. 'It appears Fanchette thought Gerard Fontenay's pockets would be deeper when he made an honest woman of her, hence her interesting petition for my help.' He pursed his lips and raised one eyebrow. 'Now that we have a replacement for Jack Noble and – if Emily plays her cards right – access to the diplomatic pouch, perhaps we can help each other.'

LISTLESSLY, Emily remained in her bed at Honeyfield House.

Grieving. And plotting.

The death of Jack's child had taken with it any necessity for Emily to have a husband.

She need not have married Angus. It was a bitter reflection.

Jack had tapped the deepest of passions within Emily. Passions she'd not known existed. The fiery responses he'd aroused had been shocking and profound. What she'd felt with Jack was real love: the explosion of the senses, the heightened sense of living. No man in her life could ever again compete with Jack. No man could arouse the sensations Jack had aroused.

With growing certainty, as she wallowed in her misery and tossed, despairingly in her bed, she reasoned it was unfair on Angus that he be afflicted with a wife who could never love him.

Finally, she roused herself, and reached for her writing box.

Perhaps, she suggested in a letter to her Aunt Gemma, a bargain could be reached in terms of the dowry her aunt had intended granting Angus for Emily – a sum which obviously had not yet been paid.

With the child dead – another man's child – she was certain an annulment could be procured, with her aunt's assistance.

Her final argument in the letter – of which multiple drafts had been written – was that this marriage was as unfair on Angus as it was on Emily. He was a good man who deserved better in a wife: a wife who could love him.

Having sent her letter, a little of the terrible weight of grief fell from Emily's shoulders.

❄

A WEEK since Angus's departure turned into two. She forgot that Angus had been kind and patient and had seemed to genuinely grieve over the death of the little one. While Emily's grief remained overwhelming, her husband was becoming a distant memory.

If she felt troubled that Angus may object to her plan of an annulment, she thought of his mistress, Jessamine. He'd had other women in the past and no doubt he'd find some worthy woman to make his wife in the future. He'd soon forget Emily.

Caroline put her head around the door and said with a smile, 'Perhaps you'd feel strong enough for a short walk this afternoon, Emily. It's a beautiful day.'

But when Caroline began to sing the praises of her brother-in-law as she drew the curtains, Emily deflected her seemingly favourite topic of conversation by asking the tantalising question which seemed to paint Angus's dealings with women in an uncharacteristic light. 'Please tell me about Jessamine.'

Yes, it was scandal and surely not a topic Caroline would consider fitting for the ears of Angus's wife, but it was something to dwell on, other than the baby. Besides, the brief reference to Jessamine in the carriage indicated Caroline clearly knew more than Emily did.

'Jessamine?' Caroline repeated the name in a tone of deep disquiet as her hand dropped from the curtain, and Emily felt a twinge of shame because Caroline had shown her nothing but kindness.

Caroline chose her words carefully. 'Angus *told* you about Jessamine?'

With studied carelessness, Emily traced the embroidery on the bed linen. 'He said she was long dead.'

Seating herself beside the bed, Caroline took her hand. 'You mustn't be jealous, Emily. Angus—'

Emily cut her off with a laugh. 'I'm not *jealous*.'

Caroline frowned and in the silence Emily could imagine her thoughts whirling round inside her head. Emily used to put Lucy on the spot like this, after she'd realised Lucy no longer wanted to tell Emily the stories of her father's heroic background.

Caroline appeared to be vacillating over how much to say. Then clearly decided to say nothing. 'Jessamine is dead. Let's leave the past as is, shall we?'

Emily, a second ago, had been prepared to dismiss the subject. Now she was deeply interested in the reason for Caroline's clouded brow.

'She was a camp follower, wasn't she? Angus met her during the Corunna retreat. I gather she was Spanish.'

'French,' Caroline corrected her, absently.

'How did she die?'

'She took her own life.'

Emily was unprepared for such an answer.

'*Killed herself?*' That meant she lay in unconsecrated ground. A fate baby Jack would have shared had Jonathan not buried him in his own churchyard.

Caroline rose, adding shortly, 'Angus found her.' She pretended to busy herself, rearranging a drooping flower and changing the subject as she said, falsely bright, 'I received a letter from Angus today. He's returned to England but has had to go to London on business. He asked me to convey his love and says he anticipates being home in three or four days.'

Three or four days! Emily's shock at the nature of Jessamine's death turned to horror at this latest news.

Her mind worked quickly. Surely two weeks after her miscarriage was too soon for him to expect his conjugal rights? Until she received instructions from Aunt Gemma as to how to proceed with her application for an annulment she must find any excuse to keep Angus at bay. She ought to be a free woman. She had not wanted to marry Angus two months ago and even less did she wanted to be married to him now.

Caroline smiled and brushed away a strand of Emily's dark hair. 'He is so looking forward to seeing you again,' she said, and despite herself Emily closed her eyes, enjoying the rare sensation of being caressed. She was truly fond of Caroline and sorry she would be disappointing her.

Better to do it earlier, though. 'Poor Angus,' whispered Emily. 'His honourable actions towards me will cost him dearly, I fear, for I am not the wife to make him proud – or happy.'

The following day her response from Aunt Gemma arrived.

Snatching the sealed letter from amongst those the parlour maid delivered on a silver salver to the drawing room and with only a cursory nod at Caroline, she hurried to the privacy of her room.

Quickly, she slid her nail under the wax seal and scanned the few lines, her heart racing.

Dear Emily,

Perhaps you have forgotten the number of people who witnessed your delicate condition. There were, also, two witnesses in church who would testify to the advancement of your pregnancy.

Major McCartney is a gentleman who is anxious to secure your happiness, though not at the expense of his dignity. You seem to forget that his gallantry towards you was the only means by which you salvaged your reputation and could have kept your child.

An annulment is out of the question not to mention a shabby way to treat a good man.

Quite frankly, I find your efforts in soliciting my help in that direction grubby and beneath yourself.

You also seem to be labouring under a misapprehension. While it is true I offered financial inducement to Major McCartney, he refused my offer.

I am sorry for your misfortunes but you are, ultimately, responsible for your rash behaviour.

Wishing you all the happiness for which you are prepared to strive towards in your new life,

Yours, GH

Emily crumpled the thick paper and squeezed shut her eyes as she climbed the stairs to her bedchamber.

She felt helpless and trapped.

Trapped, as she never had when Jack's baby offered hope for some future happiness.

Now not only had she lost her baby, but Aunt Gemma denied that Angus had taken her money.

An eternity spent sharing a lumpy mattress with a soldier husband she did not know while she ruined her hands to get the fire lit each morning loomed ahead.

In her bedroom she threw herself, face down, on the bed, and sobbed.

She wanted Jack and she wanted their baby, but her only consolation in not being shunned and destitute as a result of being intimate with the man who would have been her husband in just a few days was … Angus.

And he was a poor substitute.

❄

ANGUS RODE into the stable yard four days later.

'Emily!' he cried, seeking her out from amongst the family members and staff who had come to greet him.

Dismounting, he removed his hat, smiling as if she could be nothing other than delighted to see him. He carried himself with ease, tall and erect in the saddle. He seemed confident, different from when just the two of them were together.

She'd expected to feel nothing but despair, perhaps even contempt, when she laid eyes on him after such a long separation. Curiously, she found herself admiring his straight-backed form, wondering about the old scar she'd never asked him about. Indeed, he looked every inch the brave, competent soldier she'd been told he was.

'Hello, Angus.' Emily tempered her smile to reflect a modicum of welcome. She felt wary and very vulnerable, a moment later acknowledging with shock the surprising warmth that swept through her as he took her hands in his strong, determined grip.

'I hope your journey wasn't too onerous.' Still she strove for the right tone: polite, formal. Distant. She did not meet his eye. It would be wrong to encourage him in view of her determination to leave him – for she *was* determined on that– yet she was surprised at how much she *didn't* recoil.

'It would appear you've not ridden post haste from the docks.' She'd intended for her words to contain a veiled criticism, despite the fact she'd given him no reason to hurry home, yet he did look awfully good. There was a ruddy glow to his cheeks and his mouth, which she was surprised to notice for the first time was full and well shaped. His eyes sparkled like one in the peak of good health or perhaps riding the crest of good fortune or buoyed up by enthusiasm. His light-brown hair was ruffled, making him appear more boyish and approachable, and his coat, though a little mud spattered, was of the finest cut. In short, her husband looked handsome and well turned out in his buckskin breeches, as if he'd visited the finest tailor before returning home, specially to please her.

Three-year-old Jane raised her arms to be picked up. 'Hamsum Uncle Angus.'

Swinging her onto his shoulders, Angus's gaze lingered upon Emily, but when it was clear Emily had no further greeting for him, he hung back to match Caroline's pace, saying over his shoulder. 'Not too onerous, thank you. I've just returned from London where I was required to submit a report.'

Abandoned, and instantly regretting her coolness, Emily walked behind them, listening to her husband answer Caroline's volley of questions. Most of these he adroitly bypassed, concentrating on his pleasure to be at Honeyfield and to find everyone so well.

He'd just finished thanking Caroline for her care of Emily when he turned, his expression warming instantly as he looked searchingly at his wife.

'Emily, I have a surprise. I've secured us a house.' When no immediate response was forthcoming he went on, 'I think you will like it for it is within easy visiting distance of here and not far from the village.'

At Emily's restrained, 'How nice, Angus,' he sighed and his tone lost its enthusiasm. 'The lease came up unexpectedly, though of course if it's not to your taste we won't take it. I thought the proximity to Caroline and Jonathan would be'— he waited for Emily to catch up so he could walk beside her —'helpful.'

'They have been kind,' Emily murmured, trying to maintain the sense of isolation and emotional distance she should feel. But all she could think was how well her husband looked. And handsome.

She gave herself an internal shake. She had not wished for this marriage and the fact remained that she was his to command, all on account of the tiny, perfectly formed infant that should have been the first of many warm soft bundles of pleasure created from a loving union with Jack.

After a few moments of awkward silence, Angus gave up trying to thaw her reserve and rejoined Caroline and Jonathan as his sister-in-law led him through the house to show off her newly decorated drawing room.

Emily could see his admiration was genuine as he cast his eye over the purple drapes and embroidered muslin curtains which framed the French doors opening into the conservatory. It was a daring colour scheme which Emily acknowledged worked superbly and Caroline deserved to look pleased with herself. 'Jonathan was horrified when I showed him the drawings,' she said with a smile, 'but I think he's come round.'

'The poor reduced husband was hardly in a position to object.' Jonathan squeezed his wife's slender waist, causing Caroline to feign an exasperated sigh.

'As if you don't have the authority to control my fortune as you see fit.' Despite the tartness of her tone she was unable to maintain her frown at Jonathan's hangdog expression. Shrugging off his arm to continue her argument, her mouth twitched as she chided, 'How often must I remind you that I find your references to my fortune and your lack of one in exceedingly poor taste?' She directed an arch look at Angus. 'Not even my substantial dowry was sufficient to compensate for my lack of face and figure until Jonathan took pity.'

'And haven't I paid dearly for it?' enquired Jonathan with exaggerated despair. 'Three beautiful children, an exquisite, well-run home and a wife—'

Emily had expected him to continue his bantering tone.

Whereas she'd once felt uncomfortable listening to their more intimate exchanges, she now found them endearing.

She glanced back from her contemplation of Caroline's handiwork and her heart skipped a beat as she intercepted their look. Jonathan continued, his tone gentle and sincere, 'who is the most beautiful woman *I've* ever seen. A queen amongst queens.'

At Caroline's maidenly blush, Emily slid her eyes across to Angus. Some indefinable emotion crossed his face which made Emily quail inwardly. Did he really think *they* could be like that?

He turned to Emily with a smile that looked as if Caroline and Jonathan's domestic cosiness were contagious. 'I think you will like our new house, Emily. Like Jonathan, I'd happily give my wife free rein to decorate as she pleases.'

Emily was confused by the unexpected pang of hope and excitement she felt.

Immediately her suspicions were aroused. How could Angus suddenly have come into funds? He'd told her his new appointment was dangerous and secretive, but his remuneration couldn't be so large and immediate, surely?

Bypassing Emily's bland smile, Angus resumed with undampened enthusiasm, 'It was only quite by chance I heard Wildwood Manor was available during the crossing over. I remember how highly you thought of the place after you were invited there by Admiral Chesterbrook last summer, Caroline, so I inspected it immediately following my return to England.'

'My, my, little brother.' Jonathan's tone was admiring. 'How your fortunes have changed.'

Emily slanted a suspicious look at the two of them. Was she being taken for a fool?

'I'm afraid I haven't the first idea about decorating,' she said, faintly.

Caroline looked at her, oddly.

'Perhaps, Emily, you'd like to accompany me to the schoolroom to hear the children read,' she said.

'Lovely,' Emily echoed Caroline's falsely cheerful tone, nodding as the men repaired to the billiards room to pass the time until the dinner gong sounded.

'Caroline, I'm sorry I was unkind,' Emily began in a rush the moment they'd gained the sanctuary of the long gallery. 'I *know* my aunt's money paid for this apparently wonderful new home of ours, yet Angus didn't even consult me.'

She *had* to believe it was true. Her aunt must be lying. It was the foundation for her hopes of dissolving this unwanted marriage. It was what she'd channelled all her efforts into achieving since Angus had left, and just because she felt this odd reluctance didn't mean a clean break wasn't ultimately in their best interests.

'If you're piqued Angus didn't consult you I believe he elicited your feelings earlier but your lack of enthusiasm suggested he should do as he felt best.' Caroline tucked Emily's hand into the crook of her arm once more, adding, 'You can't have it both ways.'

'You make me sound like a spoilt child,' Emily muttered, and Caroline laughed.

'With a great cross to bear. I'm prepared to concede that, my dear.' She smiled. 'Remember what I told you before? You stand to be a much happier woman if you try to put in the effort.' Fleetingly, she touched her face. 'Believe me, Angus is worth it.'

A strange jolt of hope came close to breaching the defences guarding Emily's vulnerable heart.

What did she really want? she wondered.

Love and protection, like any woman, but were those things really possible after all that had happened? To give in to Angus's best efforts to win her round meant denying Jack the loyalty she owed him, surely.

OBEDIENCE HAD BEEN DRUMMED into Emily from infancy, though her father and a succession of governesses claimed wilfulness and stubbornness were her greatest failings.

She'd thought he'd never forgive her for rejecting his first choice of bridegroom, so her astonishment had been great when, after a year's social isolation, her father had without warning entered the drawing room where she'd been embroidering one evening, and introduced Jack. The instant flare in Jack's eye told her that he liked what he saw, and to her even greater surprise, her father had left them alone together.

Major Noble, he'd told her, was lodging at The Four Swans while conducting business in town, and he'd be a regular visitor.

Soon Emily was in the throes of fiery, passionate love. Jack was a man of courage and great moral integrity and, astonishingly, he loved her back.

Angus was kind and decent, but he was not Jack and she could never love him like she loved Jack.

He certainly was, however, making a brave effort to insinuate himself into her affections.

'Wildwood Manor is only twenty minutes from here by coach, Emily.' Angus's eyes glittered with enthusiasm from beneath the chandelier as he faced her across the table. 'Much quicker if you ride, of course, and you've told me you're fond of riding. The house is comfortably furnished, so ready for immediate occupation. We can repair there as soon as you wish.'

Immediate occupation. Emily's heart thudded to her feet

even as she reminded herself of Caroline's truism. No, she could not have it both ways. But while they were guests of the Reverend and his family she felt safe from her husband's advances. She need never be alone with him, if she didn't wish. She tried to blank her mind to the surge of feeling she'd experienced earlier when he'd smiled a sudden disarming smile at her. It was an aberration.

She forced a smile. Perhaps, if she conveyed her real feelings and discussed it with him in the right way, Angus may be amenable to an annulment.

Caroline leaned over to touch her arm, not hiding her excitement. 'Emily, we will be neighbours. How delightful. I shall send out invitations for a tea party to celebrate your entry into local society.'

Angus looked at her expectantly. They all did.

Suddenly her bold desires to independently retreat from this holy union were revealed for what they were: the hopeless daydreams of a powerless woman. The law was on Angus's side. What had she to fight with? She had no money, no allies. She was in too deep, Angus clearly wanted the marriage to continue and judging by Caroline and Jonathan's enthusiasm, he had a veritable army ready to fight his cause.

Yet was that such a bad thing? While Angus had been absent, thoughts of severing their union had given her focus. Now that he was back, she wasn't sure what she wanted.

'Whenever you wish, Angus.' Confusion made her voice leaden. 'You make the decisions.'

There was little point in delaying the inevitable. They would go to Wildwood and there Angus would claim his husbandly duties with relish while her heart cried out for Jack. She felt a moment's guilt at Angus's fleeting, stricken look before he composed his features, turning to respond to something Jonathan had said to fill the awkward silence. Pudding was cleared away and Caroline rose, the sign that she and Emily would withdraw, leaving the men to their port and coffee.

But Emily had no desire to listen to another lecture on the virtues of her new husband from her sister-in-law. Not when her own feelings were in such disorder.

'I have a terrible megrim. Will you excuse me?' She passed a languid hand across her brow. 'Angus, you must have a great deal to discuss with your brother. I promise I won't pry into details about your journey. I'm sure there is much information with which your wife ought not be entrusted.'

She sent Angus a wavering smile, for she did feel bad. Later, if he were interested, she'd try to explain the complicated state of her heart. Six months was not long enough to mourn the greatest love of her life.

Not when he'd died saving the man who'd won her by default.

CHAPTER 10

'So at last we are able to speak frankly.' Jonathan leaned back in his delicate chintz-upholstered chair by the fire and, as was his habit, laced his hands across his stomach. 'Not a love match, I take it.' Then, as Angus opened his mouth, cut in, 'On Emily's part, I mean.'

'I can't imagine Angus marrying for anything but love,' Caroline said. 'Remember, Emily is in a fragile state. She's mourning her baby. Cruelty is born of powerlessness. Give her time.'

The fire gave out a comforting glow in the dim room. After a silence, Angus reflected morosely, 'Time is my only ally.' He was conscious of the dull ache in his breast. It had been largely absent during his time abroad. The excitement of clandestine meetings with the *Chevaliers de la Roi*, some in prison and others at society events, had given him little time to ponder the wisdom of his union with Emily. He'd had no idea until he met the Delons of the network or scope of the operation in which he was now involved. It was exciting, invigorating and hugely daunting, but he would play his part in bringing peace to England. It was his greatest role yet.

And along the way he would be a good husband to Emily. He would win her respect and, ultimately, he hoped, her love.

'No. Your kindness and patience are what will win her over.' Caroline reached across to pat his hand. 'Then your charm and dashing spirit will make her your slave.'

Both brothers laughed.

'It's true,' she protested as Angus looked at her fondly. He was at his most relaxed with these two. There was never any pretence and matters were dealt with in the most down-to-earth fashion. 'What a pity you don't have a sister, Caroline,' he jested.

'If I had, she'd not have suited you, Angus. You are drawn to those with a flash of spirit and you have an eye for beauty, despite the image of yourself you like to project.'

'You mean I always hankered after what I could not have and thus leapt at the opportunity to take advantage of Emily's predicament?'

'I thought as much,' pronounced Jonathan at which his wife said, derisively, 'My dear, as if that were not as plain as the nose on my face. But,' she added, turning to Angus, 'your competition is fearsome. The dead betrothed has become a martyr.' Caroline's fingers beat a tattoo on the arm of her chair. 'She carries his letters to bed with her and reads them each night.'

'Still?' His hopes were dashed even further.

Jonathan grunted. 'You've not yet told her the truth about this false fiancé?'

Predictably, Caroline pounced and Jonathan explained what his brother had told him of the circumstances surrounding Jack Noble's death.

Caroline threw up her hands. 'Why Angus, if Emily's Captain Noble had been dallying with a camp follower – or any other woman for that matter – of course you must tell her. Why must you always play the hero?'

Angus gave her a laconic smile. 'Caroline, for someone so wise, is it not perfectly plain? Would it elevate me in Emily's eyes to hear me call Jack faithless? Do you really think she'd believe me if I told her the truth: that he consorted with women of all ranks on a regular basis?' He shook his head. 'You know it wouldn't and that I'd only damage my own position further by tarnishing what she believes is the one true and good thing that's ever happened to her. She'd assume I was knocking Noble off his pedestal in order to elevate myself.' He gave a wry smile. 'Though don't think I haven't contemplated it.'

They digested this in heavy silence. Finally Jonathan said, 'You'll just have to become a hero, abroad, won't you? Pleasant little sojourn, was it?'

The word hung, unsaid, in the air. Espionage. Perhaps the only way for England to ultimately defeat the Corsican pretender who held such control over Europe and whose Continental Blockade threatened England's prosperity. Six years earlier, Napoleon Bonaparte, having conquered or allied with every major European power, had established a trade embargo against Britain. The difficulty of importing and exporting for the island nation had pushed up prices and caused great hardship.

'Really, Jonathan,' interposed Caroline, 'Angus has to be discreet if he values his position.'

'And his neck,' Angus supplied. He waved a hand the length of his newly and splendidly upholstered form. 'Behold the Gentleman of Fashion. I move in different circles on the Continent. It has been opportune, in view of my recent marriage, to be able to afford a coat of decent cut.'

Caroline raked her eyes over his immaculate rig-out. 'Your funds have come through then, Angus?'

Angus chose his words carefully. 'My new clothes are courtesy of my employer, and my decision to lease Wildwood was on the expectation of the remuneration discussed with regard to my activities abroad'—he hesitated—'supplemented by funds realised from selling my commission.'

He'd never quite forget the bleak horror in Emily's expression as she'd cast her eye around his lodgings. 'Naturally, I want to supply Emily with a home where she can be comfortable. I was also led to believe my late father left me a small bequest, however there've been more important matters demanding my attention. My first priority is Emily. It'll be a while before I can leave her again.'

'She mightn't feel the same way, Angus.' Caroline twisted her lawn handkerchief around one finger, as if weighing up whether to speak further. Finally, directing him one of her famous candid looks, she added, 'Angus, she's not a porcelain doll. Emily needs and respects a strong hand. If you tiptoe around her, trying to please her, she'll only despise you for it.'

'What are you trying to say, my dear?' Jonathan sounded almost embarrassed. 'Angus never tiptoed around anyone in his life.'

Caroline turned to him. 'He does when he's around beautiful women.'

'I don't believe I've ever tiptoed around you, Caroline,' Angus remarked mildly.

Caroline dismissed this. 'I've never been a beauty. I can see Emily has the potential to make you tie yourself in knots. Don't give in to her, Angus. You're her husband. Show her you're in charge.'

'That's right.' Jonathan laughed. 'See how well it's worked in our household.'

EMILY LISTENED to the discreet rapping on the door, her heart pounding.

It was four o'clock and she was sitting at her exquisite walnut-inlaid dressing table on the third day in their new home. Just now she'd been gazing out through the large sash windows at the lovely garden, watching the team of gardeners at work. She felt an imposter amidst the luxury which surrounded her. A wife, as yet in name only.

'Won't I go and open it, miss?' Sukey, her maid replaced the silver-backed hairbrush on the dressing table and looked enquiringly at her mistress's reflection.

'I'm not dressed to receive guests.' Emily clutched her peignoir closer around her.

'It's the master, o' course.' Sukey knitted her brows, as if her mistress were queer in the attic.

The rapping came again. Polite, but insistent. Obviously Angus was not going to go away this time. He'd tried to visit her the previous afternoon, but Emily had ignored him on that occasion, also. Later, at dinner, she'd lied that she'd been taking a walk in the garden when he'd asked her over the oyster soup where she had been.

Before Emily could stop her Sukey was at the door, greeting Angus in her friendly, uninhibited country fashion. She heard his voice, kind, but with an underlying note of authority not even the most fiercely protective lady's maid could act against. 'Good afternoon, Sukey. I wonder if I might have a moment, alone, with my wife.'

'Dinner is less than an hour away,' Emily murmured, staring at him in the looking glass as he smiled across at her, 'and I've only just begun dressing.'

She glanced at her hands, now clasped in her lap to stop their trembling.

She hardly knew this man and here he was to … What?

She felt the fine hairs on hers arm rise at the very prospect that he might touch her. Yet would that be so terrible? It was just that …

She hadn't the words to articulate, even to herself, the plethora of mixed emotions she felt.

'I can see you're about to work magic on your mistress's hair, Sukey, but if you wouldn't mind leaving us now.' With a smile he dismissed the maid, holding open the door for her to leave.

To Emily's amazement the girl gave a little giggle as she passed through.

'I didn't know you were in the habit of flirting with the housemaids.' She regretted the words – and the tone – the moment they were out. It was almost as if habit and a sense of forced loyalty to Jack were lacing her words with a hostility towards Angus she no longer felt.

Angus crossed the room to stand behind her. 'My mother,' he said, 'is notoriously difficult to please. My brothers and I became accustomed to placating tearful housemaids.'

'You think I am notoriously difficult to please?'

Her voice sounded sharp in the silence. She tensed as his hands rested lightly on her shoulders, subtly pushing away the silk shawl. It was the first time her bare skin had come in contact with him in anything other than a medical emergency.

She caught his expression in the looking glass. He wasn't looking at her, but at her long, dark hair cascading over her shoulders and down her back; frowning, as if uncertain about touching it.

Remembering Jessamine, she flinched. Jessamine who, being French, quite possibly had had long dark hair. Had Angus been drawn to Emily through some perverse memory of his old mistress? She remembered sensing something that was more than just reluctance when she'd questioned him about her.

The thought made her feel appalled and indignant at the same time. Or was she manufacturing these emotions? The truth was, she hated the idea he might gaze at her and recall his mistress – a prostitute who followed the army, going from one protector to another. Jack had spoken with disgust about the vice and vermin-filled creatures.

Emily drew herself up proudly, but before she could register her aversion through honeyed barbs sufficient to send him scuttling back through that door, he'd picked up the brush.

Good Lord, was he going to brush her hair? The act seemed hideously intimate.

And at the same time she relished it.

The silent admission sent a wave of guilt through her. She closed her eyes, telling herself she relished it because it would only prove he was clumsy and without finesse.

No doubt he would tug, and the brush would tangle her tresses and it would be far from the romantic gesture he'd planned.

Emily closed her eyes, prepared to wince at the first opportunity.

But he did not tug and pull.

'Emily, we have not spoken properly about the baby.' His voice was soft as he combed gently from the crown to the ends with long, even strokes. To her surprise, she found herself calmed by the contact.

Mention of the baby had not provoked the hysterical tears that she would have expected.

'I feel like my heart has frozen and it will never thaw,' she murmured. She kept her eyes closed. While she didn't have to look at him she could pretend it wasn't Angus soothing her while they discussed this most painful of subjects.

'It doesn't help to be told that one day you will feel again?' Angus continued the rhythmic strokes through her thick tresses.

Emily shook her head. 'The mind and the heart do not

always communicate.' She swallowed past the lump in her throat. 'My head reminds me of the gratitude I should feel for you …'

She registered his stiffening before he supplied, quietly, 'But your heart rebels.'

When she did not answer – could not, he replaced the brush on the dressing table with a sigh. 'I am a patient man and I do not want what would only be reluctantly given, but I am your husband, Emily.'

She felt the tears rise. Opening her eyes, she saw the panic in their reflected depths in the looking glass before her. 'Everyone tells me you are good man, Angus, and I wish I could …'

She shook her head, the tears finally coming, not resisting when he drew her up from her seat and took her into his arms.

'… love me?'

Emily felt the warmth of his breath and trembled, though not from disgust, she knew that.

It was a strange and not unpleasant sensation being comforted by him. A stranger, still, but not such a daunting one.

'I will try to be a good wife,' she added earnestly, raising her head to reassure him, and feeling a strange warmth that was more than simple gratitude pooling in her lower belly. 'I … I'm so grateful to you for understanding my need for more time to get over my losses, but one day'—she drew in a quavering breath—'I shall be a dutiful wife.'

She felt the tremor of his amusement. 'A thrilling prospect,' he responded with more than a hint of irony as he set her away from him.

He stooped to kiss her forehead and she was surprised by his delicacy.

Extraordinarily, another frisson of sensation shot from

her heart to join the curdling that now extended beyond her lower belly; a strange, confusing sensation she had no right to feel.

'And now I shall leave you, Mrs McCartney, as the dinner hour is nearly upon us and you are not yet ready.'

Ready.

Would she ever be?

She'd convinced herself she could never love this man, but now her insides roiled with a cocktail of conflicting emotions. Nowhere could she identify revulsion.

CHAPTER 11

Emily gazed with satisfaction at the effect created by the morning sun as it streamed through the muslin curtains of her elegantly decorated green and yellow drawing room. She had not yet admitted it to Angus, but three weeks after taking up residence, she truly believed Wildwood Manor was the most wonderful home in the entire country.

'Major Woodhouse!' Smiling, she waved the handsome soldier into his seat as she breezed through the double doors to greet the visitor she'd been told was awaiting her.

'Mrs McCartney, you're looking well.'

It might have been mere gallantry, but Emily acknowledged the compliment with a surge of gratification. Today she felt very well. Her health had fully returned and her fears had not been realised regarding unwanted overtures. As long as she and Angus remained congenial housemates she could enjoy her surroundings and his company without the niggling guilt that assailed her whenever Angus got too close. For she was increasingly unable to play the ice maiden which loyalty to Jack required.

After three weeks of deep, rejuvenating rest, Emily had woken this morning refreshed and feeling better than she had in months.

'This is a pleasant surprise, major.' She felt the extraordinary power at being mistress of her own home going to her head as she sank into the chair opposite. However, as she saw the awkwardness he was unable to hide she was reminded uncomfortably of his last visit when she had been only a few days married and heavily pregnant. 'My husband can't have been expecting you as he is away on business.' She forced her gaiety back to the fore. She had nothing to be ashamed of and she refused to feel at a disadvantage. 'He left several days ago.'

Major Woodhouse raised his eyebrows. 'Indeed?'

'He's seeing his solicitor on a matter to which he had hoped to attend earlier, before you sent him away so peremptorily.'

Her tone was playful, bantering. Like it had been in the old days when Jack …

She bit back the thought as she noticed Major Woodhouse had not responded to her light-heartedness as intended. Embarrassment washed over her. She could feel the heat in her cheeks and wished she didn't sound so breathless as she indicated the room with a flourish. 'As you can see, our circumstances have changed. We've been here three weeks now.'

Rather than admiring the décor the major glanced at her flat stomach before saying awkwardly, 'My condolences, Mrs McCartney.'

She inclined her head, keenly aware that he had not even pretended real sympathy.

'I hope you will stay for some tea and Madeira cake at least, Major,' she managed. 'I'm sorry your journey has been in vain.' Signalling to the parlour maid who had come in to replenish the fire, she ordered refreshment.

Since Angus had left she'd had no visitors, other than Caroline who had called yesterday.

The fact that Major Woodhouse appeared about to decline made her even more desperate he should stay. How dare he make her feel embarrassed? She was a respectably married woman and she wanted to play hostess in her fine new house.

'Are you back long?' she asked as the tea things were set before them.

'I await orders.' He shrugged, apparently reluctant to discuss the war, though Emily was always eager to hear news.

With a bright smile she began, 'I hear—'

'I'm glad to note the change in circumstances,' he said, indicating the room with a sweep of his arms. There was an almost desperate note to his tone. Emily blinked, surprised. 'Yes.' She swallowed, her awkwardness increasing before anger rose to the fore, making her incautious and trip out the words she'd once used as a weapon against her impotence. 'My aunt was generous in my marriage settlement, Major Woodhouse,' she said, adding with a smile, 'I've no doubt my husband has distinguished himself abroad for he certainly knows how to seize the advantage at home.'

She regretted the words immediately they were out. What had possessed her?

Angus was this man's friend. Emily was doing herself no favours belittling her husband with sentiments that no longer reflected her feelings, besides.

She felt both ashamed and deserving of the look he sent her over the rim of his tea cup.

'A man in your husband's position is unable to reveal the nature of his work. He must, however, be confident of the discretion of his wife who bears her own responsibility towards the security of our country.'

White hot rage surged along her spine at this veiled dressing down, which absently she realised was a defensiveness for the knowledge she'd put herself in the wrong.

Still she could not help herself. 'Jack Noble was a hero – I know that, major – but I know little of my husband's exploits.' She shrugged. 'I am not criticising him. Quite simply, he tells me nothing, you may be assured on that score.'

She turned away from his narrowed gaze to pour her own tea, surprised when he said with a change of tone that was more conversational than was warranted, 'I believe your mother is French, Mrs McCartney. The events of the past years must have made family relations ...' he drew out the pause, 'difficult.'

Replacing her cup upon the saucer with a clatter, Emily said, 'I was born in England, Major Woodhouse, and though my mother prefers to converse with me in French, her loyalty is towards England. Unfortunately her relations across the channel did not survive the revolution.'

'With the exception of her sister.' Emily felt her jaw drop.

'I have never met my Tante Fanchette,' she murmured.

In response to the look she sent him, he replied, 'In the interests of security it was standard procedure to look into your family background, Mrs McCartney. Please do not be offended. Besides,' he added, 'your father has long been of interest to us.'

'You insult me, sir.'

'By speaking plainly? I am sorry, Mrs McCartney. It is perhaps time for me to leave.'

He stood and Emily, caught up in a maelstrom of shock, indignation and confusion, rose also.

'I'm glad to find you enjoying more comfortable

surroundings. A beautiful woman brought up in the comfort of Micklen Hall could hardly be expected to endure soldier's lodgings for long.' He nodded curtly. 'Fortuitously for you, Major McCartney's late father's bequest was unexpectedly generous, though it was through other means your husband leased Wildwood. I'm surprised he did not tell you. Naturally, though, I'm glad your aunt has done her part in assisting the newlyweds for I've heard your father was neglectful in that regard.'

She stared at him.

'In this business, Mrs McCartney, it is imperative to keep abreast of such matters, for the safety of all concerned.'

Emily felt herself sway. Major Woodhouse's insinuations regarding her family were deeply disquieting … but Angus's father's bequest? Unsteadily, she said, 'Angus's father is not dead. Jonathan was here only yesterday. He would have said something.'

'Angus has not told you?'

To her surprise the major looked disconcerted. 'My apologies, ma'am. I thought you knew.'

She could not believe the change in attitude. A deep flush stained his cheeks. He cleared his throat while avoiding her eyes. 'It is in keeping with your husband's character that he would see to the comfort of his wife before attending to what others might consider more urgent matters.' He bowed. 'I came here, purely to pay you and your husband a social call, and now it appears I have been indiscreet. Pray, forgive me.'

'If Sir John is dead why was I not told?' she whispered.

'No, Sir John is not dead.' Agitated, Major Woodhouse ran his hand through his hair. 'This is something you need to discuss with your husband. I had assumed you were aware of Major McCartney's background …'

He darted a look at the door.

She fixed him with a level stare. 'It is not indiscreet to

apprise me of what you intimate "everyone" – except me – apparently knows.'

The major signalled his defeat by exhaling on a sigh. 'This morning I was told by your husband's half-sister, Lady Catherine—'

'Half-sister? Angus has only brothers. At least, so he told me.'

The major hesitated before saying slowly, 'You should not be hearing this from me, but I have said too much already. No doubt Angus would have told you in good time that it is common knowledge the Earl of Netherfield acknowledged him as his son, though Sir John brought him up as his own. During my ride earlier today I met Lady Catherine, the earl's legitimate daughter whom I have known since childhood. You may recall she eloped several years ago with a subaltern. Now she is expecting their second child.'

Emily remembered the scandal which had riveted the *ton* for weeks. Lady Catherine had been on the verge of marrying the Marquis of Bruton's heir.

This new knowledge regarding her husband's paternity was infinitely more shocking.

The major went on in a resigned tone. 'Lady Catherine told me her late father had left Angus an enormous bequest while making paltry provision for her.'

Gasping, Emily indicated the lovely drawing room with a sweep of her arm. 'So that is how he afforded … this?'

'Your husband is being well remunerated for his work.' Major Woodhouse did not trouble to hide the fact he considered her remark contemptuous. 'He also sold his commission. I know, Mrs McCartney, that he was very anxious to provide you with a home where you would be comfortable.'

She had not the strength to watch him ride off. Sinking into a chair by the fireside, Emily buried her face in her hands. Each time she expressed criticism of Angus or his actions it was she who was made to feel ashamed.

Hold your tears, she berated herself as she heard the maid enter the room to replenish the fire. A megrim, that's what afflicted her, though what did the servants care? They showed far more warmth towards the master and little wonder for it. Emily was the cold and resentful wife he did not deserve, she thought with a self-pity she acknowledged for what it was.

'Fetch me some chamomile tea, Mary,' she whispered, not raising her head from the cushion upon the sofa arm, knowing with a dull hopelessness that nothing could soothe her disordered spirits.

Indeed, Angus did not deserve her.

CHAPTER 12

At the sound of Angus's boots upon the tiles in the hallway the following afternoon, Emily lowered her head and tried to control the rapid beat of her heart.

Dread borne of shame. Her fingers worked feverishly over the infant's garment she was enlarging for Elizabeth's daughter Jane to wear, while her thoughts were in turmoil. She had wronged her husband, grievously. The time had come to atone.

She recalled the distinctive ring of her father's shoes upon the flagstones that had made her mother visibly blanche. His entrance was always the same.

'Margeurite,' he'd rasp as if displeased to find her in the drawing room when it was where he confined her for most of every day. So much derision and contempt contained in the one word. Usually he'd not address her again. In earlier days he'd turn to Emily with a smile and ask proudly, 'How's my little beauty, today?'

When had he stopped saying that? When she was about twelve, on the cusp of becoming a woman. By then he'd fostered in her the fawning desire to please him. If he no longer praised her, she was determined he'd not deride her as he did her mother, though it seemed his displeasure grew with each successive year. It had confused her, for he'd loved her and she tried so hard. 'The girl now looks like *her*!' she'd once overheard him say in response to some whispered exhortation for discretion from Lucy, who did her best to shield Emily from his angry outburst or snide remarks.

The thought filled her with terror. If she looked so like her mother, could she one day become similarly afflicted?

She reasoned her mother must once have been very beautiful and rich to have captivated her father.

'Beauty,' her father had once told her, 'is a woman's only defence. Use yours, Emily, while you can, for you have little else to recommend you.'

Now Emily was hunched over her tatting just as her mother had once cringed at her husband's return; though Angus could not be more different from her father.

For one thing her father never spoke cheerfully, either to his family or to the servants, she reflected upon hearing Wallace the butler laugh at his exchange with his master as he divested Angus of his multi-caped coat in the hallway. Then her husband strode into the room, making it seem suddenly much smaller.

His smile was brief, distracted, eye contact maintained only for as long as it took to say, 'Good morning, Emily, I hope you don't mind that I stayed away longer.' He stooped to kiss her cheek before relaxing with a smile in the seat opposite her. He wore riding clothes, and his face had a healthy glow. Emily drew herself up, murmured an appropriate response, and wondered why he seemed so different today.

'Thank you, Wallace.' Angus gathered up the accumulated correspondence from the silver salver the butler held out.

Breaking the seal of the first letter, he began to read. Unaccountably, Emily was piqued. She'd been building herself up to meet this moment. She had tormented herself as to how she would offer an oblique apology without having to prostrate herself and leave herself vulnerable. This was an unfair way to look at the matter, she knew. Angus would not take advantage, but she hated being in the wrong.

Now Angus was attending to daily business as if they were a long married couple, with barely a glance in her direction.

'Major Woodhouse called yesterday.'

He smiled briefly at her over the top of his correspondence.

'Your sister told him of the bequest from your father.' That got his attention, she thought, satisfied at last, waiting for him to lose his composure.

Pretending interest in her handiwork, she watched him carefully beneath lowered lashes.

He did not immediately respond, though the studied look on his face as he stared at the page in front of him indicated he was shocked.

'Why did you not tell me the truth, Angus?' Emily raised her face above her tatting.

'Would it have made a difference?'

The bluntness of his question made her squirm. Blushing, she dropped her eyes at his inference that she'd have accepted him more willingly had she known he was the Earl of Netherfield's only son and not merely one of Sir John's numerous brood.

He answered his own question. 'It seemed of little importance when I had no expectations we would benefit in any way. I met my natural father only twice.'

It was extraordinary the effect his interested gaze had upon her. She felt the blush rise up her throat. This was not the diffident Angus who had asked for her hand. Now she wanted to claw her way higher in his estimation.

'It was ill done of him to overlook his daughter,' Angus said, finally, still studying her with neither smile, nor frown. 'My solicitor in Habersham confirmed the size of the bequest when I visited him.' He transferred his gaze over Emily's shoulder, to the garden which seemed to flow right out of the house. Tapping the thick cream parchment, as if weighing up something of great importance, he said, 'I made over part of it to Lady Catherine. I hope you don't mind, Emily, for we have more than enough, and she had all but nothing.'

'Did she approach you?' The question was prompted by curiosity in the light of Angus's altered family relationship, but it sounded calculating, she realised, as Angus looked at her strangely.

'Of course I don't mind about the money,' she said hurriedly. 'That's not what I meant.' Taking a deep breath, she galvanised her courage. 'I'm sorry I misjudged you about accepting Aunt Gemma's funds.'

His expression, as he slowly rose, took her by surprise. Standing tall and straight in the centre of the room, his dark-brown eyes kindled with something she couldn't quite determine. Included was certainly a measure of warmth.

He seemed handsomer, more commanding and for a heartbeat she responded with a smile that came naturally.

'You were angry.' He shrugged, smiling that curious smile to which she was increasingly far from immune. 'No doubt feeling helpless, too, and that's not pleasant.' He gave a short laugh, breaking eye contact, turning to gaze out of the window. 'I know that feeling better than most. I was a prisoner of war for six months.'

Good Lord! What torture and privations must he have endured that he'd never spoken of? Or had he, but she had not attended him? He'd have had excuse enough to have considered there was little point when Emily was so disinterested. Admiration struck her as she stared at the back of his head, wondering at the fact she'd never felt his close-cropped curls and had no idea if they were coarse or silky; taking in the long, lean lines of her husband's physique and for the first time acknowledging that in comparing him with Jack she did not find Angus wanting.

No, she'd not been interested, before, but now she was consumed by curiosity.

She opened her mouth to frame her question, but the words did not come. Instead, she experienced an extraordinary and unexpected response to her husband's warm smile when he turned, akin to sweet syrup feeding through her veins and into her heart.

Shifting uncomfortably in her chair, she was aware of her greatly altered feelings when he crossed the room towards her.

Her tatting fell unheeded in her lap while her eyes travelled up the length of his top boots, over his Nankeen-clad legs. Impulsively, she raised her hand to touch the sleeve of his well-cut riding coat.

'Emily.' He tilted her chin up so he could see her face, and as her body betrayed her with that familiar kindling in her belly that should only be reserved for Jack, her mind came to the rescue.

Anger, cold and cutting. Because of this man's actions, Jack had died. Innocent though Angus's involvement may have been, he'd walked off with the prize while Jack now lay cold in his grave. Her loyalty to Jack demanded this of her.

She turned her head from him as she shrank back into her chair, and Angus's hand fell away. She heard him sigh. Heard his footsteps cross the soft carpet until he'd positioned himself to gaze once more out of the window.

Remorse came too late as she picked up her tatting, using

the rhythm of the stitching to repeat the litany of Jack's name. He said, conversationally, 'Caroline thinks you are in need of some diversion. She fears you are mouldering away in the country and has asked if you've expressed any interest in this tea party she's organising.'

Emily's mind was still on her response to her husband.

Her withdrawal seemed petty, an abuse of power in a parody of a childish game.

'Of course. Caroline is very kind to take such an interest,' she murmured. 'Tell her I'm in a fever of delight.' Her voice told a different story, but that was the way she was these days. Contrary. She wasn't proud of it.

'Emily, what must I do to make you happy?'

Shocked that he'd give voice to it, as much as at the desperation in his tone, she jerked up her head to find him towering over her.

'Nothing.' The beating of her heart terrified her. Her voice sounded thin, puling, unlike her. 'The house is beautiful. I tried to thank you—'

'You did not.' His hands came down on her shoulders as he crouched before her. This time there was no warmth or sympathy in his expression as he searched her face. 'Mere platitudes. Emily, you are my *wife*.'

She wriggled out of his grasp and struggled to her feet. Taking a faltering step backwards, her hands went to the locket around her neck. Jack's locket which contained an inky black curl belonging to the hero who'd died some six months before.

'Yes, your wife, your property. I feel forever under siege.' It's what she'd felt when he'd married her, but she was not prepared to think too deeply on her response to him only minutes before. She took a shallow breath, pressing on with her denials, her self-justifications, even though they sounded old and tired and no longer relevant. 'Do you not realise that every moment in your company I am reminded of your rights over me? Do you know how that makes me feel?'

She saw the tightening of his lips, the bleakness in his eye, but still she went on, trotting out the lines that had once run endlessly round her head but which now sounded hollow; she was unable to stop now that the floodgates had been released. 'If you smile at me, I wonder, will it be tonight? I can't bear it. I am your wife, yes, and I have no choice. We made a bargain. *I* made a bargain. We have been at Wildwood three weeks and as the sun sets each day I cannot breathe for fear of what the night will bring. I cannot expect you to wait forever so for God's sake, let's get it over with.'

'Excuse me, ma'am,' Mary interrupted, hovering in the doorway. 'Mr and Mrs Micklen have arrived.'

If the previous conversation had destroyed her composure, Emily felt completely undone as the blood drained from her head in a physical reaction only her father could produce. 'My father?' she repeated, looking at Angus as if he would refute it. For how could her father be here when he had cast her off? Bartholomew Micklen did not forgive.

'Your mother, also.' Angus had taken her arm, obviously for fear she might fall, so obvious was her distress. She felt the tenseness in his grip though his tone was conversational for Mary's benefit, while his eyes searched her face. 'You did not receive my letter telling you of their visit?'

'You invited them?' Oh, how she wished he hadn't, but there was no opportunity to say it for now the tall, white haired old man was waving through the servant who carried her mother like a child. Directing him to the chair closest to the fire, Angus moved forward to assist.

'Good afternoon, Emily. You look surprised to see us.' Her father's thin smile barely reached his eyes.

Emily did not know what to say. She'd expected never to see her father again. Her mother she'd intended to visit clandestinely. What could Angus have said to induce the old man to relent? Her mind churned with mixed reactions. She should be overjoyed, yet she was not.

'Mama.' Bending, she kissed her mother's cheek before crouching to wrap her useless feet more cosily. Just as she'd done a thousand times.

After greeting his in-laws Angus turned to Emily. 'Mary has already prepared the blue room. I hoped your parents' visit would be'—he lowered his voice as the Micklens settled themselves—'distracting. Mrs Micklen,' he crossed the room to his mother-in-law, 'are you too close to the fire? Yes? Certainly I shall move you back a little.'

It was strange hearing him enquire after her mother's comfort when she'd never heard her father do so. She was even more astonished when that evening Angus took a seat at right angles to his mother-in-law and carried on a lengthy and lively discussion ranging from fox hunting to the war with France. Patiently, he awaited her slurred answers, his look interested, before adding his own response. This left Emily facing her father, wondering, awkwardly, what she could talk about. She could not remember having dealt with him in such a setting.

She certainly could not remember him having ever relented on a punishment when she'd transgressed. The last time she'd seen him was moments before she'd been dispatched in a dog cart with one trunk. His parting words still rang in her ears: 'This house is forever barred to you for you have proved yourself beneath contempt.'

Now he smiled at her as he never had, and enquired after her health. Having her parents as guests in her lovely, grand new house, was extraordinary. She just wished she felt less like a trapped rabbit, and put it down to the conflicting emotions she felt at the change in her relationship with her husband.

❄

EMILY WAS UP EARLY the next morning, leaning over the railing of the jetty by the ornamental lake where Angus found her. She'd spent a fitful sleep in her own apartments and had risen with the sun to seek solace for her disordered thoughts. Terrifying though it had been to face her father again, he'd gone to pains to make it clear she was forgiven. This gave rise to the most unexpected relief and gratitude on her part. Gratitude that extended towards Angus. He had, carefully and consciously, worked towards a reconciliation, recognising it was an important step in her recovery.

Grief, she acknowledged, was like a painful canker that healed slowly.

Angus joined her at the railing, a faint smile curving his lips as he stared into the glittering waters, as if yesterday's exchange had not taken place. For the benefit of her parents they'd been civil, almost conversational, over dinner.

Angling his body to face her, he said, 'I thought I might find you here. It's lovely at this time of morning, isn't it?' He raised an eyebrow. 'However, you don't want to be late for breakfast, Emily. I suspect your father does not like to be kept waiting.'

His proximity was disturbing, for the hands he rested upon the railing were close to hers, but he made no attempt to touch her. It was a shock to acknowledge that every time he'd come near her since he'd returned from abroad she'd deliberately recalled Jack's image as some kind of safeguard against the curious, mixed feelings that kindled within her when she found herself alone with her husband. Surely it was wrong that she had to remind herself where her true loyalties lay?

'It was kind of you to invite my parents.' She felt afraid to meet his eye as a gust of wind ruffled the surface of the lake.

'You've nothing of which to be ashamed.' Angus rested his chin on his fisted hand as he relaxed against the railing and she turned her head, heart hammering suddenly to meet his gaze, dark with the intensity of his feelings. 'I've told you that, Emily, and now your father's confirmed it. You're beautiful and clever and witty and you have your future before you. You can make as much or as little of local society as you wish. Caroline is your ally. We all are.'

She gaped at him. What did he know of her ability to charm? And what did he know of local society? She was terrified of her inevitable initiation. Would people know? Suspect? Would there be whispers? The cut direct, even?

'Witty? I don't think I've ever made you laugh, Angus.' It was a self-deprecating statement which she bore up with, 'I've been nothing but churlish and ungrateful. I wonder you can still speak in a civil fashion to me.' The words were catharsis. She felt a curious flowering in the darkest recesses of her heart.

'We've not had an auspicious start and you've not been shown to advantage, it's true,' he conceded with a candour that took her aback. She must add 'plain speaking' to her husband's list of recommendations. 'But remember, I saw you at the Regimental Ball when you'd experienced none of the trials life has thrust upon you during the past six months.' He straightened, pretending a study of the half- moons of his fingernails. Almost shyly, he said, 'I saw the impression you made on people.' When he glanced at her with his clear-eyed gaze she felt the inexplicable desire to put out her hand and trace the line of the scar upon his cheek.

She stopped herself, cocking her head as he continued. 'Not just the men. The women sent you envious glances. You were dazzling. I was dazzled.' He gave a short laugh. 'You looked so happy. As if you had the world and its moon at your beck and call ... and I wanted you so badly.'

'You ... did?'

'Emily, you will have the same effect on local society as you did back then. You can enjoy a good, rich life here ... if you want.'

She was silent as she pondered this, aware of his closeness and aware of how much she wanted to bridge the distance between them.

He broke the long silence, saying in a lighter tone, 'Your mother is astute. Amusing, too.'

'I ... never really thought much about it.'

'She obviously enjoys little society, but she reads and listens. I was impressed.'

The warm glow in Emily's heart intensified. No one had ever praised her mother whom her father never lost an opportunity to belittle. She was about to tell him what that meant to her when he said abruptly, 'Major Woodhouse wants me to go away again.'

'So soon?' She was shocked by the extent of her dismay.

'I have been home three weeks, Emily.'

'Where are you going this time?' she murmured. 'There is much you keep from me.'

Though his hand was less than an inch from hers he made no attempt to touch her. His shrug was almost imperceptible. 'For your own good. Ensuring your wellbeing is the only reason I do not unburden myself. Not mistrust of you.'

It was what Major Woodhouse had intimated, but she didn't want to think of him. Angus's smile – wistful, as if he wished she appreciated his concern – nearly undid her and she found it difficult to concentrate on his next words, so busy was she trying to make sense of her desire that he take her in his arms.

'Not only is my work important for keeping us in comfort, Emily, both now and in the future, it is vital for the security of our country.' He touched her cheek with the barest of caresses and she shivered, disappointed when he withdrew his hand and fixed his thoughtful gaze upon the lake. 'Napoleon has been cutting a swathe through Europe unchecked for so long, we cannot take for granted our way of life here.' His jaw was clenched and his gentle look hardened. 'We cannot take anything for granted and we all have a duty to safeguard what we hold dear, for ourselves and for those we love. The threat may seem diluted now, but it is real and there are enemies amongst us who would see Napoleon have his way'—his gaze held hers as if he wanted her to share his concern—'at the expense of all we uphold as good and reasonable.'

'There are some who say England's only enemies are the enemies within. What about the revolutionaries who smash the machines which would see England prosper? Those men who are destroying the new looms? The army had to be called in. Are they not more of a threat? You are a brave man, Angus.' She put her hand on his. 'You risk your life because of your loyalty to England, and to me, but you are fighting for a foreign cause. I suppose there might be some benefit to restoring the French king, but Napoleon will never reach England. If you are more concerned with protecting those you love, would you not be better choosing a cause closer to home?' She sighed and when he prompted her to go on, saying that he wished to hear more of her thoughts on the crises at home and abroad, she realised she was only spouting Jack's beliefs. Still, Jack had told her more than Angus ever would.

She glanced at their hands, hers resting almost tentatively upon his, and made sure to wipe the uncertainty from her tone. Angus clearly had different beliefs and she was beginning to doubt her own. 'Jack wanted to confine his work to England but, like you, he was in the pay of the British Government so had to follow orders.'

'Then Jack was an odd choice for the kind of work he did.' Emily flinched at the scorn in his tone as he went on. 'I would be wary of Jack's version of the truth.'

Emily raised her chin, her tenderness for her husband fast evaporating. Removing her hand from his, she gripped the railing and tried to steady her voice. 'Are you calling Jack a liar?'

'If I said I was'—a note of frustrated weariness had entered Angus's tone—'the conversation would end, Emily, for you would turn your back on me and flounce back to the house.'

She gasped in outrage at the same time as acknowledging the truth of it. *Rein in your temper, Emily*, she exhorted herself. *You've played the ice maiden so long it's little wonder Angus thinks you still care only for Jack. He's deriding Jack because it's the only way he knows how to knock down the barrier between you and him. Do not be drawn.*

However, the lessons she'd learned when responding to her father's taunts deserted her. Most of her life had been spent subsuming her inner desires, stifling her impulses. Jack had lifted the lid on her passions. Now Angus was tapping the well of her need to give sway to her deepest emotions.

Struggling for a deep breath, she pushed her shoulders back. 'So Jack was a liar, was he?' She tossed her head to indicate her scepticism. 'You believe he and my father underestimated the foreign threat to our country?'

'I don't pretend to know what Jack believed in, Emily, but I believe he told you what it pleased him to tell you as it served his own ends.'

Her throat was suddenly very dry. She swallowed as her fury rose to fresh heights. 'The only threat,' she said, her tone crisp to match his, 'as I see it, is the threat Jack's heroic nature poses *your* situation. He cannot defend himself for he is dead while you have gained everything from his death. A death that occurred only on account of you!'

She'd not meant to bring it up, ever, for of course it was not Angus's fault that brave Jack had intervened in his defence.

'Stop, Emily!' He gripped her shoulder as she flung away. 'The story I told you to explain Jack's death—'

'Oh, so that's not true, either?' If only the force of her outrage could fell him on the spot. She hated him. How could she ever have started entertaining tender feelings for this calculating husband of hers? She managed to twist out of his grip, but he was too quick for her.

'Listen to me, Emily.' He jerked her forward, bringing his face close to hers. She heard the flapping of a bird's wings as it settled on the railing nearby, as if to gain amusement from their altercation. His breathing was fast and shallow. She heard it as she felt her own fear at what he might say.

'Emily, there is something I should have told you before.' His voice was urgent. 'Perhaps it's foolish of me to bring it up now when you are still mourning Jack and I'm about to go away again, but I've said too much and I will go on.' Distract-edly, he raked a hand through his wind-ruffled hair. 'God knows, six months is not a long time and yet it is time enough to reflect with calm and reason. I need to tell you something, Emily, and even if you choose not to believe it'— his eyes were bright, imploring—'promise me that you will listen calmly, without flying into the boughs. That you will hear me out and not dismiss my words as an attempt to achieve my own ends at anyone's expense.'

His words struck terror to her core. She needed all her defences for this. Stepping out of his grip, she said, 'You can tell me now.' She knew she sounded ungracious. 'I am your wife. I will hear you out. You can tell me anything, have I not already told you? Jack trusted me enough to tell me his thoughts, his ideas and dreams ... even his secrets.'

Was it the prickliness of her tone that made Angus appear to give up on their exchange?

He sighed, his shoulders sagging and his voice leaden as he stared back over the water. 'I sail the day after tomorrow. You will have several weeks to enjoy your freedom. Though I would prefer – for your own good – that you did not know where I am going, I believe it only right to tell you that I shall be lodging, as I did on my last mission, at the home of Monsieur Delon and his daughter.'

She was silent for a heartbeat as she digested this, angling her body round to face him once more as she leant against the railing. 'You are a replacement for Jack in all things, are you not?'

Her irony was not lost on him. 'Not all things, Emily.' Gently he rested his hand on her shoulder. 'There is something you must know about Madeleine—'

'Madeleine?' She cut him off, her mind churning, still unsure what she felt to discover that Angus had taken up where Jack had left off, not just in the marital stakes. The men were so different yet Angus seemed to have stepped so easily into Jack's shoes.

She cut him off with a forced smile. 'There is a book of Children's Verse I had bought Madeleine and which Jack was going to take with him on his last visit.' She was determined to be placatory, as much to win Angus round as to learn more. 'Now you can take it to her for me, and with my best love.'

He shook his head, his eyes bleak. 'Save your gift, Emily. I will not take your Book of Children's Verse. Madeleine is not—'

'You will not take my gift? Why? Because I should know nothing of what you do? Because I should be kept in ignorance of everything, just as Major Woodhouse implies? Am I considered *so* untrustworthy?'

He stared at her, as if weighing up something of great importance. Once more he slowly he shook his head. 'I would trust you with my life, but I will not entrust you with the truth if it endangers you.' He straightened. 'Or if you are not ready for it.'

'Come back!' she demanded, following him as he retraced his steps along the jetty. *Oh why was he leaving after saying so much and ultimately so little? Why did she have to respond with such defensiveness to anything Angus said that pertained to Jack?* She tried one final desperate gambit to draw him back to her. 'What was it you were going to tell me? Jack told me everything and we were not yet married. I know *nothing* yet I am your wife. Why should it be considered a breach of security for you to convey a simple book to a little girl?'

His expression, which usually softened when he gazed upon her, was hard with anger. 'When you are in this mood you are not inclined to accept the truth if it is not what you want to hear.'

Outraged, she stamped her foot. 'How dare you?'

'Save your gifts, Emily,' he muttered, stepping onto the gravel path that wound round the rose garden. 'When I return from France I'll give you all the evidence you need to enable you to decide where your loyalties lie. To the *memory* of your dead, *false* fiancé who could not have loved you else he'd not have deceived you as he did, or to your husband who loves you with all his heart.'

SHE BARELY SLEPT, she was so outraged by his allegations. Angus had thrown those last few words at her out of pure cruelty just to keep her in a foment of angry curiosity.

He'd tell her when he got back. *What* was he going to tell her and who did he think she was? Some biddable little innocent who'd meekly accept everything?

So what if Jack had uttered a white lie here and there to protect her? It was in his nature to adopt a casual approach for the greater good, whereas brooding Angus was such a defender of the truth he'd consider the slightest white-washing by Jack as evidence of poor character.

In the morning Angus was gone on business leaving Emily to fret and fulminate, though one unexpected consolation was her father's interest in her affairs. For the first time the sour expression beneath the shock of white hair warmed as it had not done since she'd been a child.

He was interested in her. Concerned with her thoughts on how she intended to make an impression on local society. Of course she knew impressions counted for a great deal in her father's eyes otherwise she'd not have been relegated to such a hopeless position and forced to marry Angus. But his interest seemed for the first time to encompass her feelings. Including, strangely, her feelings about her husband. He must be more concerned for her happiness than she'd thought.

'He has been good to you, Emily?' Facing her from his seat opposite in her elegantly decorated private sitting room, while her mother was resting upstairs, he picked up a small painting of Wildwood which Angus had done. 'Indeed, Angus has been very good to you, Emily. More so than Jack would have been.'

The statement shocked her. Her father had *loved* Jack. He'd sanctioned the match when Jack had neither wealth nor illustrious connections.

Unconsciously, he stroked the frame of the little picture as he bent forward.

'Jack was involved in dangerous operations abroad, Emily.' The blue eyes beneath the thick white brows darkened. 'I suspect you'd have been alone a great deal. Jack's political interests would always have come first.'

This was not the Jack she knew. Jack spoke lightly of the secretive work he was engaged upon, of being nothing but a slave to the British Government who paid the bills but who should have been more concerned with fighting the enemy at home.

Jack always put Emily first. She was astonished her father knew anything about Jack's priorities.

'Jack spoke to you about this?' Her heart hammered. Was her father privy to information Jack had not confided to her? It was like a betrayal. Angus's words of the previous day returned with an ominous echo.

'Jack commonly sought my trusted opinion, Emily.'

'Jack trusted me, too, Papa.' She wished her voice sounded stronger. 'He told me everything about his work and the people with whom he lodged.'

Her father leaned across and patted her hand which tapped in agitation upon the arm of the sofa. 'A husband must confide in a wife, Emily.'

Unconsciously she pulled away. 'Angus has me in his confidence.' It was a lie, but it seemed suddenly imperative that she carry it off if she were to maintain her elevated status in her father's opinion. 'Major Woodhouse chose him as Jack's replacement.'

Immediately the words were out, Emily regretted them.

Angus would not wish her to divulge this to anyone.

She was glad her father betrayed no surprise, suggesting he already knew.

'Major McCartney strikes me as an effective and loyal servant of the British Government, and a good choice for such a role.'

On the heels of her wish that she'd not been so indiscreet was the undeniable power in bringing a look of interest to her father's face. He who had been singularly *dis*interested in her for most of her life.

Her father ran his hands thoughtfully over the arms of the fashionable Egyptian sofa Angus had bought Emily. 'He lodges with the Delons when he is abroad?' Nodding at her shocked acknowledgement, he went on, 'Jack told me about the Delons, Emily. Monsieur Delon is a faithful ally of the English.'

Guilt engulfed Emily. She stammered, 'I don't think Angus would like to know we were speculating about Monsieur Delon. He is very secretive about his activities.'

'How would your husband know we were speculating?' Her father's expression was benign, yet there was something uncomfortable about their discussion Emily could not put her finger on.

Her father leaned towards her, his manner conspiratorial. 'Every husband must be master of his household, Emily, and yours has the added responsibility of ensuring both your safety and that of his country. Angus is a worthy husband, yet a wife must shore up her own position.'

Emily squirmed at the manner in which his eyes raked her, hiding her embarrassment when he added, 'Now you've lost the babe – Jack's babe – you have never been more desirable to him.' He chuckled. 'Use it as a weapon, Emily.'

She felt her mouth drop open while her skin prickled and she felt suddenly self-conscious in her fashionable sprigged muslin, with its skirt revealing every curve. Was her father truly referring to her body? When Emily had complained as a sixteen-year-old at the ugly dresses she was forced to wear, Lucy had muttered that to flaunt herself would upset her father.

Her father continued speaking. 'A woman's powers of attraction are her only weapons. You are clever, Emily, but you allow your heart to rule you. That is a mistake. Jack is dead. Angus is your husband. You must learn to play him and that means using your powers of attraction to discover all you can. For your own survival.'

Her face burned. Was he intimating that she must play some wanton creature merely to gain information?

He raised an eyebrow. 'Your Aunt Gemma told me you'd solicited her help in seeking an annulment.'

Emily's embarrassment was replaced by shame.

'I'm glad the matter went no further, Emily, for look what you have gained from this marriage.' He made a sweeping motion with his arm. 'Would you prefer to return to your old home and live out your life under my roof, spurned by society?'

She couldn't look at him. He would see how intolerable such a notion was. 'But father, how can I do as you tell me when—'

'When what?' he asked sharply. 'You do not love your husband?' He sat back and fanned his hands as if he'd already supplied her with the answers and she was a fool for needing clarification. 'You live in a world of make-believe, Emily. We exist on this earth to survive as best we can— alone. In truth, we can trust no one for there is no one who will not betray us when their own self-interest trumps the transient affection that occurs with unexplained randomness. Our survival depends on the material world and you, Emily, would have nothing if your husband had not fallen in love with your pretty face. His honour was aroused by what would have disgusted most men.'

Including her own father. She wished one of the servants would interrupt them and bring an end to this horrible discussion.

'You used to send small gifts to the child, Madeleine Delon.'

She flushed. 'How did you know?'

'Jack and I spoke often.' He looked at her searchingly. 'Has your husband told you about Madeleine?'

Emily shook her head, embarrassed. 'He … said he wouldn't take my gift to her because it would put me in danger and that he'd explain everything when he got back. Jack was very fond of Madeleine, I know.' The memory of the ribbons he and the little girl had chosen together for her sent a flood of nostalgia through her. She brushed away a tear. 'He spoke of her often.'

Her father frowned while his lips formed a faint smile. 'How interesting,' he said softly. To her astonishment he reached over and caressed her cheek. 'Your husband obviously loves you very much, Emily, yet I sense that all is not well between you.'

Emily, embarrassed by the almost unprecedented intimacy, watched him stare thoughtfully at the ceiling. Her mind churned with confusion.

'Let me pour your more tea, Papa.' Relieved to withdraw from such close proximity, she reached for the teapot.

Her father smiled suddenly and his tone was different, as if he'd come to a decision. 'Inevitably there will be things your husband will tell you that you do not wish to hear, Emily. Such is the way of life.' He nodded as he accepted the dish of tea she offered him. 'However, your happiness depends upon the harmoniousness of your union. You must be a loving wife, in whom Angus feels comfortable confiding. Promise me you'll try?'

Slowly, as required, Emily forced herself to nod. She was still angry with Angus for his wounding words though she'd decided it was only natural that her husband's long frustrated need to bring her into accord with him would lead him to denigrate Jack. Once he'd laid the facts before her she'd confidently dismiss them all. After that …

She swallowed down the lump of excitement as she

reflected on the musings of her long, sleepless night. In the early hours of the morning she'd experienced an epiphany. The light had shone upon the path that would lead her to happiness and marital felicity. She would show her loyalty towards Jack by defending his memory with all her might, but she'd make it clear to Angus that she was ready to be on a different footing with her husband. The mere thought was enough to send the heat rushing to her cheeks.

She'd accepted other truths, too, such as the fact that the operation in which Angus was involved required the greatest secrecy. If there were any criticism to be made of Jack it was that he had been a little too forthcoming with his information during their tender moments together. Sometimes he'd surprised her with his detailed descriptions of places and people. She'd never forgotten his description of the beautiful spy that posed their greatest threat.

'She's very cunning, Emily, and very wicked, but so beautiful that no man who has crossed her path has ever had the heart to see she receives justice.' He'd made a slicing motion across his throat which had made Emily feel a little queasy before she asked, 'You've seen her?' Her distaste turned to wicked excitement when he replied, 'She reminds me of you,' adding at her pretended outrage, 'but you are virtue to her evil.' He'd laughed uproariously. 'You're of similar height, with the same lustrous dark hair. She is a French Madonna hiding a wicked soul while you're an innocent blushing English rose. And aren't you blushing now!' The exchange had ended with giggles and kisses, but Emily never forgot that she had an evil counterpart across the channel.

She bit her lip as she checked the words she was about to say. 'Papa, I have a book upstairs that I had intended to send'—she swallowed—'with Jack on his last mission.' Rallying, she added, 'I could not bear to part with it for Jack and I had bought it together, but when I mentioned it to Angus he said he wouldn't take it.'

Her father regarded her for a long moment. 'He didn't say why?'

She shook her head again and stared at her hands, clasped in her lap. 'He said he would tell me everything when he got back from his next mission in France. He leaves tomorrow.' Her misery increased as she admitted, 'Angus and I spoke in anger about it. That's why he's not here now.'

'Yet he said he would … explain … when he returned?'

She nodded.

'And what do you think that means?'

It was difficult to force out the words. She could only guess, herself. Haltingly, she told him. 'He said Jack lied to me. When I demanded that he explain in what way he said there was no point in carrying on the discussion when I'm angry but that when he returns he'll prove it.'

'Prove it, eh?' Her father's look was one of sceptical interest. 'Are you not consumed with curiosity, Emily? Have you not demanded that Angus stop keeping secrets from you?'

Miserably, Emily shrugged. 'I don't want to anger Angus. Let him say what he has to say when he returns. He'll never convince me Jack was anything other than the kindest and most loyal of men.'

Her father chuckled. 'Indeed he was, Emily, but Angus is your husband now. Now you must prove you're a cunning and intelligent wife and that it is not in Angus's best interests to keep you entirely in the dark. Why not slip the book into your husband's luggage when he's not looking? Once he's in France he'll not be able to resist giving it to the child.'

Emily rose. 'I do not wish to make Angus angry.'

'Indeed you must not.' Her father's smile was colluding. 'Remember, Emily, the more you find out for yourself, without him knowing, the greater your power over him.

Every woman seeks advantage over her husband because it is the only way she can survive.'

She could not believe she was having such a conversation with her father and took a step away, embarrassed and disgusted by his plain speaking. 'But mother—' she began, too bravely, and was glad he cut her off.

'My point exactly. Your mother is a hideous cripple.' His tone was dismissive. 'She can wield no power over me when she is confined to a chair with absolutely no powers of attraction. You, Emily, must learn to wield the weapons God has given you. Wield them for your own survival, for if you do not, you will lose the affection of your husband upon whom your survival depends.' His eyes glittered over his steepled fingers. 'The manner in which you and Angus have been thrown together is not the most auspicious and you will never know how deep is his disgust for your sin, therefore you must use all means to protect yourself for the future. Knowledge will give you power, Emily.'

She turned away as he added, 'Remember, I am your father, and blood is thicker than water.'

The brief flare of camaraderie she'd felt towards her father at the beginning of this conversation was long gone. She put her hand on the door handle, anxious to get away. 'Mama may have woken,' she muttered. 'I must check on her.'

'First, bring me the book. It would amuse me while you are with your mother. There is a small child, the daughter of a cousin, who is coming to visit and Margeurite will want to buy her a present. In fact, bring me the book now and I'll show it to your mother. I'm sure it would please her.'

CHAPTER 13

Angus turned towards the small mirror on the washstand and ran his hand down the smoothness of his unscarred cheek.

Emily's parents' visit had been cut short at Mr Micklen's sudden behest. He'd cited urgent matters requiring him at home but had not countenanced his wife's pleas that she be allowed to remain.

They'd left that afternoon and Angus would be crossing the channel tomorrow.

He knew Emily was expecting him tonight, but God, this was not the right time.

He'd certainly not expected such an invitation. Not after their recent strained relations. But if the surrender of her body, her tacit acceptance of the marriage contract, were her way of indicating she wanted a truce, he'd not complain. He'd show her how much he loved her with his tender caresses. Early in their marriage, he'd been shocked by her claim that she'd been a slave to passion in Jack's arms. Now he understood better the deeply smouldering fires of her complex temperament and how they could be ignited. He wanted to prove he was capable of the same depth of love she'd attributed to Jack. Surely, then, he would be rewarded in kind.

Scowling at his reflection, he wished he felt eager anticipation. The truth was, he had no idea what had motivated Emily to indicate in such clear terms that she would accept him into her bedchamber that night. Not after his allegations of Jack's duplicity, which he deeply regretted. He should have remained silent if he'd not intended furnishing her with the entire truth.

He did not delude himself that Emily was excited about tonight. Dull resignation was most likely her overriding emotion; and yet, they had to start somewhere.

In the dim lamplight his scar stood out, raised from the smooth surface of his face and lighter in colour. Neither that nor the alignment of his features had ever been of concern, nor were they now. He focused on the silver blade of his razor lying upon the marble surface and contemplated the long walk down the passage to his wife's apartments.

To the only woman he'd ever desired.

Emily had presided over dinner like a queen. At Wildwood she was the consummate mistress, managing the servants with skill, though conversation with her husband had been even more strained since her parents had left.

No, after nearly two months of anticipation, dreaming of how he would prove that he, not Jack, were the better man, he was not looking forward to this at all.

Knotting the heavy silk banyan around his middle, Angus strode purposefully towards the door, pausing with his hand upon the doorknob. How engineered the whole act was. There was no feeling on her part but she was submitting like the good wife she'd promised she'd be.

It made him sick.

At the same time he could barely contain his desperate hunger for her.

He heard her stifled gasp when he entered her room.

'I did not expect you so soon,' she said, rising from her dressing table and he watched, mesmerised, as her lawn-clad figure swayed over the candle she carried to the cabinet by the bed.

'Don't snuff it out.' At her side in two steps, he put his hand on her wrist to stay her. He felt her trembling. Their eyes locked; hers black, reflecting her terror. The only relief he felt was that he could see no disdain.

'Emily, I have something for you.' Lord, he sounded so desperate. The moment the words were out he knew this was not the time to present his gift. There had been no 'right time' to present it to her before, but this was about as wrong a time as he could ever have decided upon.

Her eyes went to the slim velvet box he'd placed on the dressing table, but they did not brighten and he silently cursed himself for his gaucheness. She'd see his gift in a different light altogether.

'Thank you.' Her voice was dull as she picked up the diamond choker Sir John had given him. It glittered in the candlelight.

'Let me fasten it.'

His hands shook as they never had in battle when he swept back her hair, his fingertips brushing her soft, delicate skin.

Turning, she stepped back so he could admire his gift. 'Do you want me to keep it on when …?'

At the catch in her voice he wished he could just call the whole thing off.

'Whatever you wish.'

After a pause she shrugged, removed the silver locket she

always wore, then took a step towards the bed as if resigned to her fate.

He followed, drawing back the covers. Slowly, he bent to scoop her up, placing her on the soft feather down mattress.

Mutely, without expression, she stared up at him.

He felt the tightness within him grow. It gripped his heart, the pain of longing matching that which throbbed in that basest, expected region of himself.

Their shadows twined and danced upon the walls, then slid out of sight as Angus lowered himself onto the bed beside Emily. With his elbow supporting his weight, he gazed down at her.

Lord, she was beautiful. The purity of her expression, the sweep of her throat which curved down to meet the swell of her breasts made him catch his breath. She was perfection.

When his hand grazed her bare skin as he toyed with the ribbon which tied her night rail, her tiny intake of breath was a reminder of the weight of his great responsibility. He did not touch the diamonds around her throat; did not want to look at them.

Obediently, she lay pliant beside him while he practiced the restraint of a lifetime. His lungs felt so constricted he could hardly breathe, his heart gripped by his awful responsibility, and all the while his loins were on fire, urging him to consummate the act which underpinned their marriage contract. She was giving herself to him in return for his continued protection.

Simple.

Like Jessamine had.

Raising himself above her, with just the insubstantial fabric of night clothes between them, he could feel the heat from her body, the rise and fall of her chest as she sucked in each anticipatory breath.

Her eyes did not leave his as she moved slightly beneath

him, shifting her body to accommodate his weight more comfortably.

He couldn't kiss her. Of course he could not. That would be far too intimate. Reaching down beneath the covers he found the hem of her night rail.

She arched slightly, making it easier for him and he eased the garment upwards. As his hand skimmed her thighs, a lightning charge ripped through him in response to her heat, her shudder.

Her head rolled to one side and he saw that she fixed her gaze on a shadow on the wall, her whole body tensing.

She was anticipating the pain. She'd done this before. Jack had violated her. She'd taunted Angus with the fact she'd enjoyed it, but what did a good wife know of passion?

Women bartered their bodies for the things they could not provide for themselves. Emily's unpalatable marriage to Angus was the result of having been coerced by Jack. Now the time had come when she could no longer withhold her side of the bargain.

Parting her legs obediently, her eyes seemed suddenly vacant, turning her face into an inscrutable mask.

Also like Jessamine.

All the pent-up desire, longing and desperation drained out of him.

Angus gazed at her hair spread like a dark, glossy curtain over the pillow and the resignation writ so bleakly in her expression, while the memory of the dreadful night Jessamine first came to his bed returned to haunt him.

Beneath him, Emily stirred as he rolled away, her voice a hoarse whisper, though he heard fear and confusion there, too. 'Where are you going?'

He had the gall, for a split second, to imagine she considered his retreat a disappointment.

Retying his banyan, he bent over her and gently brushed

back a strand of dark hair from her cheek. The softness of her skin nearly undid him. He wanted to curl up beside her, feel the curve of her body pressed against his and stroke her into feelings which matched his own.

Only shame and disgust at the memory of the last time he'd bedded a woman stopped him.

'I can't do this, Emily.' His throat was so dry he could barely say the words. He stooped to brush his lips across her brow. 'Sleep well.'

She said nothing but the look in her eyes slashed at his heart. She might not have wanted this but his rejection had battered her pride.

On his way out, he saw the book of Children's Verse, tied with red ribbon, on top of the escritoire near the door. Accompanying it was an envelope addressed to Madeleine and clearly he was to carry it to France with him.

Only the greatest self-control prevented him from picking it up and hurling it at the wall.

MOST PEOPLE OBSERVING THE LOVELY, statuesque Mrs McCartney as she stood on the portico of the classical rotunda high on the hill might have thought she was simply admiring the splendid view of woods and chequered fields.

Little did Emily know she had become a figure of curiosity and that much drawing room gossip centred around the tea party the rector's wife was organising. The grand lady of the manor had earned a reputation for mystique. She was also referred to as the handsomest in the neighbourhood.

Unaware, and afraid the secret of her tarnished reputation may have been leaked, Emily kept to herself, preferring the solitude of her gilded prison which she left only occasionally to visit Caroline.

On this particular day, with Angus gone above two weeks on his second tour of duty, Emily watched dispassionately as Major Woodhouse laboured up the hill.

He greeted her with a lie: 'I came to see how you were faring.'

She knew he was simply checking on her. Perhaps he wanted further proof of her disloyalty as a wife.

'That is kind of you, Major. Angus sends me regular updates on his good health. Little else, let me reassure you.'

She began to walk, forcing him to follow her, his company like a thorn in her side. She realised she'd made an enemy of him, but though she was well aware of the foolishness and unfairness of her words, she could not take them back.

'Your husband is the height of discretion.' The corners of the major's mouth tugged when she glanced at him. 'Has he asked you about your French connections?' The casual tone belied the sudden intensity of his look.

Furious indignation rose up in her breast but she managed tightly, 'We have no communication with the French side of our family, Major. I can only assume them casualties of this terrible war.'

He raised an eyebrow and she bridled at his scepticism. 'Did you interrogate my husband over his French connections?' she demanded, swinging round. Then when he appeared confused, 'Did he not consort with a Frenchwoman on the battle field?'

'Jessamine?'

His shock appeared profound, as indeed it might. What good wife referred to her husband's mistress?

Emily was not about to lose the advantage. 'So you knew?' Angrily she went on. 'It would seem my husband's association with this … Jessamine'—she all but spat the name—'who lived in France, did not constitute the same threat to national security that it appears his association with his wife, who has never set foot in France, does.'

His composure returned, Major Woodhouse continued walking, silent for some seconds until he asked, coolly, 'So you deny having had any contact with any relatives in France?'

'Why is my past plumbed as if I were a traitor?'

He cocked his head as he rested a hand upon the Greek column which supported the folly they'd been traversing.

'An accident of birth does not make one a traitor. Only one's intentions and actions. I am asking questions, not to satisfy my personal curiosity, Mrs McCartney, but because I think it's important. I'm sorry if you feel I am interrogating you.'

Emily tried to steady her breathing, still deeply unsettled. 'I have nothing to hide and my husband certainly does not regard me with the unfair suspicion you obviously harbour,' she said softly. 'Despite my incautious words to you last time we met, I love and admire my husband.'

'Bravo, Mrs McCartney.'

Emily regarded him through narrowed eyes while she gathered her courage to pursue what would under normal circumstances be a forbidden topic. 'Since you brought up the subject, Major McCartney, I would like to know what else you know of my husband's former mistress.'

She registered the flare of shock in his eye at her unlady-like words. Maintaining an air of cool control as she resumed walking, she prompted, 'Naturally I am curious at the circumstances surrounding my husband's association with the … enemy, and as you instigated the topic I believe I am entitled to pursue it.'

'That is, indeed, direct, Mrs McCartney.'

The discomfort in his tone felt like a point in her favour. She picked up her skirts as she carefully negotiated the steps that led down the hill towards the house. 'You're a man who believes in the truth when it doesn't compromise the security of our country.' Stopping on level ground when they'd reached a small terrace built into the hillside, she turned with a smile that hid her pique at his reluctance to answer her. This man had insulted her. He'd all but called her a traitor. She dragged in a breath. Simply asking the question about Jessamine branded her the creature beyond redemption he must think her for her previous sins.

'What was Jessamine to my husband and why did she kill herself?'

'I'm afraid I can tell you nothing, ma'am.'

Beneath the cloud-studded sky, his look was evasive. Rather than her tormentor, he appeared to her suddenly as no more than a young man driven by conviction, whom she had highly embarrassed. Self-righteousness drained from her. So did her anger, for she had nothing to hide and Major Woodhouse's questioning had clearly been motivated by overzealousness. She relented as she contoured one of the smooth pillars which edged the terrace with the palm of her hand. 'It's all right, Major Woodhouse. I behaved abominably the last time we met and you have every reason to be wary of what you say to me.'

The humiliation of Angus's rejection was still raw. Was there some deficiency in herself she was unaware of? As she'd waited for him to come to her, she'd reflected that her timing in requesting their marriage contract be honoured the night before he left for France might not be auspicious. However, her father's strictures were still ringing in her ears. The extraordinary thing was that the moment she gazed upon Angus's strong, lithe body in the candlelight and imagined his warm mouth and body pressed against hers, she'd been flooded with a fierce, hot desire that had nothing to do with enticing her husband for the reasons her father had told her were so necessary.

She'd been ashamed by the force of her ardour during those moments of anticipation. Would Angus believe her wanton for the lustful impulses she'd be unable to hide once sexual congress were begun? What would he make of the ice maiden who suddenly proved she was every bit the depraved creature who'd allowed herself to be seduced outside of wedlock?

So many confusing thoughts and feelings had been whirling through her brain and body when he'd gazed into her face with that tender look which made her heart perform some extraordinary contortion she couldn't begin to explain.

Then, without warning, without explanation, he'd withdrawn. With such terrible suddenness.

It was only after his departure from her bedchamber that Emily, trawling for explanations, wondered if her husband had actually been in *love* with Jessamine. She remembered Caroline, in the carriage, whispering to Jonathan that 'love' had nothing to do with Angus's union with this woman, but could Caroline have been wrong?

Major Woodhouse, silent beside her, blocked the weak afternoon sun. There was little love lost between them but she thought she saw some relaxing of his features at her veiled apology.

'The wind is rising, Mrs McCartney. I think we should return.'

Reluctantly, she acquiesced when he offered her his arm, though Emily chose the path that led towards the ornamental lake instead of returning to the house.

The major, still so young and boyish in looks, had survived the weary, soul destroying retreat from Corunna at

Angus's side. He obviously knew more about Jessamine than he was prepared to reveal.

Emily was not about to relent. 'My sister-in-law tells me this woman was a camp follower Angus met during the retreat to Corunna.'

He glanced at her, his expression set. 'Few who lived through the horrors of Corunna choose to talk about it. If your husband doesn't, you must respect that.'

She waited, watching him filter his thoughts. 'Then I have no choice but to think the worst.'

They walked, Emily still clinging to his arm as they negotiated a small, narrow flight of steps. When he finally spoke it was as if he were narrating an ancient saga and his voice was carefully devoid of emotion. 'So many heroes died in the mud and cold, denied a glorious death in battle. Jessamine—' He hesitated. 'My apologies, ma'am, but I do not think I knew her last name. She had been the – er – companion of an English foot soldier. From these parts, I'm told, though that is all I know about the woman.' He stopped, obviously struck by doubts regarding the wisdom of continuing. 'I think, ma'am, that if your husband chose to keep this information from you—'

'I have been supplied half-truths from various sources. You would be doing my husband a service if you gave me the honourable version.'

With a sigh, the major gazed across the sweeping lawns. 'Angus deserves the comfort and security he has found. He is one of my dearest friends and I would go to great lengths to ensure his wellbeing … his happiness.' He sent her a sharp look, as if he doubted that Emily was doing much to contribute to that. Indecisiveness crossed his face. Then she heard his breath escape in a soft sigh, as if he'd made a decision. 'If it will help you to understand some of the conflicts that torment your husband, I will tell you this.'

At last …

'Several days into the retreat, with bodies dead and dying amidst the snow, soldiers wounded and wives and camp followers struggling to survive the distance to the shore where British troops were waiting to transport them home, your husband came upon Jessamine tending to her dying protector. The man would not survive his injuries. The enemy was on their heels and his sufferings were acute.'

Tensely, Emily waited in silence for him to go on.

The major's tone changed. She thought she heard pleading in his voice. 'To elaborate on the nature of this soldier's injuries would be too much for your delicate sensibilities, Mrs McCartney, and yet I would want to do so in order to exonerate those actions which your husband was called upon to expedite'—he paused—'entirely as a result of decency and humanity and the urging of the wounded soldier himself and his woman. Death was inevitable, either through cold and deprivation or the advancing enemy.'

Emily pressed her hand to her heart. Dear God, was this the burden her husband lived under? The premonition of what Major Woodhouse was about to say was almost overwhelming and without realising it she pre-empted him in a whispered rush. 'Jessamine prevailed upon my husband to put hers out of his misery?'

Major Woodhouse inclined his head. 'Consequently she was left without a protector. She believed she owed your husband a great debt'—his tone grew dry—'though it took her some time to persuade him to agree to the contract.'

After a tense silence, he changed the subject. 'I hope you are reconciled to Major McCartney's need for discretion.'

Emily's reply was distant. She could think only of the woman Angus had taken reluctantly into his bed after she'd begged him to kill her husband. The liaison had been formed through duty and necessity, not love.

When Angus had come to Emily's bed the night before he left, she wondered how he'd felt, knowing he was about to make love to the second woman whose husband's death he was responsible for?

'I'm sorry, Major Woodhouse, what did you say?' She struggled to attend to him. 'Oh, discretion? Have no fear, Angus speaks in only the vaguest of terms about his work.' She was still in shock but she forced herself to turn, saying with a grim smile, 'Tell me, Major Woodhouse, should I be concerned for Angus's safety?'

'I will offer you no platitudes, Mrs McCartney. There are always risks in defending one's country.'

Sadness washed over her. 'Poor Jack. He should have died defending his country. Instead, he died defending my husband.'

'I beg your pardon?' Major Woodhouse jerked his head up. 'Is that what Captain McCartney told you?'

Startled, she replied, 'Have you heard otherwise?'

He flushed to the roots of his brown curls. 'I will not refute what he has told you. Angus was chosen for his discretion, ma'am. It's not my place to elaborate where he chooses to keep his own counsel.'

She struggled to understand him. More untruths? 'Even if his wife is kept in ignorance?' she whispered.

'Especially if he deems it *safest* to keep his wife in ignorance.'

There was no arguing that Madeleine Delon was a beautiful woman. Irresistible to the majority of men, perhaps.

Angus was conscious of the pride that radiated from Monsieur Delon as they watched his graceful only child descend the stairs into the hallway of the Delon residence.

Except Madeleine wasn't a child and therein lay the problem.

She was a lush, sensual woman, completely aware of her seductive allure if the look she trained upon Angus was any indication of what was going on inside her pretty little head. She'd changed out of the simple muslin morning dress she'd been wearing when she'd greeted Angus in almost sisterly fashion. With the dimming of the light she'd become the grand temptress. Her gold lutestring gown with its gauze trimmings brought out the lustre of her skin and the amber of her sparkling eyes. They were sparkling at Angus right now and he seriously questioned whether he would have had the strength, were he not emotionally engaged elsewhere and ignorant of Madeleine's true character, to resist their pull.

What man could resist the allure of a beautiful woman who single-mindedly set about luring him? Especially if he was not used to such attention and lived with a disinterested wife?

Jack Noble had been unable to resist and Angus wasn't about to go the same way. He was quite certain Mademoiselle Delon's motives for her interest in him went beyond simply notching up another conquest.

'She is a rare prize, is she not, Major McCartney?' her father demanded, blinded by his daughter's beauty. 'Count Levinne is a lucky man, *non*? My daughter has made the catch of the century.'

Yes, she was a beauty, a rare prize, but she was no substitute for the wife Angus had left behind: the young woman he still hoped – God knew how – would somehow grow to love him. Painfully he reflected on their disastrous bedroom encounter the night before he left.

With her oblique references to being ready in half an hour to greet Angus 'as a husband would wish to be greeted by his loving wife', Emily had all but insisted that he come to her.

He hadn't felt it was the right time in view of their earlier strained relations, but he could hardly reject her outright. And God, how he wanted her.

In the flickering candlelight he'd searched Emily's face in vain for some sign that she truly welcomed him with love in her heart. While he'd not read revulsion she'd certainly not greeted him with joy. Emily had simply been going through the motions. The reflection of Jessamine doing the same was enough to pour cold water on any feelings that went beyond simple protection.

Madeleine placed her dainty, gloved hand upon Angus's forearm and slid him a sly glance from beneath her dark lashes. With her vibrant smile, her glossy dark hair, straight little nose and small but generous mouth there was a far greater resemblance between her and Emily. The confident, dazzling Emily, he amended.

'The count is indeed a catch and I must pretend the honour is all mine,' Madeleine said, her tone brittle as the doors opened to the street outside, and with a glance at her father, as if to ensure he'd not heard.

Madeleine had indicated to Angus before that this marriage was not the wonderful match her father clearly regarded it. Had she not voiced her reluctance in such a plaintive tone as she'd pretended to pick lint off his coat, and had Angus not been told by Monsieur Delon that Madeleine's wishes regarding her marriage partner were paramount, Angus would have felt sympathy.

If Madeleine felt such aversion towards marriage to the count, avarice was clearly motivating her to the altar.

In the flagstoned reception hall of the fortress where the ball was being held, Angus prepared to act his part: that of a regional painter visiting galleries, both public and private. Count Levinne's was reputed to be among the best in France, and mission aside, it gave him a thrill.

Although Angus's French was perfect and his charade close enough to the truth had he followed his painterly inclinations, he was always mindful of the potential for error. Above all, he must not reveal himself as an Englishman.

This was his second mission. His first had been straightforward: to deliver Allaire's papers.

The dangerous female spy of whom Major Woodhouse had spoken during their first meeting was now the focus of this, and perhaps subsequent, missions.

In just one month Madame Fontenay had slain two English agents. In each case the dying men claimed they'd been lured into a honey trap, drugged and poisoned. They'd both described the woman with whom they'd thought to enjoy untold pleasures making off with their official documents. The descriptions indicated the perpetrator as Madame Fontenay and subsequently the identities of numerous other agents had been revealed. Some had fled the country, others had been arrested.

The consequences for national security were devastating. Angus had been recalled to France shortly after Madame Fontenay had been spotted in the Saint-Omer region where she was believed to be intending to lure a newly arrived English recruit into her clutches.

The young man, a twenty-four-year-old posing as a diplomat, had been apprised of the danger and would be meeting Angus this evening as both were briefed on their intended roles by Count Levinne.

Madeleine nudged him as they waited to be admitted to join the other guests into the grand saloon. 'Genuflect, Monsieur. Levinne has seen us.'

Angus followed her gaze as the stern, gaunt young man, eyes bright with purpose above a hawk-like nose, bore down on them.

'Mademoiselle Delon, Monsieur McCartney, I have been waiting.'

Levinne bowed over Madeleine's hand. The saloon was already near capacity and much of the discussion, Angus presumed, concerned Napoleon's defeat at Leipzig the previous week. The reports filtering in told of hundreds of thousands slaughtered. Napoleon had fought hard to retain his hold on the country but after several victories earlier in the year he had miscalculated. Speculation was rife as to what this meant for France.

Madeleine tilted her head, arranging her smile for the count's benefit and Angus saw the flare of lust in the young man's eyes as she said, coquettishly, 'My apologies if I've kept you waiting, Levinne. I'm aware I must expect to be punished for my lack of punctuality once we are married.'

She touched her betrothed on the arm in a show of intimacy and he gripped it, trapping it there for a moment while his eyes roiled with an emotion Angus was all too familiar with: an as-yet unsatisfied desire for that which was his due.

'Allow me, Mademoiselle Delon.' The count's slender fingers caressed Madeleine's neck as he unfastened the bow which tied her cloak beneath her chin and Angus registered the spasm that crossed the young woman's face at her fiance's touch.

Quickly he turned his head away so as not to betray his surprise at seeing the filigreed silver locket Madeleine wore. 'This way, please.' The count ushered them into the midst of the throng, hovering over his beautiful future-wife like a spider with a fly, yet Madeleine seemed unconcerned by this display of jealous attention, charming men and women alike.

Tonight she wore her glossy jet hair pinned upon her head in the Grecian style with curls about her forehead and cheeks. Without a doubt she was the most beautiful woman in the room, though she would rival Emily, thought Angus, striving for dispassion as his host's daughter smiled up at him when they danced together. He turned his head away, wishing Emily would smile at him like that and wondering how he would bridge the impasse that yawned between them.

With the truth, he supposed, though he had no idea how Emily would react to proof of Jack's duplicity. She would start by refusing to believe anything Angus said, but in the end she would have to concede the weight of evidence was overwhelming.

Would she love Angus then, when Jack's noble edifice crumbled before her eyes?

At the end of the quadrille Madeleine drew Angus into an

alcove a few feet from the count, who was sympathising with an elderly gentleman's tale of peasant treachery.

'I am honoured, am I not, to ally myself to a man such as Levinne?' She did not wait for him to reply, her agitation apparent as she twitched the curtain tassel. 'It has always been my fate. I've known it since I was a child. I was given a reprieve due to a death in the family, but I fear there will be no further reprieves. The most strategic members of both our families are in robust health.' She smiled sweetly. 'I saw you admiring my locket, Major McCartney.'

She was flirting; drawing him into her orbit as she no doubt did every man who fulfilled her need for admiration. What did she hope to gain by her coquetry? Was it simple venality, for how could he feel sorry for her when he knew she could sever the connection if she chose?

A sudden thought intruded. If Madeleine's heart had been broken by Jack then Angus owed it to Madeleine to reveal the truth about Jack's duplicity just as he intended to reveal it to Emily.

'I have seen its copy recently.'

'Are you an expert on women's jewellery, Monsieur?' she asked with a toss of her head. 'The piece is simple but I treasure it infinitely more than the diamonds my future husband will expect me to wear to add to his consequence.'

'The giver is always more important than the gift.'

Madeleine sent him a wary look before glancing at Levinne. Lowering her voice, she said, 'You think it dangerous to wear this when it contains a lock of hair belonging to another man?'

'As long as your heart does not belong to another man, Mademoiselle Delon.' Angus put his hand beneath her elbow to steer her back into the throng. 'Do not marry if your heart is not engaged.'

Though who was he to be giving such advice, knowing how much Emily had railed against marrying him?

Madeleine narrowed her eyes, the coquetry quite vanished now. 'You think I am marrying Levinne only for his money and title, don't you, Monsieur?'

Angus shrugged. 'I do not trouble myself over your motives. You must live with the consequences.'

She sucked in an angry breath. 'I have no choice in the matter! Do you know how hard it is to have discovered what love is – and to know I will never enjoy it with the man fate has decreed I must spend the rest of my life with?'

'Your father told me—'

'It is not my father who compels me, it is duty.'

Angus raised his eyebrows. 'You had not struck me as such a dutiful young woman.'

She glared as she tapped her heart. 'You think duty is the preserve of plain and dull but good wives such as yours.'

She must have seen the shock that reverberated through him, for she hissed, 'Jack told me all about Emily Micklen. How dreary she was but what a good wife she would make.'

He swallowed. 'Perhaps you should have married Jack, then.'

'I would have if it had not been my destiny to marry Levinne.'

'Nobody is forcing you.'

'It is my mother—' She stopped, her look frightened. Clearing her throat, she whispered, 'It was always my mother's wish that we should marry.'

She was fingering her locket once more and Angus stared at it, remembering his own feelings when he'd laid eyes on it hanging round Emily's neck before she'd removed it to wear his diamonds.

'You should know that Captain Noble gave more than one of these away.'

The vivid colour which contributed so much to her beauty tonight faded to a waxy pallor. She caught her breath and he felt her falter beside him.

'He gave one to the … Micklen creature?' Her devastation was real.

Gently, Angus asked, 'Did Jack Noble lead you to think his heart really belonged only to you? That his intended marriage to Miss Micklen was just a sham?'

She lanced him with a look from beneath sweeping lashes, her little ivory fan affording her the protection she needed from Levinne's scrutiny. 'Jack Noble loved me. He knew me long before he went in search of the Micklen slut. Do you know how eagerly she responded to his address, how easily she succumbed to his advances?'

Angus winced and she blushed at her coarse language. 'Jack loved *me* but it was expedient to wed an Englishwoman.'

'You were not yet married and nor was Jack.'

'No, we were not yet married and no, I could not have been Noble's wife, for it would not have been sanctioned by … by anyone who mattered.' Trembling even more, she added, 'How he laughed to recount the ease with which he wooed her. She was not backwards in coming forward, he used to tell me.'

'Was it necessary for Captain Noble to acquaint you with all the facts if he was concerned with your happiness?' Angus asked. It pained him to hear it as much as it obviously pained Madeleine. 'I think Captain Noble enjoyed making you jealous, Madeleine. Just as he enjoyed exercising his power over Miss Micklen.'

'Miss Micklen was a fool. She knew the risks and she paid for them. When I was given the news of Jack's death I heard she'd been forced to marry some soldier she cared nothing for to salvage family honour.' Madeleine's mouth puckered. '*You*, Major McCartney, I believe.'

Angus didn't know if she was sneering or trying to stop from crying. 'Serves her right if her forced marriage makes her so unhappy,' she said bitterly. 'I hope she rots in hell.'

'My dear, are you well?' The count was at Madeleine's side having obviously observed her distress. Grasping her elbow, he cut a path for them through the throng.

Angus watched them disappear onto a balcony. He was relieved when Monsieur Delon appeared and introduced him to the young diplomat, Monsieur Boulais.

Monsieur Delon's murmured warning brought him back to the present. 'Monsieur Boulais has just been welcomed with unusual felicity by one of our prime objects of interest, that gentleman over there. *Le Petit Trione*, they call him.' He pointed to a sandy-haired exquisite dressed in pale blue, in conversation with a slender young woman who might have been his sister. 'He was seen in company with Madame Fontenay last week and as he is also known to be courting anyone suspected of being English, on the pretext of sympathising with anti-French causes, we believe that he may lead us to her.'

Angus studied the young man who was speaking with extravagant hand gestures and kept sweeping his fair locks back from his high forehead.

'The consummate fop but don't be misled by appearances. He's dangerous.' Pretending nonchalance for the sake of the public arena they occupied, Monsieur Delon patted his neat, rounded belly as if commenting on the food of which he'd just partaken in the supper room where he'd followed *Trione*. 'In two days he travels in secret to Dover. We need you to tell us who his English hosts are. Before he leaves we also need to know his informers. He is, as you call it, piggy in the middle. We cannot get rid of him until we know with whom he is trading information.'

Though it was not late, Angus sagged with relief. In two days he would return to England. Granted, he would find little relaxation in the prospective surveillance operation, but he was desperate to see Emily again.

'Who arranged the match between Madeleine and Levinne?' Angus asked his host, now alone on the balcony.

Delon turned with a genial smile. The Frenchman would be considered a traitor by his countrymen but there was an air of gentleness about him. Angus could not believe he would pressure Madeleine into marriage.

'She said her mother …' Angus prompted.

Surprise crossed Delon's face. 'Madeleine was very young when her mother died.'

'I see.' Angus nodded.

'She is adopted, you know,' Monsieur Delon went on. He seemed happy to share confidences with Angus away from the throng. 'Madame Delon and I were unable to have children. After twenty years we thought we never would.'

Angus hesitated. 'She knows?'

'Yes, it is common knowledge. My wife had a companion of whom she was very fond. The woman —' he hesitated. 'She got herself into trouble and, as she was unable to provide for the infant, we offered to bring her up as our own.' His smile did not falter. 'Madeleine brought us great joy, but sadly, my wife died when Madeleine was five.'

In the early hours of the morning, as the guests began to drift away, Madeleine and Levinne joined Angus and Monsieur Delon, who were conversing in desultory fashion now inside near a curtained alcove.

'What a successful evening, Papa.'

Her complexion was hectic, as if she'd indulged either in furious weeping or frantic kissing. Angus recognised the forced gaiety and was not surprised when Madeleine avoided his look. She nodded at the count. 'Good evening, Levinne. It has been delightful as ever.' With great gallantry he bent to kiss her hand then, taking her father's arm, Madeleine descended the steps to the waiting carriage.

Once home, Monsieur Delon sleepily excused himself and Angus would have done the same had Madeleine not stopped him with a hand on his elbow. 'A drink, Monsieur?'

'Another time.'

'No gentleman declines the company of a lady who desires to unburden herself.' Her voice was low and although Angus would have preferred to have gone to bed, he realised it was an opportunity to understand how much Jack Noble had compromised himself.

While he poured them both a glass of brandy, Madeleine paced in front of the fireplace.

'The count is delighted to entrust you with the *Trione* boy.' Fingering the locket at her throat, her eyes darted to his face. 'Not that he needs chaperoning all the way to Dover and beyond. Do you know how many men *Le Petit Trione* has killed? Even more than Madame Fontenay.' A deep sigh followed her brief laugh. 'It makes me happy when the count is pleased.' Her words were stilted. She was highly agitated.

'Then you will be a dutiful wife.'

'It would be to my detriment were I anything else.'

He saw her hands clench. 'I am a woman, Monsieur. I have no say in my future. My fate is a plaything in the hands of those who control it.'

'Ah, but it is always the fault of the men who control the lives of women,' Angus murmured, thinking of how he'd grant Emily any latitude if he could only make her happy.

'It is not only men,' she huffed. 'Some women have a great deal of control, too.'

Angus took a sip, ignoring her while he wondered if

Emily's distaste for her husband truly was as strong as Madeleine's clearly was for Levinne. His skin burned and his heart clutched to think of Emily sharing intimate confidences with Jack as Madeleine was doing with him.

'Now, Monsieur, since you have offered me no comfort in respect to the unpalatable marriage I am about to contract, tell me about Mademoiselle Micklen instead of taunting me with your enigmatic silence. Jack did not love her. Will you tell her that?'

'Please sit down, Mademoiselle.' He knocked back his drink to prepare himself. 'You are making my head spin.'

Obeying, she regarded him tensely from an upholstered walnut armchair opposite, her foot tapping. '*Is* Miss Micklen beautiful?'

'Very.'

She tried to hide her dismay, turning her head quickly. 'More beautiful than I?' Her voice was thick with jealousy.

'You should be flattered to know that you and she are very similar in looks.' He smiled at her pout. 'On first appearances only, I should add.'

Madeleine's eyes flashed disgust. 'How dare you! She is a mouse! Jack needed a wife who would not question his actions abroad. That's why he chose her.' Angus watched her bare her pretty white teeth before she hissed, 'A lovely little lapdog. Those were his words. It has always been my destiny to marry Levinne. Jack knew that. He knew Levinne would have had us both killed if he discovered ...' She shook her head in defeat, unwilling to put into words her risky amour.

Carefully, Angus said, 'If Captain Noble was not in love with Miss Micklen he was a fine actor.' Angus saw he'd struck a nerve and wondered if he'd been incautious in pursuing this line.

She was quick to revenge. 'And you swept Miss Micklen

off her feet and were a welcome replacement for her dead fiancé.'

He forced himself to appear unaffected by her scorn. 'No, Mademoiselle Delon.' Angus felt her eyes following him as he went to the sideboard to pick up the brandy decanter. 'I knew she did not love me and could not for some time. But I also believed I knew what I was doing. I'd taken on the task of delivering Captain Noble's letters to Emily when I informed her of his inglorious death. You know he died in a brawl over a camp follower.'

Turning at her predictable gasp of outrage, he went on. 'Let the truth be some solace. Why harbour false ideas if you must wed elsewhere?'

'You are very blunt, Major McCartney.' Her chest heaved. He was tempted to believe it an act to display her fine bosom sheathed in its revealing gold silk, but Angus recognised the bleakness in her tone. 'Were you so good as to similarly acquaint bereaved *Miss Micklen* with the true nature of her betrothed? I should hate to think that *she* still holds his memory dear.'

Angus was not prepared for the emotions her careless, wounded words unleashed.

Her truncated laughter was like a lance. 'I would suggest that you do not know what to do with your lovelorn, bereaved wife who mourns another man, do you, Major McCartney?'

With hands not as steady as he would have liked, Angus refilled their glasses. When he turned back she stood in the centre of the room, hands on hips. Her cheeks were flushed, her pretty white teeth revealed to less advantage as her lip curled derisively. 'You offered yourself as Miss Micklen's saviour.' Picking up the little ivory fan she'd placed on the side table, she used it energetically as she paced. 'Lily white

Miss Micklen is the bereaved fiancé and I am the villain for salvaging my pride at her expense.'

He said, carefully, 'You and Jack considered it sport to deceive Miss Micklen.'

Dropping the fan, she reached for her brandy and took a convulsive sip. 'Jack needed to see how far she would believe him. *You* must understand how necessary it is for the future wife of a'—she lowered her voice—'spy to believe everything her husband tells her.'

'Not if the information is no more than childish, vengeful games.'

Madeleine glared before the corners of her lush, full mouth turned up. She regarded him for a long moment. 'Miss Micklen had the benefit of my good taste.' Her angst fell away and she laughed. 'Silk ribbons of every hue. You have no idea what sport it was.' Her feigned good humour dissipated. As her mouth sagged, Angus had a glimpse of what she would look like when she was old and disappointment had marred her beauty. Slumping into a chair by the fire, she ran a hand across her brow. 'Tell me, Monsieur McCartney, how satisfying a wife is poor bereaved Miss Micklen'—she glared at him—'when her heart belongs to Jack?'

He was surprised by the force of his reaction; heard his voice brittle with pride as he replaced the stopper in the decanter, muttering, 'Time is assuaging her grief.'

Madeleine raised an eyebrow. 'Grief must have been the least of her considerations if she entered into marriage with you before Jack was cold in the ground. She was big with child and you were a lovelorn fool who couldn't own her any other way. Am I not right?'

With a loud chink Angus put down the decanter as Madeleine asked in gloating tones, 'Will you tell her? About me and Jack? Should I sleep with a rapier beneath my pillow to protect me from Miss Micklen's – I mean, Mrs Mccartney's – terrifying thirst for vengeance?'

'Vengeance is not part of her nature. You need not be afraid.'

'Then why haven't you told her the truth?' The words were honeyed now, not forceful. With studied carelessness, his wife's nemesis wrapped a curl around her finger as she leaned back in her chair. 'If you're such a defender of the truth, *Major*, why didn't you tell your wife that Jack was my lover and that he deceived her from the start?' With a sly smile, she answered her own question with terrible acuity. 'Because you were afraid she would shoot the messenger, weren't you, Monsieur? Because she does not love you. Her heart still belongs to Jack.'

Draining his drink, Angus put down the glass and strode to the door.

'Major, surely you are not leaving. I am so disappointed. Not even a present for me? Miss Micklen was always such a conscientious correspondent. Jack never left me empty handed. But then, you are so fond of keeping secrets.' She simpered up at him from her casual pose. 'Or perhaps you call it keeping your own counsel while you justify that it's for her protection. Perhaps that is why poor deluded Miss Micklen remains in the dark. Just as Jack told her nothing about us, you tell her nothing of your activities. What a hero you are, Major.'

Angus paused with his hand on the door knob. 'She knows what is safe for her know.' Madeleine's charge rang uncomfortably true. 'Emily is intelligent and naturally curious. If you are accusing me of deception through omission it is only to safeguard her and spare her feelings.'

Madeleine feigned a sigh of relief. 'Ah, so even if Miss Micklen were the avenging kind, I need not fear being slain in my bed since she will not know where to locate *Chez Delon* because Jack wove her fairy tales and you believe that honour equates to silence.' She knocked back the last of her drink and ran an unladylike hand across her mouth. 'Believe me, Major, if I were in Miss Micklen's pretty little slippers and knew where to find me, I'd be on the next packet with a dagger bound to each ankle. It is fortunate for both of us Mademoiselle Delon is the timid sort.'

'She is not timid.' Angus reflected on Emily's pride-induced invective and Mademoiselle Delon slanted a suspicious look at him. He realised he was smiling.

'Jack said she was, and mother ...'

She turned her head when Angus looked curiously at her, but when she said no more he bowed. 'Good evening, Mademoiselle. I must go to bed,' he said, excusing himself and leaving with relief.

In the morning he could have sworn someone had gone through his trunk.

A LIGHT MIST swirled through the churchyard and collected like dew on the black gauze of Emily's veil.

Dew? Or tears?

She shed none, however, as she lay her little posy upon her son's grave then straightened to read the inscription:

Jack McCartney

Less than an hour old but how lucky she was that kind Jonathan had organised the transport and burial of her little darling so Emily could visit him with ease.

The soft damp earth muted the sounds of approaching

footsteps so that she turned with a gasp to find Caroline nearly upon her.

Her sister-in-law smiled as she placed her own flowers beside Emily's, squeezing her arm. The touch was comforting. 'Are you all right, Emily?' She led her away, back to the waiting carriages. 'I hoped you'd offer me some tea while I tell you that all the ladies invited to your tea party have accepted. They are so looking forward to meeting you.'

Emily smiled. 'You're very kind, Caroline,' she said. And meant it.

Tea was served in the drawing room. The day was gloomy and the light dim so they sat near the large French doors that opened onto the garden and enjoyed the open vista of sweeping lawns.

'Angus chose well.' Emily made a sweeping motion of the lovely room, determined to speak highly of him to the sister-in-law who championed him so fiercely.

Fixing her with a level look, Caroline chose to misconstrue her meaning. 'He thinks he did, Emily. Once you allow yourself to move past your grief, you'll both be very happy.' Emily put her hand to her heart. 'There will always be a little piece of me that grieves, but you're right, time is healing my sorrow. Angus is a good man. I am looking forward to his return.'

She directed an expectant look at her sister-in-law, but Caroline looked unimpressed.

'I'm glad of it. A passionate heart does not shrivel and die at the first tragedy and you have a passionate heart. As does Angus. I think you are well matched.'

'I respect my husband,' Emily murmured.

Caroline took a sip of her tea before setting down the cup and levelling another of her famous frank looks upon Emily. 'It's a good start, but he deserves more than that.' She paused, adding, 'Like the pure and honest love of a woman worthy of him.' She cleared her throat then added, 'And not too proud to show it.'

The soft falling rain overlaid by the sound of carriage wheels on gravel sounded in the silence.

Before she could stop herself, Emily said with a half-smile, 'If I didn't know better I could almost think you were in love with him, yourself.'

To her shock Caroline's porcelain skin took on a fiery hue. 'Oh my goodness,' her sister-in-law gasped, laughing. 'I'm glad Jonathan isn't here to witness my discomposure. What must you think of me?' She stopped, gathered herself, then spoke carefully. 'I am five years older than Angus and a good fifteen years older than you, Emily. I am well versed in the ways of the world and I can honestly say that I would strive for contentment over passion any day.'

Emily was listening. Passion had been relegated to the grave and contentment was certainly more desirable than the misery which was her companion. But Caroline and Angus? She studied her sister-in-law with renewed interest.

'Because I'm so plain, and obviously older, Angus saw me differently from other women, and treated me accordingly.' Caroline shrugged. 'I fell in love with the man he could have been had he been matched with a wife who stirred him. I was also wise enough to recognise from the outset that such feelings would doom me to perpetual misery and so I threw myself into stirring up Jonathan's interest once he'd begun his half-hearted courtship.'

Emily felt something stir in her own heart as she digested this. The smile Caroline directed at her was not tinged with poignancy, but it came from the heart: the open smile of a woman more than contented with her lot.

'Jonathan is the perfect husband for me,' she said, and clearly she meant it. 'I never expected such happiness, Emily, when I embarked upon our marriage.' She reached out to touch Emily's arm. 'And now it would appear you have visitors,' she added, turning as Mary announced Aunt Gemma.

Emily gripped the arms of her chair and her heart quailed. The last time she'd seen her aunt was at her wedding. The last communication from the old lady been a cutting reminder to Emily about duty and the fact that she had made her bed.

Emily doubted this visit from Aunt Gemma was a social call.

CHAPTER 15

Angus followed *Le Petit Trione*, the ginger-haired exquisite in blue, to Calais.

In a dark corner of a tavern near the docks, he and Monsieur Delon, heavily disguised, drank their porter and watched the pretty young man rise to greet the ripe, raven-haired beauty who swept into the room close to midnight.

Monsieur Delon nearly spilled his porter in his excitement. '*Mon Dieu*, it is as we thought. As we hoped.' A battle-stained envoy had passed on the information to Angus in his tap room an hour earlier that one of Bonaparte's generals had been closeted in the private parlour the previous evening with a woman fitting Madame Fontenay's description. Suddenly Angus shared his host's excitement.

He turned. 'Half our work is done. Do not let *Trione* out of our sights. His compatriots will give us an idea of who to keep under surveillance when they all convene at the Chateau Pliny in a weeks' time.' His elegant accents roughened as he muttered, 'It won't be long before these foul enemies of peace are dancing at the end of a rope.'

Rumour had it that the grand masquerade ball was to be the venue for an exchange of intelligence regarding Napoleon's military intentions. Recent defeats had rocked French supremacy and Woodhouse had made it clear gaining access to this information, together with an understanding of who the key conspirators were, would be crucial in hastening Napoleon's end. *Trione's* visit to England would hopefully lead them to one link in the chain while Angus would be returning to Pliny in a week with Madeleine as his consort in a bid to infiltrate the military machine and lighten the burden of secrets held by a particular French General.

Keeping a slippery fellow like *Trione* in his sights was more difficult than Angus had anticipated.

By the time he'd watched the young man board the packet back to Calais after several meetings on English soil, then followed the respective traitors back to their farmhouses, Angus was exhausted.

Arriving to a warm welcome at the rectory, he slept a full nine hours in Caroline's Blue Room and woke with just enough light to see him back to Wildwood Manor if he left without too much delay.

He'd agonised over whether to go directly to Emily, but the combination of fatigue, uncertainty over his reception and his travel-stained state had decided him in favour of Jonathan and Caroline's assured welcome.

Caroline told him not to arrive home unannounced so Angus had duly sent one of the grooms ahead to tell Emily he would be home within the next two hours.

Caroline had also informed Angus that Emily's Aunt Gemma had paid a visit so what advice that lady had dealt out to her niece was anyone's guess.

Despite Angus's directive he'd want only a light supper, Emily had waited dinner for him and it was quickly apparent she'd carefully schooled her reception into one of contrived pleasantness. There was no inference they'd parted on diffi-cult terms though the knowledge of it swirled about them.

She asked him general questions, clearly mindful she must not delve into the real reasons for his absence. She remarked on the fine weather they'd been enjoying and said she hoped he'd enjoyed the same, wherever he'd been. She said he was looking well, that his current activity seemed to agree with him now that he was out and about more. The tone in which she said it implied he was under less pressure on His Majesty's Service than pandering to his demanding wife.

In an agony of indecision as to whether to cut through the charade and have the conversation he'd promised them both, Angus replied politely at first, only objecting to this last insinuation.

'If you think I enjoy these prolonged absences, you're wrong, Emily—'

She cut him off, rising and saying, 'It's late, Angus. You've been away a long time and you deserve a proper wifely welcome.' He saw the difficulty she had in formulating her next words. 'We parted on … difficult terms, but …' The furrows that creased her brow indicated her confusion, 'I don't believe it was entirely my fault.' She half raised her hand, as if to grip his arm. Dropping it, she asked, 'Shall we retire for the night?'

The enigmatic look she sent him stirred his blood and energised his dormant pulses, but his mind revolted.

He'd promised himself he'd tell Emily the truth, as if it would be some kind of weapon that would slice through the falsehoods Jack had told her. Only with the truth revealed would Angus have the right to claim her.

But the truth would be unpalatable. It would take Emily time to adjust to an altered emotional landscape.

Emily, however, was so determined on returning to the

bedroom that when he cautioned, 'Perhaps, we should wait, Emily,' she faced him across the room, head high, eyes proud, almost defiant, and shook her head.

'No.' Yet her mouth trembled and he saw the effort with which she drew out her next words. 'Please, Angus, don't make this harder than it needs to be. I want this and surely you do, too. I'm your wife.'

Her tone was pleading, almost as if she harboured doubts as to his feelings for her and so was reminding him of *his* duty.

What could he do? Grave misgivings tempered any enthusiasm he might earlier have felt, yet he couldn't reject her a second time.

Still he hesitated, recalling her from the door where she stood poised on the threshold as the maid entered with Angus's brandy. 'Emily—' His tone was gentle once they were alone again. 'We need to talk first.'

She must understand his reluctance had nothing to do with a lack of desire for her and everything to do with shattering what fragile truce existed between them.

'We can talk later.'

She didn't hesitate to hear what he might have to say and he watched her graceful exit with mixed feelings. After taking several steps down the passage, she returned, putting her head round the door.

'You *will* come?'

He nodded with little enthusiasm though his heart pumped like he'd just swum the English Channel.

When she'd gone, he picked up his brandy, knocked it back in one burning, unsatisfying gulp, then made slowly for his own apartments to prepare himself.

EMILY FORCED herself to display no outward signs of agitation as Sukey brushed out her hair and helped her into her night rail, yet surely the girl could hear the drumbeat of her heart? Finally dismissing her maid, she slumped onto her stool at the dressing table and rested her forehead in the palm of her hand.

Tonight she would become Angus's wife in more than simply name, and she was hungering for him.

Jack had loved and adored her, but he was dead. In his arms she had experienced the greatest of passions. Knowing the depth of his love and how joyfully he would have embraced fatherhood would sustain her forever.

But Angus was her future. He was a kind, decent man and he'd done everything he could to cherish and protect her.

She owed him her heart and now, finally, she was prepared to give it.

Her Aunt Gemma had thought to counsel Emily on how to do her duty, but her visit had been unnecessary.

Emily was ready to embrace her duty with a full heart and a body throbbing with eagerness.

While she waited, she reflected on the little lurch of her heart that had accompanied Angus's arrival into the dining room that evening. He'd looked good. Handsome, healthy and confident.

She recalled her husband all those weeks ago, torso bare as he wielded his axe, the glistening sweat coating his bulk of muscle as he'd split wood. Even then she'd begun to feel the first stirrings of felicity, knowing she owed everything to his kindness.

In the interim Angus had become a gentleman of means, but that was not why she loved him.

Aunt Gemma had been so determined to drive home the importance of Emily doing her *duty*, Emily had nearly laughed.

How matters had changed since she'd implored the old lady to help her secure an annulment.

Aunt Gemma had reminded Emily she was equipped for *nothing* but to be a dutiful wife and mother, but Emily knew her value to Angus was much greater than that.

She jumped as the clock on the landing struck the hour. Angus would be here in a few minutes and the thought sent tingles of excitement from the tips of her toes up her arms. She imagined the scene one step further than the last time. The weight of his body pressed the length of hers as he looked down into her eyes. The skim of his hands the length of her bare thigh.

Desire roared in her ears. No, there was no revulsion in the prospect of the forthcoming intimacy.

Angus was her present and Jack was her past and there was no need to denigrate her old love to induce Emily fulfil her role as Angus's wife.

Jerking to her feet at his knock, dismissing Sukey, she uttered a welcome, forcing a smile as he entered the room. The candle flickered on her dressing table, sending shadows dancing across the blue and gold counterpane and upon the walls. The bed, high, its curtains drawn, looked inviting, she thought, wanting this union to be as comfortable as possible. A satisfied husband was the best recommendation of her abilities as a wife. Her Aunt had said it. Her father had intimated it.

Emily had few bargaining chips. Angus had taken her with nothing – except another man's child in her belly.

Yet, tonight's union was so much more than a business contract and the need to cement her position.

He stepped into the room and she was conscious of the way her insides contracted when he looked at her. He'd paused by the tall oak chest of drawers, his head a fraction to one side as he regarded her as he might a painting worthy of his attention. Emily kept very still. She wanted him to admire her; she really did. Wanted him to think her desirable and beautiful.

Vanity, perhaps, though she didn't think it was that, alone.

No, it was the need to know she still inspired *his* desire.

Following him as he took a step forward, she parted her lips in a smile of invitation, her insides curdling at his soft, 'My God, you're beautiful, Emily.'

His banyan was knotted around his middle, exposing the dusting of dark chest hair. She wanted to run her hands through it and feel its softness. Instead, she settled her gaze on his mouth. It was a beautifully shaped mouth: a gently curved juxtaposition of tender masculinity. She clasped her hands together to stop them trembling as the sweet smile he levelled upon her ruffled her composure even more.

Fleetingly, her hand went to her throat. *Please, don't let me have forgotten to remove Jack's locket*, she thought in sudden panic. Relieved to find her neck unadorned, she glanced at the surface of her dressing table for the quick reassurance it was out of sight, resolving in the same instant never to wear it again.

She felt Angus's eyes on her. Saw his gaze follow her hand as she gripped the edge of the table to steady herself, her breath quickening, dismay and fear coursing through her that he'd just seen what she heartily wished he had not: the red ribbon that trailed from the bundle of love letters she'd pushed to the back of the little walnut table.

Oh, why had she been so careless? The letters had always been there, though she no longer read them every night or cried over them.

Now, seeing them through Angus's eyes, the ribbon was like a stain of reproach, the well worn parchment a testament to the reluctance with which he might think she received him as a husband.

He stopped a few feet from her, his eyes roaming over the pots of unguents and lotions, the orange flower water she liked to wear and the silver backed hair brush he'd wielded with such gentleness all those weeks ago.

'Emily—'

Cheeks burning, she locked eyes with him.

'Angus, I'm sorry.' She felt hopeless. This was no way to start. No way to go on.

He saw that she referred to the letters, and sighed. 'They don't matter, Emily.'

Another step closed the distance between them. Gently, he put his hands on her shoulders. The touch, featherlight but heavy with promise, made her gasp as sensation speared through her.

Tentatively she brought her hands up to clasp his arms, her hands skimming the heavy brocaded silk of his banyan. She raised her eyes to his face and her heart shifted at his expression.

He touched her lips with one forefinger, then gently contoured her face with his hands, as if committing her image to heart. Lowering his head, he whispered, 'I understand your grief, but we have a new life together.' He swallowed and the sincerity in his voice made her heart thrill. 'I loved you from the moment I first saw you, Emily. You know that.'

She closed her eyes, swaying towards him and wishing he'd enfold her thoroughly in his embrace. She was letting go, at last. And it felt good.

'I've been an ungrateful wife, Angus.' She curved her lips, wanting to feel the touch of his against them.

At last he pulled her into his arms and kissed the top of her head, saying with a smile in his voice, 'This is a good start to making good, then.'

She wanted to get the words off her chest. To wipe the

slate clean before they began. 'I blamed you for not being Jack.' She raised her head to look at him. 'For marrying me for material advantage and for being the man for whom Jack sacrificed his life.' She was desperate to make full atonement. If she could rid her heart of all its bitterness through confession perhaps they could forge a new beginning.

'Emily—' His voice was thick with emotion.

She put her finger to his lips. 'I don't blame you for any of those things,' she whispered. 'Not any more. I want us to be happy.'

He did not smile with relief or gratitude as she'd expected. His grip tightened and he appeared to be waging a battle with himself. Finally he said, quite gently, 'Emily, I had nothing to do with Jack's death.' He stroked her cheek, his expression tender, almost as if he were preparing her for something. 'I told you a lie in order to spare you pain when I came to deliver Jack's letters, though I cursed the words the moment they were out.'

She stepped back, breaking his grip, shock robbing her of a more considered response. 'You *lied* to me?'

He held up his hand as if to stay her anger as he went on. 'Jack was killed in a skirmish, it is true, but I arrived on the scene too late to help him.'

She shook her head as if to clear it, opening her mouth to try to push out the words, a coherent question he could answer and so end her confusion.

Angus looked deeply troubled. 'I wanted to spare you, Emily.'

'From the *truth*?'

He recoiled at her gasp, before drawing himself up. 'Jack was consorting with a woman. She was married and when her husband demanded to know where they were, I, fool that I was, indicated the direction of their tent.'

'Oh God …' She felt herself sway and quickly caught the edge of the dressing table.

Wearily he ran a hand across his brow. 'I knew he was to marry you and wanted Jack to be taught a lesson.' He exhaled on a sigh. 'I had no idea it would end so badly.'

Emily rasped in a breath. 'Jack was *unfaithful*? You told me Jack had lied to me but you never said he didn't die a *hero*.'

He shook his head, his wretchedness increasing, as well it might. Miserably, he repeated, 'How could I, Emily, when you believed in him so completely. You had enough burdens to carry.'

Her horror was compounded by confusion. 'All this time I believed Jack died saving your life. And you let me continue to believe it.'

'I never thought I'd see you again so I said what I thought would bring you comfort. Once the words were out, there was never a right time to take them back.'

He made no move to comfort her when she so badly needed him to. Now his arms hung limply at his sides, his head tilted to one side as he watched her.

'You let me believe a lie all this time?' she whispered. How much easier this marriage would have been if Angus had told the truth from the outset.

She realised the unfairness of this when he said, 'Emily, you'd have thought I was bringing Jack's character into disrepute in order to build myself up in your estimation. You must know I couldn't do that. I'm a proud man. I want you to love me on my own merits.'

She was about to murmur that she did, she truly did, despite the cruel betrayal Angus had just documented, when he tapped the book of Children's Verse which lay near the letters. The book he had refused to take with him to France.

'There's more, Emily.'

She slanted a glance at him. She wasn't sure if she was ready for too much more, just yet.

Doggedly, he went on, his expression even darker, the gulf between them growing. 'If I lied to spare you pain, Jack lied to you about so much more.'

The silence was heavy with premonition. She waited, bracing herself, while in her head a little voice taunted, 'Jack never loved you.'

'Madeleine Delon is not a child of six.' His look was clouded with the pain of what he was delivering. 'I'm sorry, Emily, but Madeleine Delon is a woman of twenty. A very beautiful woman.'

It was like the truth was seeping coldly up through the floor and into her bones, flooding her body with a betrayal she did not think she could withstand.

Hugging herself, she began to pace, murmuring to try and make sense of this new truth. 'Then Jack and Madeleine Delon …' She didn't need to say it. Angus confirmed it through the sympathy of his look.

She started to tremble though she managed as proudly as she could, as if by allotting blame it might help, 'Why didn't you tell me before, Angus?' Sinking down upon the stool by her dressing table, she rested her forehead in her hands, cognisant enough, despite her wounding, to whisper, 'I'm sorry, that was unfair of me.' She felt so drained she wondered if she'd ever be able to get up again. With an effort she raised her head to look at him, acknowledging, 'I'd more likely have railed at you for delivering the news and refused to believe what you were telling me.'

'If proof is important, then—'

She cut him off, saying wearily, 'I believe you, Angus.' The emptiness inside her was beyond tears. 'I understand everything. Jack deceived me. Jack never loved me.'

Angus put his hand on her shoulder. 'I believe he did,' he

murmured, but she shrugged out of his grasp. Such words were barbs of pain, not comfort.

'How could he? I can't bear to hear any more. Not now, Angus.'

He bent to kiss her lightly on the top of her head, his touch some small comfort. 'Regardless of what Jack was,' he whispered, his breath tickling her ear, 'he loved you, Emily, for how could he not?' Gently, he placed his forefinger beneath her chin and raised her face to his, his eyes bright with fervour. 'But I love you more.'

Angus put Emily to bed and sat holding her hand as she stared at the Chinese wallpaper. Only when her breathing became even did he deem it more expedient to leave than to climb in beside her and hold her, as he longed to do. The lancing of a woman's pride was an unpredictable thing.

Shortly after dawn the next morning he put on riding clothes and headed down the passageway towards the steps that led to the kitchen, intending to access the stables via the scullery, but on impulse, after passing Emily's apartments, he doubled back.

He would remove the detested Book of Children's Verse that threatened to greet her like a foul reminder of her pain. Another thought occurred to him. It was early. The clouds were limned with pink, heralding a glorious day, but it would be several hours before the servants intruded upon Emily's slumber. If he slipped into her bedroom, safely dressed, she'd not be afraid. It might even be possible she'd welcome him if her night's reflections had favoured him over Jack.

Her room was bathed in soft morning light as he quietly crossed the threshold.

Except Emily wasn't in her bed. He glanced through the adjoining door into her private sitting room, but there was no sign of her.

When he'd waited a few minutes and ascertained she was not returning, Angus picked up the book of Children's Verse from the escritoire with a baleful glance at the pile of Jack's letters which were lying beneath the discarded locket.

The love letters were neatly bound by ribbon. He felt their weight – the weight of faded dreams and hopes – and wished he could throw them into the embers of the small coal fire the maid would stoke up later in the morning.

After returning them to their position, he was about to leave when the sight of his name jumped out from amongst a torrent of close-set writing, much smudged, and obviously discarded. Clearly it was a draft of a letter Emily had written not so long ago to her Aunt Gemma.

He knew he should shelve his curiosity and depart. Reading another's correspondence was as unconscionable as eavesdropping, but it was impossible to leave unsatisfied his desire to know how Emily had communicated her thoughts regarding her husband to her Aunt Gemma.

Aunt Gemma's unexpected visit during his absence had perhaps been in response to this very letter. It must be assumed Emily had been counselled to be a dutiful wife, perhaps prompting Emily to request he visit her in her bedchamber, but how had Emily petitioned her?

The letter protruded from the little desk drawer and Angus needed only one stroke of the forefinger to slide it into view.

With a dry mouth and a heart that was soon hammering fit to deafen him, he read:

Dear Aunt Gemma,

I am in torment and I beg your advice in ending this marriage forced upon me, now that the reason for contracting it in the first place no longer exists.

Tears made the next two paragraphs impossible to read, but the ending was even more damning.

Angus is everything Jack was not. Jack was easy-natured, charming and gallant. Together we looked forward to a future of joy and a brood of noisy children.

I do not believe I can survive the compromises I am forced to make, and the quiet, unsettling intensity of my husband.

Our marriage is unconsummated, and the child which was the reason for contracting it is dead. Surely there is some way an annulment is possible ...

ANGUS HAD to take a couple of rallying breaths before his vision came once more into focus. Beside this letter was Aunt Gemma's reply.

He had no scruples in reading it. Just what had Emily's cold and calculating Aunt Gemma advised her desperate niece?

A woman must play her part. If he loves you, as you say he does, then that is your greatest weapon. Perhaps your only weapon. Play on it. You need the continued goodwill and affection of your husband if you are to survive.

Forget your despair, forget that you despise him, that his nature is anathema to you. Forget everything except the one thing you need to cling to if you are not to be thrown onto society's dung heap: that without an independent fortune a woman has only her body with which to barter the necessities of life.

You are not clever, Emily, and you are certainly not brave. Angus loves your pretty face while your vulnerability arouses his protective instincts. His pride and protectiveness are what you must appeal to if Angus is to want to remain in this marriage.

You claim an annulment or separation is what you want, Emily, but you don't know what you're saying. If Angus were to agree, or to be the one to instigate one, you'd be left with nothing: nothing but a ruined reputation and perhaps a few years more youthful bloom. And that, might I remind you, is no consolation if your reputation is sullied.

Angus returned the letters to the exact position he had found them. Fingers of pain and horror seemed to crawl all over his body as he lingered by Emily's escritoire, waiting. He wanted to confront her with what he'd just found. He needed to hear from her own lips what she truly felt about him and about this marriage of theirs.

Raking his hands through his hair he paced the small, elegant room, digesting the sentiments which had mocked him from the parchment; sentiments which sneered at his feeble attempts at trying to turn himself into the kind of husband Emily might want. Desire.

Desire! Ha!

She might want him through *need,* and as Aunt Gemma reminded her so brutally, through simple necessity. Only he could offer her salvation.

But at what price?

He spun once more on his heel and ran a hand across his

fevered brow. The price of her body which she would offer him minus her heart.

And certainly with no particle of desire.

You're a man, he reminded himself angrily when the reflection made him want to howl his anger and despair like some primitive creature. *Not some lovelorn schoolboy, for God's sake.*

Gathering himself, he stared out of the window at the sweeping lawns that swept out from the lovely, well tended gardens. He'd imagined peaceful times here with Emily once he'd finished his mission. He'd be entitled to some deserved rest and domesticity.

Domesticity. He'd craved it for years. Years when he'd soldiered and bivouacked in dangerous, inhospitable terrain. When he'd existed in his squalid bachelor's quarters, some-times – though not often – allowing himself to dream of a companion who shared his interests. A wife who loved him as he loved her. Simple things. Mawkish, perhaps, and which didn't usually factor amongst what soldiers like him discussed amongst themselves.

This beautiful home … He looked appraisingly at his surroundings. He'd thought he'd reached the pinnacle of masculine consideration when he'd secured Wildwood for Emily. Obviously, however, Emily felt he'd simply gilded the cage he'd compromised her into occupying. It might be a step up from his original dwelling to which he'd brought her, but she still had to share it with a man for whom she felt nothing.

Nothing but aversion.

Emily did not return so after a few more minutes of anguished waiting, Angus left the house to saddle up Saladin and to embrace the early morning chill and the pain of the wind whipping his cold, tired face.

CHAPTER 17

Dawn heralded a new beginning for Emily now that she knew the truth.

A truth she would not have been ready to receive before. But now she was ready to embrace the future. To receive with a heart full of love everything he would offer her, she decided as she pushed her feet into slippers and wrapped her shawl closely around her. The house was still dark but growing lighter as she hurried down the passage, heading for Angus's apartments. She needed his comfort. No, she needed more than that. Last night he'd recognised exactly what she'd needed. Then, his comfort had been enough. Now she longed to feel his arms about her, the contours of his body pressing against hers. His patience and understanding made a powerful aphrodisiac for a young woman who'd received little enough of those in her life.

He was not in his apartments. In his dressing room she saw evidence of his having risen and dressed. Probably he'd gone riding.

Surprised by the extent of her disappointment, she returned to her own chamber. Perhaps they could talk over breakfast. No, the servants … They could walk together. That's what she'd suggest. She knew last night had been difficult for him, too, but surely he realised how much her feelings towards him had changed?

He might be distant or hesitant to begin with, but he'd willingly oblige her when he saw how much she needed to tell him everything that had gone on in her own heart during the painful few months of their marriage. It would be *just* what he wanted to hear.

But Angus did not appear at breakfast and, in view of the events of the previous night, she was surprised when his valet told Emily the master had advised he'd be gone until the evening.

After agonising all day as to exactly what she'd say, Emily was glad Angus missed dinner. With the servants hovering, it would have been a stilted affair.

Finally she heard the sound of his arrival in the hallway long after she'd gone to bed. Instantly she sat up, her nerve endings leaping to life at the thought of the welcome she intended to give him. Last night she'd been prepared to accept Angus into her bed when she'd known nothing of the truth. When she'd thought Jack better than he was, and Angus guilty of actions he did not commit.

Jack's deception had been a terrible shock. Strangely, though, she'd been better prepared to face it than she'd thought. Angus, through quiet doggedness, had proved himself. Without her even realising it, he'd inveigled himself into her heart. His bravery abroad and his compassion at home were just part of what made him a decent man and a good husband.

She lit a candle and waited. Angus had been so gentle and sweet to her last night that she was certain he'd come directly to her after having been away all day.

Her disappointment when he did not almost sapped her

courage, the distant chiming of the clock in the hallway sounding like a call to arms. Emily strained her ears; listening not for the final chimes of the midnight hour but for the sounds of creaking floorboards. Sounds that indicated Angus was on his way.

The silence dragged out, lonely, reproachful.

Disappointing.

Angus was showing *too* much restraint. As the eleventh chime faded away Emily threw back the bedclothes and wrapped her peacock blue shawl about her shoulders. By the twelfth she was hurrying down the passageway to Angus's room for the second time that day. She felt excited and breathless, as she had so many times; but not through fear. No, this was very definitely anticipation and she should have been feeling it a long time ago.

'Angus,' she whispered as she pushed open the door.

Good Lord, had he been asleep? She heard the bed creak as he rose, fumbling in the darkness for the tinder box before a soft glow illuminated him.

'What is it, Emily?'

His question checked her. That and the lack of answering passion in his voice. He was querying her as if she must have some life or death purpose for visiting him.

Shame at her past behaviour made her curl her toes and clench her fists, but she was determined to make him understand.

Understand what? She forced herself to ask the question.

That she wanted *to be here.*

'Angus, I—' She gazed at his short, light-brown curls which she'd never run her hands through. Tousled with sleep he looked young and vulnerable. And immensely desirable. Did he not understand, as she did, that last night everything had changed between them?

When she could not get out the words but simply stared,

his voice was almost rough. 'Go, Emily, you'll catch your death. You have nothing on your feet.'

'Then warm me in your bed.'

Saying the words sent a rush of desire through her. She felt her nipples tingle and a roiling in her womb.

To her astonishment, Angus pulled the covers back over him. It was tantamount to shutting the door in her face. She stepped back, confused rather than appalled and said the words she'd once practiced but which sounded all wrong, now. 'I am your wife, Angus. I'm here to … to …' How could she say the words she truly felt: 'make love to you'? Instead, she managed, 'To fulfil my part of the bargain.'

'I don't want you to fulfil your part of the bargain.'

She could tell from the derisive, almost hurt note in his voice that he assumed she came through duty alone. That, indeed, he expected she felt aversion, though why that would be, she didn't know, since she was the one to instigate a visit he'd certainly be making himself in the next little while.

Rocked by indecision and burning with embarrassment, she bit her lip, contemplating simply crawling in beside him, but he looked not the least bit like the loving husband who'd faced her in her bedchamber the night before. She couldn't understand the change in him.

She took a step forward.

'No, Emily.' He reached for his banyan as he got out of bed, quickly covering himself before he put his hand under her elbow to guide her back to her own apartments. 'Go to your own bed.'

Devastation washed over her and brought the sting of blood close to the surface of her skin. She could hardly speak the words which came out as a puling thread of sound. 'You don't want me?'

'I don't want you thinking that bartering your body for the things you need is your only means of survival.' There was no tenderness in either his voice or expression. 'You need to eat and you need a roof over your head and you need respectability. You've had them with no demands from me for all these months. Why come to me like this, now?'

His words harked of Jessamine's boldness and Angus's reluctance in taking her as his mistress in a similar exchange of food and security.

Disgusting thought! She tried to erase it from her mind, but it struck a note with what was happening here.

'I am not like Jessamine. I am not here for those reasons.' She tried to sound proud but it came out merely defensive.

'Jessamine?' He repeated the name as if he couldn't believe she'd even think it, dropping his hand and glowering down at her. In the lamplight his scar stood out and his eyes were black with emotion. She tried to read desire there. Surely he wanted her?

In response, her own desire for him roared in her ears. He was brave and noble. Beneath the blue silk banyan his young body was hard and lithe and she wanted to feel it wrapped around her in more than just the tender comfort he'd offered her last night.

She wanted him as a lover more than a husband. She wanted to run her hands over the planes of his face and through his hair and explore the smoothness and hardness of him while he did the same to her.

The desperate need for release pulsed through her, but he simply looked at her like a usurper until she had no option but to step back and *make* him want her.

Untying the ribbons of her nightrail, she gripped the thin fabric and almost tore it off herself.

Then, breathing heavily, she stood in front of him, naked, defiant, offering him what she knew, or at least hoped, he wanted so much he'd be unable to resist.

For a long moment he simply stared at her. Not like the

tender husband he'd been all this time, or the lovelorn suitor whose only bargaining chip was that she had no choice but to accept him.

But with a great, unsatisfied hunger that both terrified her and exhilarated her.

'I am your *wife*, Angus.' She almost hissed the words, so desperate was she for a response.

And respond he did for he was a man, he was her husband and he could *not* resist what she was all but forcing upon him. With a groan he swept her into his arms, one hand supporting the back of her neck as he kissed her face, her neck, her breasts.

The desire that had been lapping at the periphery of her consciousness, despite her fear and uncertainty, swept through her, gaining force as he suckled one nipple, his short brown curls soft against her stomach as she tangled her fingers in them. She felt the swelling hardness of his manhood against her belly; and her senses raced with excitement at the prospect of being joined as one with this man.

Yet there was no sign that his heart answered hers. No tender avowals of his love.

He was silent, the fierceness of his expression unrelieved by his familiar smile as he lay her almost unceremoniously on the bed, then joined her, pinioning her to the mattress with his long, lean body.

Her gaze skimmed the length of him and her heart seemed to skip a beat. He was magnificent. Hard, lean and eager ... for her?

She'd make him want her, she thought briefly as she registered his hesitation.

For the briefest second his face held a question but her actions brooked no doubt. Brazenly she arched her body against his rampant erection, more than ready at last for his response.

And his response was fierce, passionate, unequivocal, though it seemed he would not take her yet.

Angus had learned the art of pleasuring a woman. She'd not expected it.

The scrape of his cheek across her tender skin was catharsis. She wanted no cloying softness.

Where was the comfort in half-truths? There were so many of them, swirling around them. Lies and half-truths that needed unravelling, but for the here and now she wanted ...

No pretence. Something real. This.

She wanted her husband's single-minded passion. Wanted to feel hungered by him.

Her own responses took her by surprise. This gradual escalation of sensation, intensifying at every plateau.

Throwing her head back, she gasped as his mouth trailed hot, passionate kisses the length of her throat before taking a nipple once more into his mouth while his hands stroked her naked body, unleashing a tide of sensation.

It seemed impossible that this man she'd held at bay for so long with her contempt and disdain could whip her senses into such a frenzy.

Still he did not speak as he pleasured every exposed, sensitive piece of her, feasting on her eyes, her throat, her lips.

Touching her, kissing her, whipping her into whimpering ecstasy.

And she thrilled to it as she twined her fingers in his hair as she'd so often wished to do, arching against him, wrapping her legs round his waist, desperate for the same release that she believed, hoped, he wanted, too.

His breath, fast and shallow like hers, was hot and moist in her ear, tantalising her nerve endings and doubling her cravings for more and yet for release. Her body was on fire, consumed by feelings she'd not known possible as she gripped his shoulders, throwing back her head to gasp, 'Yes!' as she felt him breech the final barrier she'd erected against him all these months.

And as he thrust into her and she felt her body clamp around him, her cry was one of triumph and exultation.

This was desire. This was … love … and she'd been a fool not to have recognised what had been staring her in the face. As her husband collapsed on top of her, spent, his breathing still fast and heavy, Emily held him tightly, never wanting to let go and filled with the joy of knowing she could finally offer him her heart.

They slept the sleep of the deeply satiated and when he awoke, Angus raised himself on one elbow and gazed down at Emily and felt his heart nearly break at the sight.

She was his, now. In body and soul.

Fear assailed him, even while he revelled in the brief joy allowed him.

His at what cost?

She looked so tempting, her dark eyelashes sweeping her cheek, her mouth gently curved as if she were enjoying a pleasant dream.

He was reminded of when he'd gazed at her on their wedding night. His heart had been so full of love and so mauled by the sight of Jack's love letters beneath her pillow. All the same, he'd sketched her image as a kind of masochistic act to remind him that her heart did not belong to him.

What of the state of her heart now? Yes, he'd read the letters she'd exchanged with her aunt. The pain of discovering her aversion went so deep was a gut-wrenching blow, yet he could not reconcile a dutiful, unloving Emily behaving with the passion she'd poured into their loving, last night.

She'd offered him her body with more relish than would be suggested by a blithe transfer of allegiance.

Either she was a consummate actress or she really hadn't detested physical relations with Angus as much as either he or she had expected she would.

But her heart?

The question nagged at him. He'd learned too much to be confident of Emily's acquiescence of her altered situation. A wife in more than just name – with no turning back.

He did not wait for her to awaken. Mounting Saladin half an hour later he threw his pent-up energy into a bracing ride as he tried to untangle how much Aunt Gemma's advice to her niece had dictated Emily's behaviour last night.

A wife must use whatever wiles she had at her disposal to keep her husband in thrall, she'd said. Yet surely Emily could not feign that level of enthusiasm?

Branches whipped his cheeks and he rode as if the devil were at his heels. Faster he went, reliving the exhilaration of last night when he'd given in to what no man could resist: the warm, welcoming embrace of a wife he'd desired for so long.

God, he was confused.

Yes, he should have waited until Emily had woken so he could ask her, plainly and directly, what had prompted her brave and epic journey to his bedroom. The uncomfortable truth was that he was a coward. There was no other excuse for it.

Perhaps he was afraid of seeing the telltale stain of acknowledgement when she replied in answer to his question that of course she loved him, and Aunt Gemma had nothing to do with her taking the initiative.

He was surprised to see Emily leaning on the fence as she waited for him at the entrance to the park. She looked so lovely as she raised her hand in greeting but there was a haunted look in her eye. Was she regretting last night?

Fear spiralled through him. Was she about to tell him that she had wanted the consummation of their marriage to fulfil her expectations but that Angus was not the lover or husband for which she'd hoped?

Angus dismounted and tethered Saladin loosely to the gatepost.

'Is anything the matter?' he asked, the casualness of his tone so at odds with what he was feeling.

'I wish you would stop asking me that. Every time I approach you, it seems you're imagining I must have some ulterior motive.'

He gave a short laugh, feeling wary but also hopeful. Her manner was light rather than portentous. 'You'll have to persuade me there's not, then.'

Her mouth dropped open. Clearly, it was not what she'd expected to hear after last night.

After last night. Everything was changed after last night, and yet everything was the same.

He had to be straight with her. Secrets were only for keeping if they saved another pain. 'Emily, why did you come to me last night? I saw the letter your Aunt Gemma wrote you about the need to be a good wife.'

She blanched and took a step back, gasping. 'You saw that?'

'Of course I should never have read it, only it came out, staring me in the face, when I picked up the book of Children's Verse lying on your escritoire.' He felt she would have no answer that would satisfy him. Tensely, he waited to hear her out. Would she rail at him? Blame him for being underhand? Indeed, that charge held water, now. He felt shamed but glad he knew, nevertheless. They needed this conversation.

Emily looked down at the ground, clenching and unclenching her fists, as if she didn't know where to start.

Finally she raised her head and said, 'What Aunt Gemma advises and what I feel are not the same thing.'

'But you *did* what she advised. After telling her my presence was anathema.' God, it hurt to say the words out loud.

She gasped again, her face crumpling as she clutched her shawl about her shoulders, almost, it seemed, for protection. 'Don't you believe that I love you, Angus? After last night?' She took a tremulous breath. 'If you hadn't read Aunt Gemma's letter perhaps you'd be a contented husband right now.'

'But I *did* read her letter.'

Her hand strayed to his which rested on the gate post. He forced himself not to flinch. Was this part of the act?

Emily's expression was searching. 'Would you believe me if I told you that I wrote the letter some weeks ago in the midst of grief and despair but that your kindness and patience finally won me over?' Her mouth relaxed into a smile and his heart performed a strange contortion when he saw the tears in her eyes. 'Even before I knew the truth about Jack I'd started to open my heart to you. I just felt so guilty towards Jack's memory about doing it.'

He shrugged. 'I'd *like* to believe it.' He couldn't help himself, gently caging Emily's hand with his free one. 'Yet I have to remind you it was mere weeks ago you asked your aunt if she would help you obtain an annulment.'

She snatched her hands away and put them to her face. 'I felt so differently then, Angus. I was still in love with Jack. I still resented you.' Her expression was strained but sincere. 'I *want* to be with you, Angus. As a wife. In all ways. Do you believe that?'

Angus regarded her carefully. He thought of how sincere she'd been about *not* loving him when he'd married her. She'd never lied about her feelings. Why would she start now?

He nodded, though he could still picture the words which

branded his soul from the paper on which they were written. 'I could almost believe that, Emily … after last night. Nevertheless, it is true what your aunt said about an annulment harming your reputation. That a reputation and a pretty face is all the insurance a woman can look to in this world. I want to believe that your feelings for me were pure—'

'You surely can't accuse me of play-acting in your bed, Angus!' she flared.

'No, I won't do that.' He sighed. 'I'm sorry, Emily.' He truly was. 'I wish I'd never come upon Aunt Gemma's letter.' Miserably he looked down at his balled fists. 'Knowing how much you detested the sight of me, just weeks ago, is painful to my pride. I wonder how you can have changed your feelings towards me so quickly.'

Through gritted teeth she asked, 'And what about the knowledge that you married me because I reminded you of your former mistress?'

'Jessamine?' Startled, he saw her distress was genuine.

'You married me because of Jessamine.' She spoke crisply, as if resorting to this false pride were one means of taking control of her feelings. 'You married me for atonement … not because you loved me.'

Saladin snorted. Angus loosened the reins so the horse could crop the grass at their feet, then he raised his head to meet the confusion in Emily's expression.

Clearly she had investigated Angus's relationship with Jessamine more thoroughly than he'd realised. Resigned, he watched her shoulders sag.

He couldn't let her labour under such a misapprehension. 'You're wrong. I married you because I *loved* you. I'd loved you for two years.'

He raised his hand to stay her response. He'd been a fool not to acknowledge he must one day confront what he'd spent four years trying to forget. It seemed only right that it would be for Emily's benefit.

'But you already know that. You cannot have been blind to what I've felt here—' He touched his heart as he smiled at her. 'Now you want to hear about Jessamine.'

Emily's look was challenging, her mouth set, her eyes dark with angry pride as she waited, as if she truly believed Jessamine had been a contender for his affections.

'Jessamine took her own life,' he said, and so he began with her death because he knew so little about how Jessamine had lived before she'd met him. Wearily, Angus sketched the few details his late mistress had shared with him: the taunts that she was Robespierre's bastard she'd endured from the innkeeper's family who'd fostered her in Paris. The hard life which had not become easier after her birth mother had reclaimed her when she was ten, for although she then lived in comfort, her mother wanted to take control of her mind. Then her escape from her mother, hoping to find refuge with a relative.

'But something terrible happened because Jessamine had recurring nightmares in which she'd scream that the tide was coming in to drown her. Almost every night.' Embarrassed, he glanced at Emily. He should not have been so revealing, yet it was something that had always troubled him. Jessamine's terrors had been profound as had Angus's inability to bring comfort. 'She was terrified of small dark places and said she'd have died in one had it not been for her unlikely rescue by an English soldier, the man who then claimed her as his wife and brought her to Spain.'

'If honour was so important to Jessamine,' Emily asked after outlining what Major Woodhouse had told her, 'why was she prepared to be your mistress?'

Angus hid his shock that Woodhouse had revealed so much. What must Emily think of him for taking a man's life?

Haltingly, he replied. 'She believed honour required her to offer the only thing she had in return for my protection. It's true that she would have starved without me. And, ultimately, I *had* been responsible for her protector's death.' Thoughts of the war evoked terrible memories but this was perhaps the worst. Forcing back the mud and blood-soaked images, Angus muttered, 'Yet I couldn't leave him to die painfully from his mortal wounds, or fall into enemy hands, in which case Jessamine would have died at the end of a bayonet, too. I don't believe I had any choice.' He drew in a difficult breath. 'Still, I should not have allowed her to … force her attentions upon me for there was little love on either side.' He dropped his eyes and said more softly, 'She was desperate for something more from me that I couldn't give her. *That* is what haunts me.'

When he raised his head once more it was to find Emily's eyes locked upon his face and knew she intended puzzling out what he wanted to extirpate from his mind forever.

Steadying herself upon the gate post, she asked softly, 'What did *you* do, Angus … that she would take her own life?' She was worrying her lip with her teeth, trembling; and he wanted so much to take her into his arms to warm her, now that his anger was directed at himself. How badly he wanted her approbation, but he feared she would withdraw once he satisfied her curiosity.

Emily reached out her hand, dropping her arm before she'd touched him. 'You've felt the need to make amends ever since, haven't you? You were driven to rescue someone who needed your help, not because you loved her – Jessamine or me – but because you couldn't live with your guilt.'

He did not deny it though there was so much more to it than that.

'Last night you made me your wife, Angus.' Her voice was strained. 'Yet you attributed the basest of motives to my coming to you.' She looked miserable as she snapped the slender frond of an overhanging tree branch causing Saladin to startle.

The noise galvanised Angus into a response stronger than the hopelessness that held him victim.

'I admit it was wrong of me, Emily, to keep the truth about Jack from you for so long. I admit, too, that I was wrong to read that letter.' He balled his fists and shifted his weight to his other foot. 'But I did and it changed everything.'

Puzzled, she shook her head. 'I do love you, Angus, but why is it so important when marriage is a contract? We made a good start last night at fulfilling our contract. I came to you out of more than just duty. Do not tell me that your feelings have changed because you doubt my love for you.' Her voice, which had sounded a reasoning note, suddenly turned harsh. 'On account of a silly letter written at a time when you knew I did not love you ... weeks ago! Did your love turn to scorn the moment you discovered you could have me, after all?'

'No!' He gripped her shoulder, then let his hand fall. 'No, Emily.' He tried again, and succeeded, the anger gone from his voice now. He even managed a smile. 'Foolishly, I imagined I could win your heart through gallantry.'

He was relieved she did not draw back when he put his arm around her shoulders and clasped one of her hands. In fact, she moved closer and he felt a surge of warmth he'd never expected to feel again. He might even have kissed her had the *unfinished business* not continued to swirl about them. 'You need to hear how Jessamine died.' He stilled. Like the calm before the storm, he prepared himself to make a clean breast of everything. Jessamine's death had shocked his sense of self. It had never fully recovered and Emily needed to know the worst of him.

She raised her chin and said with surprising perspicacity, 'If it'll ease your guilt, then tell me. Otherwise, I don't need to hear it.' And then she put her cheek briefly against his chest and he felt her love like a conquering force do battle with the demons that lurked within him.

For a moment he nearly backed away. Was truth always the only way?

In this case, it was.

He began carefully, his arm still around her shoulders, the other clasping her right hand, standing in the dappled shade of an elm tree while Saladin cropped the grass nearby.

'Let me begin with the death of her hopes and dreams for I killed those when I delivered the bullet which ended her husband's life. Don't be afraid, Emily.' He heard the bitterness in his laugh. 'I did not kill Jessamine ... at least, I didn't kill her like I killed her husband.'

'I did not think you did.'

He cleared his throat for the words were so hard to dislodge. 'Jessamine killed herself because I refused to play the gentleman.'

The truth was like a knife, twisting his entrails. He had no excuses. After he finished backing up this damning assessment it would eradicate any lingering charitable thoughts Emily might still entertain.

'Jessamine appeared on my doorstep because she had no one and nowhere to go. After what I'd done, I could not cast her off. She was bound to me, yet her grief, her silent determination that she warm my bed in return for the essentials of life, were intolerable.' With a sweep of his arm, he swatted at a fly, needing distraction, wanting to pace, some kind of release. Emily said nothing but he could not meet her gaze which was fixed upon his face.

'For months we cohabited. She cooked my food, tended to my needs as a good wife would. But I never loved her and I hated the burden of guilt she'd forced upon me. It was a blessed relief when I could finally tell Jessamine I was returning to England but that I was unable to take her with me for I had not the means to keep a woman. I insinuated she was beautiful, there were others who would gladly take her on, look after her. I insulted her. She was not like that. She had *married* the soldier I killed. She was not a common doxy.'

Emily placed her palms on his chest and tilted up her face.

The sympathy of her expression made his heart clutch. 'You were in an impossible position, Angus. You can't blame yourself for not feeling as she'd have wished you to feel.' As he rested against the gate post, holding Emily lightly, his burden grew heavier. Her sympathy was ill-placed and soon she'd know it. 'I was young and ignorant.' He glanced at his wife. She knew all about *that*. 'With no sisters I could not comprehend the helplessness to which I was consigning her, so when Jessamine told me she was carrying my child—' He stopped at Emily's gasp. Was there any point in going on? *Could* he? He felt unutterably weary but he had not told her the worst of it, so when she filled the silence, her eyes dark with sympathy, saying, 'So that's why she hanged herself—?' he shook his head.

'She didn't hang herself.' Moistening dry lips, he said softly, 'I killed the joy in her when I shot her husband but I killed all hope when I told her that having my child did not alter my resolve to leave her.'

Emily's voice was a whisper. 'So that's why you married me? I was a desperate woman and finally you could offer me and my child a future? To atone for Jessamine?'

He toyed with his signet ring. It wasn't so simple. He did not deserve the forgiveness she seemed prepared to allow him. He forced himself to continue, to relive that fateful last conversation.

'After I told Jessamine I was leaving her, she cooked my

food as usual, sat down at the table, and then reminded me she was carrying my child. Would I still leave her?' Angus focused his gaze over Emily's shoulder. 'The look in Jessamine's eye was a challenge to my honour and decency. I did not reply. I took my coat and hat and left to go to the officers' mess where I proceeded to drink a great deal.'

Emily waited.

'When I returned she was still sitting at her place at the table. I thought she'd not moved.' He could picture it still; the tragedy in her luminous eyes which pierced his soul. 'I hated her for putting me in such a position. For her misery which sucked the happiness out of me. She looked up as I came through the door and asked if I'd changed my mind.' Raising a hand to his brow, Angus remembered the flint in her eyes as she'd repeated her question.

He clenched his fists as he went on. 'I said my resolve was unaltered but that I would find the funds to support her and the child. She didn't speak but I turned when I noticed that she reached into the pocket of her skirts. I saw her put something in her mouth. I was suspicious and asked her what she'd done.'

Carefully Angus levelled his eyes upon his wife's, anticipating the horror which reflected his own. But he could read nothing.

'Jessamine told me she'd sold the pistol I used to shoot her husband in return for poison which one of the infantrymen kept in a vial around his neck in case he fell into enemy hands.' He closed his eyes, his nostrils flaring at his last memory of her. 'She said that as *she* had fallen into enemy hands she needed a way out of her torment, too. Then the poison began to act. I did what I could but it was quick,' he muttered, 'though not quick enough for what she suffered.'

Emily turned her footsteps back towards the house while Angus nodded farewell before riding in the opposite direction. She had said what she could but her words were not enough. It was true, she was deeply shocked, but greater was her dismay on Angus's behalf. He was still haunted; she could see that by his retelling of those terrible events.

Angus blamed himself for killing Jessamine's husband, for killing Jessamine's hopes and for Jessamine's death.

She tried to reason out what else he might be feeling.

Did he want to kill Emily's good opinion of him because last night, when she came to him, he could not accept the joy of finally seeing his own hopes of love realised?

Or had his memories of Jessamine rekindled disgust and suspicion that Emily might be trading on the only means at her disposal for his continued protection? That when she offered him her body she was doing so in base imitation of Jessamine and with no love in her heart?

There was no way of knowing.

Angus probably did not know it himself.

All Emily could do now was to prove that she loved her husband.

When she entered her room after her walk the first thing Emily saw were the letters – Jack's and hers – in their usual position. For months they'd sat neatly stacked in the corner of her escritoire, a testament to the lie on which she'd based what was supposedly the most wonderful thing in her life.

With a cry of rage she seized them, casting the bundle into the fireplace with all the force she could muster.

But the fire was not hot enough and the parchment did not catch. If ever she needed a reprieve, an opportunity to act upon second thoughts it was now, but she was resolved. She picked up the bundle of her letters to Jack, untied the ribbon, and letter by letter, began feeding them into the fire.

When the dinner gong went she was part way through dealing with her past and ready for luncheon and a new beginning.

Unfortunately over luncheon she encountered another impediment to carrying through her determination to prove to Angus that she loved him with a pure heart.

For over the mock turtle soup Angus told her that Major Woodhouse required his services for the culmination of the important mission on which he'd been engaged. He would leave the following morning.

CHAPTER 18

Caroline's visit within an hour of Angus's departure was ostensibly to finalise details for Emily's much-delayed entry into society, but Emily was certain there was a good deal of curiosity regarding her marital relations, also.

A cool autumn breeze stirred up the leaves on the gravel walk as the two women walked, arm in arm, about the rose bushes and Emily told her sister-in-law that Angus was in Dover, awaiting this afternoon's packet.

'Of course, he told me nothing that would compromise my safety,' Emily said, smiling despite the irony in her tone, 'but he's told me enough to satisfy me.'

Caroline squeezed her arm and commented with a question in her tone, 'You seem happier, Emily.'

Emily had obliquely intimated to Caroline that she and Angus had made their peace, yet despite the more gentle union that had resulted in the bedroom last night, a sense of disquiet lingered. Not that she'd admit that to Caroline. Instead she said with quiet force, 'Angus has all the qualities of a fine soldier and has been a good husband.'

'*Has* been?'

Emily smiled. 'And no doubt will continue to be,' she amended for Caroline's benefit, wishing her sister-in-law was not quite so perspicacious when she asked, 'But that still is not enough for you, Emily?'

'Oh, I am perfectly satisfied.' Emily made sure there could be no doubting her sincerity. 'Over the past couple of days you might say the scales have fallen from my eyes. I've been in ignorance about a great many things which have now been made clear.'

'That is good.' The way Caroline said it made Emily wonder if her sister-in-law knew the truth about Jack before Emily did. 'I hope that when Angus returns it will be for a long time. The two of you can then begin to forge a future filled with children and happiness, as Jonathan and I have done. Emily, what is it?'

Emily heard the nervousness in her own laugh. 'I will not betray secrets but suffice to say that Angus is on his way to lodge where Jack used to stay. I worry about his safety for it is a dangerous mission.'

'Napoleon has suffered important losses recently,' Caroline remarked. 'It's thanks to heroes like your husband that we can look forward to the cessation of so many years of hostilities. And for hopefully soon ending the blockade that's pushed up prices and caused so much hardship.'

Emily nodded. She was in accord but her concerns were more personal. 'Apparently the daughter of the house bears a great resemblance to me.'

Caroline raised an eyebrow. 'You doubt Angus's constancy when he keeps company with another great beauty?'

Emily frowned, puzzling it out as she spoke. 'I can't put my finger on it. It's not that I doubt Angus's constancy, yet I gather this young woman is part of the operation in which Angus is involved and in which Jack also took part.'

'Angus told you all that?'

Emily's smile broadened. 'I had to know if I were to understand certain matters … about the past. Yet all I really know about the future is that Angus is in Dover awaiting passage to France and that the next few days brings the culmination of some very dangerous operation. That alone fills me with dismay, but so does the knowledge that a certain incomparable and thoroughly deceitful Mademoiselle Delon is up to her neck in it, too.' She looked squarely at Caroline.

'Jack had told me she was a child, but Angus says she's a beautiful young woman about a year or two younger than me. It's not Angus I mistrust … it's Mademoiselle Delon,' she said and was cross to receive a blithe laugh in return.

'You don't understand, Caroline,' Emily said, twisting the ends of her shawl. 'This young woman – Madeleine, her name is – was Jack's …'

Burning, she turned her face away. She couldn't finish. How could she possibly admit such a thing to Caroline? Fortunately she was saved further embarrassment when Caroline gripped her elbow, saying with great wisdom and revealing clearly that she knew the truth long before Emily, 'My poor Emily! What a disconcerting discovery to make at such a time.'

'I've made a lot of disconcerting discoveries over the past few days.' Emily was not about to reveal them all, but she was glad of Caroline's understanding.

At the top of the hill by the rotunda they stopped to gaze at Wildwood, beautiful and gracious in the distance.

'I have almost everything I could want.' Emily tried to sound satisfied and hoped Caroline wouldn't pounce on her for the wistfulness in her own voice.

'Indeed you do,' Caroline said firmly. 'A beautiful home and a husband who loves you.'

Emily clamped down on her trembling lip and whispered, 'Perhaps, Caroline, but he doubts me. He doubts that I feel as I tell him I do. Because he saw them in black and white, I suppose. They were in a letter I wrote to my aunt. A draft I should have thrown away. *Many* drafts.' Miserably she looked at her feet. 'In effect I decried everything Angus is: sober, serious, considered, saying I wanted someone like Jack who was spontaneous and carefree.' She searched Caroline's face. 'Yet now I am quite changed. Jack betrayed me and I am in love with Angus's sober, serious, considered nature. I can't tell you what pleasure it brings me here'—she touched her heart—'when he bestows upon me one of his unexpected, illuminating smiles, or when he laughs. It's like I've truly earned it and it thrills me, whereas Jack laughed at everything. He was never serious and … he never meant what he said.'

'No doubt Angus's mind is occupied with what he must do. When he returns you can concentrate on building your future together.' Raising one eyebrow, she added, 'Just as long as you don't doubt *Angus's* constancy with regard to this other woman.'

Emily shook her head.

'I'm glad to hear it.' Caroline smiled. 'Then short of buckling a sword and scabbard around your hips and chasing Angus to France, you'll have to be satisfied with the conventional approach.' She encompassed the flowing garden and distant house with a sweep of her arm. 'Be patient, Emily, and accept what every woman must. This is our arena and this is where we must prove ourselves.'

Caroline's good sense made Emily feel infinitely better.

When her sister-in-law had departed in her carriage with

an invitation to afternoon tea the following evening, Emily went indoors to change.

Disconsolately she mentally went through her wardrobe, wishing Angus would be at dinner so she had some reason to make an effort.

'What shall I lay out for you, ma'am?' As if reading her thoughts, Sukey looked up from rearranging the items on Emily's dressing table.

Emily sighed. 'The master isn't here so—'

She was surprised when Sukey cut in, saying, cheerily, 'My auntie told me that when her husband was away fighting the war and her spirits were poorly she used to put on her grandest gown.' Sukey turned to Emily's wardrobe and started going through the options. 'She said the funny thing was she never dressed fancy for him when he were home, only it just made her feel better.'

Emily laughed. 'I suppose if it worked for your auntie, I could try it. Go on, Sukey, lay out my best gown and I'll pretend to have a house full of illustrious visitors to entertain in great style even though we're being country bumpkins tonight and dining before five.'

Sukey was a cheerful girl and delighted to be responsible for raising the mistress's spirits.

'Oh, my goodness, won't I look grand for dining alone?' Emily laughed when she saw the low-necked blue silk gown her maid had laid out. 'And the diamonds?' She picked up the necklace of glittering stones which Sukey had rushed to retrieve from their hiding place beneath a floorboard in Emily's dressing room.

'The diamonds are the only jewels that will set off your gown, ma'am,' she declared firmly, helping Emily to dress.

Obediently Emily raised her arms and Sukey slipped the dark-blue sheath of silk over her underdress of silver net. It slithered to just below the knee, beneath which the silver net fell in scallops to her ankles. These were bound with matching silver laces to set off her slippers.

'Oh ma'am, you don't look half beautiful,' Sukey breathed. 'I bet the master can't wait to come back. 'Ere, let me just attend to this curl.' She rearranged Emily's hair which was threaded through with a pearl-encrusted silver cord.

When she'd finished she stood back, shaking her head. 'What a picture,' she declared, and Emily smiled at the reverence in her tone as the girl added, 'If only the master were here.'

This was a sentiment Emily silently echoed when Major Woodhouse was announced.

'At this hour?' she stared at Wallace as she put down her knife and fork having just finished her Dover sole.

'Yes, ma'am.' His tone indicated that he shared her disapproval.

Then she remembered that Angus had recently visited the major for a briefing before travelling to France and her heart gave a little lurch. Perhaps Angus had charged him with a message for her before he left. Or perhaps Angus was returning and the major was giving her advance notice of the fact.

'Thank you, Wallace, I'll see him in the drawing room.'

Quickly she attended to her appearance in the long mirror above the sideboard, not because she wished to impress Major Woodhouse but because he seemed always to find her wanting and the least she could do to ameliorate this, the better. At least he'd find no fault with her attire, considering the lengths to which she – or rather, Sukey – had gone to ensure she looked as fine as possible.

'You look well this evening, Mrs McCartney.'

It was as close to a compliment as Emily was ever likely to receive from the Major. She glanced down at the diamonds Angus had given her and managed to sound more enthusiastic at playing hostess to the major than she felt.

'Thank you, Major. Would you care to take a seat and tell me what this is about? I trust Angus is well.' No point in dancing around the niceties. The major was a straight talking man who no doubt had as much desire to call upon Emily as she did in entertaining him.

When he did not immediately respond after settling himself into an elegant wing back armchair, she repeated with a stab of real fear, 'Angus *is* well, isn't he?'

Major Woodhouse gave what no doubt was supposed to pass for an apologetic smile. 'Forgive me, Mrs McCartney, yes, he is well. I was simply surprised to see you were expecting guests.'

She supposed it natural that her grand rig-out would lead him to think such a thing. 'I was dressing to lift my spirits since my husband is to be away for some time, Major.'

He quirked an eyebrow. 'I'm sorry your spirits are so cast down by your husband's absence. I'm also glad you're not expecting anyone, Mrs McCartney.' Nevertheless, he looked sceptical, as if he expected some lover to be lurking in a cupboard. 'What we need to discuss may take a while. First, though, my apologies for calling at such an unfashionable hour.'

Absently, she nodded, troubled by his tone.

When he asked with no warning, 'What do you know about Madeleine Delon?' she drew in her breath quickly and clutched at the diamonds round her neck. The question was like an unexpected lancing.

'Nothing, Major Woodhouse,' she whispered, which was for the most part true.

'Come on, Mrs McCartney,' he prompted, almost cajoling, though there was a menacing gleam in his eye, she noted. 'Clearly the name struck a chord and as we're talking about

233

your husband's safety I'd hoped you'd be a little more forthcoming.'

'My husband's safety!' she gasped.

She felt like slapping him when he chuckled. 'I'm glad you are so concerned about your husband's safety. I'd suggest the more you tell me about what you know, the better the outcome will be for everyone, not least you, Mrs McCartney.' *Was she understanding him correctly? Was there a veiled threat here? An insinuation that she was lacking in her loyalties? To Angus?*

'Madeleine Delon,' he repeated. 'Tell me what you know about her.'

With a shaking hand Emily pulled on the bell rope. 'Wallace, please will you fetch the major a drink. Brandy? Yes, brandy, thank you. And a glass of Madeira for me.'

She needed to remind herself that she was hostess and that everything was going to be all right.

Only when she'd taken a sip of her wine did she answer the major's question. 'I believe you are asking me to confirm what I suspect you've known for some time, Major. Madeleine Delon was my former fiancé's mistress. Do you wish to humiliate me further?'

'I have no wish to humiliate you, Mrs McCartney.' Smiling, the major toyed with his drink. There was a calculated gleam in the boyish green eyes. The look of a child who is relishing the anticipation of revealing his brother's truancy or some other misdemeanour to a parent.

'I am sorry for Jack Noble's disloyalty to you, but it is in fact his disloyalty to something far more important that concerns us. We hoped you might be able to help.'

'Me?' Again she gasped and he leaned forward, his smile falsely reassuring. *Dear God, he honestly thought she had something to hide.*

'I'd appreciate it if you cast your mind back to conversations shared with Jack Noble or your husband pertaining to their work in France and Switzerland.'

Jack and Angus? Their work was secret. She was supposed to know nothing and certainly Angus had told her very little. Emily looked squarely at Major Woodhouse. He had never liked her. No, that was not true. He had admired her like the rest when she had been Jack's intended. Since she'd incautiously criticised Angus he'd clearly lost all respect for her.

His impatient toe-tapping riled her. He had no idea to what extent she'd been made a confidante and she'd rather keep him guessing. For once she held a modicum of power. He was testing her. Angus wasn't in danger.

'I'm sorry, Major Woodhouse, but neither Jack nor Angus told me anything that could be of help to you now.' She smiled her regret, indicating to him with a tilt of her chin that she had nothing further to add and that their interview was over.

She knew all about Mademoiselle Delon and she did not need to have Major Woodhouse rub her nose in it.

'So you claim to have never met Madeleine Delon. Please, Mrs McCartney, we have serious concerns about this operation in which the young woman is to play a major role. If you are not prepared to cooperate we will need to find other means of discovering the information we are seeking. Less pleasant means.'

Emily gasped. 'How could I have met her, major? She lives in France and I have never been to France—'

'You were born in France,' he interrupted. 'Your mother is French, as is half your family. Have you ever communicated with Mademoiselle Delon?'

Emily raised her hands and looked at him helplessly. 'No,' she said. She was not about to lay bare the extent of Jack's deception and the books she used to send to the young woman she'd believed was a child. The wound was still too raw. 'I was not born in France. Nor do I understand how I can be of assistance, Major. Angus is conscientious about keeping from me anything of a sensitive nature relating to his activities abroad.'

'Jack Noble was not so conscientious'—the major fixed her with a long, level stare—'was he?'

Damning shame stung her, flooding her face and throat with incriminating colour. 'Jack risked his life for his country,' she whispered.

'Your late intended risked more than that.' Major Woodhouse began his toe-tapping once again. 'Captain Noble sent us much valuable information when he was first recruited. Until he was compromised.'

Suddenly she understood. Her breath left her in a rush. 'You believe Jack was a spy *for France?*' She felt sick to her stomach. The man in whom she'd placed so much trust had betrayed not just her but her country? 'That he was compromised?' Emily rose, covering her face and began to pace. 'How? But of course, Mademoiselle Delon!' She clapped her hands to her mouth as she swung round from the fireplace to confront him. 'Then Angus may be in danger!'

To her astonishment she saw the major was regarding her with cynicism. 'Bravo, Mrs McCartney,' he said with a desultory clap. 'Your concern is touching. However you've told me nothing we don't already know and I have just communicated to your husband my concerns regarding Mademoiselle Delon.'

Mademoiselle Delon. The name filled her with loathing. 'I, too, have told him he must take care. What is the operation, Major? Why is Angus in danger? Surely you can tell me that since you assume I know so much?'

'Really, Mrs McCartney, you stretch credulity too far.'

Puzzled, she shook her head.

'You know exactly what role Mademoiselle Delon plays in this unfolding drama and don't try to pretend otherwise.'

Still she stared, silent, anxiety coalescing into terror as the major pulled out a sheaf of documents.

'You might do a reasonable job at feigning concern for your husband, Mrs McCartney, but how will you react when I inform you that Madam Fontenay and her husband were apprehended in Paris last week.'

She stared at him blankly. The name meant nothing to her.

Raising his eyebrows, the major looked disconcerted for a second before he burst out laughing.

'Good Lord, Mrs McCartney, but you can play a role to perfection. Not a shadow of emotion crossed that pretty face of yours to learn that your mother has been caught as a spy and that the operation in which you, she and your sister are all implicated is doomed.'

Emily gripped the back of the sofa to steady herself as she sucked in a gasp. 'My *mother*, Major McCartney? My *sister*? My mother is at Micklen Hall and I have no sister. You are speaking nonsense to me. Explain your meaning.' The room began to swirl. She put her hands to her ears to try to block out the nightmare but the major was insensible to her distress.

'You do not deny your mother is a Laurent, of Noble Normandy stock, I believe she's proud of citing.'

'Margeurite Laurent,' Emily murmured. Then, her voice growing stronger, she asked, 'Have you met my mother, Major? If you have you will discover how ridiculous this assertion is for my mother is a cripple, all but incarcerated at Micklen Hall.'

'Margeurite Micklen is your *aunt*. Your *mother* is her sister and we have intelligence, both in the form of documentation as well as verbally – under duress, admittedly –

that your real mother is Fanchette Laurent, now the notorious revolutionary Madame Fontenay who has murdered more than a dozen of our finest in the course of their duty to England.'

Terror forced itself out as rage. How dare he tell such lies? He was trying to implicate her in something she knew nothing about, simply to get her out of the way because he considered her a disloyal wife to Angus. It could be the only explanation. The Foreign Office did not trust Emily and they wanted her removed.

'These are lies! You know it!' She turned angrily towards the fire to gather her wits.

The major gave a snide laugh. 'Fanchette Laurent – now the notorious Madame Fontenay – fostered out both you and your sister so she could continue her revolutionary activities.'

Major Woodhouse sounded so sure of himself but her breath was so constricted she could barely get the words out. 'It cannot be.' She was conscious of her hands tensing and relaxing, tensing and relaxing. She felt like an old woman with no strength to do more than protest weakly, 'Madame Fontenay cannot be Fanchette Laurent. I have never met this woman. My mother lost touch with her sister years ago.'

'*You* did not lose touch with your sister, did you, Mrs McCartney?'

The outrageousness of this assertion gave her strength. 'I do not have a sister,' Emily repeated grimly.

Clearly irritated, the major rose. 'You are well trained in discretion when it's required to save your own skin, Mrs McCartney.' He extended his arm to indicate that she must come with him. 'Conversation is getting us nowhere. Let's see what we can find, shall we? If you have no objections, perhaps we could peruse correspondence between you and the late Captain Noble.'

The awful thought occurred to her that somehow Jack had implicated her in this nightmare.

'I burned Jack's letters.' She would not admit that Sukey had retrieved at least half the bundle which Emily had pushed to the back of a drawer. 'My apologies, Major Woodhouse.' She nodded, dismissal in the gesture. 'It would seem we have nothing further to discuss.'

The major looked unimpressed. 'Your lack of cooperation doesn't surprise me. I saw from the start that you were a reluctant wife to a good husband. Major Noble was a charismatic companion, clearly. He had your love and loyalty though he plotted against England for – what? Nothing more than material gain as far as we can surmise, seduced by the charms of your sister. Two sisters across the channel, it would seem.'

'Mademoiselle Delon is not my sister, Major McCartney, and Madam Fontenay is as unknown to me as ... the Queen of England. It is outrageous that you would to try and implicate me in a plot that would also see harm come to my husband.' Emily refused to follow the major when he rose and walked to the drawing room door. From her chair she said, 'I admit I was a reluctant bride and I made the foolish mistake of inferring to you my lack of delight at the new situation in which I found myself. But you go too far to try and implicate me in such a ... a ludicrous scenario.'

The expression on the major's face when he turned was both sorrowful and satisfied.

'It is easy to verify that which you refute, Mrs McCartney. Records prove that your mother had two daughters whom she fostered out. Madame Fontenay *is* your mother and Mademoiselle Delon *is* your sister. In fact, the likeness between the two of you is quite extraordinary.'

Across the channel there you have a wicked counterpart.
A spy who looks just like you.

Jack had teased her about it. Angus had remarked upon her resemblance, also, to Madeleine Delon. She tried to steady her breathing. As soon as the major had gone she would go to her mother – her *real* mother, Margeurite Micklen – and verify that the major spoke nothing but lies.

'Now! Let us see these letters, Mrs McCartney.' He held the door open for her and, resigned, she saw she had no choice but to go with him.

He accompanied her upstairs to her private sitting room and waited while she took the remaining letters from her writing desk.

When she demurred as she stared at Jack's familiar handwriting, once so beloved, Major Woodhouse became impatient. 'This is a national matter. Lives are at stake, including your husband's.'

'These are love letters, Major McCartney,' she muttered. Nevertheless, she began to read them – those that had survived – envisaging a young woman of twenty rather than the child of six she had believed Madeleine to be when Jack wrote of their exploits. At each reference the pain sliced deeper.

'April 14. Madeleine and I went to the Pont du Sur to feed the ducks. They were bold and greedy and in her excitement to get away Madeleine nearly fell in. I caught her in time but she nevertheless had to change her stockings.'

Major Woodhouse rifled through his notebook to check the corresponding date in his notes, announcing with satisfaction, 'On April 14, Noble, in company with Mademoiselle Delon, was observed by one of our agents meeting a woman matching the description of Madame Fontenay at the bridge. Something was exchanged, Mademoiselle Delon appeared to take fright and lost her footing, landing in several feet of water.'

He indicated for Emily to go on to the next letter.

Trembling, she picked up the well worn piece of parchment and began to read. 'I took Madeleine to the fair today where she begged so prettily for a new blue ribbon. She's such a dear child, darling Emily, that I was unable to resist her sweet charms, especially as she insisted I buy one for you, also. It accompanies this letter – with all my love.'

There were many references like this. Some which were only part legible though she knew them by heart and others which no longer existed and could not be matched up with the notes in Major Woodhouse's notebook. So many contained references to Madeleine.

When she reached the end of the final letter, Emily leaned back and faced the young major.

She felt drained. It took several moments before she could speak. 'Why did you not act before if you had the information? Jack sent these letters almost a year ago.'

He waited until the maid had tended to the small fire and left the room before replying, 'Our suspicions were aroused some time after Noble's death. Initially Captain Noble supplied us with prompt and accurate information but as time went on his responses were slower, which caused the death of several fine men. Then the information he sent became unreliable. It was not until Major McCartney took his place and voiced some of his own concerns regarding what Jack had reported, and about the Delon girl, that the puzzle began to fall into place.' He glared at Emily. 'There is more. A single page of correspondence found amongst Captain Noble's personal effects, which had been mislaid, was recently brought to our attention. In it he makes the clear association between you and those we are seeking.'

Where was Angus when she needed him? Shocked, Emily hugged herself. Her palms, when she pressed them together, were cold and clammy while heat prickled the back of her neck. She'd never felt so frightened and alone. 'If Angus believes that Mademoiselle Delon is my sister and that I am implicated,' she whispered, 'he would have charged me with it, himself. Why is he not here defending me?'

'Come now, Mrs McCartney.' Steepling his fingers, the major stared at her over the tips. 'You and your sister are adept at winning over the men in your lives. Your husband does not know I'm here otherwise his misplaced loyalty would have him compromising the entire operation. No, he is in Dover, soon to escort Mademoiselle Delon to the Chateau Pliny for the event of the year which, as you very well know, takes place in three days. I am here because your mother's latest husband proved surprisingly forthcoming after he was apprehended. We now know the role Mademoiselle Delon will play in the operation. Or rather, I should say, your half- sister, for we've lately learned that Monsieur Delon and his childless wife adopted the infant who was the child of Madame Fontenay when she – your mother – worked as a companion to Madame Delon. After that lady's death, Madame Fontenay re-established contact when the child was about ten and recruited her to her cause. No doubt this is not news to you, however.'

Emily's mouth dropped open. 'It's not true,' she whispered, imagining she was the moth currently singeing its wings in the flame of the candle the major had placed on the escritoire. 'Madame Fontenay might be Mademoiselle Delon's mother, but she's not *my* mother. How is it that I'm a part of this fanciful tale? Surely neither Monsieur Fontenay nor his wife … Madame Fontenay … claimed such a thing? And Jack's letter? If it was incomplete you must have misunderstood his meaning.'

The major shrugged. 'You can ask Madame Fontenay that yourself when the time comes. In the meantime I need to find out from you everything I can that provides a background to the breadth and depth of the Fontenays' network so we can protect Angus at this masquerade at the Chateau Pliny. We want the information he is there to obtain, but we also want him alive.'

Angrily, Emily flared, 'You let him go when Mademoiselle Delon poses such a threat?'

The major responded with a snide smile. 'Your husband knows how to look after himself, Mrs McCartney. Your attempt to persuade me of your concerns are worthy of Sarah Siddons. Major McCartney will simply be at Pliny to take note of the people with whom Mademoiselle Delon communicates and to pretend to pass on the information he is given.'

Through its own stupidity the moth had incinerated itself. Bleakly Emily watched its death throes on the wooden surface in front of her. 'What good will that do?' she asked dully.

'We need to know who constitutes the threat before we act. Our hopes are that Mademoiselle Delon will communicate with Madame Fontenay before she is to consort with one of Napoleon's trusted generals. We understand information will be exchanged. We have agents on hand to apprehend her when the time comes, though if we are able to apprehend Madame Fontenay then all our troubles would be over.'

'I thought you'd already done that.'

The major looked uncomfortable. 'Madame Fontenay escaped from custody. Fortunately she does not know her idiot husband was apprehended shortly after her flight and that not only does he know a great deal more about her clandestine activities than she thinks he does, he was decidedly forthcoming. He has furnished us with a great deal of information regarding the masquerade at the Chateau Pliny as well as background as to how Captain Noble – and, of course, you, by the double association – came to be implicated in the operation.'

Wearily Emily asked, 'What operation and how was I implicated? I would love to know.'

'Don't be droll, Mrs McCartney.'

'My sister, then. How did Jack meet Mademoiselle Delon?'

Major Woodhouse sighed. 'Perhaps you have been spared certain details, Mrs McCartney, relating to Captain Noble. A fond mother might choose to soften the truth when a ruthless operation like this is complicated by affairs of the heart.'

Clearly, Major Woodhouse had no compunction in laying that painful truth bare. He went on. 'Captain Noble was sent by the British Government to France to lodge with Monsieur Delon, who has been a long-time ally of Britain. Because Mademoiselle Delon had already been recruited to her mother's cause it was inevitable Mademoiselle Delon would be instructed to use her ... natural attributes to ... persuade Noble to sympathise with her aims.'

The familiar rage at mention of Madeleine's name rose up in Emily's gullet but the major took the wind out of her sails with his amused response. 'My dear Mrs McCartney, I don't know why you appear so outraged. *You* were the one to have married him. Mademoiselle Delon and Jack Noble were keen to marry, but your mother had already arranged a match for her with the most important man in the English/French alliance. Count Levinne.'

'So what if this is true. I don't know any of these people. Except Jack.' Emily tossed the letters onto the escritoire and rose. 'What do these letters tell you, Major McCartney? Nothing! You've read into them everything you believe, or perhaps what a fanciful Frenchman, or one who will say anything under duress, would have you believe. I think your intelligence gathering leaves something to be desired for I was not born in France, as you have suggested on more than one occasion.

Calmly Major McCartney recounted, 'There is no record of your birth in this country, Mrs McCartney. Furthermore your father's long-term employee Lucy Gilroy asserts that you came to Micklen Hall as a small child directly from the revolution in France with your parents.'

She hid her shock. 'It does not mean Madame Fontenay is my mother.'

The major frowned at her. 'It does not,' he conceded, slowly. 'However we *will* find the link, Mrs McCartney. Now, in the interests of your husband's safety, would you please allow me access to his library, a request, I might add, for which I have his authority.' He smiled a thin, cold smile. 'That is, unless you have something you wish to tell me.'

Her bravado was fast diminishing. She paused halfway across the carpet. 'How do I know you have Angus's authority? You say he does not even know I am being interrogated. If he did I know he would be here defending me.' Yet doubt assailed her even as she made the assertion. She thought back to the night she'd appeared in his bedchamber. Only three nights ago they'd lost themselves in a surfeit of lust, and she'd exulted in the abandonment. Her husband's subsequent cooling had been properly explained and last night they'd shared a more gentle love, and confidences, though they were not as easy with one another as she'd have wished.

Was there another reason for the emotional withdrawal she sensed in Angus? Had Woodhouse spoken to him of his doubts about Emily and a possible collusion with Jack with regard to this operation? Did Angus believe Emily a traitor?

She turned quickly so the major did not see her fear. He'd misinterpret it, of course.

'You'll just have to take my word for it, Mrs McCartney.' He led the way to Angus's study, pulling out a chair so she could sit before opening the drawer of the bureau. 'If there is nothing to hide there is nothing to fear. I wouldn't put it past you to use your husband's desk as a convenient hiding place for your own correspondence when he is away.'

'I want Angus's authority in writing. This is preposterous. Have him sent for immediately. He will defend me.'

'You protest too vehemently, Mrs McCartney. The evidence is stacked against you. Your mother established links with England through Captain Noble when he was recruited to the enemy side through your sister. You were affianced to Captain Noble before disgrace forced you to wed the honourable Major McCartney whom you made no secret of despising. His usefulness soon became apparent when, fortuitously, he was recruited to take Captain Noble's place in this operation.'

The major shook his head as if he thought her disingenuous. 'Do you really think you can make me believe you are ignorant of the whole operation?'

Emily did not reply. Dully, she stared at the remains of Jack's letters, charred and disintegrating, like her hopes and dreams. The major had come to her for evidence to support his outrageous claims, but what did he expect to find? An incriminating letter in her handwriting? A record of payment for disseminating false information?

'What's this?' Major Woodhouse had picked up the book of Children's Verse and opened it at the front page where she'd written her greeting to Madeleine.

Sickened by the sight, Emily replied, 'A gift Angus was to take to Mademoiselle Delon. Jack used to take parcels from me to'—bitterness welled up in her—'the child I thought Madeleine to be. Angus refused ... and then told me the truth.'

'Of course,' Major Woodhouse said in a tone which suggested he didn't believe her for one moment. 'Your husband is known for his honesty and plain speaking.' He started flipping through the pages, adding conversationally, 'Jack Noble had no such virtues. I'm sorry you find this intrusive, Mrs McCartney, but I am confident I will find *something*— What is this?'

Emily looked over his shoulder. Her stomach clenched. From between the pages he withdrew a sheet of vellum. 'I don't know—'

The major began to read, carefully and in a tone of disbelief as he angled himself towards Emily, '*M – Your information was most useful. Six months on we have another conduit. Major MC. Continue to be good to him. You know what to do. Once he has delivered the information supplied to him he is no longer needed. Your father will be protected. Rest assured I have destroyed your letter. Tell F she can anticipate funds shortly.*'

It made no difference that Emily looked helplessly at him. That the letter was unsigned. Her innocence was clearly interpreted as play-acting.

Slipping the book into the leather pouch he carried, the major's look conveyed his satisfaction.

Emily heard the panic in her voice. 'Angus is in danger and ... I don't know where that letter came from—'

'Really?' He smiled. 'Tell that to the court.'

She rose from her chair and took a step towards the door. The room felt hot and close. Her love for Jack had been a lie and now this—

'Where do you think you're going, Mrs McCartney?' The major's hand upon her shoulder was heavy and shocking for its lack of deference. 'If you're so keen to convince me of your innocence, let us see what *exonerating* material I might find.'

Pushing her back into her seat, he turned again towards the large desk where Angus kept his papers in drawers and cubby holes.

'Please feel free to speak. You're more likely to escape the hangman's noose if you're prepared to shed light on those we're investigating.'

She didn't answer, her mind whirling with possibilities. Angus? Could he have planted a letter implicating her in these activities? Jack had betrayed her when she had believed the sun shone out of him; when she'd have given her life for him. But Angus? He was the antithesis of Jack, yet her judgement had already cost her dearly.

If not Angus, then one of the servants? She tried to breathe evenly, watching Major Woodhouse continue his careful search. Had *he* planted the evidence to entrap her?

The major's voice cut through the mists of desperation. 'Perhaps you'd care to tell me who *this* woman is.'

He'd tossed upon the desk a number of sketches Angus had drawn and Emily felt the pull of her heartstrings as she recognised the hastily but beautifully executed charcoal likeness of herself. She remembered with a mixture of pain and remorse her wedding night when she had cried herself to sleep clutching Jack's letters.

Angus had drawn her as the picture of serenity, long dark lashes curled upon her cheek, almost childlike in repose.

It was not painted by a man who saw vice and corruption but was tenderly, beautifully drawn ... by a man who saw his wife's devastation at her lot evidenced by the ribbon which protruded from beneath the pillow concealing a dead lover's letters, the red ribbon a symbol of the knife wound to her new husband's heart.

And now Emily's.

She brushed away her tears. Weakness. Her father abhorred weakness. She realised with shame how weak she'd been during the past months and rallied her attention. The major had not been referring to this tenderly rendered likeness of herself.

One impatient finger stabbed at a small oil painting. It was a woman, familiar but difficult to see clearly in the gloom. He moved the painting closer to the light of the oil lamp and the shock she'd felt at the discovery of the illicit letter was nothing compared to the fear she felt now.

Leaning over the desk she studied the artist's rendition, so familiar but so out of place in her husband's study. It was not a recently painted picture. The clothes were not of the fashions of the last five years.

The woman, dark-haired and golden-skinned, wore a jaunty smile. The familiarity of expression and her luxuriant beauty made Emily gasp.

Emily knew exactly who this woman was, for she had seen this very picture, or at least one almost like it, on the wall of her mother's dressing room.

She glanced up to see the major staring at her with hard eyes. 'You know, don't you?' He made it a statement. 'Fanchette Fontenay,' he intoned. 'Your mother. Perhaps there's something on the back,' he suggested and when he turned it over Emily's shock was compounded, though it went some way to explaining how it came to be in her husband's possession.

'*To Jessamine,*' he read, '*from Mama. 1808.*'

CHAPTER 19

Locked in her sitting room, Emily's nightmare worsened as the evening wore on. She could hear sounds that indicated the major was moving furniture, no doubt searching through everything in Angus's study, and her stomach knotted with fear.

She had been branded a traitor on the basis of an incriminating letter supposedly from herself to Madeleine.

The major claimed Fanchette was her mother but Emily knew she was her aunt. He claimed Emily had been born in France but Emily had never been out of England. He claimed Madeleine was her sister. There was not a shred of evidence to bear out such a claim.

Now, apparently, she had two sisters. 'Your mother fostered out two of you. Why not three?' he'd replied to Emily's arch question.

Major Woodhouse continued searching the house for more evidence to shore up his belief she was a traitor. She'd become a creature beneath contempt long before the discovery of the letter in the book of Children's Verse.

If only she knew who had written the letter. She had to find out.

Angus would not, could not, have done such a thing. He was not in league with a traitor. His association with Mademoiselle Delon was innocent in a way that Jack's – on all levels – had not been.

And Madame Fontenay? Even thinking the name aloud made her feel sick. Her *mother*?

She shook her head, trying to reason out the impossible connection.

Her mother was Margeurite Laurent, wife of Bartholomew Micklen who had saved her from the guillotine during the revolution in France. Major Woodhouse based his assertions regarding Emily's parentage on wild supposition.

Hugging herself as she rocked on the bed, she acknowledged that the major did not believe himself mistaken. He'd long ago written Emily off as a faithless wife. In his eyes she'd transferred her loyalties too quickly and easily from Jack to Angus; he'd seen her pregnancy as a crime for which she had not received proper punishment. Now he intended seeing Emily pay the highest price for her sins.

With a moan, she buried her face in her hands. Could a letter she had not written and a painting that was not hers be sufficient evidence?

The wind whipped a tree branch across the window pane. Emily reached across the sofa to see the catch was secured properly, though a tree branch through the glass was hardly a calamity under present circumstances.

She could tell by the keening outdoors that a storm had blown in. Through the window she saw the major's coachman draw his muffler more snugly around his neck beneath his greatcoat as he waited for his employer. No doubt he'd not have expected his evening to be so protracted. If it were to be no more than a short visit he'd have gone into the kitchen but clearly he was under orders to remain with the horses.

Pacing like a caged animal, Emily tried to subdue her fear. What would happen to her when Major Woodhouse's search was completed? Would he bundle her into the carriage or allow her to remain in her own house?

Either way, she was a prisoner. She'd tried both doors. The only way out was through the window and she could hardly...

She caught herself up as she reformed the question. Why could she not ...?

The mere idea of behaving in such an outlandish and unladylike manner struck as much fear into her as the thought of landing up at Newgate.

Yet nothing could be worse than being convicted for a crime she did not commit while Angus was in danger.

Unlatching the window, she leant out, reaching for the tree branch which swept within a foot of the pane. It was not a perilous drop if worse came to worst, she thought, as her silk slippers at first failed to find a purchase. But within seconds she was discovering that a childhood ability to climb trees was a skill one retains for life if one's agile or desperate enough.

She was relieved she had not fallen so she could address the coachman looking like a lady. A quick glance told her that her silk dress remained unspoiled while the diamonds commanded respect. Behind her back she clasped the painting of her aunt.

Covering the last few yards at a run she cried out, glad of the keening wind which muffled her voice from those indoors.

'Major Woodhouse has had a seizure. Quick!' She waited impatiently while the coachman jumped down from the box to open her door and put down the steps, adding, 'My maid is with him now. Follow the road to London until I tell you to stop. I'm going to fetch the best doctor I know.'

Little matter if he thought it an odd delegation of authority. He was a servant and it was not his place to challenge her.

ANGUS CONTEMPLATED the storm ruffled waters that had delayed his departure to Calais. Sleep had proved impossible so he'd done what he should have done a long time ago: written Emily the truth. For though he had every intention of delivering this in words, face to face when he returned, a mission such as he was embarking upon always carried dangers. And Emily deserved the truth.

He turned at the rapping on the door. At this time? Dawn was still many hours away.

Immediately his thoughts returned to Emily. They were never far from her. Their last night together had been satisfactory, but after what he'd experienced the night before that, he'd wanted so much more.

The fault was his. He knew he'd not done a good job in reassuring Emily that he was unaffected by his discovery of her correspondence with her aunt. He'd not responded to her protestations of her newfound love for him as she'd have wished, but he just wasn't terribly good at play-acting and Emily's quiet desperation that he reassure her with words and kisses had been too similar to what Jessamine had wanted from him.

God, his feelings for Emily could not be *more* different. He *adored* her. And he was reasonably reassured she loved him. But learning that his very nature was anathema to her –

or had been mere weeks ago – was something he still had to reconcile.

Nevertheless, hope that it was Emily was in the ascendant as he flung open the door.

'I hadn't expected to see you again,' he muttered when Woodhouse shouldered his way in.

Woodhouse tossed his hat upon the bed, raked his hands through his wet and mud-streaked hair and went to the window, turning a highly agitated face to Angus.

'Yesterday you didn't want to hear that your wife is up to her ears in this sorry business,' he said, without preamble. 'But hours ago I discovered in your own house numerous pieces of evidence to implicate her.'

He was breathing heavily, his mouth working, as if he didn't know whether to appear triumphant or sympathetic. Because he'd been Angus's friend for so many years he obviously settled upon the latter, adding, 'Sorry, old chap. I take no pleasure in being the harbinger of bad news. But now that we know, we are far better placed to deal with this threat, once and for all.'

Angus, lowering himself onto a chair at the tiny table, noted his friend bore the signs of a desperate journey on horseback. Forcing emotion from his voice, he asked, 'Where is Emily now? I trust she is safe and you've not transported her to Newgate on a mere suspicion.'

A glance from beneath his lashes before he conveyed his porter to his lips showed the indignant flare of Major Woodhouse's nostrils before the other man said crisply, 'I found clear evidence Mrs McCartney is the daughter of Madame Fontenay. A letter contained within a book you were apparently to carry from your wife to Mademoiselle Delon indicates the connection between the two and hints at grave danger for you, McCartney.'

'Drink, Woodhouse?' Angus offered with a smile, indicating the jug.

Angrily, Woodhouse pulled the offending piece of parchment from his coat pocket and thrust it at Angus. 'Read that. Perhaps then you'll agree it's time for the authorities to rein in that wife of yours, who some hours since demonstrated her innocence by climbing out of her sitting room window and stealing my carriage in her desperate bid to escape justice.'

'By God, you go too far!' Fury that Woodhouse's strong-arm tactics had driven Emily to such desperation made Angus rise so abruptly he knocked his chair over as he glared at Woodhouse. 'Where is she now?'

'I don't know, but she's guilty as sin.' Woodhouse maintained the courage of his convictions as he brandished the letter he'd found. 'I presume we'll find her at Micklen Hall, but as Dover was not too great a diversion I felt that, as your friend, you should be apprised of the situation before you set sail and before your wife is arrested – as will inevitably be the case. The weather is fair and you will be at the chateau in Pliny in time for the masquerade in less than seventy-two hours, though in the name of friendship I will allow you to see Mrs McCartney before she is condemned.'

'Are you out of your mind?' Angus scanned the letter before casting a fulminating stare at Woodhouse. 'There is nothing to indicate my wife wrote this letter.'

Major Woodhouse mutinously defended his beliefs. 'There is more. A painting of Madame Fontenay with the inscription on the back which reads "To Jessamine from Mama". It's dated 1808. We know Madame Fontenay had two daughters – both bastards and both fostered out at one stage or another. Madeleine Delon is one of them, your wife is another. I would suggest, based on this painting that clearly belongs to your wife, that your former mistress, Jessamine, was a third.'

Quietly, though his heart was beating rapidly, Angus said, 'That painting came into my possession through Jessamine, the woman who was once my mistress. Emily has never seen it. Nor do I believe she knew anything about the letter found in the Book of Verse. It must have been placed there by someone else.'

'Who else? The connection is too strong. You wife is clearly related to Mademoiselle Delon and now, it would appear, also to Jessamine.'

Angus began to pace, muttering as he racked his brains to remember what Jessamine had told him of her past. Jessamine? How on earth could his dead mistress be implicated?

He recalled the shrill cries of the gulls and the shouts of the dock workers overlaid by the salty tang of the breeze as he'd prepared himself for bed. Jessamine had recounted her terror of that very combination. Well, minus the dock workers. What had she said?

I went to England to find my half-sister after learning she lived on the Kentish coast with mama's sister.

But the only person I met was my uncle, who entombed me in a cave by the sea, for he said I was too dangerous to live.

The story had horrified Angus, but the extent of the horrors Jessamine had lived through could not make Angus love her.

Now, in this altered context, and with its implications for Emily, her story resonated terrifyingly.

'Oh, God, Emily …' he muttered, only half to Woodhouse. He swung round to his friend, dread turning to icy fear. 'You've been to my brother's house?' he asked.

'It was the first place I looked.'

'Then the only other place she'd go is Micklen Hall.' The

pieces of the puzzle that were slowly being assembled before his very eyes pointed to Micklen's involvement. First with Jessamine's attempted murder and now the wide-reaching operation in which Madame Fontenay played centre stage.

His fingernails dug into his palms as he silently intoned, *Please, don't let Emily have returned to Micklen Hall. Not to her father's house.*

'I presumed the same but I thought she'd come to you first if she thought she had the means to prove to you her innocence.'

Angus clenched his fists and tried to work out how long it would take him to ride to Micklen Hall. An hour perhaps. 'Micklen Hall,' he muttered. '*Dear God*, I pray she has not gone there.'

'If you find her, then you have no choice but to hand her over, Angus, so that she can prove her innocence.' Major Woodhouse clearly did not share his concerns that Emily was in great peril.

Angus ignored him as he strode to the door.

He heard Woodhouse's boots upon the floorboards coming after him and swung round.

'You have been a good friend, Woodhouse,' he snarled, 'but I swear I will never forgive you if harm has come to Emily.'

There was no sympathy in the look Woodhouse returned. 'She has manipulated you, Angus, just as she manipulated Jack Noble. I should have kept this from you until we had her safely under lock and key and every piece of proof documented and beyond doubt.'

Angus exhaled in fury as he strode up the corridor. 'Leave me to find Emily,' he said over his shoulder, 'and I swear I will see she gives a good account of herself, but I'll be damned if you accompany me, breathing down my neck.'

'Why should I trust you?' his friend demanded, bearing down on him.

Angus turned abruptly and slapped a hand on the other man's shoulder. 'Because I have never let you or my country down,' he answered quietly, his voice gaining strength as he added, 'God damn you, Woodhouse! You have no idea of the danger you have put her in. It's Bartholomew Micklen you want, not Emily. Micklen tried to kill Jessamine because he said she was a threat. A threat to what? I have yet to find out but it's at the centre of everything. Do you know how much greater the danger is to Emily is, thanks to your interference?' He sucked in a breath. 'I will go now, but let me tell you I will leave no stone unturned in order to exonerate my wife!'

CHAPTER 20

'This is a surprise, Emily.'

Her father's greeting was restrained, despite Emily's obvious agitation as he led her into his study. 'I trust everything is all right?'

She'd considered seeking refuge at Honeyfield House. Jonathan and Caroline would help her, protect her. But what did they know of her origins? Major Woodhouse maintained he had irrefutable proof linking Emily with a notorious spy.

Only her mother and father could tell her the truth. 'Something has happened?' He raised his eyebrows and, strangely, his coolness was comforting rather than daunting. 'A little brandy to calm your nerves?' He resumed his favourite seat by the fireside while she chose to stand. He'd always been a commanding figure with his thatch of white hair above broad shoulders, and he was commanding still, but age was taking its toll. He seemed more stooped than she remembered, though his face was still the cold, inscrutable mask that used to strike dread into her when one of her governesses forced her to confess some misdemeanour. 'Then you can tell me what has upset you.'

Emily took the tumbler of amber liquid he handed her, wishing her hands were not trembling so much. Her father respected cool nerves and she needed all her defences.

'An odd time to call, Emily, though you look rather fine.' He nodded at her blue silk and net gown.

'Father, Major Woodhouse has just been to visit me.' She finished the brandy in a couple of gulps and the fire that burned her insides made her feel much braver.

'He accused me of being a spy, said he had proof I'm the daughter of a French woman called Madame Fontenay and that I have two half-sisters called Jessamine and Madeleine who are both spies, too. When he went through Angus's study he found a letter which I did not write contained in a book to Madeleine Delon. Remember, she's the … daughter … of the family with whom Angus lodges, only Major Woodhouse says she's my sister!' Emily took a break to calm the rising hysteria. 'And now he's found this.'

She brandished the painting before her father. 'It's Tante Fanchette, I'm sure of it, but Major Woodhouse says it's a painting of my mother whom he says is a spy he calls Madame Fontenay. On the back is a dedication to Jessamine.' She nearly added that Angus had had a mistress called Jessamine, but the admission was more than she could manage right now.

Let her father digest the details of Major Woodhouse's shocking allegations first.

Emily had hoped for a reassuring denial and a genial endorsement that Major Woodhouse was clearly as deluded as Emily believed him. Instead she was surprised by his sudden waxy pallor and the strain of his voice when he snapped, 'Of course it's your aunt Fanchette!'

He motioned her to hand it to him and he took it with furrowed brow and trembling fingers.

Slowly, he said, 'Though it is not the same as hangs above

your mother's rosewood desk. Where did you find it, Emily?' This was far from the reaction Emily had expected. She saw the blood vessels stand out in the whites of his eyes. His breathing was agitated. 'You came to me first? You have been to see no one else? Angus is away, of course. But his brother is ignorant of the matter?'

'Major Woodhouse locked me in my sitting room but I escaped. I came directly to you, father.' She swallowed, wondering why her father should be more concerned as to where she found the painting and who knew about her predicament than the fact itself.

'Where did you find it, Emily?' he demanded again. 'You say Angus had it? Then where did *he* find it? Washed up on a beach, perhaps?' He seemed as perplexed as he was horrified.

As Emily was.

Emily sagged with relief. 'I knew Major Woodhouse was wrong. He said this painting was of a spy in France. A notorious woman who has been wanted by the English for years. When he learns he is wrong—'

Her father cut her off. 'Yet it was in your husband's possession?' Frowning, he studied the painting and again Emily weighed up whether to speak of the connection between Angus and Jessamine. 'Emily,' he said sharply, 'You are not to show it to your mother or to repeat to her anything of what you've just told me! Do you hear!'

She jerked back at his anger. 'But Papa—'

'Do you not realise how it would upset her?'

Emily nodded. Her father had always had the ability to make her meek before him.

'Everything will be all right, won't it, Papa?' she asked, hating the fact her voice had the same thin puling sound to it she remembered from when she was a frightened child. 'Of course.' But he wasn't listening; he was studying the painting as if for further clues.

'Major Woodhouse says Angus is in danger from Madeleine Delon and also this Madame Fontenay. He thinks I'm a party to some conspiracy to take Angus's life.'

Her father glanced up. 'You never loved him, Emily.'

She gasped. Could she have heard him correctly? 'I do now. Father, Angus is to attend a masquerade at a chateau in Pliny, I believe. Can you help me get a message to him in France somehow? Or maybe the packet was delayed by the stormy weather and we can still reach him in Dover!'

Her father stepped forward, a great giant of a man, dominating her as he had when she'd been a child. Intimidated, she nodded weakly when he asked, 'Major Woodhouse verified all these details? He knows everything?'

'I told you that Major Woodhouse found a letter referring to Madame Fontenay in the book I asked Angus to take to Madeleine,' she repeated. 'He says it's proof I'm involved in their spying operation, but it must have been planted by one of the servants. Someone in our household is a spy, but Major Woodhouse believes it's *me*.' She forced back the tears. 'Angus will know what to do.'

He began to pace, the painting held in his hands clasped behind his back so that the jaunty smile of her Aunt Fanchette danced in his grip. 'Yes, quite right. And Major Woodhouse will no doubt search for you here,' he said. 'We must hurry, mustn't we?'

Her bones went soft with relief. 'Give me two minutes with Mama while you organise the carriage, Papa,' she said, going to the door.

'Don't tell her anything – do you promise? It would be unfair to agitate her when you are about to rush off into the night. Besides, she's been in a lot of pain. The tonic has addled her wits. She'll not attend to you as you'd wish. Rather wait until the matter is dealt with properly. I shall follow you up in a couple of minutes after I've organised the carriage and several other matters.'

His advice seemed reasonable.

'MAMA! It's Emily. Sorry to disturb you,' she whispered, putting her head around the door to her mother's chamber.

'Darling girl!' Margeurite Micklen struggled upright on the day bed while faithful Lucy gave a cry of joy to see her young charge again. Emily hugged them both, horrified by how shrunken her mother was.

Gently, Emily settled the older woman against a pile of pillows, smoothing back the grey hair from her head and taking her hands in hers to rub as she had done so many times before.

'I can't stay long, Mama. Papa is organising a carriage to take us to Dover.' Though guilty at revealing what she'd not intended, she nevertheless went on at her mother's questioning look, 'Angus is there and—'

Her mother smiled. Clearly she had no idea what time it was. 'Angus is a lovely man.' Her words were slurred and when Emily slid her anxious gaze to Lucy, the maid indicated the laudanum bottle by the bed, whispering by way of explanation, 'Your mama was in a lot of pain this evening.'

Best, then, thought Emily, that her mother not be worried more than necessary.

Lucy leaned over her mistress to smooth the covers and Emily acknowledged for the first time in her adult life that Lucy was more than just a servant. She alone was responsible for her mother's meagre comforts, if not survival.

Her mother blinked and the fog seemed to lift. 'Isn't it late to be visiting Angus in Dover, Emily? Is something the matter?'

Emily looked between the two women before deciding to reveal a little of the truth. 'I need Angus to help me, Mama. It's about some ridiculous claims Major Woodhouse is making about Tante Fanchette and a couple of other little matters I need Angus to help me sort out.'

She did not repeat the claim that Tante Fanchette, in addition to allegedly being a spy, was also supposed to be her mother. Her mother was drug-addled and confused enough as it was.

'Fanchette? What does your husband know of Fanchette?' She was surprised at her mother's sudden lucidity. Major Woodhouse's claims were so ridiculous she'd felt sure of – and had hoped to be reassured by – her mother's dismissal of them.

'A painting of Tante Fanchette was found in Angus's study dedicated to her daughter Jessamine, and—'

She jumped at her mother's gasp.

'Jessamine? In your *husband's* possession, Emily?'

Her mother seemed even more discomposed than her father had been. Clearly the laudanum didn't help. Emily stroked her forehead as she struggled to explain. 'Angus rescued a woman called Jessamine at Corunna.' Carefully she added, 'She and Angus became very … close … after this woman's husband died during the retreat.' Jealousy needled her and she had to brush away the tears. 'I can only imagine that is how the painting came to be in Angus's possession.' Taking a breath, she asked, '*Did* Tante Fanchette have any daughters?'

It was Lucy who whispered, sharply, 'Jessamine? It is not so common a name.' She glanced at her mistress, as if uncertain whether to divulge more; but drew in her breath at the sound of footsteps in the passage.

With a creaking of hinges the door opened and Bartholomew Micklen strode into the room.

Emily put a protective hand on her mother's shoulder, all questions forgotten as his expression overrode her anticipation for their imminent departure. She must remember that her father was a stern man. It was only because Angus was kind and gentle that she had grown used to a less fraught existence.

'Are you ready, Emily?'

She started to follow but her mother surprised her, struggling to force out the words, 'Do not take her, Bartholomew!'

'Mama, I must reach Angus before he sails—'

'No, Emily! Don't go—!' Seized by a fit of coughing, Margeurite gasped for air as her daughter turned. Bartholomew pushed Emily towards the door, barking at Lucy though she stood only a foot away, 'Your mistress needs you! Fetch her water! Come Emily.' He snatched up a dark cloak that hung from the back of his wife's door. 'Take this. We must go.'

Distressed by her mother's hacking cough and the horror in Lucy's parting look, Emily hung back, but her father seized her by the wrist and hustled her into the corridor.

'There's nothing you can do for her that Lucy can't. Major Woodhouse will be here soon so we must hurry. We'll take the cliffside route. He won't think to come that way.'

Torture though it was to leave at such a time, Emily felt only relief by the time she stepped into the carriage which waited at the bottom of the steps. She was glad the waxy moon threw enough light to see the road.

Angus would convince Major Woodhouse of Emily's innocence. The servants would be interrogated and the puzzle over the letter would be solved. Emily's mind was in such a whirl over the events of the past couple of hours she no longer knew what to think.

Soon, though, she would be with Angus. He would know what to do.

CHAPTER 21

It was some time before Emily glanced out of the window. 'Papa, are we going in the right direction?'

They were skirting the shoreline, steep cliffs plunging from the left side of the road to the foaming sea below, gleaming in the moonlight. Emily strained to identify her surroundings. She'd not walked this far alone before and the landscape was unfamiliar.

Her father leaned across and patted her knee. 'We must lose Major Woodhouse at all costs, Emily. I've told the servants to send him in the wrong direction but he won't be easily fooled and you are clearly anxious that we reach Angus before he does.'

'Why is John stopping here?' Wrapping her mother's cloak more closely round her shoulders, Emily stared out of the window. The carriage had slowed to a standstill so close to the precipice that all she could see was darkness edged far below by a frill of white foamy waves.

'There is something I must show you.'

Her chill deepened as she let John assist her to the

ground. 'What do you want to show me, Papa?' she asked, glad the fear was not revealed in her voice.

'You will see. Come, Emily.' He held out his hand and she took it for she had no choice, ashamed that she should feel relieved at the words exchanged between her father and John the coachman. Her father must have good reason to lead her down the narrow path that zigzagged over the cliff face. She must not show the skittishness which would only make him lose patience with her.

'Smugglers, Papa?'

He gave a grunt of laughter as he walked in front of her, 'Yes, Emily, and all related to the plot in which your husband and, indeed yourself, are implicated. When you see, you will understand.'

'Then there *is* something? And you know about it?' Emily wished her father would explain rather than drawing out the suspense. Still in her finery, her slippers were ruined and the hem of her skirts torn and dirty by the time she reached the small shaley stretch of beach at the bottom, though she dared not complain.

She was dismayed to hear the waver in her voice as she asked, 'Are you involved with the smugglers, Papa?'

'I turn a blind eye, Emily, in return for the occasional barrel of rum.' He stopped, twisting to face her. To her surprise, he smiled and touched her cheek with his finger-tips. 'John's family have been dancing rings around the excise men for generations. He knows a word from me could see them all hang. Now, Emily, you must pick up your skirts and follow me into that cave. I know it's dark and the rocks will make the going difficult, but I'll go ahead and light the way. Are you coming?'

After a pause, Emily did as he asked. He was testing her. Giving her an opportunity to show she was made of sterner stuff than he believed. Determined to rise to the challenge, Emily scrambled after him, her brain whirling with possibilities. How was this connected with the operation in which Angus was involved? Was there some link between the smugglers and the spy ring? What could be so important that her father would take her to this secret location in the dead of night?

Climbing out of her sitting room window had seemed the height of daring, but this was a challenge harder to meet in her flimsy evening dress and her torn shoes.

Once inside the cave, Bartholomew raised his lantern high and pointed to the tumbled rocks in the far corner. They reached to the top of the cavern. 'Do you see that tunnel, Emily?'

She could only nod. Fear made it impossible to speak.

He brought his face close to hers, the shadows from the lantern contorting his features so she had to force herself not to step back in alarm.

'I need your help, Emily.' His voice was grave. 'You've asked for my help, but first I need yours.' He put his hand on her shoulder and pointed. 'You are the only person I can trust small enough to reach inside that opening, yet strong enough to pull out the chest which is concealed near the entrance.'

She stifled a gasp. 'You want me to climb up those rocks?'

'If you are brave enough, and prepared to render your father the greatest service of your life, then yes, Emily, I am asking you to do that for me.'

The crashing of the waves outside the cave was almost deafening. Emily hesitated, frowning up at her father, too afraid to ask him to explain.

He put down the lantern and cupped her face. He had never been so tender. She closed her eyes and his voice caressed her fears away. It was as she'd dreamed he'd be when she was a child.

'If you can do this for me, Emily, you guarantee my safety.'

'You're in danger, Papa? Why did you not say?' she cried, opening her eyes and clasping his wrist. 'Tell me what's happened.'

'Later.' Resting his hand in the small of her back, he gave her a gentle push. 'Now go, Emily. This great act of yours will save my life, but I need you to hurry before the tide comes much higher and cuts off our return.'

All her adult life Emily had feared him, and although she still did, she knew he would regard her differently once she met, without hesitation or complaint, the challenge he set her.

She began to climb. Her feet hurt and her dress tripped her up, but her father was with her all the way, his breathing laboured as he moved heavily from stone to stone so that halfway up she became afraid for him and said, 'There's no need to use your energy, Papa, for there is light enough if you want to stop here.'

'Perhaps I will. I'll hold the lantern steady. Ah, you have reached the top. And the entrance is clear? Well, that is fortuitous. Well done, Emily. Now, crawl in and tell me what you see. It was a good thing I came so high with the lantern after all, wasn't it?'

Emily crouched in the mouth of the tunnel, her head touching the roof, and cast around for signs of a chest but she could see nothing.

'Is it there?'

Her father's voice echoed eerily round the chamber. Disappointment cut deep. Her torn dress and slippers faded into insignificance compared with the fact she had failed to discover what her father was so desperate to find.

'It's not here, Papa.' She swallowed down her disappointment. Yet again she had failed to meet his expectations.

'I know it's there, Emily. Perhaps it's further down the tunnel. I cannot get so high to cast the light, but I beg you, Emily, go a little further and see what you can find.'

Fear did not enter into her decision as she crawled on her hands and knees deeper into the tunnel. If her father was convinced that what he sought was here, she would find it.

She heard his voice calling, 'Can you still see a little way? Do you have enough light?'

It was not pitch black, for the lantern, even from so far away, sent a faint glow from the midst of the cavern.

'A little, Papa,' she called, from about ten feet into the tunnel, turning at the sound of shifting rocks, before gasping. 'The light is completely gone now, and I can find nothing! Something has happened. Papa, are you all right?'

Turning with difficulty in the cramped space she struggled back the way she had come. What if her father had stumbled and fallen? What if he'd been crushed by falling rocks? Her horror increased at his silence. 'Papa, where are you? Are you alright?'

Why was it suddenly so very dark, despite the full moon which had contributed its share of the soft glow?

Her forehead connected with something rough and solid. Stone. She must have stumbled blindly into the side of the tunnel. Putting out her hands, she felt the cold, damp rock which blocked her passage.

On three sides.

Fear pumped through her veins and she screamed. 'Papa, I can't find the opening!'

She was almost certain she was at the entrance where she had begun, but the opening was blocked. She pushed and felt the boulder yield a fraction.

'Papa, help me!' she screamed again.

There was no answer. Her pleas sounded muffled, unable to penetrate the thick rock which imprisoned her. The blackness of her mind coalesced into blinding red, hurting her eyes though they were squeezed tight shut. What had happened? She had entered the passage, gone only a short distance, then come back again.

To find the entrance blocked.

Her father? No. She would not believe it. Yet the more her mind ran over the limited scenarios this seemed the only possible one. If there had been a serious rockslide, she'd have heard it, felt it. After a minute she gathered her strength for a renewed assault on the boulder, but she was not strong enough to shift it.

Her brain tore through the possibilities as she screamed and screamed again.

But still there was no response.

Then the chill that held her in its grip tightened its icy hold as realisation dawned.

Her father had entombed her.

He had never loved her. She always knew that, though she only acknowledged this now.

But like a little lamb she had followed him to slaughter.

Clenching her fists, she hunkered like a cornered animal and screamed until her lungs rasped with pain.

When she opened her eyes she saw a sliver of light penetrated the gap between the boulder which lodged in the opening. Her father must still be there.

Yes, he was, but she no longer expected him to help her.

Collapsing with her head against the stone, a shard of weak light filtering through, she whimpered. He was just on the other side for now she could hear his breathing in the silence.

All her life she'd tried to please him, but she had sinned and Bartholomew Micklen never forgave.

That must be what this was all about, though she needed to understand it from her father's lips. For a few minutes she struggled through the pain, trying to form words that would not come until finally she managed, 'What have I done, Papa, that you hate me so? All my life I have tried to be a good daughter.'

His voice came to her from only a few feet away, his tone patient, regretful.

'Ah Emily, I too am sorry it had to come to this. And if you *had* been my daughter perhaps it would not have been possible to act against the fruit of my loins.' He sighed deeply. 'But you were neither mine nor Margeurite's and now the threat which you unwittingly pose is so great I cannot risk exposure, no matter how blameless you are.'

Not his daughter?

Numb with fear and caught up in confusion, she tried to digest this. 'What are you saying, Papa? You brought me up as your own. Why should you now do this to me – *now*? What have I done?' Her head spun and in the darkness she felt as if she were being sucked into a vortex of horror. This man was the only father she had ever known. He had not been always been kind, but she did not imagine he was a monster compared with other parents. He had been indulgent in her youth.

She tried to swallow past the lump in her throat. 'Whose daughter am I? Would you see me die with such a question unanswered?'

'I feared you would ask me and, indeed, I am not *so* unfeeling as to leave you entirely in the dark, in all senses of the word.'

She tried to be brave but was unable to hold back the sobs which choked her. Only when her father began to speak did she stop. She needed to hear what he had to say. While he was still talking she could cling to the hope that he may relent and allow the girl he'd at least brought up as his daughter to live.

CHAPTER 22

No, Emily was not his daughter. Bartholomew Micklen spoke in the tones he might use if he were telling her a fairy story, relaying the long ago history of the orphaned Laurent sisters, Margeurite and Fanchette, who lived in Paris and relied on the charity of their overbearing great-aunt, Baroness Angevine.

But this was no fairy story. It was a tale turned dark and Emily was reminded of the gruesome cautionary tales Lucy sometimes told her when she was a child in the hopes of keeping her meek and obedient.

At the age of sixteen the elder, revolutionary-minded Fanchette disgraced the family with her liaison with a radical member of the National Assembly some claimed was the feared Robespierre. An illegitimate child resulted who was quickly spirited away, for the immoral Fanchette was not fortunate like the sinning Emily, her father reminded her.

'Indeed, Emily, you have no idea just how fortunate you have been, for Fanchette was disowned by her aunt and forced to earn a living as a hat maker, while your transgressions,' her father reminded her, 'resulted in an offer of marriage from the noble Angus McCartney. Not that you appreciated your good fortune, my dear.'

Not at the time, Emily silently agreed.

'Was Fanchette beautiful?' Perhaps she would please him with her interest in her father's ... lost love? She chewed at her knuckles, trying to remain calm. If she could maintain the normal, civilised modes of behaviour despite her peril she could perhaps engineer her release.

Micklen appeared to relish the opportunity to talk about Fanchette.

'Beautiful, Emily? She was the most beautiful woman I had ever seen and I met her the day after I arrived in France in November 1791.'

Her father had obviously settled himself on a boulder not far from the entrance to Emily's prison. His voice was warm as he reminisced. 'I saw Fanchette across the chamber. She was listening to a debate in the gallery at the National Assembly and I was entranced by her passion, her fervour ...' She heard the smile in his voice as he added, '... her loyalty to a cause I could believe in: liberty and equality for all.

'In her I found a compatriot, a fellow revolutionary who wanted to change the unequal society in which we lived. For that, Emily, was what drove us: liberty and equality for all. Each day I went to the National Assembly, she was there, shouting down moderates like Lafayette and cheering her hero Robespierre. Each day my admiration grew.' The glowing tones hardened as he added, 'I had no idea of her moral depravity: an illegitimate child fostered out the year before. Jessamine was her name. I only met her once and she's now long dead.'

Shock coalesced into pain at the revelation. But what was Fanchette to Bartholomew Micklen other than the Laurent sister he preferred above Emily's mother? Above Margeurite.

'Yes, father, I know,' she whispered, wanting to prompt him into further disclosure.

'Not knowing Fanchette's fickle nature, I left her in Paris so I could travel, listen to the mood of the country, work with other revolutionaries. When I returned a year later to claim her as my own, I discovered she had another babe at her breast'—his voice turned to a snarl—'that was not mine.

A child she'd named Emily, the result of Fanchette's brief infatuation with one of Robespierre's acolytes.'

Emily exhaled on a gasp. '*Me*, father?' All that had begun to make sense fractured into nonsense. She truly was *Fanchette's* child? The same Fanchette Major Woodhouse claimed was the notorious spy, Madame Fontenay? Then who was her father? *One of Robespierre's acolytes?* It was ludicrous! Fanchette was her aunt. The mother – apparently – of Jessamine. Fanchette was her father's – no, this man's – former mistress. She might believe that.

But Fanchette Laurent, now known as Madame Fontenay, was her *mother*?

Her skin prickled with horror while her breath came in short, shallow gulps. If what she was hearing *were* true, then she and Jessamine were half-sisters, just as Woodhouse claimed.

But how in the world had Jessamine crossed Angus's path? How had *their* fates become entwined?

Her father would be unable to answer these questions, but he could answer the question that screamed in her head: 'If you hated Fanchette so much, why take me … when you must have hated *me* so much more?'

He still did. He always had, but it was never clearer than now. Emily shrank into her cloak, which provided no respite from the chill.

'You'll understand, Emily, if you let me finish my story,' he told her. 'Soon you will die, like you should have twenty- one years ago had I not rescued you and Fanchette and Margeurite from the mob who threatened to tear you apart when you were imprisoned in the Abbaye.

'I returned to Paris during the Terror in '92,' Micklen continued. 'Fanchette had just been delivered of her babe. A fatherless babe. Make no mistake, I ensured Fanchette would have no other protection than myself.'

'You *killed* my real father?' She did not know why she made it a question when the truth was so clear.

Micklen made a noise of impatience. 'The streets of Paris were running red with blood. No one trusted anyone, anymore. Power shifted with the wind and common people butchered anyone whose opinion ran counter to theirs … and got away with it. You would have died of starvation by your first birthday, Emily, or the mob would have dashed your brains out against the prison walls had I not rescued you, your mother and your Aunt Margeurite.'

Emily buried her face in her hands. The horror of her present was matched by her past.

Except that she had survived. She was familiar with the tales of bloodletting and state-sanctioned violence told by emigrés who'd escaped the guillotine.

'Why were they – we – in the Abbaye?'

Micklen snorted again. 'Why was anyone in the Abbaye, Emily? Everyone was betraying everyone else. No one was safe and certainly not in the Abbaye. Fanchette was there with her Aunt Angevine and the rest of the family. For two nights the mob breached the prison to rape, torture and murder. Friends were torn apart before each other's eyes while the authorities looked on. Everyone expected to die.'

Emily pictured this long-distant time. She could understand the desperation to stay alive so it came as no surprise when Micklen said, 'Fanchette swapped favours to escape death and gained a pardon.'

However she was not ready for the knowledge that her *mother* then condemned her Aunt Angevine and the rest of the family to the guillotine with her allegation they were traitors to the revolution. 'Fanchette's fortunes were assured when her aunt's were confiscated.' Micklen's tone was full of pride.

How much more must she listen to? Her *mother* had done this? Through dry lips she repeated, 'So my mother survived. Why didn't she keep me?'

It made no sense … unless her father – this man – had gained from it.

Of course he had. 'Fanchette was in love with revolution, not with me. She had no desire to be encumbered with an infant. The only person she loved was her useless sister, Margeurite. Yes, Emily. In return for a handsome sum she saddled me with Margeurite as a wife and you as our child.' Emily's mouth dropped open. Grief washed over her as she muttered, 'She might as well have abandoned us. You never loved me and you certainly never loved mama. I mean, Tante Margeurite.'

Micklen chuckled. 'True enough, but few marriages are based on love. If you were less idealistic you'd have appreciated your *noble* Major McCartney better, and run clear of your *i*gnoble Jack Noble.' He drew breath and answered, crisply. 'I did it, Emily, because I needed money and Fanchette threatened to expose activities which would have prevented my return to England. As it was, I was ready to return and a docile, grateful – and crippled – wife suited me quite well.'

Her brain was working like an abacus. There was still so much to piece together. Jessamine, for one thing. Hesitantly, she said, 'So after you took us back to England, Fanchette collected her other daughter – my half-sister Jessamine – and began her life as a revolutionary in earnest.'

She heard his gusty sigh. 'It was a few years before Fanchette's maternal instincts came to the fore. She claimed Jessamine when the girl was about ten, but Jessamine was plain and placid and a disappointment. She told me her mother was not kind to her.'

'*She* told you?'

'Yes. Jessamine appeared on my doorstep'—he paused, obviously to calculate, before adding—'about five years ago. She'd learned of the existence of her aunt and half-sister and arrived one night begging me to assist her. She'd walked for days, in rags, and appeared like a beggar. I could see she was Fanchette's daughter but without her mother's beauty or her grace.'

Emily remembered the night she'd seen the beggar arriving at the house and her father's carriage rumble down the driveway bearing the two of them away. With dawning clarity she whispered, 'But you didn't assist her, did you, Papa?'

'Like you, Emily, Jessamine posed too great a threat. Fanchette had betrayed me once. I wasn't about to offer refuge to her spawn who clearly risked my past being unearthed. There was a bounty on my head before I left England but, thanks to Fanchette's funds, I returned a gentleman; and, once I'd familiarised myself with the opportunities in these parts, a very wealthy one.'

The sound of small stones dislodging indicated he had risen. 'So I took Jessamine here. You are not alone, Emily, if that makes you feel any better.'

The realisation was shattering. Burning bile rose up her gullet. Micklen believed that Jessamine, the other offspring of the woman who'd betrayed him, had met her death here. Emily was not about to tell him otherwise.

For if Jessamine had survived, it gave hope to Emily that she, too, may survive.

'Several years after that,' said her father, 'Jack Noble arrived, introducing himself with a letter from Fanchette.'

'*Jack*? Sent by Aunt Fanchette? I mean, my *mother*?'

'Jack was on His Majesty's Service and had fallen in love with the daughter of Monsieur Delon with whom he lodged in Saint-Omer.'

'Madeleine,' Emily supplied, dully.

Acknowledging this with a grunt, her father went on, 'Madeleine was the third of Fanchette's bastard daughters and she'd been adopted by Monsieur Delon. Like you, she was beautiful, but unlike you, she was obedient to her parent. Fanchette had kept in secret contact with Madeleine and was determined the girl would marry Count Levinne, so Madeleine rejected Jack Noble's offer of marriage and she and Fanchette sent him here, to Micklen House, to court you, Emily.' A certain reluctant admiration crept into his tone as he said, 'Fanchette is a determined woman and she ensured I would benefit from assisting her in her aim of bringing you into her fold through Noble.' He gave a snide laugh. 'Noble's task was easy. He had only to look at you and you melted at his feet.'

His words brought back afresh the pain of Jack's betrayal. Jack had seemed smitten. Love at first sight, she'd truly believed.

But like everything in her life, it was a lie.

The sound of dislodged pebbles sounded the ominous note that her father was preparing to leave her.

'You're going?' she cried, as the light was extinguished and the sound of Micklen scrabbling to get a foothold on the rocks signalled there would be no last-minute reprieve. 'Don't go! Please!'

'The tide is rising, Emily, and I must cross the shale to the cliffside. I've told you everything you need to know.

Answered all your questions. It's unfair of you to detain me further when my feet might get wet.'

'You can't leave me, father!' she screamed, tearing at the rocks with her bare hands. 'What will John say when you return to the carriage without me? He'll know you've left me here. He's my friend. I've known him since I was a little girl.'

'John will ask no questions when I tell him you're waiting for a secret lover to spirit you away.'

'He'll never believe you.'

'Of course he won't. And he'll be sad for you, Emily, but he knows I have the power to see his entire family dance at the end of a rope. A little illicit trading carries harsh penalties and he know the risks they take.'

Everything felt raw. Her throat, her face, the tips of her fingers. She imagined them as bloodied stumps, stinging as the sea water rose and swirled her about her dark prison.

'How much longer do I have? Just tell me that?'

His voice echoed back, faint and indistinct. 'A few more hours for reflection, Emily. It'll be quick. It's a pleasant death, I'm told. There'll be no pain.'

CHAPTER 23

Lying on his stomach near the summit of a hillside damp with dew shining in the moonlight, Angus scanned the outbuildings and surrounds of Micklen Hall. He felt as if he were in Spain again, just before he'd been captured and made a prisoner of war for six months.

Dawn had not yet broken. The previous night's storm had swept through quickly and the ground was scattered with debris. He'd hoped the weather had prevented Micklen from leaving his home with Emily, but after quickly scouting the stables, Angus had been dismayed to find the carriage was absent. He prayed that Micklen had left town on other business before Emily arrived.

Emily was clearly an innocent pawn. The fact she was Jack Noble's betrothed and perhaps Fontenay's daughter did not make her a traitor, and Angus would prove it.

But first he needed to find his wife.

From his position on the rise, about twenty yards away, Angus was surprised to see a thin woman emerge from the kitchen, onto the back steps. She put her hand to her forehead and appeared to scan the hillside, as if looking for someone.

Although he'd only met her twice, he thought it looked like Lucy. The maidservant had been concerned enough for her young mistress to risk the master's displeasure all those months ago when she'd told Angus and Jonathan that Emily needed help – which meant she was the only person he could trust who might be able to help him now.

He had to take the chance it was Lucy.

With a furtive look to satisfy himself she was alone, Angus emerged from the shelter of the trees and strode down the hill, astonished when she ran towards him.

'Major McCartney! Sir, you've come quicker than I'd hoped!' she cried as he drew her into the cover of the beech wood. 'As soon as the master took Miss Emily away I sent the bootboy to find you, only there weren't no way he'd get to Dover quickly with no horse and I had to hope to the lad's cunning.'

'I came of my own volition, Lucy, when I learned Emily had escaped here after being held on suspicion of spying for England.' If Lucy had sent for him, the situation must be as grave as he feared.

Lucy grasped an overhanging branch and covered her mouth. 'I could tell you a thing or two about the *master* but ain't no time now. He's taken Miss Emily away with him and I fear for her life, sir, and that's the truth.'

'When?'

'Late last night, sir. He put her in the carriage and drove north along the cliff road.'

Angus felt sick. Emily had been in Micklen's hands for hours.

Quickly, he untethered Saladin. "Lucy, will you ride with me and show me the way?" he asked, adjusting the saddle for an extra passenger when she agreed. 'And then you can tell me why you think Miss Emily is in danger from her father?'

'The master's not all he seems,' Lucy said as Angus pulled her up in front of him. 'Mr Micklen's got that many secrets – don't ask me what they are – I jes know he'll do anything to keep them and I'm afeared he'll do to Emily the same as he did to the lass that he took away 'bout five years ago.'

'Jessamine?'

'I never knew her name. Charlie and I were in the kitchen when she came a-knockin'. She were French and so bedraggled, which is why it were that strange the master would put her in 'is carriage and take her off, alone. I told me bruvver to follow in secret. He'd come on 'is own horse, which were lucky for he were able to keep up, though 'e had to wait some time till the master had left again, but Charlie got to the cave in time to rescue the girl before the tide came in. If ever there were a hero it were Charlie Gilroy. He kept her safe and then took her to Spain with him.'

Gilroy. Jessamine had taken the name Gilroy when she'd married the English foot soldier who had rescued her. Her final words of so long ago came back to haunt him and he shivered. 'Charlie Gilroy was the only hero I've known. He saved me from drowning in a cave while you, Angus McCartney, would see me dead!'

Lucy's voice broke. 'But Charlie died out there in Spain and I don't know what 'appened to the girl, only now I fear my Emily is going to the same dark place. Take the right turning 'ere, sir. We're on the coastal road and must turn north. Lordy knows how I'll ever find it when there are so many secret caves, but Charlie said it were about four miles past the crossroads. I'll pray for a sign, sir.'

A faint mist dampened Angus's face, chilling him to the bone as the inevitable questions churned in his mind. Why would Micklen murder his own daughter?

They passed another rider coming in the opposite direction. Angus decided not to stop him. Who could he trust when Micklen exerted so much influence in the area? What secrets needed to be guarded so closely that he'd be prepared to murder to protect them? Smuggling was the obvious one, in which case half the coastal population in these parts was probably in some way involved.

When Lucy tugged at his coat to indicate for him to slow down, they both scanned the coastline. It was empty and offered no clues.

Dull hopelessness lodged in the pit of Angus's stomach. The steep cliffs were riddled with caves. If Lucy didn't know exactly where Micklen had taken Jessamine, how on earth would they find Emily in time?

Emily was made aware of the breaking dawn by the sound of calling sea birds. She opened her eyes and could see the grey sky through the chink between the stone and the tunnel wall. Stiffly, she shifted position. She'd hoped to fall asleep; hoped that death might carry her away without pain. But she was still a prisoner. She still had death to look forward to, for rescue would not be forthcoming.

In the dark Emily had explored every inch of the tunnel as best she could. Her fingers were numb, her throat was sore and her head throbbed. The boulder had been firmly wedged into the opening and she'd found no other exit.

If Jessamine had been rescued it must have been because Micklen had been followed, but hours had passed since Micklen had lured Emily here. It was clear he had not been followed this time.

Which meant Emily was doomed.

For a few minutes she allowed herself the catharsis of

tears, but then her mouth grew dry and she realised she was desperately thirsty.

In a short while there'd be no shortage of water, though not the kind she needed. The sound of the sea as it lapped the rocks just a couple of feet lower down taunted her.

She wondered if Angus would ever learn what became of her. Was he in Calais, fired up with the excitement of a mission soon to be completed? At least Major Woodhouse had warned him of Madeleine.

Madeleine.

Her half-sister.

Her nemesis.

What did Emily feel? She was too cold to feel anything.

No, that wasn't true. She was frightened. Death would be here soon and in the short time remaining she had only the solace of knowing Angus had loved her. He'd been entranced by her happiness, not her beauty, for, oh, how happy she'd been when the brave and handsome Jack Noble had led her proudly through the Assembly rooms after she'd agreed to be his wife. But Emily had been nothing to Jack. He'd been in love with Madeleine since she'd tempted him over to the traitor's side. No wonder Jack had prolonged the engagement. He'd been so in love with Madeleine he'd do anything for her.

Even marry a woman he didn't love. Emily.

Why?

Because Emily was similar enough in looks to Madeleine to please him, and Madame Fontenay – Emily's *mother* – wanted to bring Emily back into the fold. She thought she could convince Emily to turn against England and it would please her to have a loving daughter in her twilight years.

Then Jack died and Angus was conveniently made Jack's replacement.

Emily had no wish to dwell on either her mother or

Micklen. She'd try and think happy thoughts about Angus. 'Oh, Angus …' Taking a deep breath, she shouted his name once more but the sound was muffled. It did not even give her the satisfaction of echoing as it would have had she been in the cavern of the cave.

Everything she might try would be futile. Angus was already on his way to Calais, if not there already. Lost to her. Forever.

She began to cry again, taunted by images of the horrors of the recent past interspersed with the unhappiness Micklen had unleashed by his long-ago actions when he'd saved the Laurent family from the Abbaye. She imagined the horror Jessamine must have experienced when she'd been lured to this very place. Jessamine, who'd lived on to perhaps experience brief happiness before—

No point dwelling on Angus's role in Jessamine's life. She did not blame him for acting as he had done.

It all came back to this cave. Perhaps even this narrow, cramped tunnel where her half-sister had crouched, like her, in terror.

Jessamine.

Emily tried to quash the irrational anger and feel sorrow for the girl but she could not when she knew Jessamine had survived beyond the cave but Emily would not.

Because of Jessamine, Angus had married Emily. Perhaps because of Jessamine, Emily was here now.

A STRONG HEAD wind slowed them but since they had no clear direction it didn't matter. Somewhere nearby Angus's wife was imprisoned, but the fact he did not know where nearly drove him insane. Soon, he'd have the blood of both Emily and Jessamine on his hands.

After another fifteen minutes' hard riding, Lucy signalled Angus to stop and he slowed his mount, urging it towards the cliff face. He sensed Lucy's doubt as they stared at the hopeless scene below. Several paths in the vicinity led down to the shore but the tide had swallowed up the shaley beach. Foaming white waves broke over the rocks.

He felt Lucy tremble as he placed a hand on her shoulder and the face she turned towards him was bleak. 'I thought I could tell you, sir, truly I did but— Oh me Gawd!' She broke off, shrinking into his arms.

'What is it?'

Her voice was a thread of terrified sound. 'It's the master. We must get out o' here!'

Angus tightened his grip to stop her sliding as he turned to see Bartholomew Micklen's carriage lumbering towards them on the coastal road, a small speck lit by lanterns, which grew larger as it rounded a bend about half a mile away before coming to a stop. White hot fury powered through him. He wheeled his horse back to the road and galloped to meet it, ignoring Lucy's pleas to turn tail, squinting against the wind as he watched the coachman jump from the box and run to the edge of the cliff. The carriage was now identifiable as Micklen's and the man a servant to judge from his serviceable brown coat and muffler and the brown felt hat that was swept away by the wind as he collapsed to his knees as Angus and Lucy drew near.

'John!' screamed Lucy as Angus reined in his mount, helping her down before she tumbled. They ran to where the coachman was crouching, his hand shading his eyes as he scanned the angry sea below. Tears coursed down the old man's face as he looked up, but he did not speak.

'Where's Emily?' Angus hauled the thick-set fellow to his feet and John stabbed a finger towards the beach. 'The master made me take him all the way to Dover the moment we left here. There weren't no chance o' coming back to save her. I'd a done so, God's honour I would have. Only, he knew it, too ...'

Angus had to let him go. He bent double, hands on his knees as he felt the bile rise up his gullet.

He twisted his head and stared into the foaming sea which roared into the entrance of a large cave a little to the right. The track that led down the cliff face was entirely swallowed up by the swirling water.

John's tone was hopeless. 'I thought I might get here before the tide was up and if I could swim, God's truth, I might still do it, too—'

'Is there a way, John?' Angus knew he was clutching at straws as he heard the fevered hope in his voice. 'Where *exactly* is she?'

'There's a tunnel near the roof of the cave.' John ran a grimy hand over his face which was streaked with mud and tears. 'The master lured Miss Emily into it then blocked it up with a stone, knowing she'd drown when the tide came up.'

Angus strained to see where John was pointing and hope clawed a jagged path through him as he realised the top of the cave was not entirely inundated.

'There might be hope!' he shouted over the wind. 'Look.' 'But the sea is fierce, sir.' John turned away, shaking his head, already conceding defeat. 'Even if you could swim you'd be dashed to bits against the rocks.'

Angus ignored him, peeling off his jacket then tearing off his boots.

'Careful, sir,' Lucy cried after him as he began to descend the path that led to the cave, although the last couple of yards which led directly to the cave were well under water.

He chose a launching point as close to the entrance as possible, plunging in and gasping at the cold. Immediately, he sought something to cling to and felt a long, flat ridge of rock. A split second later the force of the current sent him spinning against a far less hospitable outcrop. Unless he formed a better strategy he would be slashed to ribbons and then what use would he be to Emily? Taking a deep breath he dived beneath the surface and propelled himself as far into the cave as his breath would allow. He had to believe that John's information about an inner tunnel were true.

Debris swirled around him and he could see nothing until his out-thrust arms came into contact with a ledge of some sort. He hauled himself out of the water, choking, and dashed the water from his eyes as he looked about him, thanking Providence for the rays of breaking dawn that supplemented the moonlight. The cave curved around on three sides, large boulders reaching to the ceiling. Raising his head, he searched for possibilities. An oddly wedged rock, just a few feet beneath the ceiling of the cave, caught his attention and he began to climb.

'Emily!' he shouted. His voice sounded oddly truncated, battling with the roar of the sea. He didn't wait for an answer but grappled over the boulders until he reached what hope and instinct suggested might be the entrance to the tunnel he was looking for.

Several smaller rocks had been used to secure a much larger boulder in place. He slid his fingers into the narrow space on either side to inch them out.

Straining his ears, he thought he heard a sound, but then all his concentration was focussed on withdrawing the boulder in the few minutes left before there was no air and the chamber was entirely submerged.

With a final grunt of effort he fell backwards as the rock dislodged. Already the water was swirling at his ankles for the tide was rising fast.

'Emily!' He peered into the gloom, the brief exuberance

he'd allowed himself tempered by the fact he could see no sign of her.

Despairingly, he cried out her name again, pushing himself into the narrow tunnel, aware that mere minutes would seal his fate, condemning him to a watery grave.

'*Angus?*'

Disbelievingly, he straightened then plunged his arm into the darkness. '*Emily?*' He felt something warm. Warm and damp. His fingers closed around what he believed … hoped … was his wife and pulled.

Pulled until he had dragged her to the entrance where she tumbled and splashed, sobbing, into his arms.

For a brief moment he allowed himself the joy of holding her like this: throbbing with life and wanting him as she wept, 'I thought you'd never find me. I thought I would die. I prayed you'd come, but I thought you were in France and I'd never see you again.'

'Hush,' he calmed her, gripping onto the boulder to maintain balance for them both while her warmth and closeness filled him with the hope and energy he needed to get them out of here alive. The water that was already up to his knees kept knocking him off his feet.

'I'll always be there when you need me, Emily.' Fierce tenderness rushed through him, carrying fear and urgency in its wake.

She buried her head against his chest, balling her fists beside her face as he held her, but now she drew away with a gasp as she looked around them. 'It's too late.' Reproach mixed with the deepest terror. 'Why did you come? I do not deserve your love.' She gasped as the reality of the situation appeared to sink in. 'Now we'll *both* die.'

'I could never leave you. But Emily, we still have a chance. Can you swim? Well, thank God for that. If you can hold your breath and keep with me for about a minute … perhaps two … we can make it.' The knowledge that they must negotiate about 30 feet of eddying water, then further perils before dragging themselves onto the rocks – if they were lucky enough to reach that far – struck cold terror into his heart. Her trusting look galvanised his determination that he would not fail her. He gripped the back of her dress. 'I'm going to have to rip this off, Emily. You'll die otherwise.'

He grasped both sides of her bodice and tore, shredding the once-elegant evening gown from neck to hem. She twisted in his embrace as the current carried the garment away, twining her arms around his neck and murmuring into her kiss, 'God be with you, Angus, but don't sacrifice yourself for me—'

Before he could respond she signalled her understanding of their peril by tugging his wrist and plunging deeper into the water.

'Hold onto me, Emily,' were his last words. 'And don't let go.'

Taking a deep breath he kicked off with as much force as he could muster, going deep to best navigate the churning waters.

… until his lungs were fit to bursting and he had no choice but to surface, thanking God Emily was still with him.

But not for long. A wave caught them as they reached open water, tearing them apart and hurling Angus upon a mercifully flat rock where his seeking hands found the handhold he so desperately needed. Dashing the water from his eyes, he cast around for sight of Emily. Nothing. Oh God, he'd been so close. Where was she?

By the time he'd located her she'd been carried further down the coast. John was already at the spot where her body had lodged against a huge boulder while Lucy's anguished cry, torn away by the wind, struck terror into his heart.

He hauled himself onto dry land, negotiating the rocks

and boulders on frozen feet until he reached the pair, waist deep in water, arms outstretched. Emily's motionless body bobbed, face downwards, eluding them by a couple of tantalising feet.

Barking orders to link hands, he lunged forward, grasping Emily by the hair in order to drag her to the edge. The wind lashed them and gulls swooped, a mocking tone to their cry as the trio struggled to manhandle Emily's unconscious body up the rest of the cliff and onto the flat. There was no life in her, he saw, and when he rolled her on her side and pushed back her dark hair he saw a bloody gash across her forehead. 'Emily!' he cried, raising her to his chest and squeezing her tightly, despair turning to joy as she choked and spluttered in his arms.

CHAPTER 24

The publican's wife found dry clothes for both of them and put them in the best bedchamber while John and Lucy returned to Micklen Hall.

Emily and Angus now sat before the fire, wrapped in nothing but linen towels, shivering while two young maids filled a large tub with hot water.

After they'd left, Angus rose, extending his hand towards Emily. The catharsis of finding her alive and having her close by him was more than he could put into words.

'You first,' he said softly, taking her by the shoulders and leading her towards the welcoming tub of steaming suds. 'If you die from a chill it would be a poor way to repay my exertions.'

His words broke through the silence that had settled upon them now that the danger was over. The smile she forced was distant and he could see she was in shock, so when her legs buckled he whisked her into his arms.

Her hair was damp against his bare shoulder and her warm breath against his cold skin made the hair on his chest and the back of his neck prickle into awareness.

The linen strip had fallen away and he cupped her breast, his eyes meeting hers as she responded with sudden awareness.

Her arms tightened around him and she buried her head in his chest.

'Oh, Angus, I can't believe you found me,' she whispered, clinging to him with all her strength. 'My father tried to kill me. Only ... he's not my real father.' She choked on her loathing.

Shocked, he gripped her shoulders before scooping her up to place her into the bathtub. A moment's reflection decided him there was room to join her. Though cramped, it would be the best place to question her, giving her the time she needed to answer. And by God it was heaven to feel her limbs pressed against his. He took her arm and gently began to soap it.

'Micklen is not your father?' he repeated, shaking his head. 'I suppose that explains a great deal.'

'My whole life has been a lie.' Her voice broke. 'When I thought I would die, that didn't matter.' She bit her lip, resting her head on his shoulder. 'But ... now it changes everything.'

Angus dropped the sponge to take both her hands in his. He had to reassure her. 'Emily, I loved you for what I saw with my own eyes, not what I believed you to be. Your parents may not be who you thought they were, but you are entirely innocent. Don't think Woodhouse and his like can hurt you.'

She squeezed his fingers, dropping her gaze as she whispered, 'The man who brought me up is a murderer and my real mother is a traitor. Oh yes, and a murderess, too, it would seem. Both would see you die, Angus and they have killed other brave men like you.'

Angus moved position so he could put his arm about her

shoulder. Then, after giving up the attempt to keep the bath water from sloshing all over the floor he drew her onto his lap. Tightening his embrace he whispered against her ear, 'You have been raised in innocence, Emily. Major Woodhouse and everyone else who matters will realise this.' The uncomfortable truth hung between them. Emily remained a traitor in the government's eyes unless her innocence could be proved.

'Jack was a traitor, too, Angus, and not just to me.' She clenched her hands together as if to stem some terrible pain and Angus waited for her to finish. 'Jack was already in love with Madeleine when my mother – this woman, Madame Fontenay – sent him to find Micklen and ... to court me.'

A sob truncated her words before she poured out what Bartholomew Micklen had told her, some of which Angus knew already, some of which he'd suspected.

Stroking her hair, he let her talk. It was important to establish the facts before he took Emily to bed. That would be a glorious respite before he continued his journey to France on the next tide. If he could learn as much of the truth as could be pieced together, he'd better know how to proceed.

So Emily told Angus everything Micklen had revealed and when the bath water had grown cold and she was shivering against him, Angus lifted her out and held her, both of them naked, before the heat of the fire.

Emily studied her handsome husband surreptitiously beneath lowered lashes as he crouched to stoke up the fire. His long, lean flanks and muscled chest were bronzed by the glow of the firelight in the dim room and his clean, strong profile hinted at the intensity of his thoughts. He'd deposited her onto the bed where he was about to join her but, practical as ever, he needed to ensure their continued comfort before he could act upon the desire she knew consumed him.

Jack would have hurled himself upon her and she'd have been overcome by the force of his uncontainable passion. Foolish, naïve child that she was, she'd have taken that as a greater avowal of his love than the thoughtful self-containment of this man who was her husband.

She felt proud in that moment. Eager and desperate for him in the next. When he smiled unexpectedly as he turned and caught her eyes upon him it was like the sun had found a chink in her armour and was pooling inside her. Soon, there'd be no more darkness within.

Then she remembered that she was the traitor, the reluctant wife, believing at one time or another it seemed, everything but the truth.

Soon Angus would climb under the covers beside her and love her.

Her happiness, however, depended on convincing *herself* that he believed in her.

He put down the poker, eyebrows raised at her attempt at a smile, perhaps misinterpreting her uncertainty when in fact her need for Angus was like a fierce beast within her, raging to be released.

'Come to me, Angus.' She was glad she'd said the words rather than waiting, pliant, for something changed in his expression.

His smile gained warmth. Swiftly he crossed the thin hearthrug to the bed and she stretched out one arm to greet him as he pulled back the counterpane and slid in beside her, his warmth and the smoothness of his long, muscled limbs making her tremble.

He gathered her in his arms and she curled into him, revelling in the touch of moist, heated skin on skin as she twined her hands through his soft, light hair.

This was her husband in the guise she should have recognised from the start: tender, sure of himself, the brave protector.

Swiftly, he touched his lips to hers, gently, without hesitation while he contoured her face with his hands, as if committing her outline to memory. For the knowledge that soon he would leave her hung between them.

'I'm so proud you're my husband,' she whispered.

Passion simmered between them as he murmured against her ear, 'I'm so proud of the wife who did what she had to in order to survive.'

'But do you trust me?'

She tensed for his answer though she knew it already. He had to say he did, but doubt would lurk in the wings when he'd withdrawn. It would be their constant companion as he travelled across the sea and as Mademoiselle Delon cast her lures, the beauty who would enslave him: to herself and her cause.

She raised herself on her elbows, cupping his face and looking deep into his eyes, cutting short his answer.

'You go to France to extinguish that great threat, Madame Fontenay – my *mother*, Angus – and you rely on the support of Madeleine Delon, my half-sister: a traitor. The lover of *my* dead fiancé. Can you trust *me*?'

He rolled over, breaking her clasp and rising above her to cage her body with his. The tender understanding in his expression nearly broke her heart. She had no doubt that he loved her.

He cradled her within the sanctuary of his warmth. 'You have grown up in ignorance. It's what saved you from being my enemy and England's enemy and it's what will save you when Major Woodhouse pushes you to answer his allegations.' Still supporting himself with one arm he used the other to cup her cheek. She'd never seen such fierce tenderness. 'I will protect you, Emily,' he whispered. 'I swear.'

She nearly wept at the fire in his eyes and her heart answered his desire to sweep aside all that might stand between them. 'I will protect you because I love you *and* I trust you.'

Tears welled up behind her eyes. She smiled. 'Thank you.' Then she gripped his wrist as anger at her past rose up inside her. 'Do what you have to, Angus. Do what you must to bring those foul traitors to justice.' She steeled herself from putting into words the misery which lay heavy on her chest. *Kill my mother if you have to, for she is nothing to me and a threat to everything I hold dear.*

'I may have no choice, Emily.' He stroked her face and she trembled at the featherlike touch. His gentleness was the prelude to so much danger and violence. For if traitors did not die, the innocent would.

With a sigh, she raised her arms to pull him down to her. It was time. It was real. Real in a way the other times had not been.

He recognised the signal, for he deepened his kiss and she felt the fire within her combust and burn more fiercely. She grasped his buttocks and wrapped her legs around his waist, rubbing her body against him, willing him to end this exquisite agony by claiming her wholly.

Still, he made sure to control his own urges before seeing she was lost in a sea of desire for him, as he kissed her deeply and suckled her nipples and stroked her into fierce arousal. Only when Angus finally abandoned his self-restraint and became fierce and single-minded in his possession of her did Emily let herself go, plunging into a mindless oblivion of love and lust that swept away everything but her sense of union with this man who'd made her whole.

PEACE. Perfect peace.

Beneath the thick green eiderdown Emily nestled against her husband and wondered if she'd cut off all circulation to his arm which curled about her.

She judged it to be early afternoon. Soon Angus would ride off, and on the evening tide he'd board the vessel that would smuggle him across the channel.

He stirred and in a whisper she voiced the fears that had plagued her since she'd woken.

'Angus – I'm afraid for you.'

Glorying in the aftermath of such extraordinarily intense lovemaking, Emily cupped his cheek as she gazed at her husband, still half asleep, his expression surprisingly gentle in repose. All the fears she'd entertained for her own life just hours before were now reserved for Angus. 'You are returning to a nest of vipers. Madeleine—'

Instantly alert, he caught her wrist and twisted onto his side, resting on his elbow so he could look at her. His scar stood out in relief and his eyes blazed with so many things: sincerity and the need to put her fears to rest.

'Let me worry about Madeleine,' he reassured her, though she did not miss the flicker in his expression that hinted at a deeper emotion. 'I know how to guard my back.' His gaze darkened. 'The irony is that you must be protected from Major Woodhouse until I have the evidence to exonerate you.' Emily jerked up into a sitting position with a gasp. 'He may already be on his way here.' The terror was back, sucking her brief joy into a black void.

'We're probably safer here than anywhere for the moment.' Angus's smile was clearly calculated to soothe her. 'Major Woodhouse will be seeking you further afield. He'll think you've gone with your—' He checked himself. 'With

Micklen. Woodhouse is probably in Dover, though he may have followed Micklen across the channel when he sees I did not make today's rescheduled packet. Micklen will have found a place on board. While you were sleeping I altered my plans. A boatload of men are waiting to take me once darkness has fallen.'

For a serious man, assessing life-threatening risks, his grin was surprisingly boyish. 'I should have been gone now, my love, had there not been more important things to do.' He reached up for her and pulled her back under the covers, holding her tightly.

All senses on high alert, she quivered, her body crying out for him once more.

He did not disappoint her, his hands skimming her body, sharpening her senses.

His mouth quirked. 'I have but ten minutes, though perhaps we can to go over everything we did earlier in that time.' He kissed her deeply. 'Not the talking, Emily, but the loving. And then I shall settle funds upon the landlady to ensure you are well looked after and kept hidden while I am gone.'

She curled into him, as if to absorb his warmth, his strength and all the goodness he could offer her, mourning the sudden coldness of his retreat for just an instant; relishing what was to come.

'I have taken every precaution for your safety,' he whispered as he rose above her like a demigod in the flickering firelight. 'I'll let no harm come to you and I'll return soon.'

Molten heat pooled in her lower belly as she felt his erection press against her thigh; preparing himself, readying her. He was reassuring her that she had nothing to fear.

And while he was close and loving her, she had none.

CHAPTER 25

A ngus had left Woodhouse with assurances he would discover the truth.

He'd left Emily with avowals of the same.

Now, in the grand chateau at Pliny, he believed he was on the verge of finding the evidence to exonerate Emily.

And so much more.

Angus answered to both Levinne, the French spymaster, and Woodhouse, the English coordinator of a network uniting regime-weary French, English and other nationalities in the common goal of bringing an end to Bonaparte's empire.

If all went well, the mission at Pliny would unmask the network of collaborators who would neutralise these anti-French agents at the same time as revealing Napoleon's next strategic initiative.

Madeleine's guile and beauty made her the ideal candidate to set a honey trap for Napoleon's ageing, trusted general, Bethune, who came directly from a military meeting with the emperor and who possessed a map the English would very much like to get their hands on. Angus, from

Levinne's point of view, fulfilled the criteria for the so-called husband who would protect his betrothed, though Angus was under no illusions as to their respective roles.

Madeleine had a different agenda. Information supplied by Monsieur Fonentay suggested his wife would be at Pliny to oversee Madeleine, who was under orders to deliver to Angus a false map and information he would dispatch to England.

And unless Angus could unmask Madeleine for the traitor she was with proof of her connection to Madame Fontenay, Emily, his adored wife, was a branded woman, unsafe on English soil.

Emily's life depended on the subtlety with which he managed Madeleine tonight.

So as he and Mademoiselle Delon strolled side by side in the gardens while their trunks were being unpacked in their respective chambers, Angus assumed an air of polite indifference and prayed Madeleine would not test his resources too early.

The evening was closing in with lighted lanterns along the formal walks, lending a romantic air to the entertainment, but Angus's thoughts were far from romantic – except when they strayed to his tender parting with Emily.

Emily, who was hiding in a tavern not far from her childhood home.

Fortunately Angus had credible information that Woodhouse was in France, perhaps even here tonight. No doubt his erstwhile friend feared Angus had fallen under the influence of his 'turncoat' wife. Perhaps he was even sketching out the preliminaries of Angus's court martial.

Madeleine was in a flirtatious mood as she plucked at a flower amidst the herbaceous borders. 'You, Monsieur McCartney, will be the handsomest man at Chateau Pliny tonight.' She slanted a sloe-eyed smile at him, adding, 'Yet I am supposed to be insensible to my *husband's* charms while I run my hands all over the fat general.' Her coy regret disgusted him and prompted a surge of longing for the lovely wife whose safety depended on him.

'Look at that fat burgher's wife dressed up like a princess.' Madeleine halted on the manicured gravel pathway amongst fountains and topiary-edged terraces and pointed to a carriage which had drawn up in front of the sweeping steps to disgorge its fabulously garbed occupants. 'A pork chop! Will I not be irresistible to General Bethune this evening?'

'You'll have to be, otherwise our plans are nothing.' Madeleine was to render the general insensible from drink, then steal the key he kept on a chain around his neck when she helped him to his room. It was believed the general's desk, which he took everywhere with him, was the most likely place to find the documents and maps he'd brought from his meeting with Napoleon.

Preening at Angus's grunted assent, Madeleine squeezed his arm. 'I passed him in the hall. When I said I admired a dissertation he'd given at Madame Picard's salon in Paris he was vastly flattered.'

'With the array of tricks up your sleeve, Mademoiselle Delon, you are assured of success.' Angus strove for gallantry before adding drily, 'Just don't try them on me.'

She slanted her wicked amber eyes up at him once more. 'You are less susceptible than most,' she conceded, 'but then, you are recently married.' She made a noise of disgust. 'Was it a love match?'

'On my part.' Immediately he regretted speaking so frankly.

'Perhaps, *mon mari*, I could pull out some of these tricks you refer to from up my sleeve and show how you might win this heart of Miss Micklen's which still belongs to Jack. You are a very attractive man, but clearly your wife does not appreciate you.'

'Save them for the general, Mademoiselle Delon.' Steering her back in the direction of the house, Angus was relieved it was time to part. 'You are a beautiful woman, but I don't need your help beyond the requirements of tonight.'

'Ah, tonight,' she purred and Angus regretted his poor choice of words. He'd stopped thinking of himself as clumsy with the opposite sex, but he realised how careful he must be to navigate the next hour with Madeleine until they were in public territory. Especially when Madeleine trailed an elegantly gloved forefinger the length of his arm and whispered, 'You need much help from me tonight, my handsome husband, and you know it.'

Madeleine took his hand and led him behind the high yew wall of the maze. 'A moment's privacy, my lord, so we may review our strategy now that we are at our location? It will be our only chance.'

It was true but he must be careful. Madeleine might decide now was the time to try to recruit him to her cause like she recruited the susceptible Jack Noble.

The moment they were shielded from prying eyes she rounded on him, her eyes flaring with challenge and disdain. 'Tonight you play the role of my husband, but I think you do not know how to be anyone's husband. Do you?' she added, with an air of hauteur when she failed to elicit more than a sardonic smile.

'Emily can answer that, Mademoiselle Delon.'

Clearly she was irritated at failing to whip up more of a response. 'That little dormouse? You are a fool, Monsieur! You think your Emily will love kind, tame, patient Major McCartney like she loved charming, devil-may-care Jack Noble?' She seized his hand and pulled him along the path deeper into the maze. 'Is her *gratitude* sufficient for a man of your depth of feeling?'

He had not mistaken Emily's desire for gratitude and nor was it a question worth considering when right now he had much more cause to be afraid of Madeleine than Emily's feelings for him.

'What kind of a *man* are you, Major McCartney!'

Against the backdrop of yew trees which reached high above their heads, Madeleine with her flashing eyes in her scarlet gown was an arresting sight. She took a couple of agitated steps then angrily swung back to face him, her scarlet skirts frothing at her ankles.

So, thought Angus, this is when she tries to win me over, as she did Jack Noble.

'Has Emily ever looked at you like this? With aching want of you blazing from the depths of her soul?'

Her breathing was quick and shallow and for a moment Angus was mesmerised, not because he was susceptible but because she was such a malignant version of Emily's confident grace.

'A woman likes admiration, Major, and to be comfortable and cosseted, but there are times when she appreciates firmness.' Madeleine stepped close, her eyes focussed on his as her small hand crept up his arm. He imagined it was Emily's, her light, exploring fingertips conjuring magic, thrusting his emotions to combustible levels. He felt the blood pounding in his head and down to his extremities, then Madeleine's short, outraged intake of breath as he set her away from him, his voice sounding distant to his own ears as he murmured, 'In that case, you will appreciate my reminding you, Mademoiselle Delon, that we have an important job to accomplish tonight which precludes dalliance.'

Her mouth fell open. Perhaps she really had not expected

he would reject her. Certainly Angus did not expect the stinging slap to his cheek she delivered.

'You are a fool, Major McCartney,' she hissed, spinning away from him. 'Your tragedy is you do not know just *what* a fool you are.'

DESPITE HIS EARLIER REJECTION, it was with grudging admiration that Angus, who had made a conciliatory and fairly successful attempt to reconcile Madeleine, watched her insinuate herself into the general's circle.

Her feline grace and the effortless allure which instantly found its mark when she targeted Napoleon's fat and trusted acolyte, went some way to easing Angus's disturbed feelings. What had Madeleine hoped to achieve back there in the maze? If he had succumbed, was he guaranteeing his safety?

He'd been fairly confident it was too early for Madeleine to attempt to kill him, for he was needed as the conduit for the false information she and Madame Fontenay intended would be sent to Britain. Later tonight he would have to be more on his guard, and after such a round rejection Angus had no doubt he was a marked man. He only wished he knew exactly who his enemies were. Madeleine and the mysterious Madame Fontenay, to begin with. *Emily's mother.* He put it out of his mind. One thing at a time and first he must ensure Madeleine carried out her prescribed role.

But what of Levinne? And Monsieur Delon? He was all but certain they were not traitors, but how could he be sure? Pausing beneath a sconce of beeswax candles as the ballroom filled with fabulously garbed guests in full masquerade, Angus wondered how Madeleine could exude such apparently genuine desire for the grey-haired mausoleum. The general, a portly war veteran in his sixties, was clearly flattered by the attention she lavished upon him, leaning towards her to catch a remark she'd made, ensuring her glass was replenished, and once, Angus was shocked to notice, brushing a stray lock of hair from across her breast after she rose from what appeared to be the less than discreet adjusting of her garter.

Madeleine was a consummate actress. Levinne must know it which was why he'd assigned her the role when hitherto he'd been reluctant to place his intended in any overt danger. Had Madeleine truly loved Jack Noble when they deceived Emily, or did she not know how to love?

Irrelevant right now, he thought, moving between the knots of guests while keeping Madeleine in his sights. Like a scarlet butterfly in her Lucrezia Borgia gown, she hovered about the general who was seated at the far end of the room with a bottle of claret at his right elbow. Even from a distance Angus saw how her eyes shone and her lips, slightly parted, glistened in the candlelight as she listened, rapt, to the general's monologue.

The woman was skilled at pretending feelings she did not harbour. Fleetingly, doubt returned as to whether Emily's feelings for Angus were strong enough to survive a lifetime. Without a dragon to slay or a churning sea from which to rescue her, would she remain content with a man less forthcoming with his feelings than easy natured Jack Noble?

A man whose very personality had, only weeks before, been anathema to her?

What had passed between them in the inn reassured him on every level. Now he just had to prove who the real villains were in order to ensure Emily's continued wellbeing.

CHAPTER 26

Angus.

Already he'd be travelling across the rutted roads of a country Emily believed she'd never visited. Towards danger and if she was not the direct cause, she was culpable.

Exhaustion and fear on her own account had been replaced by fear for her husband and a growing conviction that she was in a position to lessen the risks he faced.

That she needed to do *something*. Angus was too precious to lose.

Now, warming her hands in front of the fire in The Seagull's front private parlour, Emily glanced edgily at the door.

Captain Whibley would attend to her as soon as he returned, she'd been promised, though she had no idea if he would take her aboard *The Dundas*.

After Angus had left she'd slept the night through in a deep and dreamless slumber from which not even the fight in the taproom downstairs could wake her. She'd only heard about it later.

When she rose she felt refreshed, re-energised and

bursting with the knowledge that she was on the cusp of something truly remarkable and that her life would never be the same again.

Then the terror kicked in that her life would only be truly remarkable in a *good* sense if no harm befell Angus and if she could provide sufficient proof to avoid a remarkable end dangling from the hangman's rope.

But Angus was in even more immediate danger and only she could mitigate the threats he faced. She, with her perfect French and her resemblance to the Delon woman who plotted to kill him.

As for her mother, Emily felt nothing but loathing.

Caroline had intimated a woman must be content to prove herself within the domestic arena. But Emily had to prove her loyalty – to Angus and to her country – and that meant going to the Chateau Pliny.

Her brain whirled with plans as she absently watched the maidservant tend the fire. Wisps of red hair fell across the girl's face from beneath her grubby mob cap and her home-spun skirts and burlap apron were patched and darned. Angus's warning to keep a low profile and to wait for him to fetch her rang in her ears as she smoothed the fabric of the silk gown the publican's wife had found for her. Nervously she fingered the diamonds at her throat. No, she'd not change her mind. She had to go. What alternative did she have, for how would Angus prove her innocence when Major Woodhouse had all the evidence he believed proved her a traitor?

If Madame and Emily were half-sisters who looked so alike, it was enough to bolster Emily's belief that she could succeed in her mission to foil the plot which threatened Angus.

She had only to find her way to the Chateau in time. Chateau Pliny was clearly a grand residence, so she had to hope she'd not have too much difficulty getting directions once she was in Pliny. Surely, once there, she'd find a way to diminish or eliminate the threat posed by Madeleine and in the process prove her innocence and protect Angus.

If she remained hiding in the tavern, meekly waiting until someone claimed her, that person might not be Angus.

She must have made some noise for the maid glanced up from stoking the fire and said with evident surprise, 'You bin here all the time, ma'am? I was waitin' to tell you the cap'n will be about five minutes.' The girl's eyes lingered upon Emily's dress and her diamonds.

'Thank you.' Emily glanced nervously towards the door, the foolishness of her charade suddenly terrifying her.

'Sure he won't be long, either,' the maid said chirpily, 'for he's bin 'specting you, I hear and—'

'What!'

The girl raised her large brown eyes at Emily's tone and repeated, 'Bin 'specting you since a feller was here to tell him he was to specially look after a beautiful dark-haired lady what looked like you, ma'am. Oi! What yer doin?'

Emily sprang from the window seat and clutched the girl's shoulders. 'The captain's been expecting me, you say? Who was here asking after me? What do you know of the captain?'

'He does his business here, ma'am, seeing passengers what want to come aboard his boat.' The girl looked frightened by Emily's intensity. 'I ain't bin here so long. I only knows him by sight and I only heard there was a feller lookin' for a fine lady with black hair.'

Of course Woodhouse would think to look for her here – and her father, too, if he realised she'd escaped. Why hadn't she been more discreet? Emily thought quickly as she released her grip and the servant girl edged backwards.

Dear Lord, if the captain detained her …

'I saw you admire my dress?' The words came out too urgently. 'Would you like it in exchange for yours?'

The girl stared at Emily as if she were a madwoman. 'Course I like your dress, ma'am, but I hardly think—'

Emily grasped the mantelpiece for support while her head spun. 'Take me to one of the rooms upstairs. I feel ill, I need to lie down. Quickly!'

She could hear the bluff greeting of the captain as he put his head in at the tap room down the passage. Desperately, she continued, 'Tell the captain I need to put myself to rights and I'll be down to see him in—' She caught herself up as another serving girl entered the room. 'No! Tell your friend to pass on the message. I need your help in attending to me. Now!'

Emily was a lady and their job was to pander to the desires of The Seagull's patrons, however odd.

Once inside a sparsely furnished chamber on the second floor, she latched the door and ran to look out of the window.

If the captain had been told to look for a girl matching her description then she was doomed.

Whipping round to face the serving maid, Emily decided upon honesty. Angus had been generous to the publican but she had no coins to pave her way, leaving her vulnerable and ill prepared. Recruiting the carrot-haired maid seemed her only chance.

'I heard the other girl call you Susan,' she said. 'Yes? I need your help, Susan, to get to France ... but I am fleeing a bad man and the captain mustn't recognise me.' As she spoke she struggled with the catch of her diamond necklace. 'These are real diamonds ... I have no money so I'll have to pawn it.' She thrust it at the girl who stared at it stupidly. 'It's imperative I sail on the next tide and if you help me I will reward you handsomely. We'll need to swap clothes first.' She didn't wait for the girl's answer, knew that she could expect nothing more than the wide-eyed disbelief with which she was regarded as she hastily undid the buttons down the front of her gown before putting out her hands.

With a squawk Susan jumped backwards.

'*Please!*' Emily advanced towards her. 'Help me out of my dress then give me yours and take me somewhere I can get money for my jewels. I won't get what it's worth but I'll pay you a good sum up front and double it if you accompany me to France. I'd wager you'll get more than you'd earn in a year.'

It was apparently enough of an inducement and after a few minutes of frenzied activity Susan was out of her dirty cotton print and coarse burlap apron, pulling Emily's blue silk gown over her own head. When she objected that she could hardly carry off her charade as a lady Emily told her to say nothing. Emily would play the maid and speak for her mute mistress. Nobody who might be after her would look twice at the thin, plain red-headed maid dressed in her fine clothes.

By the time they heard Susan's fellow serving maid trudging up the stairs, possibly at the captain's behest, the two of them were already hurrying down the back steps to a pawnbroker with premises down a nearby back lane.

In a poor bargain, Emily handed over her diamonds for a sum of money and made a quick selection from the second-hand gowns hanging from the walls. These included a dark dress which might once have belonged to a parlour maid and an elaborate, old fashioned sacque gown her grandmother might have worn. The gown would be ideal to wear for the masquerade, as would the powdered wig she discovered that had gone of out fashion forty years before. These she bundled into a bag purchased for the journey, together with a few other necessary items.

With her maid's cap pulled down over her ears, Emily,

secured passage for her and her 'mistress' from the tavern, then she and her hopefully loyal companion were rowed out to *The Dundas*.

At first Susan could barely contain her excitement at wearing the gown Emily had been given by the publican's wife, fingering the coins which jingled in the purse that hung at her waist. She seemed a simple, good-natured girl and Emily prayed she'd remain so and not decide she preferred the role of mistress, since Emily had encouraged Susan to treat her with the disdainful manners of a superior to deflect attention from herself. Their roles would be reversed once more when Emily donned the elaborate sacque gown which was made of pink lutestring and adorned with yards of lace, bows and furbelows and which would be perfect for the masquerade.

Her impulsive decision to make the crossing disguised as Susan's maid was bolstered by the intensity with which the captain's rheumy gaze scoured the passengers on deck. By the time the boat drew anchor, Emily and Susan were safely ensconced in curtained bunks in the centre of the vessel.

Depending on the winds they might be in France in a little over three hours. A bad crossing, or if they were becalmed, made it anyone's guess. After that, they would have to negotiate the frightening unknown in order to make their way to the Chateau de Pliny.

While many of her fellow passengers bespoke lodgings at one of the ramshackle inns once they'd docked, Emily was glad she'd not been similarly weakened by seasickness. She needed to press on while she could. When she'd asked Angus how he intended making his way to the chateau she'd had no idea she would be following him within twenty-four hours.

He'd intended stopping a night with the Delons and thereafter would travel to the chateau in Madeleine's company. Emily knew that he would be dressed as a cardinal. The long, flowing robes could conceal a weapon and, if necessary, a sheaf of documents, but would Emily recognise him?

His height and military bearing might distinguish him amongst the crowd, but she had no idea how many guests were invited. With a surge of longing, she willed the coachman to drive the horses faster.

When it grew dark they stopped at another ramshackle inn and for an exorbitant amount slept the night through on mouldy sheets before resuming their long journey.

The sun was low on the horizon by the time Emily and Susan were set down at a crossroads not far from the chateau.

Darkness offered protection and as they walked they were passed on the road by a procession of carriages heading, Emily presumed and hoped, for the Chateau Pliny. Behind the hedgerows near the entrance to the estate Susan had changed into the unassuming clothes of the serving class and Emily donned her elaborate masquerade costume.

As the chateau rose before them, Emily felt a jolt of amazed self-satisfaction. She'd dared what most young women would never have dared. And she'd achieved the first, difficult part, which was to travel, unchaperoned, across a foreign country.

Certainly the danger increased the closer she got to the chateau, but with so much activity deflecting attention they were able to access the building, Emily in company with a group of well dressed guests, and Susan via the scullery. When they met on an upper floor without incident, Emily heaved her first sigh of relief. Angus could not be far away.

After quizzing several servants, in French, Emily was able to ascertain the location of Mademoiselle Delon's bedchamber.

Some guests were making their way to their respective chambers but others milled about in silks and diamonds and demi masks or elaborate masquerade costumes.

By a stroke of luck, Emily learned though several discreet inquiries that Madeleine had already gone downstairs to the saloon, giving Emily access to her adversary's bedchamber.

'Look for whatever you can find, Susan,' she directed once she'd closed the door softly behind them. The girl had been helpful and amenable the entire journey and Emily felt she had no option but to trust her fully. She'd imparted the necessary background to her escapade and Susan, no doubt strongly motivated by the fortune she carried with the expectation of soon doubling it, was fired by the adventure. 'Anything suspicious. Letters, weapons ...' Emily rose from a quick search beneath the pillows. 'Madeleine Delon will baulk at nothing, I assure you. We need to outwit her if my husband is to stay safe and we are to foil the real villains ... and I am to pay you.'

As Susan redoubled her efforts at ferreting out something to please her mistress, Emily made for the door. 'I must find my husband now, but if you hear anything you are to pretend you're a servant attending to the fire in Mademoiselle Delon's chamber, is that understood?'

ANGUS RAN a weary hand across his brow as he watched Madeleine sitting on the general's knee. The general had downed another bottle of claret and laughingly, Madeleine dabbed at his moustache with the hem of her rich brocade gown, revealing the scarlet garter that tied the white stocking of her shapely right leg in the process and exciting the general mightily.

She was succeeding nicely in getting him drunk.

In his guise as a man of the cloth Angus raised his eyes heavenward.

What happened after Madeleine enticed the general to his bedchamber? The question had consumed him from the moment he'd led her away from her father and Count Levinne. Were *they* to be trusted?

'Will you hear my confession, Father?' A familiar voice speaking deplorable French caused him to whip around and he found himself face to face with Woodhouse dressed as a monk.

His friend raised his cowl slightly and, after seeing they were unobserved, narrowed his eyes and muttered in English, 'I didn't expect to find you here. Not after choosing the safety of your traitorous wife over the integrity of this operation.'

Angus glanced at the disinterested guests nearby then took a contemplative sip of his champagne. 'Had I not, Emily would now be dead.' The curl of his lip and the flare in his eye would, he hoped, leave Woodhouse in no doubt as to his fury at the man he'd once considered his closest friend. 'Tonight will prove Emily is no traitor.'

'What, by proving Madeleine Delon *is*? The women are *sisters.*'

Angus finished his champagne and fought for calm. Putting his head close to Woodhouse's, he hissed, 'Emily escaped to her father's house and asked Micklen for refuge. Do you know where I found her?' When Woodhouse merely raised one eyebrow as if a flaw in Angus's logic could be found in any answer, Angus gripped his friend's shoulder and shook him. 'Emily had been lured into a cave in the cliffs by her father and entombed. By the time I reached her the tide was high. We both nearly drowned.' He pointed to a graze across his temple.

Woodhouse digested this in silence. Finally he said, 'She

had to take a risk to prove her innocence and you bought it. Wait, I'm sorry.'

Angus had been about to shoulder his way out of their conversation but he allowed Woodhouse to continue. 'Of course, if you can prove the allegations I've made against her are false then I have no case. But she is not a loyal wife, Angus. She wanted to marry Jack Noble, not you. She could not have made that more plain when I met her shortly after your vows.'

'She made it very plain to me, too.' Despite himself, Angus felt his expression reflect the warmth of his feelings as he added, 'Things have changed.' He turned and indicated Madeleine with a jerk of his head. 'There's the *only* traitor we need to concern ourselves with right now, though Madame Fontenay is no doubt lurking in the shadows. Mademoiselle Delon is behaving very nicely while she has an audience but what about when our backs are turned? She has no loyalty to Levinne, although it's possible she put on a good show so as to elicit my sympathy.' Angus gave a rueful grin. 'I don't pretend to be an expert on women.'

'You know that we have it on good authority Mademoiselle Delon plans to kill you once she's satisfied you've dispatched the information she *supposedly* elicits from the general,' Woodhouse said bluntly. 'That's the point at which we'll have the most chance of proving her disloyalty. Believe me, Angus, my greatest fear is for your safety. You are surrounded by enemies and we have no idea when Fontenay or Mademoiselle Delon will act ...' He hesitated, adding, 'and if you can disprove all the evidence I found to link Mrs McCartney with Mademoiselle Delon and Madame Fontenay then I'll be as pleased as you.'

Angus snorted. 'A mere accident of birth does not make her a traitor. Is it not enough that Micklen tried to kill Emily?' Woodhouse put a placatory hand upon his shoulder.

'We'll talk about that later,' he said. 'In the meantime, tell me what you anticipate as regards Mademoiselle Delon.'

Reluctantly, Angus dropped his defence of Emily and answered the question. 'Once the general is drunk enough she intends to accompany him into his bedchamber – for our benefit, of course.'

Woodhouse agreed. 'The maps and documents will be those that Madame Fontenay and Napoleon Bonaparte want the English to have. Once you've dispatched them to a trusted courier your job will be complete. With the false documents on their way to England and you an easy target, here, you need to guard your back closely. Rest assured, *I* will be.'

Grimly Angus clapped Woodhouse on the shoulder. 'Any advice as to how I avoid the final outcome would be welcome.'

Woodhouse looked so like the old comrade Angus had fought alongside in France that he chuckled when his friend raised the overlarge wooden cross that hung around his neck.

'God will be watching you, Angus,' he said, tapping the crucifix with a meaningful look.

It was hollow and Angus grinned, despite the imminent danger that confronted him, saying, 'I'll ask no more and be satisfied that God works in mysterious ways.'

Still, once Major Woodhouse had departed and as Madeleine continued her ovation-winning performance at the other end of the room, Angus could think only of Emily. She'd insisted her head wound was a mere graze, but what if that proved not the case? What if Micklen had not gone to France and instead had discovered her whereabouts?

He could do nothing but console himself with the knowledge he'd tried his best to cover every contingency.

For now, he must concentrate on the task at hand.

To deflect attention from his lone state, he engaged a powdered and bewigged clergyman in conversation while keeping Madeleine in his sights. Her flirtatious behaviour bordered on outrageous but the general was enthralled.

When the clergyman introduced a third man into their midst Angus bowed and excused himself to seek a quiet corner beneath a sconce of candles. In the distance Madeleine slanted a self-satisfied look in his direction as she curled an arm about the general's neck.

'Monsieur, I have a confession to make.'

Startled, he gazed down upon a woman in an elaborate pink Madame de Pompadour court gown decorated with yards of lace, bows and furbelows. A powdered and curled wig and a demi mask made her unrecognisable but the glint in her eye and a glimpse of dark hair beneath the wig caused him to step back in disbelief. A plethora of mixed emotions rose up to consume him as he gasped, 'Good God … *Emily?*'

'Hush, Monsieur,' she whispered, touching his hand only briefly as if afraid of drawing attention to herself. 'It was too dangerous for you to be here alone and too dangerous for me to remain where I was.'

Horror and joy roiled inside his gut. He'd never been so overjoyed to see anyone, but in the same instant he was deeply dismayed. 'I'd have come back for you, Emily. I'd have protected you.' Angus glanced over her head and when he was satisfied Madeleine was too occupied with her own charade he returned his attention to his wife. She was smiling, her small, white teeth sparkling in the candlelight and the sudden urge to hold her close and keep her safe was almost painful. The guests that milled around them seemed like circling wolves.

'Come to my bedchamber. You'll be safer there. Follow me discreetly.' He exited through the nearest door and in the passage a minute later he caught her hand and pulled her round a corner. Still, he kept his head down and his voice low, careful to reveal no emotion nor to excite the interest of the occasional passing guest. 'You've taken a huge risk. Emily, why? It's much more dangerous here.'

'For you, yes, for your life is in danger ...' She tugged at his hand and whispered, '... from a woman who resembles me, Angus.'

In his bedchamber with the door closed behind them, an oil lamp turned low upon the desk and the gentle glow of the fire it was like some strange paradise created just for them.

'Angus, Madeleine is my sister and we look alike. I can help you.' She threw herself into his arms and he felt the tension seep away as she sagged against him. Her voice broke. 'I couldn't bear to think of you in danger.'

'Emily, you have put *yourself* in grave danger,' he muttered, stroking her hair and revelling in the sensation of being wanted while all the time alert to the impending danger each faced. 'How can your presence possibly reduce the risk Madeleine Delon poses?'

'Maybe it can't, but while Major Woodhouse believes me a traitor to England, a traitor to my husband, how else can I prove my loyalty?' Her clear gaze implored him to understand her. 'Do you not see why I had to come? To prove to you, Angus, in the only way I know how, that I am none of these. And to prove it to Major Woodhouse.' Her hands twined behind his neck and her breath fired his senses as she contoured his jawline with a trail of kisses. 'And that I love you.'

Fire powered through his loins.

In more overt terms than ever before, the wife he'd desired since he'd seen her on another man's arm all those years before was asserting in the most passionate terms how much she loved him.

'What risks you have taken to be here, Emily!' he muttered, holding her tightly. I understand you want vengeance against the woman who deceived you with Jack—'

'I don't care about that ... about Jack.' She sounded angry as she pulled back and raised her face to his. 'I care about *you* and the harm that woman may do you when you least expect it. Kiss me!'

He was not going to refuse. Every nerve ending was poised for such glorious relief and with a sigh he dipped his head. She clung to him, her mouth flowering beneath his, her slow, deep exhalation further proof of the change in her feelings over the past few days.

She'd taken huge risks to prove it.

But time was short and it took every ounce of his willpower to put her away from him, gripping the hand that looked in danger of stroking his cheek and imperilling his good intentions. 'We are in danger and the safety of England rests upon our task tonight. Madeleine is in the ballroom and—'

'*Madeleine.*' It was more a hiss. Closing her eyes, Emily whispered, 'How can I let you walk out of here and into that woman's orbit when I know she intends to kill you?'

'Because you have no choice. Right now Mademoiselle Delon is downstairs insinuating herself into the affections of a very drunk general in Napoleon's army and I can't afford to take my eyes off them for very long because soon she will lead him away to procure the information we need.'

'Seducing him like she seduced Jack and like she plans to seduce you ... otherwise she will kill you.'

Angus held her face between his hands. 'Madeleine intends passing on false information which I will dispatch with the courier and then she will strike. In the wings, we anticipate the woman she's reporting to will be watching.'

'You mean my mother.'

He felt her shudder, look away and then whisper as she gazed at the wall, 'The traitor who would run you through with a rapier with impunity. My *mother*. You are courting death, Angus.'

He sighed. 'I am forewarned and well armed. It's the best I can do, Emily. We must reconcile ourselves to the fact we may be unable to lay our hands on the real information – the maps which the general keeps in his desk – but if we can apprehend Madeleine and Madame Fontenay, discreetly, and spirit them back to England, England will be all the safer for it'—his gaze softened—'and you will no longer be the traitor Woodhouse has branded you.'

'*I'll* get you the real information you want.'

He stopped his derisive grunt when he saw Emily was serious.

'I'll pretend I'm Madeleine.' She fixed him with a steely stare. 'If the general is drunk he won't notice—'

He took her shoulders and shook her gently. 'You can't possibly. You wouldn't know how to flirt like—'

Her moment's silence was punctuated by a short laugh. 'I would not pretend for your sake, Angus, when I didn't love you, but I can pretend if your life depends upon it, if the success of the operation and'—her eyes glowed with a different light: the desire for vengeance—'if it will expose this woman Madeleine for the witch she really is.'

Angus laughed, stroking her cheek and tucking back the

strands of dark hair which had escaped from her elaborate, powdered coiffure, but she pulled away from him.

'I am guilty by association.' She looked helpless. 'Tell me what else I can do, Angus, to be exonerated? It's immaterial if you believe me, but Major Woodhouse doesn't and he has enough evidence to see me hang.'

Tenderly he cupped her face. 'Keep yourself safe, Emily, and leave the exonerating to me.'

She seemed to shrink into herself. 'Why won't you let me take over the role Madeleine is performing? Don't you trust me?'

Desperately he tried to explain. 'Your safety means more to me, Emily, than anything else and to swap roles with Madeleine is madness.'

'Not if the general is drunk.'

Never had he wanted to allay her fears with more than a few inadequate protests, but time did not permit. 'Just because Micklen and Fontenay are connected with you, and they recruited Jack Noble—'

'Madame Fontenay is my mother ...' She choked on the words and threw herself into his arms. 'Oh God, Angus, I don't know how I can live with the truth. I thought surviving after being in the cave was my greatest trial. What am I to do? I am tainted—'

He held her tightly and kissed her brow. 'You're not tainted, and all that matters is whether *you* are true ... to me and to Britain and that we get out of France safely.' He kissed her hard on the mouth then and set her away from him once more. 'Now stay here. Sleep. You are exhausted and I cannot believe the bravery and resourcefulness you have shown in getting here.'

'Not unless you kiss me again, Angus.'

She raised her head and he took her in his arms. She was trembling but not only through fear, for her tremors increased as he brought his mouth down to hers.

It was meant to be a kiss of reassurance, for time allowed nothing more. Instead the burning touch of her lips seared him with the promise of how much more she was willing to offer him; and in return he offered her his brand of owner-ship and protection, his promise that he would not fail her and that he believed in her ... to the end.

CONFINED TO ANGUS'S BEDCHAMBER, Emily paced, her wide skirts swishing alternately against the fire screen and the escritoire at each turn of the room. It didn't matter what he'd said, Emily knew the only way to ensure their safety was to masquerade as Madeleine – vanquish her, if possible – and locate the information the British needed regarding Napoleon's forthcoming offensive.

Only someone true to the cause could retrieve the real maps and not the erroneous battle plans that were to be supplied to Angus.

Only *Emily*.

Vitriol pulsed through her veins. Madeleine had stolen Jack and now she threatened her husband's safety. Madeleine would happily see Emily swing and so, it seemed, would her mother. Madame Fontenay was only interested in ties of loyalty to her traitorous cause.

No, Emily could not remain passively in Angus's chamber while Madeleine continued her path of destruction at Emily's expense.

'Has Mademoiselle Delon returned here?' she asked Susan in a low voice, putting up her hand to allay Susan's fears as she slipped in through the door to Madeleine's chamber. Then, 'Good, for surely a woman of such vanity would return and attend to her appearance before she embarks on her final deadly onslaught.'

Susan was decidedly more reluctant to carry out Emily's latest plan than she had been any of the other escapades upon which her new mistress had led her.

'Attack her when she comes back and tie her up and strip off her clothes?' she asked, aghast, hands to her cheeks. 'A grand lady? It'll be the gallows at Tyburn for sure, just like them highwaymen, for we'll be no better.'

'You'll be handsomely rewarded for your services to the security of England and given a medal of bravery to impress your friends and family,' Emily contradicted her. 'Now hush, someone's coming! Stand by the door, Susan, for we can't risk her getting away.'

Soft, satisfied humming accompanied Madeleine's arrival as she quietly entered the room and went to turn up the Argand lamp.

Was she always so self-satisfied? Emily wondered, straining from the shadows to see the features of the woman who'd made sport of her for all these years. Her half-sister.

She was beautiful, there was no denying it. Her dark hair was caught up in a simple top knot caught with a gold and diamond comb and her skin gleamed lustrous in the dim light.

Was she as beautiful as Emily? Had Jack loved her more than Emily?

Emily dismissed the thoughts almost immediately. What did it matter? Jack and Madeleine deserved each other.

The thought that Madeleine exerted any sexual allure over Angus was far more concerning. He knew she was dangerous, but had he felt any attraction?

Again, what was the point in even wondering when the plain fact was that Madeleine was her nemesis with the power to destroy the foundation of Emily's life? She'd nearly succeeded once already.

'Madeleine Delon?'

Madeleine's gasp was followed by a polite but quizzical smile as Emily stepped out from the shadows. Obediently Susan had taken up position by the door. Emily was taking no chances.

'Who are you and what are you doing in my room?' The regal hauteur was as Emily had expected as Madeleine raked her with a glance that seemed to miss nothing. She almost expected her to comment that Emily had a curl out of place. Emily studied her in return. In the pool of lamplight Madeleine looked like an exquisite Gallic Madonna; a very disdainful one. Her scarlet gown clung to her curves – almost certain proof she'd dampened her petticoats with water. Such a woman would stop at nothing to achieve her ends.

Emily swallowed down her fear. For so long she'd embraced this moment but with secret dread. Now her fear dissipated and righteous bravery gave her voice strength. 'I am Emily McCartney.'

She waited, studying the young woman's graceful, arrogant bearing, enjoying Madeleine's dawning realisation as she added slowly, 'Jack Noble's fiancé, Angus McCartney's wife.'

Madeleine, however, was well trained. Any shock she might have registered was muted, disguised beneath a veneer of supercilious disdain.

'Jack's fiancée,' she repeated softly as she half turned towards the fire, dismissing Emily as if she were of no importance though her appearance here could only be astonishing. 'Jack said you were tolerably presented—'

It was a barb designed to sting. Madeleine's ability to

belittle her feminine rivals was not a weapon to be sneezed at.

'—and not very adventurous,' she added with a cold glance in her direction. 'So what are you doing in my bedchamber?' She answered her own question. 'Chasing after your husband? Desperation is such an unattractive trait.'

The clock in the passage began to chime. Midnight.

Straightening, Madeleine indicated the door with a flourish. 'Please leave my chamber now.'

Emily fought for studied calm. 'I am here on business, Mademoiselle Delon, and we are to swap gowns. Please disrobe now.'

The flare of astonishment in the young woman's eyes was quickly replaced by amusement. 'Ah,' she said softly, 'you've escaped from Bedlam. That explains why poor Angus has been so unhappy.'

Emily flicked a glance at Susan, relieved the girl's determined scowl suggested she would guard the door at all costs, before turning back to Madeleine. 'I am fully cognisant of the mission with which you've been charged, Mademoiselle Delon, and I am here to ensure that the *correct* information is conveyed to the Foreign Office in London. Please, take off your gown.'

This time there was no disguising Madeleine's shock. 'Someone! Help me! There's a madwoman in my chamber!' Her prompt response took Emily by surprise but perhaps it was easier this way, she thought, as she hurled herself upon the young woman. Attacking a controlled, supercilious stranger would hardly have excited the senses to action like this.

Susan joined the fray. She was stronger and more determined than she looked and to Emily's surprise succeeded in divesting Madeleine of her gown with minimal damage.

Together they bound her wrists, stuffed a rag in her

mouth and shoved her beneath the bed, her muted cries fading to nothing as they closed the door.

ANGUS HEARD the clock chime midnight and glanced once more at the three doors which led into the grand saloon. Where was Madeleine? The general was swaying on his feet. The effects of too much claret would soon have him snoring in his bed, though perhaps it was easier this way.

Yet Madeleine's disappearance was worrying.

Edgily he surveyed the entrances once more. It was not like Madeleine to disappear unaccountably. Had she had second thoughts about betraying them? Was she consulting a third party about the direction the operation should take?

A flash of scarlet sidling through the far double doors caught Angus's eye. Despite the brilliant candles, he squinted to see better. Madeleine, dark eyes bold and challenging through the slits in her demi mask, sashayed through the throng, exuding confidence and sexual allure.

She certainly knew how to excite a man's pulses, he thought sourly, aware of the male interest she aroused. It almost crackled through the air. He saw her slant a glance up at a raven-haired guest and the gentleman's response as he stooped to catch her question. Lower and closer than necessary as he pointed towards the general.

With languid grace she moved in the large gentleman's direction. The general was slumped on a banquette by the wall but he roused himself, putting his lorgnette to his eye as Madeleine approached. She turned, for a second displaying her glorious full-breasted silhouette as she hesitated, perhaps weighing up the right approach having been gone so long.

There was no doubting the general's desire. The grandly upholstered belly lengthened as he pushed himself out of his slump, his hands eagerly patting his portly thighs. Madeleine folded her slender form and perched daintily upon his knee. Gracefully she brushed her ostrich plume back from her mask and put her lips to his ear.

Something inside Angus screamed to attention. Something that wasn't right and that he should have seen long before.

The gloriously elegant creature now making up to the colonel wasn't the dangerous Madeleine Delon.

He narrowed his eyes and pushed his way past several knots of guests, deeper into the throng in the midst of the room.

Oh, dear God, what was she about?

He wanted to part the crowd with a shout and whisk her to safety on the spot.

Not Madeleine. She excited no such emotion.

However this woman, though so similar in looks, could not have been more different.

The lustrous tresses with the sheen of a raven's wing which curled over one creamy shoulder and tickled the swell of breasts designed to send a man mad with wanting belonged not to Madeleine Delon but to his dangerously vulnerable wife. Helplessly, he saw the two of them rise, the general making the most of the creamy shoulder she offered to help him up as his fat, wet lips appeared to accidentally brush across her exposed flesh.

Emily didn't flinch. Like her gold mask, her smile was securely in place.

As she led her salivating general towards the far entrance Angus was gripped with indecision. Should he guarantee Emily's safety by challenging the general?

Or allow Emily to carry out her daring plan while he ensured that Madeleine remain a spent force which is surely what Emily wanted and must have managed? For now, at any rate.

ANGUS HURRIED ALONG THE SERVANTS' back corridor, hoping he'd reach the general's room before Emily and her escort.

The general might appear a doddering imbecile, but who knew what he was capable of within the privacy of his bedchamber? The idea of Emily being alone with any man was bad enough, but the thought she might be in danger made the short hair on the back of Angus's neck prickle and his blood fizz as he made haste like – well, he hoped – a cardinal rushing to attend to God's bidding.

Capitalising on the fact there was no one around he broke into a run.

And promptly barrelled into a servant as he rounded the corner.

The little maid gasped in English and he took a step back while the girl picked herself up, about to continue her flight. Angus gripped her arm and swung her back to face him.

Muffling her scream with a hand across her mouth he hissed, 'An English maid? I can only assume you're Miss Emily's. What's happened?'

She reared back before gasping in relief. 'You be Miss Emily's husband, ain't yer? Oh, sir, we've been discovered. We 'ad Miss Madeleine tied up in 'er chamber good and proper only a grand lady's come in an' found her.'

'Take me there.'

What was more important? Containing Madeleine or following Emily and the general? If Emily's bold plan were to succeed then he had to give her the necessary freedom while he concerned himself with Madeleine.

The maid led him along a rabbit warren of back passages before halting in front of Madeleine's bedchamber door, which still stood slightly ajar.

'I dunno if they're still in there,' she whispered, 'but chances are 'cos Miss Madeleine had no clothes on and it were only a minute ago. Then a grand lady walked in and the gamer were all up. It were luck I slipped out unnoticed!'

Angus pressed himself against the wall and listened. There was movement within. He heard soft, urgent voices.

Signalling to the girl to stay behind he gently pushed the door wider, braced himself and stepped in.

They were not expecting him. Two dark-haired women, one young and beautiful with a mouth that curved like a satisfied cat's and the other older, statuesque and arresting in purple velvet trimmed with gold, turned at his entrance.

The flare in Madeleine's eyes as she locked glances with him above the shoulder of her companion still lacing her into Emily's Madame de Pompadour dress was defiant. She knew she'd been exposed but her look told Angus she was confident he could not compete with the two of them.

'Major McCartney,' she crooned. 'Do you not knock when you enter a lady's bedchamber?'

'Mademoiselle Delon, I think you are perhaps aware of why I did not?'

'Ah ...' She nodded, straightening as the laces were pulled tight, then bending to pick up the powdered wig that had been cast onto the floor. She toyed with one of its ringlets as the other woman moved to flank her. 'Could it be that you do not trust me?'

There was no suggestion she was afraid.

Angus laughed softly. 'I never did, Mademoiselle Delon, which is why I was expecting this. And Madame Fontenay—'

He inclined his head, adding formally as if he were meeting her at a *soirée*, 'I have heard many interesting tales about you. Though not from Emily.'

'Where is the little fool?' Madame Fontenay's fine dark eyes raked him with disdain, her words delivered with the cold self-possession Angus had expected. This mother clearly had no maternal feeling for Emily. 'I was disappointed to learn of her marriage to a common soldier after the shocking loss of her … *true* love.' Her eyes travelled the length of his form as if she were sizing up a footman that might fit the old livery.

She raised her eyebrows. 'Major Noble's earlier reports on the girl were not encouraging in the bravery department; however, the fact she was biddable and so *very* in love with dear Captain Noble made her his ideal consort.' She put a hand on Madeleine's shoulder and the younger woman simpered up at her, saying in husky tones, 'I am far more *sympathetique, n'est ce pas?*' Her gaze narrowed as she turned to Angus. 'And more beautiful, though I don't deny there is a *small* resemblance.'

Madame Fontenay made no rejoinder. Her flinty gaze did not waver. 'Might I remind you, Major McCartney, that the only person to have dishonoured you tonight is your wife through her outrageous behaviour: violence and kidnapping.' She nodded at Madeleine. 'Nevertheless, Mademoiselle Delon was a fool to allow herself to be caught by surprise.'

The thinning of Madeleine's lips was the only indication of her emotions. Angus felt for his pistol and wished he'd entered, brandishing his Flintlock.

A wish more pressing as Madame Fontenay calmly produced one of her own.

'Emily has proved herself my enemy, just as you are, Major McCartney.' The smile that curved her mouth did not reach her cold eyes. She nodded towards the door. 'Please, lead us to your bedchamber so we may all welcome dear Emily when she returns from her bold mission.'

This was not far down a narrow passage at right angles to this one. He felt a fool as he obediently preceded the woman whose reputation assured him she'd have no compunction in pulling the trigger of the small, deadly weapon pressed into the small of his back.

A maid curtsied as she passed; a gentleman just issuing from a nearby chamber murmured a greeting.

Once inside his chamber Angus moved leisurely to the sideboard. 'Regrettably I cannot offer you ladies ratafia, but I have some excellent brandy.' He indicated the cut glass decanter. 'Mademoiselle Delon? Madame Fontenay?'

To his surprise, Madame Fontenay accepted.

'Mama!' cried Madeleine. 'What about the general? He is a loose-tongued buffoon. We must find the two of them and we must kill her!'

Angus, as he poured Madame Fontenay's drink, was chilled by the eagerness of his former compatriot, though there was little point in responding.

'Madame Fontenay.' With exaggerated formality he offered her the glass.

'Put it on the sideboard. I am not a fool, sir.' The woman held her pistol steady, trained on him. 'Madeleine—' Her tone was patient. 'Emily is out of her depth. Let her make her own mistakes. She will soon return to her husband's bedchamber.'

Angus took a sip of his drink while he thought. 'Do you really feel nothing for your daughter, Madame?'

'I've followed Emily's progress many years, Major McCartney. Regrettably I was unable to influence her childhood or her marriage to you, though when I learned you were Noble's replacement I allowed myself to think it fortuitous. I was mistaken. No, I am not fond of the English but Captain Noble proved himself more than acceptable to me.'

Poor Emily.

He tapped his glass. 'Emily is accused of being a traitor to her homeland, but her brave actions tonight prove otherwise. At least accord your daughter the admiration she deserves.'

Madame Fontenay snorted. 'Emily is not brave. She came here because she had nowhere else to go.'

'There is little loyalty amongst thieves and spies, Madame Fontenay,' he said, forcing down his fury in response to the cavalier way in which she dismissed her own daughter.

'Having suffered one disappointment I was ready for another. Two of my daughters were not fashioned in my mould.'

Angus shook his head as if he sympathised. 'Poor Jessamine,' he murmured. 'She said you were not the mother she had hoped for.'

In the first sign of emotion, Madame Fontenay's steely façade wavered and her hand went to the sideboard to steady herself. 'What do *you* know of Jessamine?' She frowned but said nothing more.

Ah, so she did not know ... Angus seized the advantage.

'When I rescued Jessamine at Corunna she told me she had no family. Only later did she mention you.'

Madame Fontenay blanched. Her hold on the pistol loosened but she quickly jerked it upwards as Angus moved forwards.

'Where is Jessamine now?'

He could see the effort with which she forced the words out. Jessamine was the daughter she'd claimed and who'd grown up at her side before the girl had run away. Of her three children, Jessamine was the one with whom she'd spent most time. Presumably, in view of the emotion she was unable to hide, she'd loved her. It was natural Madame Fontenay wanted to discover her whereabouts. Angus had found her weak spot.

'Ensure Emily's safety and I'll tell you.'

'I will not jeopardise this operation, Major.' Madame Fontenay's voice was a soft hiss. 'Emily means nothing to me. Her father was nothing to me and she's done nothing to raise herself in my estimation.'

Angus tried a different tack, hoping the false threat might weaken her resolve. 'Micklen will take a dim view of it if Emily comes to harm.'

'Bartholomew cares for nothing but his pocket book,' Madame Fontenay snorted. 'He railed against spending a penny on Emily from the moment I forced the child on him, despite the funds with which I supplied him before he left France.'

Madeleine slanted a look up at her benefactress. 'Emily was good for something,' she purred. 'When you sent Jack Noble to court her she was very obliging.'

Madame Fontenay did not share Madeleine's smugness. Ignoring her, she continued to address Angus. 'Emily knows too much. I'm surprised Bartholomew hasn't taken steps to eliminate the risk she poses.'

She jerked the pistol to point at his heart. 'You accuse me of being an unfeeling mother.' She shook her head, pityingly. 'I'm more charitable than that. After I have disposed of you, Major McCartney, Emily will be grateful to find a home with me. She's a marked woman if she returns to England where she'd be hanged for a traitor.'

Angus threw wide his arms in a gesture of defeat. 'Do your worst, Madame Fontenay, and you will never discover the truth about Jessamine who was once my mistress.'

'You lie!' She spat. 'You think you can exploit me by turning a brief chance meeting, or a lucky guess, into more, luring me into jeopardising all I've worked for. Well, you're a fool, Major, and I don't take kindly to it.' Without warning she snatched up her glass and threw it at him.

Angus staggered at the impact, holding his wounded cheek as whisky dripped from his coat, the smashed glass tinkling in shards at his feet.

A bruise, no blood, he thought, but he knew not to risk her temper a second time. She'd kill him without compunction, though now he served a dual purpose: a lure for Emily and the keeper of Jessamine's fate.

'Jessamine's protector was killed during the battle,' he said, blocking his mind to the manner in which this came about. 'After Jessamine ran away from you she came to England where she'd learned Micklen was rearing her half-sister, Emily. However, Micklen had no desire to see his past unearthed and so he entombed her in a smuggler's cave. Unbeknown to him, she was rescued by a young soldier who took her to Corunna. Jessamine became my mistress when her soldier husband died and she had nowhere else to go.'

'You lie!'

He remembered Jessamine's refusal to talk about her family in the early days. The girl had been a nervous, jittery creature. He suspected she'd suffered regular beatings but had assumed at the time it had been at the hands of her father or some other male with whom her mother lived. It was clear now her ill treatment had been at the hands of her mother. A mother who nevertheless loved her.

Angus continued. 'Jessamine was not beautiful. Not like Emily. Her hair was brown and her face narrow and fearful. Jessamine had a small birthmark on her neck which she thought ugly and one on her eyelid.'

'Jessamine was not your mistress. She would never have lowered herself after all I'd taught her. An Englishman!'

Madame Fontenay shifted position. The pistol trembled and her mouth worked to form the words.

'Jessamine,' said Angus, 'was nothing like you. Her nervous temperament caused her skin complaint. When she was particularly distressed I gave her duck fat to ease the itching. She said that was what you used to do.'

As he took a step forward Madame Fontenay raised the pistol, warningly.

'You could have found that out in a conversation.' Her shoulders heaved.

'I could have,' Angus conceded. 'However, I have Jessamine's locket and the painting you inscribed for her five years ago. In 1808. You wore a white dress with a tricolour sash. Jessamine said it was a hot day and you disliked the painter's desire to have the windows closed. Jessamine said she sat on the chaise longue and watched the portraitist at work, wishing she were as beautiful as you.'

Madame Fontenay's shoulders slumped.

'Where is Jessamine now?' The question was borne upon an exhalation of defeat.

Angus shook his head. 'You are naïve, Madame Fontenay, if you think I will tell you that while Emily and I remain in danger.'

Despite her shock, Madame Fontenay maintained her steady grip on the pistol. 'You underestimate my mettle, Major McCartney, if you think I would put family considerations above the future of France.'

CHAPTER 28

Sauntering into the ballroom dressed as Madeleine and asking where she could find the general had been the most terrifying moment of Emily's life.

Never had she undertaken a charade of any kind, much less something upon which so much hinged, including her life and quite possibly the future course of Anglo–French relations.

The admiring look one gentleman had sent her as he'd pointed to a portly, highly decorated old man a few feet away bolstered her confidence, and her doubts regarding this risky charade almost dissipated completely when the general brightened at the sight of her and patted his knee.

He was too drunk to notice she was not Madeleine. If Emily were bold enough, she'd complete her mission with flying colours.

The colours of the English flag.

Shortly after she'd taken him up on his invitation to perch on his knee, the general suggested she might like to help him to his bedchamber. His fleshy lips brushed her shoulder as she helped him to rise.

Fortuitously, after he'd staggered across the threshold of his room, leaning heavily on her, he collapsed onto his bed and fell asleep.

In an agony of indecision Emily stood in the middle of the carpet and wondered if she had the courage to put her hands on his person. Somewhere in his clothing or around his neck she knew he kept the key to the desk which she hoped contained the map of Europe outlining Bonaparte's military strategy.

Nervously, Emily placed her hand on his chest. He stirred, emitting a loud snore and she jumped backwards. If he opened his eyes she'd pretend she was here to assist him to undress. If necessary, she could run faster than he could, she was sure. The second attempt at undoing one of his brass buttons was more successful and, slipping her hand under his shirt, she felt for the key she desperately hoped she'd find.

It was there but of course undoing the clasp was more difficult as his bull neck pressed into the mattress and it required busy, probing fingers to complete her task.

At last she had the key, and she ran quickly to open the desk, finding to her dismay that it contained two rolled-up maps.

Closer inspection revealed that one was bound with a strip of paper wrapped around it clearly marked: *For M Delon.*

Emily gasped. So the general was part of the plan. He knew a young woman would solicit him and that he was to give her false information that she would then pass onto the enemy.

She hesitated. Should she take both? *Dear God, the enormity of the decision …*

If she swapped the *For M Delon* paper and wrapped it around the other map, the general would assume Madeleine had taken the map while he was sleeping. He'd be unconcerned when he awoke to find only one map. Probably he wouldn't even study the remaining map, assuming the false one had simply been dispatched.

But no, she thought in sudden indecision, turning back to the desk. For how could she prove her innocence with only the one?

With both maps slipped inside her bodice, Emily hurried from the room and into the passage.

Right into the path of a monk who raised his cowl upon impact so that she found herself staring into the disbelieving green eyes of none other than Major Woodhouse. Foolishly she began to run, for it may have been possible that he'd not have recognised her, she thought afterwards. But it was too late. She'd drawn attention to herself. Ducking down a narrow, darkened passage she sprinted for the stairs, veering past the heavy newel post then down another narrow, darkened passage in the hope of confusing him in the gloom. Once he grasped her shoulder but she shrugged free as she passed Madeleine's room from the servant's corridor, dashing down another corridor at right angles before finally, gasping with relief, she pushed open the door to the withdrawing room of Angus's chamber. She tried to slam it shut behind her, but with the major pushing against the door from the corridor, she was unable to shut it completely. Panic rising, she threw her weight against it but to no avail. Major Woodhouse would breach her defences within seconds and he would haul her away as a traitor, before Angus could testify to her innocence.

Angus. With a shock she realised he was in his room, for she could hear voices: a woman's and her husband's.

Madeleine? In *Angus's* room?

Oh God! Angus was in danger from a woman who intended to kill him, and if Madeleine heard a disturbance next door, it could push her into action.

Emily swung the door open and with a harshly whispered, 'Hush!' she put her finger to her lips, turning the major's attention to the voices in the next room. Snatching the two maps hidden in her bodice, she brandished them at Major Woodhouse.

'I found these in the General's desk after pretending I was Madeleine,' she told him in an urgent whisper. 'Can you see there are two, one marked for Madeleine Delon who I gather was to give it to Angus.' Trembling, trying to keep her voice low and level, she added, 'My maid and I overpowered Madeleine earlier, but I can hear her in the next room with Angus. Yes, I know now she is my sister and that Madame Fontenay is my mother, but they are traitors and I am not. You *must* believe me, Major Woodhouse.'

The major, raising his head from a quick perusal of one map, levelled an incisive look at her. 'Rooms like this are used for intrigue and usually contain a sliding panel.' He'd put down the maps and was testing the thin wooden partition as he added, in a tone that suggested he accepted they were now fighting the same cause, 'We *must* hear what they are saying. You try over there.'

And when Emily stepped upon the banquette that rested against the wall and began to test each panel, she was rewarded. At eye level she found one which, when pressured with her forefinger, yielded slightly, then slid smoothly to reveal an inch through which Emily was able to observe the events in the next room.

'I can hear every word, Major,' she whispered excitedly as she put one eye to the gap. Unfortunately it was not wide enough for visual contact, but she could hear two distinct female voices. The woman speaking was older than Madeleine. Her confident, icy tones were the first to suggest she held the upper hand. Her next statement confirmed it.

Emily beckoned to the major to stand on the banquette

beside her. As she inched the panel open wider, her fear increased. It stung the surface of her skin and her heart began to hammer as she whispered, 'Something is wrong, Major Woodhouse. Angus is in grave danger.'

'You underestimate my mettle, Major McCartney, if you think I would put family considerations above the future of France.'

Emily clapped her hand to her mouth. It was impossible to see what was happening without exposing herself, though when fully extended the sliding panel would likely be made large enough to view much of the room.

'That's abundantly clear'—the coldness in Angus's tone matched the other woman's—'since you abandoned Emily and abused and exploited Jessamine.'

'You're hardly in a position to take the moral high ground with me, Major McCartney. You married Emily when she got herself with child because it was the only way a poor soldier like yourself with no prospects could find a wife. Bartholomew told me Emily never stopped crying from the moment she accepted you until her wedding day.'

Emily shivered as she listened to the mother she'd never known push her point with seemingly characteristic remorselessness. 'I'll wager she's still crying, Major McCartney, and she'll never stop. From where you're standing, the future doesn't look too rosy.'

A short silence followed, then Angus's voice, thoughtful as he replied, 'I'd been in love with Emily for years.' Emily fancied she could hear the smile in his voice and warmth flowed through her as he went on. 'I met her at a Regimental Ball and I was captivated. After Noble's death I married Emily because I wanted a woman capable of the kind of love she'd shown her false fiancé. You say Emily doesn't love me ... Why do you think she's here?'

'Because she had nowhere else to run. She has played into our hands very nicely, the little fool.'

Emily turned to Major Woodhouse. He'd heard Angus's words and her mother's harsh assessment. Relief coursed through her. Her mother might be a traitor but at least she'd just exonerated Emily.

Major Woodhouse sent her an assessing look, then put his mouth to her ear. 'Perhaps I will have no choice but to commend you for your bravery and loyalty to your husband when this is over, Mrs McCartney.' He glanced at the maps on the table by the fireplace. 'Angus always was a good judge of character.'

For the first time since Major Woodhouse had met Emily as a radiant bride-to-be, clinging to Jack's arm with such pride, he smiled properly at her. Then dismantling the crucifix around his neck, he withdrew his pistol, turning to add, 'Stay here while I assist Angus.'

He bypassed the door which adjoined the two rooms and instead exited into the hall.

The moment the major slipped out, Emily returned to eavesdropping.

'Enough, Major McCartney.' She heard Madame Fontenay's tone change. It was hard to remember this was her mother. She was even less her mother than Micklen was her father, she thought with poisonous rage.

'Your wife's sudden appearance is motivated by nothing more than the desire to save her pretty neck and you are a fool to believe anything else. Love is for weaklings.'

Emily had no doubt her mother believed this cold and damning statement.

She waited for Angus's response. He didn't believe love was for weaklings. Emily wanted to hear it, too. Hear that Angus was every bit a proponent of the love match and that his love for Emily would see him defend her to the end.

Instead, an alert silence descended.

Had they heard a noise? Major Woodhouse, perhaps? Sweat prickled the back of her neck. Recklessly she opened the panel wider, risking her own safety, but she had to see what was going on.

Her vision was limited to Madame Fontenay, resplendent in purple with three ostrich feathers in her matching velvet toque.

So this was her mother. This ageing beauty whose lovely face and figure had been the undoing of countless men over the decades, including Emily's unknown, unmourned father. Leaning in a little further she could see her mother faced Angus across a small table. Madame Fontenay had a pistol aimed at his chest. Angus stood with studied insouciance, unarmed, while Madeleine, lacking some of her regal hauteur now she was dressed in Emily's gown of pink lace and furbelows, stood a little to one side. 'Someone's coming.'

Madeleine's voice was sharp with fear.

'Then where is your pistol, Madeleine? I cannot cover everyone.' Madame Fontenay did not hide her scorn at Madeleine's lack of foresight.

Relenting, she produced a second pistol from the folds of her skirts. 'Take this!' she said, tossing it to Madeleine.

Who promptly dropped it.

Emily's stifled laugh as she watched Madeleine scramble to pick up the weapon turned to horror when Madame Fontenay cocked her weapon with an audible click …

… at the very moment the door was thrown open and a male voice cried out in commanding tones.

Dear God … Major Woodhouse!

Madame Fontenay swung her pistol arm round, a rictus of a smile pulling taut her now thin, ungenerous mouth; and Emily saw her mother's sneer of satisfaction and the gloating power that clearly fuelled her as she pulled the trigger.

The blast burst through the silence, filling the room with acrid smoke.

A shrill female scream overlaid a male cry of surprise. Followed by groaning. The sound was terrible: a wet gurgling amidst the ghastly rasping for breath.

Oh God. Emily blinked rapidly as she tried to understand what had happened, but the room was filled with smoke and Madeleine's shrieking overlaid every other noise.

Then the shrieking stopped abruptly. A strange calm seemed to settle over everyone. Rooted to the spot, Emily watched renewed horror contort Madeleine's feline gaze as the young woman stepped backwards, pressing herself against the far wall.

Someone else had entered the room; a tall, well-built figure who stepped over the body to take up position by the doorway. From her limited vantage point Emily could see the black boots and dark clothes of the newcomer and, as the smoke dissipated a little, the upturned boots of the body sprawled on the floor.

Desperately, Emily opened the panel wider, straining to see what was happening.

The stranger's bulk seemed to fill the room with a dangerous kind of power.

It was as if everyone were waiting for him to speak. Finally, his quiet, commanding voice cut through the silence. He took a menacing step towards Madeleine.

'So this is how you repay the latitude I've granted you, *ma cherie.*'

Madeleine inched sideways, her beauty obliterated by the terror that contorted her features, the wall trapping her as she tried to slide away from the tall, dark-clothed figure.

He spoke in French, his deep mellifluous tones demanding utter obedience. Emily strained to catch a glimpse of his profile in the candlelight. He was dressed in severe evening clothes, unrelieved by any colour. Sharp eyes glittered through the slits of a demi mask and raven black hair swept back from a high forehead above a beak of a nose. He looked cruel and handsome in a bleak, dangerous way. Little wonder that Madeleine looked terrified to death if this man somehow exerted authority over her.

Madeleine was trapped but where was Madame Fontenay?

And Angus?

Emily stepped down from the banquette. Her legs felt like jelly but she had to go to Major Woodhouse ... *Oh God*, she gasped. Major Woodhouse whom she'd sent to his death.

Madeleine's voice drifted from the next room. She was defending herself in tremulous tones. 'You don't understand, Levinne.'

'What don't I understand? That you have consorted with our enemies?' There was no compassion in the hard, flinty tone. Just disgust. 'Until now, I refused to believe it. But tonight I came to see for myself. You little fool. Did you think you could deceive me?'

Emily, who'd been about to run from the room, stepped up to the panel once more. With grim satisfaction she saw Madeleine appear to shrink into herself, her eyes dark with fear in her pallid face.

But what of Angus? Her beloved husband? Where was he? This man Levinne held the upper hand now so surely Angus was safe and Emily would be safe going to him? Regardless of her safety, she had to find him.

Finding the connecting door locked, she ran down the corridor in the footsteps of poor Major Woodhouse, terrified of what she would find and that her arrival might be premature. Was she compromising everything?

'Emily!'

Angus's voice, clear, relieved and full of vigour, sent joy

spiralling through her as he appeared from the end of the corridor just as she reached the door of his bedchamber. Whirling her into his arms, he held her tightly. 'My darling Emily—' His voice broke as he kissed her full on the mouth. 'For one terrible moment when your mother swung round I thought it was you about to be shot,' he said.

She shuddered. 'Where is Madame Fontenay?'

'She escaped.'

'Oh, no!' Her cry was genuine. The evil scheming woman who cared nothing for her own daughter had got away. How Emily wished it were her mother who lay dead in the doorway.

Despite the joy she felt in her husband's arms, Emily's senses revolted at the knowledge of what she'd inadvertently done. Major Woodhouse. She'd sent him through that door. Sent him to his death, suggesting he could use the element of surprise to win the advantage.

'Is he dead?' She choked on a sob.

She felt Angus still as he pressed her face against his chest, his nod stirring her hair, then his restraining arm as she pushed out of his embrace.

'No, Emily, it's not pretty.' He caught her hand. 'It was instant.'

She tried to pull out of Angus's embrace but he stopped her saying, 'Even though you may rejoice at his death I want to spare you the final sight of him.'

'It's not true.' Horrified, Emily stared at her husband. Major Woodhouse had accepted her innocence. Emily, who had always wanted his good opinion, had looked forward to his reassessment of her when they were all safe and gathered in the drawing room at Wildwood, reflecting on the success of their mission.

She'd not wished for his death, but now Emily had blood

on her hands while her villainous mother lived to see another day.

Angus took her arm to steer her away, but did not stop her when Emily pushed past the goggling onlookers.

The body lay sprawled in the entrance, the large feet upturned, a hole through the chest and a look of shock on his face.

'Father!' she cried and Angus jerked his head down at her look of surprise as she amended, 'I mean Micklen.'

'Who did you think it was?'

She almost wept with relief. 'I thought it was Major Woodhouse,' she said as the man himself pounded into the room saying with breathless satisfaction, 'We apprehended Fontenay by the front portico. Levinne's men are conducting the courtesies as we speak.'

CHAPTER 29

ummer 1814

S Napoleon had been defeated and a new king sat upon the French throne. Angus's dreams of peace between France and England had been achieved. Now he could look forward to peace in his own life.

'I dare you.'

Emily shivered as Angus's soft whisper disturbed a wisp of hair by her ear. Raising her head from her contemplation of the still waters below the embankment, she smiled, squeezing his hand.

With a soft laugh, Angus returned the pressure as they continued their leisurely stroll by the water's edge. 'I know exactly what you want to do.'

'Oh, do you, esteemed reader of minds?' she teased.

He stopped by a thick overhanging willow branch. 'Hang your clothes here. I'll stand sentinel if you're afraid of being discovered.'

Wicked excitement bubbled inside her and she grinned,

nibbling her lip as she anticipated plunging into the clear waters below.

'Come with me,' she urged, and within minutes they were both splashing naked in the stream that ran through the woods that bordered her old home.

Afterwards they lay side by side in the sandy shallows, hands entwined as they played games with the clouds scudding across the sky.

'Can you see that horse and rider?' murmured Emily, pointing to the sky.

Angus squinted, then turned his face to hers. 'No, but I see a beautiful woman with bright happy eyes—' His voice grew husky as he trailed his fingers down a strand of damp hair to cup her breast. 'And I can't believe she's my wife.'

Emily stretched luxuriously and sighed. 'The luckiest wife ever.' Regretfully, she sat up, adding, 'I expect mama is waiting though I'd much rather stay here swimming'— she sent him a wicked smile —'and doing other things with you.' She sighed again. 'I suppose we should get dressed in case someone comes.'

'My Emily is not so timid,' Angus teased. 'Come, let's not go back yet.' He rose, showering cold clear water from his naked body as he dragged Emily into the depths.

They swam together and half an hour later emerged from the water, laughing and shivering. As Angus reached for their clothes, Emily stopped him with a hand on his shoulder, suddenly serious.

'Dance with me? No one will see us,' she said in answer to his surprise. She felt the emotion that came with memory rise up within her. Resting her head against Angus's damp, hard chest she whispered, 'Do you remember the day you came to tell me Jack had been killed? You met me on the road here after I'd thrown my boot. You asked me directions. Did you know it was me?'

'I spoke to a country lass, but Emily, I don't think I saw her face. My thoughts were entirely focused on the beautiful Miss Micklen I had travelled so far to see and whose image I'd carried close to my heart for so many years.'

Emily laughed at his confusion. She reached up to gently stroke the scar which cut his cheek. 'That day, while bathing, I'd been dreaming about my future.' She put her arms around his waist and kissed each of his nipples tenderly before resting her head once more against his chest, hard with muscle and dusted with fine dark hair. She shivered again as she felt his strong arms bind her against him. Love and longing surged through her as she nestled deeper into his protective embrace, revelling in the power she had to bring him instantly to a state of desire, a feeling echoed within the basest regions of herself.

Exhaling on a sigh, she whispered, 'I longed for a life of freedom and happiness and I imagined dancing naked with the man I loved.' She raised her head and her heart thrilled to see her feelings echoed in his beloved dark eyes. 'And now I want to dance with him.'

For a moment he was silent. Then in courtly fashion he took a step back and bowed with a flourish before offering her his arm. 'In that case, I would hate to cause disappointment when it is so easily within my power to satisfy your wishes, Mrs McCartney. Pray, grant me the pleasure of this waltz?'

With an answering smile and a small incline of her head, Emily stepped once again into his arms, catching her breath as he whisked her off her feet.

The serious mood was broken. Laughing, they waltzed round and over the uneven ground and grassy tussocks until they fell, exhausted and laughing even harder, on top of each other.

'And now we really must get ourselves dressed or we'll

not be home before our guests arrive, let alone have time to make ourselves presentable,' Angus said, pulling Emily to her feet and removing the bits of grass and reeds that clung to her bare skin.

After they'd rubbed themselves down, Angus pulled on his breeches before turning to help Emily with her chemise and stays.

'Point your toe, madam,' he ordered, as he went down on his knees, waving one white silk stocking.

Obediently she did so, running her hands through his silky brown hair as he eased the silk up her calves then tied the garters before slipping on her kid boots.

'I love you, Angus McCartney.'

He grinned at her matter-of-fact tone, holding out his hand to pull her up. 'And I love you too, Emily McCartney.' He tossed his boots up onto the embankment. 'I can't possibly put these on damp feet. I'll carry them—'

They jerked their heads up at the sound of jangling harness before a familiar voice cried out, 'Good Lord, what is going on down there?'

Emily squealed and hid behind Angus who still held the dress he was about to slip over her head.

Major Woodhouse, on the box of a high perch phaeton, stared down at them, surprise turning to amusement.

'Bridal tour wasn't long enough?' he asked.

Emily and Angus had taken four months to make their leisurely way back to England and a few more to settle into life at Wildwood. Now they were at Micklen Hall helping Margeurite Micklen prepare to leave her old prison forever and make her home with them.

'It hasn't finished,' Angus called up to them.

Major Woodhouse cracked his whip. 'Take your time.' His tone was wry as the phaeton moved forward. 'I'll see you at the house.'

❄

WITH MARGEURITE MICKLEN comfortably settled in an armchair by the fire, the three were in the midst of their favourite tale. Emily sat close to her husband, her head nearly resting against his shoulder, her fond gaze focused on the woman she would always regard as her mother. Margeurite Micklen was transformed. Her wizened body seemed to have uncurled a little and her face was almost radiant as she listened, rapt, to the adventure she'd never grow weary of hearing.

'So there we were, Mrs Micklen: Emily and myself, holed up in the withdrawing chamber and aware Angus was in danger'—Major Woodhouse halted his explanation to cast his old friend a look of affection—'and not for the first time.' Angus squeezed Emily's hand, concealed in the folds of the smart new Pomona green gown he'd bought her after they'd left the chateau. What a wonderful journey home it had been. Over dinner the first night, when Major Woodhouse finally realised his company was superfluous, they'd decided to make it their bridal tour. Susan, who'd been found cowering in a room further along the passage, loyally waiting for Emily, had accompanied them and was now employed at Wildwood. Meanwhile the major had delivered to the Foreign Office the maps Emily had removed from the general. The information had been regarded as a major coup.

'So I ran into the corridor,' Major Woodhouse went on, 'whereupon I spied Levinne disappearing into the distance. I was torn, but I had to go after him for not only would he be able to assist Angus, he would have irrefutable proof of his faithless betrothed's complicity. As we were returning I saw the same white-haired fellow I'd recognised from our crossing striding towards Angus's chamber.'

Emily shuddered and Angus pulled her against his side.

'You can imagine my surprise when, without even knocking, he thrust open the door of Angus's chamber'— Woodhouse rolled his eyes and they exchanged horrified glances—'just as I'd intended doing, only to be felled by a bullet through the heart.'

Emily knew Margeurite Micklen would not mourn her cruel husband, but was surprised at the venom in her voice when she muttered, 'Something I wish I'd been able to do more than once.'

Casting her a sympathetic look, Angus took up the story. 'When Madame Fontenay eluded us, pushing past Levinne who was more concerned with the betrayal of Mademoiselle Delon, Woodhouse and I went in pursuit. Then Woodhouse told me he'd left Emily in my withdrawing chamber and I immediately turned back for her.'

Emily returned the pressure of Angus's hand and brought it up to her lips, interrupting with rare vehemence, 'I'm glad Madame Fontenay'—she turned to her mother with an apologetic look—'I'm sorry, mama, but I refuse to call her Tante Fanchette ... or mama.' Margeurite had grieved genuinely for her sister, but Emily's safety was her chief concern. 'I'm glad she's languishing in a cell, for she caused so much evil. Can you imagine how hard it was to keep silent when I heard the way she tried to twist Angus into believing I was at the chateau because I was more concerned about being tried for treason than anything else?'

Heat burned Major Woodhouse's cheeks at her mention of treason. Clearly he felt the need to defend himself from appearing the villain of the story. He cleared his throat, interjecting, 'You can imagine I felt my suspicions were justified, Mrs McCartney, when I discovered the secret correspondence in the book addressed to Madeleine and, not long afterwards, the painting of Madame Fontenay. Not to mention your association with that traitor, Jack Noble.'

Now, Emily felt nothing but loathing at the mention of his name.

Mrs Micklen grunted. 'Bartholomew must have placed the letter in the book with no regard for your safety, Emily, when we came to visit you. He was the cruellest of fathers, for he fostered your love when you were a child so he would always have your loyalty.'

Angus spoke up, the sincerity of his soft words ensuring he had everyone's attention. 'Emily's loyalty is a precious gift and I am a lucky man. The moment I laid eyes on my lovely wife three years ago I thought her the most beautiful, distant and unobtainable creature ever to walk the planet.'

'I can't imagine why,' Emily said, blushing. 'If I seemed serious other than when I was with Jack it was because I was so unused to company. Father would not offer a dowry,' she forced out the words with distaste, 'but planned to trade on my looks. Although Aunt Gemma and I have never been close, I do owe her an enormous debt of gratitude.' She hesitated and dropped her voice. 'Though not as enormous as the one I owe my husband.'

Major Woodhouse clapped his friend on the shoulder as he rose. 'Time to go.'

'What a relief,' Angus sighed, once the major had left and Margeurite had been helped to her bedchamber.

'That they're gone?' Emily asked, rising at his behest and closing her eyes in anticipatory pleasure as he drew her against him. This sensation of coming home, of finally belonging, body and soul, was one she'd never get used to and one she'd never take for granted.

'Not that, but a relief that I can do this,' he murmured, stroking his hands up her arms, chest and throat to tip her head up to meet his look.

Emily gazed into his warm, brown eyes and traced the ridge of scar tissue that sliced his cheek. 'When people see this'—gently she stroked his old wound—'they see the manifestation of honour and bravery. They need not know the truth…'

At her mischievous smile, Angus laughed. 'The result of an unsuccessful manoeuvre against Woodhouse during fencing practice when we were not yet out of our teens. No, Emily, not so heroic.'

'The truth is not always apparent.' Her smile broadened. 'And certainly not in this instance.'

Angus squeezed her before whisking her off her feet to cradle her in his arms. 'The truth of my feelings for you will be completely apparent in just a few short minutes,' he promised, pushing open the drawing room door and carrying her up the corridor towards her bedchamber.

Emily clung to him and buried her face in his neck. The deep love and gratitude for the happiness that now cocooned her was suddenly shot through with the fiercest desire. Aching need curdled in her lower body as she felt the familiar throb of anticipation.

She cupped his cheek, her heart hitching at the look of adoration Angus levelled upon her.

'And you'll not be disappointed by my response, my darling husband,' she whispered, sealing her promise with a kiss.

THE END

Adelaide, Lady Leeson, is another dutiful bride who fears she may destroy the political ambitions of her noble husband if she's exposed as the inspiration for a scandalous book of poetry.
Read **An Unsuitable Alliance** - Book 2 in the *Dutiful Wives* Series.

www.ingramcontent.com/pod-product-compliance
Lightning Source LLC
Chambersburg PA
CBHW030514120726
47904CB00005B/1455